S0-BZO-867

Day Unto Day

Copyright Permissions:
In the Public Domain
   All Through the Night
   Written by Edward Jones in 1784

   Lullaby and Goodnight—33 Lullabies for Babies by Amy Robbins-Wilson
   Permission granted by Amy Robbins-Wilson, Belfast, ME

ISBN: 978-0-9846297-1-8

Library of Congress Control Number: 2010916383

Cover Design by All Things That Matter Press

Published in 2010 by All Things That Matter Press

To my granddaughter, Kira Paige Pierce—
My "Kira-Dancing"
With love

Day unto day uttereth speech,
And night unto night sheweth knowledge.
Let the words of my mouth,
And the meditation of my heart
Be acceptable in thy sight, O Lord....
Psalm 19.2, 19.14

PROLOGUE
PHILADELPHIA, PENNSYLVANIA
JUNE 1866

Oliver Terrill, head of the Pennsylvania University Medical School, removed his wire-framed glasses and massaged the bridge of his nose. For ten minutes, he'd listened to the wrangling of the two doctors on the other side of his desk. Clearly, they still vehemently disagreed. Pinching his nose a final time, he replaced his glasses and picked up the top letter from the stack in front of him. "Gentlemen." He spoke pleasantly. However, his voice carried a lifetime's authority of retrieving, during his lectures, the wandering minds of student doctors. The men paused, and he slid efficiently into the gap.

"We've thoroughly discussed this dilemma. We must decide. My wife promised roast goose tonight if I promised to be home to eat it. I intend to keep that promise." Sheepishly, the men remained silent. "We've chosen nineteen young men for our medical studies program this fall. One position remains empty. Two applicants appear highly deserving. Unfortunately, neither of you agrees with the other's choice. It's time, quietly, with open minds, to list their merits and abide by our decision. Norman?" Oliver gestured to the rotund doctor whose graying beard camouflaged his face. His uncultivated hair suggested he'd lost his comb several days ago. His precise medical work, however, far outweighed any physical shortcomings.

Hands clasped behind his back, Norman Hulbert started pacing. In his enthusiasm, his flyaway hair lifted and fell rhythmically to each bouncing step. "One, a banker's son, comes from Boston. This candidate received a superior education in the best Boston schools. He is now studying under Sebastian Cort. We know Dr. Cort's enormous contribution to the medical world with his brilliant surgical techniques. The young man is intelligent; witness the score on his preliminary examination. He will, after graduation, become Dr. Cort's assistant in seeking improved surgical techniques. Educated here, and teamed with Dr. Cort, potential future discoveries are unlimited. He clearly possesses the qualifications to become as important to the medical field as Dr. Cort." His flamboyant revelation finished, Dr. Hulbert paused and said, prosaically, "That, gentlemen, in a nutshell, paints the story of success, success to which this school will contribute."

Dr. Terrill studied his pencil. *Whose success? The medical school's financial department, courtesy of Papa the banker?* He hastily banished the impudent thought.

"Conversely," Norman rolled on, "the other candidate comes off a farm in Ohio. His application states that after graduating, he will give back to the community that fostered his start in life by becoming a general practitioner in his hometown. Most commendable."

Detecting the condescending humor tingeing his colleague's voice, Oliver shifted impatiently. At the slight movement, Dr. Hulbert, accurately reading his friend's displeasure, abruptly became all business. "However—and I say this with only the kindest motives—such a goal will waste our time and squander the priceless guidance and instruction this institution offers. How much specialized training, earned from a school with an unmatched reputation for excellence, does it take to treat broken arms and legs and a fever or two in a backwater farming town?"

Without revealing his thoughts, Dr. Terrill leaned back in his chair. "Thank you, Norman. Your points are well given." With a big smile for his opponent, and a final bounce of his hair and person, Norman resumed his seat.

"Lawrence." Oliver gestured to Dr. Cornell, the head of the ear, nose and throat department. Knowing he never spoke without careful thought, Oliver waited curiously to hear his rebuttal.

Absentmindedly, Dr. Cornell pushed a swatch of graying black hair from his forehead. Rising, he, too, began pacing, at the same time flipping into the air and catching a silver dollar, as if the habitual movement gave order to his thoughts. Close in age to Norman, Lawrence possessed none of the other doctor's bounce, literally or figuratively. Oliver noted Lawrence must be highly agitated to disagree vocally with Dr. Hulbert. Blue eyes reflecting the gravity of the situation, Dr. Cornell spoke as if to himself, not his audience of two.

"Norman expertly categorized each young man's basic facts." Catching the dryness in Lawrence's tone, Oliver glanced at Norman who, smiling, obviously considered the words a compliment. "Our presence—this discussion—affirm a decision such as this requires that many things be taken into account," Lawrence continued. "Whatever the result, the lives of both the winner and the loser will change forever. One because he is chosen, the other because he is not. Because of the life changes we will thrust on these young men, many lives will be changed, for good or ill. The lives they will touch, and the lives they won't, will be a direct consequence of the choices we make today." He turned to Dr. Hulbert.

"You urge us to select the young man from the big city, who enjoys all the privileges of an advantaged upbringing, and who will, undoubtedly, continue to have privileges and advantages throughout his life. We may reasonably speculate he will have opportunity to achieve his goals. And the young man from the 'backwater farming town' as you so succinctly put it? Are the people he will treat less important than those your wealthy young friend from Boston will encounter? You disparage the idea he'll return home and become 'only' a general practitioner. This country is crying for skilled doctors, particularly in rural areas. How many charlatans—quacks, if you will—are running around out there? Isn't that the goal of this school? To teach young doctors the skills they need so sick and dying people won't have to resort to receiving fraudulent medical care? Even if his father isn't the town banker who may reward us handsomely if we choose wisely!" He finally stopped to draw breath.

Dr. Terrill watched Norman's face turn a riper shade of purple with each fact Lawrence hammered home. He suspected Dr. Hulbert never expected to be the recipient of such a vehement challenge. Certainly not from quiet Larry Cornell. Before Norman could launch a heated protest, Oliver picked up his pencil and balanced the eraser and lead ends between his fingertips. "Thank you, Lawrence." The doctor nodded. Done pacing, he pocketed the silver dollar and sat down.

Oliver laid the pencil aside and looked steadily at his associates. "You've both expressed important facts. However, one item is not yet factored into this equation." They looked equally puzzled. "The mentor of the Ohio applicant once studied here. Because of the scarcity of knowledgeable doctors, he works a far-flung practice. 'Backwater' or not, this doctor, who trained here, I remind you, holds the highest of reputations among his colleagues and the deepest respect of his community and of this school. I know, because several of us have continued to correspond with him through the years.

"He gives the young man an excellent recommendation, although he warns his pupil isn't content with simple answers." Oliver picked up the next paper on the stack. "He says, 'He'll pester the daylights out of you until he's certain he understands a particular situation. Don't know where he picked up such an ornery disposition. Couldn't be from me. I still have mine!'" Lawrence chuckled. Norman pursed his lips as if he had just bitten into half a lemon. "Our votes count equally, and you give equally persuasive recommendations. Thank you for your honest assessments. We have been friends, and colleagues, for many years and greatly respect one another's opinions. It appears I am to cast the deciding vote." He met each of their gazes in turn before he dropped his millstone into the pond.

"I do not wish to demean either candidate. As we discussed, the young man from Boston will have many opportunities. We cannot argue that the benefits of research are incalculable. However, even with a degree from our school, illustrious as that is, he will be one doctor in a city of many medical professionals of many specialties. As for future surgical discoveries, he will, undoubtedly, receive continued guidance under Dr. Cort's excellent tutelage. Conversely, the Ohio candidate's presence—or absence—will mean the difference between life and death for an untold number of people. Saving lives, gentlemen, is what we do. Faced with the two choices, I must go with the 'backwater farm boy.'"

Dr. Hulbert started to rise in protest, but Oliver held up his hand. "I understand your position, Norman. I assure you if, for some reason, this choice doesn't work, your young man will be on the first train from Boston. You have my word."

Norman looked like he'd just swallowed the entire chunk of lemon. "What about next year? Will he be considered then?" Outflanked by his colleagues, he must live with it, but that didn't mean he couldn't throw another punch or two for his personal preference.

To hide his smile, Oliver began gathering the scattered papers. "Top of the stack." He glanced at Lawrence, who unhesitatingly nodded his agreement.

Dr. Terrill picked up the list of chosen applicants and added the twentieth and final name. MacCord Edwards.

I've walked out on a limb for you, MacCord Edwards. I sure hope you aren't behind me, sawing it off!

CHAPTER ONE
FAIRVALE, OHIO
SEPTEMBER 1866

The train taking Mac Edwards to medical school in Philadelphia huffed away from the Fairvale station. His mother Larissa smiled and held her head high as the gritty steam blew back at the group crowded onto the wooden platform.

Putting all the enthusiasm she could into it, Larissa waved vigorously to keep from brushing at the tears she could no longer hold back. Next to her, Ethan Michaels' comforting grasp prevented her other hand from betraying her. Rigidly, she focused on the swaying engine and cars that, too rapidly, became a dot in the distance and vanished, no matter how hard she strained to catch one more glimpse.

The train whistle floated eerily back to them, then silence swallowed up even that small contact. Ethan's grip tightened around her fingers. "Time to go, Larissa."

With one last wistful glance along the empty tracks, she straightened her shoulders and looked up at the tall man standing gravely beside her. His eyes, the shade of a blue jay's wing, held deep sympathy; the mouth behind the short brown beard quirked in a reassuring smile. "You did just fine."

Shakily, she laughed. "I promised myself no crying, at least until I couldn't see him anymore. I almost made it."

"You came close enough. Fact of the matter is I couldn't guarantee I'd make it."

The picture of them standing on the station platform, weeping buckets of tears while the train chugged indifferently down the tracks, curved Larissa's wobbly smile into a genuine one. She turned and almost stepped on her twelve-year-old daughter Rose, standing stricken behind her. Beside Rose, Ethan's daughter Charity wore an equally dejected expression. In spite of the severe emotional setback to her determination that their woebegone faces caused her, she reached a comforting hand to each of them. "You did just fine, too. The question is, how did Mac do?"

At the outrageous notion of Mac shedding tears over leaving home to fulfill his long awaited opportunity to attend medical school, the girls responded in duet. "He'd never cry!"

"Not Mac, Mrs. Edwards." Scandalized indignation reverberated in thirteen-year-old Charity's staunch defense of Rose's older brother.

"He certainly has stalwart supporters." Larissa turned to the white-haired man standing tactfully to the side while they regained their composure. "Don't you agree, Doc?"

Abe Rawley fingered his bushy white beard. "He certainly does. Trouble is, you were all so smiling and cheerful, he probably got the impression you couldn't wait to get rid of him." He spoke with gruff heartiness, but the shadow in his hazel eyes and his slumped shoulders betrayed his low spirits.

Larissa put her hand on his arm. "I know we aren't the only ones who've been cheering him on. If it weren't for you and all you've done, he wouldn't be on his way to Philadelphia, to study medicine the way he's always dreamed."

A faraway look veiled Doc Rawley's features. "He's the one who worked hard to make this day possible. I only gave him a boost up into the saddle. I'm going to miss him. I've become kind of used to him helping me around the office these past years." As if embarrassed by the admission, Doc studied the hat gripped in his hands. "Always underfoot. Always pestering me with questions. Wanting to know *Why this*? and *Why that*? Maybe I'll get some peace and quiet now."

Clearly, the old man took no joy from the prospect of peace and quiet. Larissa said impulsively, "Why don't you come to the farm for supper tonight?"

Doc started to decline, but Ethan didn't give him a chance to complete an excuse. "Come on back with us. It'll be great to have you."

"I don't want to intrude."

"Doc," Larissa protested, "How many times do I have to tell you —"

"You couldn't intrude if you tried!" The chorus from Ethan, Rose, and Charity proved a perfect mimicry of Larissa's often-repeated admonition when Doc declined a supper invitation for fear of taking advantage of their hospitality. She tried to look indignant at their performance, but failed miserably as a sputter of mirth escaped her. Doc's jaw dropped and he began coughing violently. With Ethan whacking him on the back, and Charity and Rose doubled up with hilarity, by the time he got his wind back, the opportunity to refuse the supper invitation had flapped away into the sunset.

"You might as well come on out right now. A hot supper will fix you up fine." With wild but nonetheless hearty optimism, Ethan dispensed his remedy.

Doc tugged at his ear, studied Charity and Rose's crimson faces and quivering lips, Ethan's determined expression, Larissa's unmistakable sincerity — and the forlornness in her dark blue eyes. "I accept your gracious offer," he announced gruffly. "I don't think my respiratory abilities could take the consequences of refusing a second time."

All joking forgotten, Ethan rested his hand on Doc's shoulder. "Why don't you come on out with us right now?"

They turned toward their buggy, but Doc gestured to Bella, his semi-patiently waiting piebald mare, hitched to his own rig. "I need to put a note on the office door where I'll be. You go ahead. I'll be along directly." Climbing into the buggy, he shook out the reins. Bella, as usual letting him know her opinion of the proceedings, started with a jerk.

Charity and Rose scrambled into the backseat of the high-topped buggy and slid along the leather cushion. Their eyes met and lowered in sudden sober realization. Without Mac taking up his rightful third portion and then some of the seat, for the first time, each girl had plenty of room.

Ethan assisted Larissa into the front, but, caught up in their own sense of loss, neither adult noticed the unusual lack of chatter behind them. The buggy swayed as he swung up into the seat beside her. Gathering the reins into his right hand, he started to reach his free hand toward her but halted the movement almost before he'd begun.

"I'm all right," she murmured. "Truly."

Privately, Ethan reckoned her measurement of "all right" compared to his about as closely as a bullfrog to a polliwog. They had acknowledged their mutual love the previous June. After careful consideration, however, they'd decided not to tell anyone of their intentions until after Mac's departure. Such reticence, they'd agreed, would enable Larissa to devote her full attention to her son during his last days at home, without being the center of attention herself. Unfortunately, when the occupants of the backseat were around, as now, this same discretion served to prevent each from fully responding to the other's emotional dilemmas.

Ethan, after an anxious glance at her set face, kept his opinions to himself. He knew from harsh personal experience how, at times, words were utterly useless. Some of the events of the weeks after Nettie died, leaving him to raise Charity, then just four years old, would forever be a blur. However, he remembered only too sharply the expectations, some subtle, some not, that he would quickly remarry and give his daughter a new mother. Even the most well intentioned suggestions had served only to heighten his sense of loss with their "she's dead and gone, so get on with your life" implications. He'd brought Charity from Croswell, Michigan to Ohio precisely to escape such pressure. He'd met Larissa and swiftly learned why his heart had so stubbornly resisted any interest in other women.

As he spoke to the horses, she set her slender fingers to tucking a wayward wisp of chestnut hair back under the edge of her platter-shaped hat. Not deceived by this casual movement, attempting to ease his acute recognition of her turmoil, he kept his eyes steadfastly on the road ahead. The old feeling of futility at being unable to help her in her darkest moments assailed him forcefully, as it had after her husband Zane died in the Civil War, now eighteen months over. With no right to interfere in her personal life during that heart-wrenching time, he had been forced to stand by while she became the target of suggestions regarding the most intimate areas of her life. She, too, had learned the futility of wishing people would stop identifying with her grief by saying they knew just how she felt. For her, however, an extra burr stuck to the saddle blanket. Society's rigid rules decreed that a woman, upon the death of her husband, must mourn him for precisely one year. Social etiquette also demanded that, during those same twelve months, the widow must swath herself in black from head to foot, to show proper grief.

All that first year after Zane died, Larissa had brazenly breached this standard of conduct by wearing subdued colors that did not include black. She'd told Ethan that Zane, his quiet ways notwithstanding, would have objected emphatically to drowning herself in widow's weeds. Society's requisite year of mourning dragged to a finish, but it did so with utter disregard for Larissa's personal timetable of grief. This burnished autumn afternoon, three years after Zane's death, she continued to follow her heart by favoring colors such as the mauve hat that matched her skirt and jacket.

The hair tucking task completed, she tipped her face to the sun's caressing rays. Ethan shifted his feet restlessly against the dashboard. *How she'll laugh if I even suggest that, in this particular outfit, her eyes outrival last night's violet-blue dusk. No,* he corrected himself honestly, *being Larissa, she won't laugh, but she'll sure as heaven be taken aback. And with good reason at such a fancy comparison!*

She couldn't have read his thoughts, but he gave a startled twitch when she said softly, "Mac's really gone. It doesn't seem possible. At least I know I'll see him again."

Unlike Zane, who, one sunny springtime day, rode away to war and never returned.

The unspoken words hung between them. "Zane would be proud of his son, today, Larissa."

Zane, who would never again share with her his pride in their son, had enlisted in the Sixth Ohio Volunteer Cavalry when the Civil War started in 1861. Unknown to him, Obadiah Beldane, Fairvale's blacksmith and farrier who, the citizenry claimed, had actually talked the ears off a jackrabbit, also joined the Sixth Ohio Cavalry. In 1862, the Army sent their unit to Nebraska Territory. Their assignment was to guard the stage stations along the Oregon Trail from Indian harassment after the regular soldiers were sent east to fight in the larger conflict. On a sunny afternoon in April 1863, Zane had died in an attack upon one of those stage stops. The events of the afternoon Larissa learned of Zane's death were forever seared upon Ethan's heart. As the remembrance stirred and stretched, he added, more roughly than he intended, "He'd be very proud of you, too."

At his undisguised support of her emotions, she sat a little straighter and pressed her lips together to keep them from trembling. "Thank you. It means more than I can tell you. I've already promised myself, but I promise you, too, I'll not be gloomy about all this. Mac is alive and well, and is now on his way to achieve what he's wanted to do all his life. Only a foolish mother would grouse about it. I hope to goodness I have more sense than that!"

He turned his head, then, to look directly at her. "You need never fear on that score, I assure you."

The twinkle in his eyes caused her mouth to quirk upward in spite of herself. "That's very comforting."

"Here comes Doc!"

At the excited pronouncement from the backseat, Larissa turned, fully intending to respond cheerfully, and gasped instead. She naturally expected to see two blonde heads encased in bonnets and two pairs of blue eyes focused on her. Instead, she viewed the flower-sprigged material covering the backsides of the young ladies. Each of the top portions leaned precariously around its respective edge of the buggy, one gloved hand clutching the hood braces, the other madly waving at the retreating scenery. "Rose and Charity!"

At her squeal of distress, Ethan hauled on the reins, unceremoniously halting Pegasus and Andromeda. "Larissa?" He twisted, seeking the cause of the commotion, and promptly joined his stern voice with hers. "Charity and Rose, turn around and sit down properly. Now." He didn't speak loudly, but the authority in his tone bore no leeway for nonsense.

The startled glance between the girls turned sheepish as they hastily slid onto the seat. Larissa seldom became infuriated with the children, but she now made up for lost time. "What were you thinking?"

"Sorry, Ma." Rose tucked her chin down.

"Me, too, Mrs. Edwards," Charity chimed in. Her father rewarded her with a look that boded no good for her previously prominent backside.

Doc halted his buggy beside them. "Something wrong?"

"Just reminding two young ladies it is dangerous, as well as unwise for pleasing a parent, to hang off the side of a moving buggy." Ethan's voice remained controlled, but Charity and Rose scrunched further back into the seat.

Doc blinked. "They were waving at me. I didn't realize they were so unbalanced." His words hung in the air as Ethan did a double take, Larissa pressed her fingers to her mouth, and the girls nervously rolled their eyes at each other.

Doc's expression radiated innocence. "Wouldn't that make a dandy first letter to Mac? 'Nothing exciting here. Except for Rose and Charity falling out of the buggy onto their heads, but we won't bore you with the details. The chickens have been unusually productive. Now, the weather—'"

Ethan's breath snagged. His abrupt exhalation sounded uncannily similar to their bull Goliath as, head lowered ominously before charging, he pawed the earth and snorted. Unfazed, Doc shook out the reins and spoke to Bella's rump, his words drifting to the other buggy. "'Thunderheads piled up ominously on the horizon, but fizzled out like a soggy match.'"

Ethan salvaged enough control to direct an "I'll remember this little prank," glower to the backseat, no easy task with Larissa sitting beside him wheezing through her fingers.

For the remainder of the ride home, Larissa, head down, didn't speak. Unfortunately, this prudent behavior did not stifle the tremors that betrayed her sincere effort not to laugh. Gritting his teeth so hard his jaws ached, Ethan focused on the suddenly painstaking task of steering the bay horses along the road they'd traveled a thousand times. At long last, the farm acres stretched before them. The golden stubble of the shorn wheat field blended seamlessly into the butter-yellow smudge in the distance that marked the apple orchard. In the chicken yard, Big Ben, whose internal clock was in perpetual need of adjustment, crowed lustily. A pencil stroke of smoke from the kitchen chimney lifted and was lost in the blue vaulty heaven above their heads.

With utmost precision, he guided the team along the curving drive beside the white-painted farmhouse, halted the buggy beside the walkway to the back door, and jumped down to assist Larissa. Still refusing to meet his eyes, she sped toward the house. Rose and Charity, hastily alighting, followed Larissa's path to the kitchen as Ethan motioned Doc and Bella over to the buggy shed. Once safely inside, his breath exploded in a soggy gurgle. Even Doc, not given to conspicuous displays of hilarity, couldn't control the rusty screen door squawks emitting from the region of his bushy beard. If they took longer than usual unharnessing the horses and tending the stock, no one mentioned it when they walked in on the kitchen's bustling work-in-progress. To the contrary, Charity and Rose were models of respectful efficiency as they assisted Larissa with the cooking and table setting.

When Larissa finally called everyone to be seated, Ethan risked a glance at her. Silly as it had been, the laughter had been an outlet for the aching emptiness in all their hearts. Larissa's cheeks were flushed, but that could have been from working at the stove. Apparently she, too, had conquered her mirth. He didn't hold out any signed and sealed guarantees for either of them that it would last, especially when she gazed steadfastly at his throat as she asked him to say the blessing.

He joined his hands with Doc on his left and Charity on his right. "Heavenly Father, thank You for Your blessings. Please be with Mac as he undertakes his cherished dream of medical school. We ask that You bless Doc Rawley, without whom Mac's venture would not be possible." He thought Doc's hand twitched, but went on hastily. "Thank You for watching over Charity and Rose, even if they sometimes forget to watch out for themselves." This time a distinct quiver came from Charity's cold fingers linked with his, but he plowed on.

"And finally, God, we ask that You be with Larissa as her heart adjusts to Mac's absence. May You grant her the serenity of understanding that, in letting him go, she has made it possible for him to come back." She raised her head, and for the first time in two hours, met his eyes directly.

"Thank you." Her lips moved soundlessly, but the words were unmistakable.

He smiled and bowed his head. "Amen."

During the meal, the lighthearted atmosphere lingered as Doc told stories of Mac's encounters with patients during the fledgling days of his apprenticeship. "I'll never forget the look on his face the first time he went with me to the Packer farm. We'd been called there because one of the girls had a bellyache. The 'girl' turned out to be Pa Packer's mule. I swear Mac's face turned almost as red as his hair. I figured he'd light a shuck for the hills, but he stayed and saw the whole thing through. I knew then he'd been blessed with his Pa's grit. And his Ma's." Doc peered at Larissa from under his untamed white brows.

She promptly blushed. To cover her loss of composure, she thrust the dish of mashed potatoes toward him. "How's Elsie Damon doing?" She asked more as a distraction for herself than anything else. Doc, who didn't really want more potatoes, meekly accepted the bowl, thus removing the danger of the hot contents landing in his lap.

"Pretty well, considering Theo hiked off to war and left her with nine young ones to support and hasn't bothered to hike back yet, even though the War's been over this past year and a half."

Ethan reached for the cornbread. "Chances of his returning now seem rather slim."

Caught up in the discussion, Doc blinked at the dish of potatoes as if wondering how it came to be in his hands, and automatically slapped a healthy spoonful onto his plate. He passed the bowl to Ethan, who started to scoop out a portion, only to discover the dish no longer contained any potatoes. Oblivious to everything except their conversation, Doc started eating the fluffy mound on his plate. Bemused, Ethan offered him the gravy boat.

Nodding his thanks, Doc dipped out two ladles full as he responded to Ethan's comment. "Chances of him coming back were already slim the day he and Kell Hollister weaseled their way into being certified healthy and signed up to go to war."

"All the other Union County men are back or accounted for. But no one's heard a word from or about either of them. You think they were killed?" Ethan asked the question gravely, aware of the personal implications for Larissa by even this indirect allusion to her husband's death. When Zane's life halted, the world had kept going along its indifferent path. Larissa, therefore, refused to demean his memory by a foolish taboo. Such topics did not come up often, but neither one shied away when the subject surfaced.

Doc snorted. "I don't think either one of that precious pair went out of his way to put himself in the path of a bullet. I have a strong suspicion they started marching one day and just kept going, claiming they didn't hear the 'to the rear' command."

Charity and Rose, shoulders shaking, studied their empty supper plates intently. With perfect solemnity, Ethan remarked, "If so, they must have marched right into the Pacific Ocean on the far side of California by now. When they needed to start swimming, do you think they got an inkling something didn't square up?"

Doc's lip curled in unbridled distain as he delivered his irrefutable opinion, garnered from years of medical wisdom. "They were all wet before they even started, so they probably wouldn't know the difference!" The girls simultaneously dropped their napkins, dived after them under the hanging edge of the tablecloth, and experienced a great deal of difficulty retrieving them. Poorly suppressed giggles, floating upward, marked their progress.

As if someone else owned the two children making such a commotion at her feet, Larissa ignored them and shook her head. "Some folks are hinting their staying away is the best thing that could happen to their families. But never knowing for certain why they didn't come back has to be a terrible burden for their wives." In the sudden silence that descended, she stood abruptly. "Would you like more coffee, Doc?"

He threaded his napkin through the pewter ring beside his plate. "Thanks, but no. I'd best be getting back to town to see who's fallen out of a tree or got himself cut up. There's bound to be something."

"I'll see you out." Ethan set down his coffee cup.

Doc paused at the door. "Thank you for another superb supper, Larissa." He frowned in puzzlement. "I'd swear I don't eat that much more here than at home. Can't figure out why I always go away feeling like I have. Must be the excellent company, and your good cooking."

"We'll expect you back soon, and no excuses." Pulling on her shawl, she followed the men onto the porch and paused near the top step as they made their way to the buggy shed. She leaned her head against the porch support post and closed her eyes. As from a great distance, she heard Ethan's farewell and Doc's response.

Aware Ethan would soon return to the house, determined not to let him catch her feeling sorry for herself, she dashed down the steps. Turning left, she hurried along the path to the cabin, where he and Charity lived. She didn't go far. Neither the candle glow from the kitchen window nor the faint starshine lightened the shadows. She figured if she couldn't see much, Ethan wouldn't fare any better and so, hopefully, wouldn't even notice her standing there. At least it would give her a few moments to get her emotions under control.

Her tendency these last few days to weep at everything in sight really annoyed her. She certainly didn't behave this way normally. So why couldn't she control her tears, now? *You're not the only woman in existence whose son went out into the world, because the time came for him to leave the nest.*

"Larissa?"

Ethan didn't startle her. She'd heard his footsteps behind her before he spoke. *He can't possibly see my red eyes and drippy nose.* She sent up a prayer that she could control her traitorous voice. "I'm here." To her relief, she sounded breathless, but otherwise normal.

He paused a few steps off. "Blacker than the inside of a cow, here," he observed mildly. "Which brings up a question I've certainly often pondered. Why are we so sure the inside of a cow is black? Maybe the cuds she chews throw off enough light, like marsh gas, to make it bright and cozy in there."

Larissa bit her lip hard, but in vain. A raspy sputter escaped her. *Better to laugh than to cry*, skidded through her mind as she turned to face him, at least to face the direction of his voice. In the darkness, he proved little more than a shadow among deeper shadows.

"Am I disturbing you, Larissa? Should I leave?"

His sudden switch to seriousness caught her off guard. "No, and no. I'm glad you found me here." Surprised at her own words, she knew them for truth. "I just came to commune with nature for a few moments before I go back inside and face the kitchen mess."

"I suspect it's going to take more than just communing with Mother Nature if you're hoping a supper aftermath that size will simply disappear. I'm betting the old girl won't settle for less than a good, old-fashioned bribe!"

"I suspect you're right. We need a magic wand, like in all the fairy stories."

He chuckled. "Seems to me in all those fairy stories, they got into more trouble than they bargained for when one of those magic wands showed up, and they ended up wishing they'd never seen the pesky thing. But if you'd like to have one, I'll see what I can conjure—I mean come up with." He searched his pockets. "Wouldn't you know?" he said in annoyance. "I seem to have left my conjuring book in my other suit. If you don't mind waiting here, I'll go fetch it."

Better to laugh than to cry. "Most careless of you," she said severely. "It's all right this once, but please be better prepared next time."

He hung his head contritely. "My solemn promise. Say, you don't have to go back to the house right this minute, do you?"

"I really should get started on those dishes."

"I meant to check on Deneb after Doc left, but I got sidetracked. It's a nice night for a stroll. Would you care to come to the barn with me to check on him?"

"Is something the matter with him?" Anxiety quickened her words. The black Morgan horse Deneb had been the pride and joy of Zane's stable. Zane took him along when he enlisted in the Ohio Cavalry. Deneb accompanied him when the Army sent him to Virginia, and later to Fort Laramie in Nebraska Territory. The war ended. Deneb came home. Zane did not.

"I'm sure he's fine. He just acted a little off his feed this evening. I'd like to check him one more time."

"Of course." She pulled her shawl more closely about her shoulders as they turned in the direction of the barn.

"Are you warm enough?"

"On this nice night for a stroll, I'm just fine."

Once in the barn, Ethan lit the tin lantern and led the way to Deneb's stall. The drowsing horse blinked curiously in the soft glow. Ethan handed Larissa the lamp and ran his hands over the gleaming black withers. "He seems fine, now. Maybe I just imagined it."

"It certainly never hurts to be sure." Her voice held undisguised relief.

With a final stroke of Deneb's muzzle, Ethan took the lantern and led the way to the door. "I'm sorry. I didn't mean to alarm you." His voice held genuine regret. He knew how much Deneb meant to her as a living connection to Zane.

She remained silent as they turned toward the porch, and once again that day she mentally braced herself, this time to face the after-supper wreck awaiting her. She crossed the threshold and stopped so suddenly that Ethan, a step behind her and closing the door, had no time to swerve.

He whacked into her and almost sent her sprawling. Only his quick grab at her arm kept her upright.

He couldn't blame her for looking bewildered. With effort, he hid his grin as his glance followed hers around the room. The kitchen, far from a tornado aftermath, gleamed with cleanliness. The dishes had been washed, dried, and stored away. The leftover food had been whisked out of sight. Candles twinkled brightly in their holders on the polished table. Ethan cleared his throat. "It appears our mischievous daughters recognized the error of their ways."

"And corrected it magnificently! They must be in Rose's room." Hurrying through the doorway to the sitting room and past the banister to her left, she paused at the foot of the stairs and called up to the girls. A muffled response drifted down. "Please come down." Behind her, Ethan quenched the twinkle in his eyes and assumed his best "stern father" expression.

Slow footsteps sounded in the uncarpeted hallway above, and two wary faces peeked around the top of the stairs. "Come down." Obviously deciding not to increase the vexation apparent in Ethan's command, they descended the steps with dragging feet. Heads down, they stopped in front of Larissa.

She reached one hand to Rose and one to Charity, cupping their chins and tilting the worried faces up to her. "Thank you," she said softly.

"You're not mad anymore?" Charity's tone mirrored the sudden hope in Rose's eyes.

"No, I'm not mad. You did a wonderful job cleaning the kitchen. Such an enormous chore to do all by yourselves."

"You didn't tell her, Pa?"

He grinned at her amazement. "Not a word."

Larissa whirled. "You knew about this?"

He hung his head. "I confess. I walked in on the girls while they were busy waving their magic wand. I couldn't say anything to you. I promised them I wouldn't." He raised his right hand as if taking a solemn oath, and studiously avoided her affronted glare.

She put her hands on her hips. "So Deneb appeared to be off his feed, did he?"

He had the grace to look completely guilty. "You must admit, we had a nice stroll."

Fortunately for him, Charity's exuberance drowned out Larissa's response. "You're not mad anymore either, Pa?"

Ethan put his hand against his daughter's hair. "I'm not mad any more, either." The twinkle he had earlier repressed bounced back. "How could I be? I bet anything Rose's Ma planned to get me in there with an apron tied around my waist to help. You saved me from a terrible fate of scrubbing and polishing!"

The girls looked at each other and giggled. Rose threw her arms around Larissa, and Charity followed suit with Ethan. "Ma, may Charity stay tonight? We'll be quiet, I promise."

The wistfulness in her daughter's tone did not escape Larissa. Or Ethan, she saw as he indicated his agreement. "All right. As long as you promise to be quiet," she said sternly.

"We'll be quiet as church mice!" Charity vowed. She gave Ethan a final hug and raced up the stairs after Rose.

"I've always wondered about the reputation church mice have for being quiet," Ethan mused. "Seems to me someone just might be pulling someone else's whiskers." Then, "It's mighty good of you to let Charity stay. I imagine you'd like a little peace and quiet, and I'm not sure now you're going to get it."

"Rose is feeling pretty down. I can tell even if she's doing an excellent job hiding it. It'll be good for her to have Charity near, this first night Mac's away."

He cupped his palm against her cheek. "I know Rose isn't the only one feeling down, even if you're doing an excellent job hiding it. I wish I could help you."

"You do help me, truly. I don't know what I would have done without you, today."

"Larissa—"

The bedroom door opening above them and a plaintive, "Ma?" caused them to jump apart before Rose's head appeared around the stairway. "Ma, a button popped off my nightgown, and we can't find it. Do you have another one I can sew on?"

"I'd better go," he said hastily.

"Ethan, wait!"

"I'll see you in the morning." He disappeared into the kitchen and she immediately heard the back door open and close.

"Ma?"

"I'm sure I have one, Rose." Her feet took her up the stairs, but her heart fled into the night with him.

CHAPTER TWO

All through the diligent but unsuccessful search for the old button, finding a new one, and getting it securely fastened to Rose's nightgown, Larissa's mind stayed only half on her task. The other half replayed the conversation on the path, the spoken words and those said simply by Ethan's presence. Eventually, the girls completed their prayers, although Larissa made a conscious effort to keep her smile in place at Rose's murmured, "Please be with Mac, wherever he is now." *Wherever he is now* evoked a too-clear image of the train hurtling through darkness, with her son a small dot in one of the lighted windows.

Resolutely tucking the quilt snugly under their chins, she dropped a kiss on each cheek, and blew out the candle. "I want you to go to sleep. No talking half the night."

"Yes, Ma."

She paused in the doorway. "Good night. I love you." Rose's drowsy murmur echoed Charity's wide awake one.

At the foot of the stairs, Larissa hesitated. Common sense said Ethan must be ready for bed by this time. How patiently he'd stood by her today, allowing her to deal in her own way with her pain over Mac's departure and, most importantly, not consoling her with empty phrases. Even tonight, he'd given comfort while leaving her the freedom to accept it according to her own needs.

Remorse elbowed her at remembrance of his rushing away when Rose diverted her attention with the button problem. *No wonder! He attempted to reassure you about facing the long night ahead, and you decided a button deserved more attention.* She'd never before sought him out once he left the house for the night, but this time, the necessity loomed too great to ignore. *I'll just go see if a light's still burning in the cabin. If not, I'll wait until tomorrow to set it straight with him.* Thus convincing herself, she snatched her shawl from the peg by the kitchen door. Greeted by the unexpectedly sharp evening breeze, she pulled the wrap closely about her.

Candlelight showing in the cabin window guided her along the path. Relief and nervousness both pulling at her, she rapped on the door. At the noise of swift movement inside, turning and running suddenly became an option worthy of consideration. Before she could consider, turn or run, the door swung open and Ethan stood before her. He no longer wore his suit coat, but revealed no other preparations for bed. The pipe in his mouth and the book in his hand indicated his intention to relax before going to sleep. He blinked in confusion.

"Larissa! I thought you were Charity. Is she all right?"

"She's fine. I'm sorry I startled you. May we talk?"

Swift relief became questioning as he stepped aside for her to enter the cabin. "Of course. Come in."

She hesitated, and berated herself for such silliness. She and the girls cleaned the cabin each Saturday, but she and Ethan had not been inside together since the day she learned of Zane's death. She'd been caught in a drenching thunderstorm down by Mill Creek, and Ethan had taken her to the cabin. Her ensuing behavior still held the power to make her blush. Ethan never faulted her or even mentioned her actions, except for the one time, at her insistence, they discussed the situation. She'd never again worked up the courage to speak of it.

Now, seeing the flush spread across her cheeks, he said lightly, "It's still a nice night for a stroll. Just let me put my book and pipe down." Suiting his actions to the words, he picked up his coat and came out on the stoop. "Shall we go along here?"

Furious at the relief swamping her, she nodded. He took her arm and they walked slowly to the spot where they'd stood earlier. "All right, now?" He spoke as casually as if she hadn't just made a complete idiot of herself.

"Yes. Thank you." She felt the heat rising in her cheeks again. *Whatever possessed you to drag him into this awkward situation? It looks for all the world like you're chasing him.* "I wanted to tell you how much your support, your being with me, meant to me today," she blurted out. "I started to tell you in the house, but Rose interrupted and you left so fast, I didn't finish." His reaction to this hastily spilled speech caught her off guard. With moonlight now added to the earlier star speckle, she saw his surprise. He started to speak but didn't. "Ethan?"

"I appreciate your telling me." An odd gravity tinged his voice. "Coming to me like this means more than you know. I want to help you. I want to be here for you." His words suddenly came out muffled. "It just seems when you need me to be here the most, I'm not."

"You're with me now. Nothing else matters." She smiled wryly. "You don't get into the messes I manage to stir up for myself, but I want to make certain you know I'm here for you, too, should the occasion arise."

He chuckled. "One official stirrer-upper of problems is plenty! Since you do such a good job, I'll continue to let you claim the honor."

"You're too kind."

"Just one of my failings," he said modestly. "I do have a few, and this is my greatest one. When I'm with you, I want so much to do this." His arms around her and his mouth against hers effectively silenced any protest she may have been considering.

"If this is your gravest fault," she managed breathlessly, "I hope with all my heart you're never cured!"

The day had been stuffed full of emotion. Compelling her heart and soul to cheerfully send Mac off, the genuine fright Rose and Charity caused in the buggy, the words at supper bringing home to her the grief of Zane's death, and, now, the wonder of Ethan's arms and his quiet strength enfolding her.

In keeping with their agreement about waiting until Mac's departure to announce their altered relationship, they'd behaved decorously in front of the children. If the young people had suspected the changed circumstances, they'd offered no comment. Through the past months, with the exception of a few private, memorable lapses, Larissa and Ethan had managed to stay reasonably straight on their appointed path. *Doing so makes moments like this all the more precious.* Larissa's hazy musing faded entirely as she raised her face now to meet Ethan's kiss.

After a lingering moment, his mouth moved to her cheek, to the soft chestnut hair at her temple. "Lizzie?" His breath warmed the region of her right earlobe.

"Yes?"

At her sighed breath, his arms tightened, his mouth returned to hers, and his resolve to bring up a vitally important subject faded into nothing.

***

The morning following Mac's departure for Philadelphia, Larissa awoke and lay a few moments, sorting out her thoughts. After keeping such a tight rein on her emotions through all of yesterday's events, she now felt only a weary emptiness.

In spite of the darkness, she reached unerringly to her bedside table for the roughly rendered, framed sketch of Zane. His Christmas present to her, he had sent it from an Army camp in Virginia the first winter of the Civil War. A traveling photographer had taken a picture of him and Obadiah Beldane. Unfortunately, he'd admitted, the requirement that he sit motionless for such a long time, in order for the shooting process to work, resulted in his "looking grimmer than all the barn owls of my acquaintance put together!" Not wanting to "scare the tar out of her," he'd made this sketch, instead. He hoped she didn't mind his not sending the original picture.

She didn't mind. She much preferred this work of his own hands, in which she glimpsed the quiet strength that had been so much a part of him. Unable to see him in the dark, she traced her finger over the glass covering the penciled drawing.

Yesterday, she'd admitted to Ethan it had proved more difficult to send Mac off than she'd expected. She didn't tell him how it brought back those moments of saying goodbye to Zane the April morning he left forever. In the last months, Mac's height, the breadth of his shoulders, and the way he tipped his head forward when a conversation intensely interested him, all echoed Zane. Still, she smiled. Mac's blazing crown of hair belonged entirely to him. The red thatch certainly didn't match Zane's dark brown hair or her own chestnut shade. She knew where it came from, however.

The years had blurred many of the events of her childhood, but one incident lingered, even after nearly four decades. She'd been no more than three the day she looked up from her play and realized Mama no longer stood at the worktable, scrubbing carrots. Toddling in search of her, Larissa heard her voice and recognized the lullaby Mama sang to her each night.

"Soft the drowsy hours are creeping
Hill and dale in slumber sleeping ..."

Wandering out to the front porch, she found Mama sitting on the top step, singing as she brushed the tangles from her just-washed hair. The afternoon sun, striking her mother's auburn locks, shot golden fire through them. Larissa had stood and stared at the wondrous halo shimmering around Mama's head.

"I my loved one's watch am keeping."

Slowly, she reached a small finger to touch the radiance. Fully aware how pretty flames burned painfully, the knowledge couldn't prevent her from seeking the source of the swirling fire. Her mother turned at the inquisitive patting and, smiling, drew her baby onto her lap. She finished her song while Larissa snuggled into her arms, never taking her eyes off the dancing flames that had not burned her, after all.

Larissa blinked, returning to the present. Her mother died shortly after Larissa and Zane married, but her memory lingered in Mac's burnished crest, which had, these past years, begun to darken from its initial fiery thatch to his grandmother's true auburn. The fact, Larissa suspected, would have pleased her mother very much.

With a last gentle touch for Zane's picture, she replaced it on the table and threw back the covers to air the bed. She'd memory-wandered too long and now must hustle to get breakfast on the table before the girls were late for school.

She hurried with her dressing and knocked on Rose's door on her way down the hall. Her daughter's voice chirped back at her, so she didn't pause. She reached the kitchen just as Ethan came in with the milk pails. She spoke, but fixed her attention on tying her apron and setting out the ham for slicing. She didn't really notice his quietness as he bent over the stove to replenish the fire he had started earlier.

Rose, with Charity lagging behind, came tumbling down the stairs in time to help make the batter for fried potato cakes. Larissa directed

Charity to set the table. She did so, but with a credible lack of enthusiasm. In a far corner of her mind, Larissa, stirring the skillet of scrambled eggs, noted the apathy, but awareness slid away as she reached for a bowl and began putting the steaming dishes on the table.

After eating only a few bites, Ethan pushed back his chair. "I'll go hitch up the buckboard." He zipped out the door before Larissa could comment on his abruptness and his failure to finish his breakfast. She sent a puzzled glance after him, but in the flurry of collecting schoolbooks and the lunch pail, and getting the girls out the door, she had no time to ponder his unusual behavior.

She stood on the porch, watching him guide the rig around the curve in the driveway. Remembering the grim lines around his mouth, uneasiness nudged her, but she reasoned if she'd somehow upset him, he would let her know. Talking things out formed one of the cornerstones of their relationship. *Of course*, she admitted with wonderful hindsight, *there wasn't much opportunity this morning for discussing problems. But fretting won't get the breakfast dishes done or the morning's work started. If something's bothering Ethan, he'll talk about it when he gets back, when the girls aren't around to interfere.*

In spite of this fine lecture, a part of her mind kept fussing as she plunged into the tasks which, inevitably, would swallow up her day. She finished the dishes, packed last evening's washed eggs into her egg cask, taking care to cover them well with the salt that would preserve them for winter eating, and went upstairs to make her bed. All the time she worked, however, her ears were tuned for the sound of the buckboard returning.

Back in the kitchen, she went down to the cellar for vegetables to add to the noon meal. Laying them in the dry sink for scrubbing, she glanced out the window toward the barn and saw both Andromeda and Pegasus in the corral. Ethan had returned, then, without coming to the house. She frowned. Whenever he left on an errand, he always checked in to let her know he'd come back, just one of the many small courtesies he extended her. The earlier uneasiness poked her mid-section with a sharp-nailed finger. Something must be seriously wrong.

Wiping her gritty hands on her still crisp apron, she hurried out to the barn. Stepping over the threshold of the smaller door, she peered into the dusky interior. "Ethan?" No answer. Swiftly inspecting, she found no trace of him in the hay mow, any of the stalls, or the manure shed. Back outside, she halted in puzzlement. Unlike him, he hadn't laid out any specific plans at breakfast for his day's activities. The sharp fingernail scratched her again. *In all honesty, he didn't have a chance to say much of anything.*

In the wheat field, the stubble glowed golden in the sun, a happy reminder that the grain had been had been cut, threshed, and sold in a market slowly recovering from the economic downturn of the war years. The corn would be harvested within the week. Perhaps Ethan had decided to check its readiness. Since she'd neglected to wear her bonnet, the autumn sunshine fell warmly on her head and shoulders as she trudged to the edge of the cornfield. "Ethan?"

Still receiving no answer, she hesitated. The apple orchard? She knew it to be a retreat for him, much as she claimed the wide flat rock overhanging the creek for her quiet place. Had he gone to the orchard to be alone?

If I find him, I won't interfere. I just want to know he's all right. Lifting her skirts free of the dusty grass, she hurried toward the orchard and finally caught sight of him. Instead of pacing the rows or examining the apples, he simply stood beneath a tree at the end of a row, his back to her, right arm raised to rest against an apple-laden branch. Certain he failed to hear her footsteps in the muffling grass, but assured he hadn't come to harm, she turned back.

Through her morning's work, she mulled the possibilities for his abstracted behavior. She could think of nothing she had done or said to upset him. *Unquestionably, he was attentive enough out on the path last night.* Her lips curved in a soft smile at memory of his attentiveness. A thought nudged her, but she dismissed it as soon as it batted at her awareness. In spite of her sureness, it slid back, curling around her consciousness like a kitten twining around her ankles.

Her hands stilled the dasher of the butter churn. Last night when she sought him out in the cabin, perhaps he'd thought her too eager. *Don't be ridiculous!* She thrust the dasher into the churn so forcefully, milk splashed down her front.

Ignoring the drippy mess, she stared at the green gingham curtains over the sink. *We're not a pair of children, embarking on our first romantic adventure.* Both had known complete, fulfilling love, as well as the indescribable agony of losing such a love. If she now responded to Ethan's ardor as she had toward Zane's, she knew no other way, and in the deepest part of her heart, acknowledged it to be right and good. She'd never questioned Ethan's manner. She'd simply accepted it as the way of a man who also knew the ultimate fulfillment in love, of giving and of receiving.

But what if--? She set the dasher thumping furiously. *No 'what if' about it!* She'd known Ethan too long, been witness to his innate integrity too many times, to doubt him now. *Whatever his problem, we'll see it through together, and no more useless fretting on my part about it.*

With her vigorous swishing, the butter came too rapidly. *Now the texture will be off.* Thoroughly vexed with herself, she turned the mass out, washed, worked and salted it, and packed it into the molds handed down from her mother. Carrying them and the jug of buttermilk to the springhouse, she set them carefully on the shelf built under the flowing water, and wiped her damp hands on her milk-spattered apron. Halfway out the door, she abruptly turned back to the spring and seized the jug of buttermilk she'd put there at the last churning. Balancing the chilled, wet container firmly on her hip, she left the springhouse and started toward the apple orchard. Common sense scoffed. *It's probably foolish to expect him to still be there after all this time.* Resolutely ignoring common sense, she turned that way, anyhow.

She didn't find him in the apple orchard or the sugar maple grove. She'd already canned, and the peach crop was stored safely in the cellar. Nevertheless, she checked the picked-bare trees and felt a thrust of frustration at not seeing him there, either. Common sense gleefully stuck out its tongue as, clutching the jug from which the chill and moisture had faded, she headed to the springhouse to replace the buttermilk in the water. She knelt above the shelf and bent to set the container down. Ethan spoke behind her.

She jumped and almost followed the jug into the water, but caught herself before taking a disastrous plunge. "Ethan," she said faintly, all her stored up, fine words deserting her completely.

"Lizzie?" Perplexity shaded his voice, but otherwise he sounded so normal, sheer relief unkinked the knot in her stomach. "Is something troubling you? When I left the woodlot, I saw you come in here. You looked exceedingly upset. Were you searching for me?" Not so often any more, but once in a while, the precise English from his days as a tutor in Fredericksburg, Virginia, sprinkled his speech, betraying his agitation even when his unruffled demeanor hid it well.

Head down, she scrubbed her damp hands on her now thoroughly rumpled apron. He dropped to his heels beside her, peering sideways so he could see her. "Larissa?" Puzzlement and dismay combined in his voice as he brushed at the single tear sliding from her tightly closed lids.

At his touch, her determination to discuss her fears with calm dignity flew the coop. "I'm sorry I've been so dratted weepy these past few days! I *wish* I'd get over it," she told a splotch of buttermilk on her sleeve. "I suspect you wish I would, too." She risked a glance up. Encouraged by the depth of caring in his blue eyes, she gathered up her tattered resolve. "I wanted to talk to you, but I couldn't find you."

"It must be a powerfully important subject, to cause all this agitation," he teased. "Actually, I want to talk to you, too. Come, let's sit outside, where it's warmer."

She dropped onto the bench beside the springhouse door and rested her head against the sun-heated wall. In the warmth, her tightly strung anxiety eased. Just as swiftly as it pranced away, however, uncertainty galloped back when Ethan retreated a step and clasped his wrists behind him.

Seeing her confusion, he scuffed his boot toe at a pebble on the path. "Were you looking for me to find out why I've not had much to say this morning?"

CHAPTER THREE

At Larissa's affirmative duck of the chin, Ethan gave the pebble a final jab with the toe of his boot. "I've never been good at snap decisions. I always end up debating both sides of an issue until one of me wins. Or loses. I've been thrashing things out for weeks now, but after last night, I can't delay any longer. I've been hunting all morning for the right words."

"Last night?" she asked weakly.

"Yes." His mouth stayed open to continue. When no words followed the lone syllable, he gave a small laugh. "Not twenty minutes ago, I worked out exactly how to ask you. Now it's gone completely. You'll have to bear with my awkwardness."

"Ask me what?" As the crowning achievement of her wretchedness, she squeaked. If he noticed, he wisely didn't let a hint of it escape as he dropped to the seat beside her.

"Lizzie, when we talked in June, I suggested we keep our feelings between us without telling the children. It seemed such a brilliant plan at the hatching, what with Mac going off and all. It would give you time to devote to him without any distractions because of an official announcement of our intentions. It worked. Almost too well," he added dolefully.

"All summer I've wanted to shout my feelings for you to the world. I knew keeping quiet wouldn't be easy, but I definitely wasn't prepared for the reality. Admittedly, some frustration comes from needing to be so careful around the children, especially before Mac left. With his medical training, he's just too blasted observant about people's feelings! Last night on the path, for the first time, it didn't occur to me to look over my shoulder to see if the children stood there, all eyes and ears. More incredibly," at his gentle smile, her heart gave a treacherous flip, "I suspect it never occurred to you, either." She blushed furiously and poked the dried-stiff stain on her sleeve.

"Lizzie." He put his hand under her chin, compelling her to look up at him. "Holding you, with no other thoughts to distract us, felt so incredibly right and good. Like coming home. Does that make any sense at all?"

On silent wings, calmness and dignity returned as she clearly saw the depth of his tenderness. She laid her palm against his bearded cheek. "Yes. It makes perfect sense."

"And that's what made the rest so hard. When we gave Charity permission to stay and comfort Rose, I didn't stay and comfort you. I should have been with you last night, moral codes be damned! I couldn't take your pain away, but I left you to fight your grief all alone." His bitter reproach sliced through her haze of joy.

"Ethan, I wanted you with me, so much. I knew you couldn't stay, but I've been so worried that, going to find you, then responding like I did, I pushed you away. Maybe my actions weren't right for you." She tried to duck her head again, but his firm hand under her chin wouldn't let her. Nevertheless, she kept her eyes cast down and scrubbed busily at the buttermilk splash on her sleeve, and thus didn't see him staring at her, thunderstruck.

"Dear God, you thought...?" He gathered his scattered wits. "If only I knew the words to tell you the oneness I feel when I'm with you. So much of it comes precisely because of how gladly and freely you give of yourself in any situation. Can you believe me?"

"Yes," she said softly. "Because I feel the same way."

He slowly rose, drawing her up with him. His arms encircled her, cradled her to his heart. He bent his mouth to hers and felt the immediate sweet fire of her response. Reluctantly, he stood her back so he could look directly at her. "I don't ever want you to worry about throwing yourself at me or whatever the term may be. The only time your actions will ever not be right for me is when they aren't right for you. I would never, could never, want you to do anything you're not comfortable with. That's not love, to demand or even to expect such giving. And I love you."

With a blissful sigh, she rested her head against his chest. His unsteady breath echoed hers as he pressed his cheek to her hair and realized how, after weeks of delay, the time of decision crouched beside him, chuckling wickedly. He spoke hastily, lest the moment vanish like morning mist in sunshine. "About us waiting for the right time. Feeling we're married. But living in the same fashion we always have. We really should consider changing this arrangement." *Quit babbling!* Chiding himself fiercely had no effect whatsoever on his effort to halt his nervous rambling. *She might not, after all, see this as you do.* "I've tried to talk to you, but something always interrupts.'"

He clenched his jaw until he thought it would crack and forced himself to speak more intelligently. "I know this isn't a decision for us to make lightly, especially on your part."

A faint flush tinged her cheeks. "Ethan, I want just as much as you to base our relationship upon giving freely to each other in any situation. Before we're married is just as important as after." The words tumbled out. "I thought we had a mutual understanding why last night, and up to now, our relationship hasn't gone further." She gripped her hands tightly together, fervently wishing she could strangle the telltale heat in her face. "Are you saying it's time it does—even if we're not married?" Her voice trailed off, the faint flush now a flaming blush in spite of her annoyed efforts to quell it.

He gaped at her blankly as his stumbling words rolled around in his skull. Comprehension dawned. He actually turned beet red. "I wasn't implying—I didn't mean married or not, it's high time we should— My God, Larissa." He pushed his hand against his forehead and inhaled deeply. "Let me start over. I've repeated this so often in my mind, it's worn a groove, while you haven't a clue what I'm talking about. What I'm trying to say, however clumsily, is with Mac gone, we should rethink my position here on the farm."

Shifting mental gears, she blinked, plainly at a loss to understand what in the world he meant. "Your position? But after Zane ... after we knew he'd not be coming home, you agreed to stay and help manage the farm. Have you changed your mind?" Try as she would, she couldn't quench the panic in her voice as she sank onto the bench again.

On the eve of war, Zane had asked Ethan to help Larissa get to her sister in Vermont, "If something happens to me." The "something" had happened. Zane died in that Indian attack on the Overland Stage way station in Nebraska Territory, two years and a thousand miles away from the family and farm he loved. The sunny May morning, three days after they learned of his death, came back to Ethan in vivid detail.

Compelled to keep his promise, he had proffered the sensible suggestion she and the children move to Vermont. She'd promptly put him in his place. A very real part of Zane lingered in the fields and trees he had nurtured. Under no circumstances would she remove either herself or Zane's children from Zane's farm. Because Ethan possessed no desire to see her move hundreds of miles away out of his life, he hadn't argued. He'd simply kept his promise to stay and help her manage the farm. They'd never discussed it again. Until today.

Now he eased down beside her. "I would not willingly break our agreement about helping you manage the place. When Charity and I first moved into the cabin, to assist with the farm work after Zane left, no questions about respectability came up as far as I knew. Did anyone say anything to you or drop hints about me living on your farm, with your husband gone to war?"

Some of her bewilderment faded into understanding as she shook her head. He entwined his fingers in hers. "Near as I could figure, particularly with the children here, folks accepted it as a wartime necessity and minded their own business. You weren't the only wife forced to make arrangements to keep your farm going." He faltered, but plowed on. "Now the wartime necessity is over, and Mac's gone, too. Rose and Charity are still here, of course, but it's not quite the same. Truth to tell, I'm concerned for you."

"Surely folks have better things to do with their time than fantasize about us!"

"I've never worried about people deciding whether to accept or reject me, but this is different. In this situation, you'd be their target." He didn't know if her sharp protest stemmed from his words or his bland assumption of knowledge of the neighbors' thought processes. But he would not risk leaving the outcome to chance. "Unsavory as the prospect is, we must consider our circumstances as other people might. Here I am, involved every bit as much as you. However, as the man, I wouldn't receive nearly the notoriety from the good folks in our community as you, The Woman." His voice tolled the last two words, the reverberations sealing their knowledge how any guilt, real or imagined, would fall on her shoulders alone.

"I don't want this for you, under any conditions. Unlikely as it seems after all this time, there is an item or two we haven't added to our given freely list of accomplishments. Although your interpretation of my fine speech has a great deal of merit!" He smiled wryly. "Mutual understanding regardless, it's not been easy, I'll admit. After all, we aren't a pair of young ones who haven't learned something about life. But your integrity is a part of you, as mine is a part of me. I'll not dishonor that integrity, Larissa, now or ever." The quiet finality in his words brought a swift mist to her eyes.

"Ethan...."

"I know I didn't say it very well a while ago. But it's the simple truth." He fixed his gaze on a red-tailed hawk circling over the apple orchard. Caught in remembering, his voice lowered, but his words came without shame or hesitation. "When Nettie and I married, knowing we were beginning our life together after the wedding ceremony, not before, strengthened our bond. We made the decision together, and we kept the commitment together. Perhaps our choice isn't right for everyone, but it defined the essence of the relationship we wanted.

"I admit it made for a bit of awkwardness because I had no more experience than she." Pensively, he shook his head at his own young innocence in those years now gone. "But we learned together, and we never regretted our actions. Of course, we were very young, with our whole lives before us and no reason to believe we wouldn't be spending the next hundred or so years together." He smiled wistfully. "Turned out we were long on imagination but short in years."

The smile faded as gravity returned. "Forgive me for discussing personal details between Nettie and me. I have no wish to make you uncomfortable with such talk. Simply put, such a choice is a part of me. Just as then, it is now."

"Thank you, Ethan."

"For what?" She'd caught him completely off guard.

"For sharing with me. You don't often speak about Nettie. I owe her so much. After all, your life with her shaped the 'you' sitting here with me today. I wish I'd known her."

He cupped his hand against her hair. "I think the two of you would have liked each other very much."

"Larissa, are you home?" They both jumped at the voice issuing from the driveway. Turning, she saw a rig she didn't recognize, halted beside the kitchen path.

The unknown visitor hallooed once more and realization dawned. "It's Martha Van Ellis."

She started to call a response, but Ethan, behind her, suddenly slipped his arms about her waist and drew her backward into the springhouse. In the privacy of its shadowy confines, he turned her to face him and bent his mouth down to hers. "So much for no interruptions this time, either," he murmured resignedly. He loosened his hold and gave her a lopsided smile and a light push. "We'll finish this discussion later. Happy visiting!"

She opened her mouth, then shut it again, but before she ducked out the door, he glimpsed her radiant smile.

Hurrying along the path to meet Martha, she attempted to remedy her appearance by tucking a pin more firmly into the heavy bun at the back of her head. The dried-stiff buttermilk splashes on her apron were explainable ... sort of, anyway. She fervently hoped Martha would attribute her crimson cheeks to the crispness of the autumn day. For the warmth within her causing the stain on her cheeks, she possessed no remedy.

Martha, halfway back into her buggy when Larissa called out, stepped to the ground. Her greeting indicated her chief concern didn't revolve around Larissa's disheveled appearance. "I'm so glad you're home! I need to talk to you."

Larissa, fully aware of the subject Martha wanted to discuss, gave her a hug. "Come on in. I'll see what the coffeepot's doing."

While she fiddled with the dregs in the pot, Martha blurted out, "Have you and Ethan come up with any solution to Shawn's and my dilemma?"

"Not yet," Larissa admitted contritely, reaching for the bag of coffee beans.

Martha bit her lip. "I'm sorry. With Mac leaving just yesterday, you've both had other things on your mind since we talked about it."

The bag slipped from Larissa's grasp, and beans promptly scattered far and wide over the scrubbed oak floor. Martha, diving to help round them up, missed the sudden red radiating from Larissa's cheeks to her hairline. *If you only knew what's been on our minds.* Hastily, she ducked to retrieve another bean.

The events precipitating Martha's innocent question had begun two Sundays ago. *Before Mac's departure.* Resolutely, Larissa tucked the thought away.

Reverend Gallaway had stood at the church door and warmly acknowledged the comments of his flock as they exited after the services. With poorly concealed anxiety, however, he'd shaken Ethan's hand. "Please stay. Martha and I would like to speak to you. It's extremely important."

A cold blade of alarm had stabbed Ethan, but before he could do more than assent, another parishioner came up, forestalling further comment.

At the bottom of the steps, Martha had put her hand on Larissa's arm. "Shawn and I can't talk to anyone else. You will stay, won't you?"

At her evident anxiety, Larissa had squeezed her fingers reassuringly. "Of course we will. For as long as you need us."

When the last churchgoers straggled away, Shawn Gallaway descended the steps. "Thank you for staying. Martha and I would like to visit you this afternoon, if you're going to be home." In spite of their obvious worry, plainly they didn't intend to enlarge upon their problem until then.

They settled upon two o'clock. As Ethan guided the team out of the churchyard, with sharply increased concern, Larissa glanced back past Mac, Rose and Charity jostling for room on the rear seat of the buggy. Shawn took Martha's hand and pressed it between his own. Glimpsing their expressions, Larissa wanted to cry. "They called each other by their first names." Ethan looked confused. "Martha and Reverend Gallaway. They called each other by name, instead of 'Mrs.' or 'Reverend.' They're always so careful to be proper, but they're so right together!"

For Ethan, the irony of the observation rang loud and clear. He considered their own circumstances, found discretion to be a most admirable virtue, and simply agreed with her, in more ways than one.

At the time, Larissa had kept to herself her own conclusion about the couple's behavior. *Something's terribly wrong if they forgot to be formal.*

When their guests had arrived that afternoon, the young people headed to the orchard to romp through the leaves. The less hardy adults gathered in the sitting room, and Shawn came straight to the point. "Thank you for having us here. As you probably guessed, we're struggling with a problem. We want very much to hear your opinions." He and Martha were sitting on the high-backed deacon's bench facing the snapping fire. Without pretense or evasion, he took her hand and inhaled deeply, while Ethan and Larissa waited. The look the couple exchanged made Larissa, in her rocking chair beside the hearth, catch her breath.

"We suspect you know Martha and I care deeply for each other." Martha's face flamed at the bold confession, but she kept her hand in his. "We want to marry. We've felt this way for some time. Her children accept me. I couldn't care more for them if they were my own." The blush now staining Martha's cheeks reflected love and joy.

"Some might not think it proper to express such feelings aloud, especially to friends who've endured their own grievous losses. But this is precisely why we feel we can talk to you. We know you have understanding of our situation." His hand tightened around Martha's. "We don't mean to intrude on your private feelings."

Ethan, standing at the far side of the fireplace, had suddenly shifted his feet, and Larissa realized he must be reflecting on their own love, not yet declared to the world. "Perhaps we have more comprehension of your situation than most," she said quietly. "I know there are times I couldn't have endured it all without your understanding, Martha. I'll gladly help whatever way I can."

"Certainly! You need only tell us how." In speaking the simple truth, Ethan's voice had betrayed none of his frustration at the circumstances keeping their own feelings secret.

Unaware of any undercurrents, Shawn said simply, "Thank you, both of you. We'll put it as straight and plain as we can. We come to you because we are faced with a dilemma seeming to have no answer. You are aware, when Ross died, the farm became Martha's. She wants to keep it to pass along to the children as their father's inheritance. I understand her feelings and do not wish her to do otherwise." He paused, searching for words. "However, as a minister, I am not allowed to own any property for myself. If Martha and I marry, even though we would both consider the farm hers, the legal system wouldn't see it that way. I, too, would be considered an owner." He smiled tightly as comprehension began to dawn for Larissa and Ethan. He clasped Martha's hand more firmly yet in his.

"In the eyes of the church, such ownership, however reluctant I am to claim it, is not permitted. It's a good rule and makes sense, but it also sets a very real barrier in the way of our marriage. Simply put, the church will not allow me to marry and have property. I refuse to allow Martha to sell her children's heritage for my sake." He smiled faintly. "She refuses to allow me to leave the ministry for her sake." Martha tried hard to look reproving at this small joke, but only succeeded in looking determined.

We have been over and over it and cannot find a resolution. We are asking you, our trusted friends, if you can see any light for us in this darkness."

Reverend Gallaway's manner of facing life's stony paths from the heart had soothed the troubled souls of many in his flock. To whom does a minister turn, Ethan wondered, when in his humanity, he needs ministering? Martha moved closer to Shawn and rested her free hand on his arm.

Neither Ethan nor Larissa spoke as they absorbed the impact of this collision of duty and desire. Ethan finally cleared his throat. "This is a ringer of a problem. In this modern day and age, it never occurred to me such a rule exists to prevent two consenting adults from marrying. I know lots of other reasons have cropped up for folks," his eyes rested on Larissa for a bare instant, "but most problems have a workable solution. I admit I'm at a loss to see an instantaneous one here. Would you mind if we discuss it between us before we give you any kind of answer? I suspect this nut is going to take some hard cracking."

Giving their grateful consent, Martha and Shawn had departed, looking a shade less agitated than when they arrived. In the days following, however, with Larissa preoccupied over Mac's leaving, she and Ethan didn't have much opportunity to discuss it, and so had reached no workable alternative.

Now, scrambling around on the kitchen floor, the two women finally captured the last of the elusive coffee beans. While the pot perked, they sat at the table and toyed with various ideas. When Martha rose to leave, however, they were no closer to resolving the question than before. Promising to keep trying to come up with a solution, Larissa waved Martha down the drive. Turning back toward the house, she caught sight of the vegetable garden. She'd rather neglected it these past days, but it was demanding her attention, now. With a sigh, she pushed up her sleeves and plunged into the task of un-neglecting it.

CHAPTER FOUR

Trouble's brewing. Rose felt it in every bone of her body at Thursday recess a week after Mac's departure. Charity was slumped on the swing. But instead of pumping, she sat statue still, staring at nothing. *She's been acting weird all week, but this is really bad.*

After Charity received permission to stay overnight last Thursday, they'd snuggled under the covers, just like always, with no hint this odd behavior lay in wait. Even with their promise to Ma, Rose fell asleep to Charity's giggling and whispering, and awoke totally unprepared for the quiet that accompanied and followed their Friday morning rising and dressing activities. Heretofore, Charity talked and Rose listened. Charity's silence had been so unsettling that, attempting to draw her out, Rose chattered like a nervous squirrel. But not even her confession that Joey McIntire said "Hi" to her two times the morning before, when he didn't have to, roused Charity's interest. *Any other time, she'd be asking all about it.*

In the rush to eat breakfast and get off to school, apparently neither Ma nor Charity's Pa had noticed her moodiness, because they'd have commented on it, for sure. In class, Charity had perked up a little, but she didn't volunteer many answers to Miss Sullivan's questions during English and geography. Usually, her hand flew in the air before anyone else's. Saturday, she'd gabbed a bit more as they worked at their chores, especially if her Pa stood near enough to hear. Sunday, riding in the back of the buggy to and from church, she talked and giggled, but Rose sensed the force behind the cheeriness.

She wanted to ask Ma if Charity's behavior seemed odd, but in the first days after Mac's departure, Ma hardly spoke, either. A time or two, Rose saw tears in her eyes. *Almost like when Pa died and Ma got so quiet and sad. I can't worry her now about Charity, too. Do I dare ask Mr. Michaels if he's noticed anything?* Contrarily enough, Charity acted cheerful around him. *It'd be beyond embarrassing to ask, then find out he has no idea what I mean.*

The week had trudged past in much this fashion. Until today. This morning, Thursday again, when Mr. Michaels dropped the girls off at school, Charity gave him a big hug and a cheerful goodbye wave. He'd scarcely disappeared around the corner, however, before she retreated into her shell. Rose had dutifully started toward the building and looked back in puzzlement when Charity didn't respond to her comment about yesterday's spelling test. Charity simply stood with sagging shoulders, unfocused gaze on the teeter-totter. Rose got the distinct impression she didn't see the teeter-totter. Or Rose, either. "Charity, come on."

Miss Sullivan, wearing her usual black skirt and white bodice, rang the bell vigorously from the top step. The other children immediately broke off shooting marbles and playing tag and trooped toward the entrance.

"Come on! We'll be late."

"I don't want to go in."

"Why not?" Rose hopped from one foot to the other as her stay-or-go dilemma increased proportionately with each student who disappeared inside the building.

"I don't feel like it."

Rose stared at her. Miss Sullivan called sharply, "Inside, girls. Right now." A hasty glance over her shoulder confirmed Teacher waited, and not patiently.

"You'll get us in trouble!"

"I don't care."

"Well, I do!" Shocking them both, Rose grabbed Charity's arm and dragged her toward the frown on Teacher's face. Sidling past the lowering brows and the sharp glint in Miss Sullivan's black eyes, Rose said hastily, "Sorry, ma'am. Charity got a pain. She's all right, now." Relief over getting Charity inside temporarily squelched the enormity of telling a lie. Miss Sullivan's thunderclouds didn't evaporate, but mercifully the gathering storm failed to materialize upon their calico-bonneted heads.

Rose, stepping on Charity's heels, forced her along the aisle to their double desk. Last year, the community had come together to modernize the school. To collect money for the building materials, the women had baked so many apple, gooseberry, and mince pies, they insisted that if set end to end, they would stretch a mile. But every pie sold at the Union County Fair. They'd also stitched a friendship quilt, which was raffled off at the fair for an unexpectedly handsome sum. The men, contributing sweat and effort, had removed the old wall-mounted shelf desks and the long benches upon which the children had sat with their backs to the teacher. They'd replaced these agonizingly uncomfortable fixtures with rows of wrought-iron and oak double desks facing the front of the room. Back-breakingly uncomfortable as the old shelves and benches were, for the first time since the improvements were completed, Rose wished they could sit facing away from Miss Sullivan in the old way.

All morning, Charity had refused to take any initiative for following Teacher's directions. Sharing the double desk, Rose pulled out the required books, pushed them under Charity's nose, and turned to the proper pages. Fortunately, Miss Sullivan didn't call on Charity, and she only asked Rose to read from *McGuffey's*, the simplest requirement possible. But as the hours crept on, Rose wondered uneasily how long their luck would hold, and knew she feared to find out.

Finally released from class for the noon break, in her worry, Rose forgot to bring her sketchpad and pencil outside so she could finish the drawing of the schoolhouse she'd begun yesterday. She dragged Charity over to the idle swing for their noon meal. In charge of the dinner pail today, she lifted the blue checked napkin and offered the contents to Charity, who didn't take even a bite of the cold chicken and sour cream biscuits Ma had packed. *And they're her favorite foods.*

Charity merely sat, hands clasped in her lap, waiting for—*what* ? Rose hadn't the faintest idea because Charity refused to tell her. Rose knew exactly what she, herself, waited for. Doom to crash into them. She could feel it pushing nearer, with no way of knowing when it would arrive. The answer came all too soon.

Last week, Miss Sullivan had informed the upper class that today she would give an oral history test, asking each student one question. She expected them to reply as fully as if they were writing the answer down in their lesson books. Passing or failing hinged on the merits of this solitary response.

As if she needed further confirmation, this test became Rose's final proof of something dreadfully wrong with Charity. Miss Sullivan called on one after another of the students and fired her yesteryear bullets at their uniformly apprehensive heads. Early on, she zeroed in on Rose to discuss the French and Indian Wars and their effect on modern day life. Rose stood, drew a deep breath, and reeled off everything she knew or imagined about the situation. She kept going so long, Teacher's eyes started to glaze. When she finally ran down, Miss Sullivan gave a clipped nod. "Thank you, Rose. You pass. You did well."

From Miss Sullivan, the three extra words conveyed an extravagant compliment. Any remaining breath Rose possessed escaped in a whoosh of relief as she fell back into her seat. Finished now, she couldn't remember a thing she'd said. Little did Teacher know, and Rose had no intention of mentioning, it had been a delaying tactic of desperation. The longer she talked, the longer she put off the turn Charity, who gave not the slightest sign to acknowledge her friend's triumph, would be called on to take.

Miss Sullivan requested proof of historical intelligence from three other students, who delivered it in varying degrees of self-confidence before sitting back limply, certain their lives forevermore could hold no greater fear. In spite of Rose's silent but urgent pleas for the roof to fall in, the moment came. Miss Sullivan turned to Charity, still slumped beside Rose like a lifeless little lump. "Charity, please name all the presidents of the United States, and their vice presidents, in the order they held office, and the years they served."

Rose felt a dizzying thrust of relief. They'd studied this exact information. Charity had even made up a silly rhyme to help them remember. Face shining with joy at the reprieve, Rose grinned at her friend. *She can answer this one in her sleep.* It appeared she might be going to do just that, and Rose's heart sank to her toes. Charity looked blank. With a touch of vinegar in her voice, Miss Sullivan repeated the question, something most unwise for a student to make her do, as even her youngest pupils learned early in their school careers. Rose shivered at the clipped tone and the glint in Teacher's black eyes. One of those reactions alone always carried enough weight to wilt the most boisterous offender. This time, even the combined assault didn't affect Charity. Desperate enough to risk the dire consequences, she nudged her.

"Rose." Teacher's one-word admonishment sent the clear signal to her pupil to stay out of it. "Charity Michaels, please stand." When Charity shifted her body and slowly got to her feet, the tiny spark of relief frizzing through Rose felt like a raging forest fire after all the previous dread. Having obeyed, Charity stood beside the desk, watching Miss Sullivan as if she'd never seen her before.

A pin dropping in the silent classroom would have reverberated like one of the mammoth oaks crashing down in the schoolyard. Rose squeezed her hands together. The roof-falling-in prayer hadn't worked, and the trees gave no indication their roots would part company with the earth anytime soon. She sent up a swift, silent plea for God to *please* help Charity answer and get her disgrace removed. For disgrace it was.

In response to Teacher's question, Charity merely shook her head and sat down. Rose's frantic bartering attempt with the Almighty rolled over, stuck its paws in the air, and died. Neither prayer, pleading nor promises could avert disaster now. Sharp talons extended, doom swooped as Rose looked from Charity's set face to Teacher's equally grim one. Miss Sullivan didn't mince words. "Charity Michaels, you have failed this test. Please stay after class." She looked at the students frozen in their seats. Even the ones not involved in the testing didn't twitch a muscle for fear she'd notice and mistakenly call on them. "Helen Olsen, please name the presidents of the United States, and their vice presidents, in the order they held office, and the years they served."

Rose, staring at Charity in bewilderment, didn't hear a word of Helen's answer. Charity neither moved nor acknowledged Rose's glance, but a single tear slipped down her cheek as Teacher said quietly, "You pass, Helen. Please be seated."

When Miss Sullivan dismissed the class for the day, Charity remained seated as Rose gathered her books and prepared to join the exodus. "I'll wait for you outside," she whispered with a quick glance at Teacher.

"Go along, Rose." Miss Sullivan's tone, although not harsh, brooked no nonsense. Adding her slate to the *McGuffey's Reader* and the hapless history book, Rose gave Charity a last, despairing glance, and fled. She sat in the swing under the spreading oak and waited miserably for Charity to appear. Time stayed as rooted to the spot as the unsympathetic trees did to the ground, but finally the door opened and Charity descended the steps. Miss Sullivan stood at the top, watching, as Rose abandoned the swing, so she didn't dare say anything until they turned a corner, putting them safely out of sight of the school building. Nerve-wrenchingly enough, Charity didn't volunteer anything.

Trudging alongside her on the east road home, seeing her friend's chalky face, she didn't know what to do. If Charity declined to share the details, she didn't want to pester it out of her. "Did she yell?" she ventured finally, unable to stand the silence any longer.

Charity nodded and pressed her lips tightly together. Since lip-pressing hindered a verbal response, Rose searched for another tactic. "Do you have to tell your Pa?"

Again, the wordless nod.

"Charity, I'm sorry." *Facing Miss Sullivan is terrible enough, but to have to tell her Pa....* Rose's shiver this time zipped from the top of her head to her toes. Mr. Michaels didn't often get mad. He became stern when Charity slid through finishing her outdoor chores properly or left her clothes scattered in the small cabin. Rose suspected "stern" would not appropriately describe his reaction to this escapade.

As she searched frantically for a new subject, a thought surfaced. She'd dismissed it earlier, since she would already know if Charity's problem stemmed from this particular issue. Now, having exhausted all other topics, Rose ventured her query. "Do you miss Mac an awful lot? I do. We should be happy, because he can't chase us into Mill Creek when we're wearing our good dresses and he's mad at us." This represented one of his favorite brotherly tactics, along with threatening to dump them into the manure pile when they refused to let him have his way.

Charity's tightly set lips quivered at Rose's guess, but she said nothing.

CHAPTER FIVE

Nearing the house, Rose feared Charity intended to keep slogging straight down the road instead of turning into the curving drive. Taking no chances, she stayed on Charity's left in order to nudge her in the proper direction. As she pivoted, Charity did, also, and continued trudging toward the house. Such relief swept Rose even her toes tingled.

Ma, just coming from the wood lot, smiled and started toward them. Rose waved, but Charity suddenly bolted. "What's wrong?" Neither answering Ma nor slacking her pace, Charity pelted headlong toward the cabin. "Did something happen to you girls?" Ma's sharp tone betrayed her anxiety of someone hurting them on the sometimes lonely road home.

"No. Nothing. We stayed together, same as always." The relief written large upon Ma's face swiftly became puzzlement. Rose braced herself for the next question. All during the walk home, she'd known it would fall to her to explain Charity's odd behavior without betraying her.

"Something's happened. You must tell me."

Escape and vagueness now both out of the question, Rose nevertheless did her best to soften Charity's fall from grace. "We had a history test today. She didn't do so good." She saw no reason to mention, yet, Charity's behavior leading up to and following the test.

Ma's gaze sought Charity fleeing past the cabin, into the grove of buckeye trees shading the east side of the building. "She must be terribly embarrassed, but we know you girls always do your best." Seeing Rose's stricken look, she said in confusion, "She did her best, didn't she?" Then, "I can see there's more. You must tell me."

"Ma...."

"It's not tattling when it's something we need to know. It's vitally important to tell so we can help her."

All the doubt and dread building in Rose for the past week suddenly overflowed. "I don't know. She won't tell me."

The forlorn confession struck a chill into Larissa's heart. The idea of Charity not confiding in Rose defied comprehension. "Ma?" Her daughter's soft plea recalled her.

"I'll go after her. Find Charity's Pa and tell him what's happened. He's probably still in the woodlot." As her daughter hesitated, she said firmly, "Do as I say, quickly!"

Rose sped for the woodlot while Larissa took Charity's earlier path. Finding her proved easy. She followed the sound of heartbroken sobbing and found her crumpled against the trunk of a venerable buckeye tree, crying so hard her breath came in strangled gasps.

Not wanting to scare her by appearing suddenly, Larissa stopped a few steps off. "Charity?" She knelt beside the girl and reached to embrace her. To her shock, Charity stiffened, pulled away, and curled herself into a tight ball. "What is it?" Again, Larissa put her arms out, but again she scrunched away, her message not to touch her loud and clear.

"You needn't be afraid. I'll help you however I can." More gasping shudders shook Charity's huddled frame from head to foot. Bewildered, Larissa pressed her hands tightly together to keep from reaching out as every instinct urged her. Not knowing what else to do, she kept talking. She never afterward could remember what she said, simply hoping the soothing words would somehow penetrate the barrier Charity had flung up.

Ethan, with Rose bringing up the rear, pounded toward them. Taking in the scene of his daughter curled against the tree, heart-wrenching sobs shaking her, and Larissa, kneeling beside her, dismay written plain upon her, he jerked to a stop. Larissa shook her head and lifted her hands toward Charity. He knelt on his daughter's other side. "I'm here now. I'm here. Whatever it is, I'm here."

At his touch and voice, she threw herself against him, wailing bitterly. He held her close and rocked her, murmuring nothing phrases, as Larissa had, letting the sound of his voice flow over her. Pain and bafflement stamped clearly upon him, he rose with her in his arms and looked over at Larissa, who again lifted her hands in wordless confusion. Cradling his daughter, he carried her to the cabin, her racking cries easing into shuddering sobs. Larissa followed, not certain what to do in the face of Charity's rejection. Rose crowded so close behind her mother they were both in danger of tripping.

Ethan laid Charity on her bed in the corner, removed her bonnet and shoes, and covered her with her favorite quilt. He gently rubbed her wrists. "Can you tell me what's wrong?" As she stared at the ceiling without responding, he said firmly, "Charity, you must answer me. I can't help you if I don't know what's wrong." Still no reaction. His eyes sought Larissa's in helpless questioning. Larissa stood back, afraid she would set Charity off again if she came too close. Ethan, unaware of his daughter's reaction to her touch, said uncertainly, "Maybe I'd better go for Doc Rawley."

"Pa, don't leave me!" They both turned, startled, at Charity's first coherent words.

"I'm just going for Doc. I'll be back as soon as I can. Mrs. Edwards will stay —"

"No!" The single word held bottomless anguish. The shock on Ethan's face mirrored Larissa's earlier reaction.

"It's all right, Ethan. I'll go."

"But—"

"It's best for right now. We'll figure it out later."

"Ma?" Rose's panicked glance skittered from her mother to Ethan.

"You'd better come with me, Rose." The girl, torn between staying with her friend and craving the comfort of her mother's presence, visibly hesitated. "It's all right. It's better if you do." Hearing the firm assurance in her mother's voice, Rose trailed her out the door.

"Larissa." Ethan had followed them. With Rose watching, he said only, "Be careful going into town. Hurry, but please don't break your neck."

The faint touch of humor, in spite of his clearly visible worry, startled her, but she succeeded in replying casually. "We'll be careful."

"The hitching up—"

"We'll manage, won't we, Rose? He must think we're helpless females," she said in a stage whisper to her daughter. "We'll just have to show him!" Rose stood a little straighter and lifted her chin determinedly. A few minutes later, Andromeda and Pegasus properly attached to the buggy, Larissa, with Rose close beside her, guided them along the drive. Once on the road toward town, Larissa glanced sideways. "Can you tell me more of what happened today? Her Pa's right. We can't help her if we don't know what's going on."

Rose hunched her shoulders. "I don't know. She wouldn't tell me anything. She hardly spoke all day."

"Why don't you tell me what she did? Maybe we'll get a clue from that."

Rose squiggled a bit, but finally poured out the story, from Charity's waking-up silence the Friday before, to her refusal all day to talk, and finally, in a trembling voice, the events of the history test. "I think Miss Sullivan yelled at her. But she didn't start crying until she saw you. I wonder why."

She wondered, too. Rose hadn't witnessed Charity's extreme reaction as Larissa tried to comfort her, so she said nothing of it, unwilling to create more upset and confusion than her daughter was already experiencing. *Time enough later to work that one out.*

Rose's halting tale took almost the entire trip into town. Guiding the team and buggy over Mill Creek's rattling wooden bridge, Larissa turned in the direction of Doc's office. She halted the rig in front of the small building. "Rose, please go get him."

"What if he's not there?"

The thought hadn't occurred to Larissa. *What will we do if he's out on a call?* "Go see. Ask him if he'll please come out to the buggy." Rose disappeared into the office. The few seconds she remained out of sight passed like an eternity to Larissa, before she reappeared, dragging Doc by the hand.

"Rose says something's wrong with Charity, but she's not sure what. Can you fill me in?"

"We're not sure, either. She's crying hysterically and shaking and won't talk to us."

Doc pulled at his whiskers. "She's not talking?" He glanced at Rose, standing beside him, hanging on every word. "This sounds downright serious. I better hustle out there and see if the cat got her tongue." Rose gave a small giggle. As he helped her into the buggy, he looked at Larissa over the girl's head. "You go on back. I'll leave a note and get my bag. Bella and I will be right behind you."

"Thanks, Doc." Larissa turned the buggy and headed out of town across the rattling bridge. Rose, having talked more than she normally did in a month of Sundays, fell silent, but edged closer to her mother as they started onto the east road home. Larissa, craving human touch every bit as much as her daughter, drew her close as the unanswered question loomed large.

Why did Charity reject my touch?

CHAPTER SIX

As they neared the farm, Rose twisted to look back. "Doc's behind us!"

Larissa strove to conceal her large relief. "Good. He'll figure out what's wrong. Problems can't hide from him for long, no matter how hard they try." She halted the team beside the kitchen path. "We'll leave them here for a bit, and tend them when we can."

"I can take care of them, Ma."

Larissa couldn't hide her astonishment. "You certainly don't need to."

"I've watched Mac and Mr. Michaels lots of times."

Larissa knew the horses were gentle. Still, her heart shivered at the thought of her daughter working with animals that towered over her. She made one of those split second decisions every parent confronts, put on a smile, and handed her the reins. "Come fetch me if you have problems."

The sudden light on Rose's face, replacing the fear and uncertainty, confirmed she'd chosen right. "I'll take care," she promised as Doc pulled Bella to a halt.

He watched Larissa watch Rose guide the team to the buggy shed. "Mac's not the only one in this family with backbone," he muttered to Bella's rump before calling out, "Charity in the house or the cabin?"

Ethan had left the door open. Catching sight of them, he rose from the chair pulled close to Charity's bed. "She calmed down after you left. But she still wouldn't talk to me. She's been asleep this last while."

Doc bent and, without touching her, studied her thoughtfully before he motioned Ethan and Larissa outside. "I'll want to examine her, of course. But she doesn't appear to be fevered or in pain. You better tell me what happened. There's an answer somewhere."

Larissa, with a quick glance at Ethan, told Rose's story as briefly as she could. Coming to the history test debacle, she understood her daughter's feelings of betrayal as Ethan looked incredulous, then dazed. She hurried through Charity's fleeing to the buckeye grove, and finding her huddled against the tree. She faltered, then, with no idea how to shape the next words.

Doc's bushy eyebrows drew together.

Puzzlement creased Ethan's forehead. "What is it?" At her stricken look, he took her hands. "Tell us." He spoke calmly. Fear looked from his eyes.

"I reached for her. She pulled away. I tried again. She refused to let me touch her. She just cried harder." The stark words, spoken in a monotone, told her listeners more than she ever intended.

"Good God." Ethan looked as if a horse had just kicked him.

Doc's piercing gaze measured Larissa's anguish and Ethan's reaction to it. He tugged at his beard. "Doesn't make sense. The child loves you, Larissa. No matter what happens, remember that."

He spoke so sternly, she blinked. Her chin lifted. "I'll remember."

"I'm going to examine her. Why don't you two wait outside." Phrased as a polite suggestion, they knew it was an order not subject to negotiation. Leaving the door ajar, Doc carefully woke Charity. They couldn't hear his words or her response.

Ethan, still looking kicked-in-the-head bewildered, drew Larissa away from the porch. "I don't know *why*," he managed brokenly, "but I'll find out. I promise you."

Bowing her head, she studied her tightly clenched hands. "Larissa." He grasped her upper arms. "Whatever this is, we'll work it out, believe me. We will work it out." His eyes locked with hers and she saw, through the lingering shock, his resolve and his love.

She clung to that love and resolve during the next miserable hour. Rose returned from the barn all in one piece, for which Larissa gave fervent thanks. Not only had she stabled Andromeda and Pegasus, but without being asked, tended Bella, too. Larissa's pride in her daughter's acceptance of responsibility provided a warm glow in the otherwise bleak coldness of her heart.

His examination finished, Doc motioned them back to the porch. At his suggestion, Rose sat beside her friend, a healing activity for her, even though Charity continued her silence. "Doc?" Ethan's dazed look had become a haunted one.

Doc assessed them. Ethan stood a little apart from Larissa, but it didn't matter. Across the room or a mile away, the link between them would be just as sure. With totally uncharacteristic indecision, he scrubbed his hand over the back of his neck. "Physically, she's all right. You've absolutely nothing to worry about there."

Ethan sagged with relief, but stiffened as Doc continued. "Took some persuasion, but she talked. I won't mince words. Partly, because I know you two can take it directly. Partly, because you won't have any choice. She saw you on the path last Thursday night, kissing." Larissa's sharp breath and Ethan's guilty-as-sin expression confirmed Doc's diagnosis. "I don't know just what, or how much, you two have been up to, and you can thank your lucky stars Charity apparently hasn't witnessed anything more revealing than last Thursday night's performance. My personal feeling about the two of you is, hell, go for it. You both deserve to be happy if anyone does. But you'll have to figure that out for yourselves. In the meantime, I suggest you quit tiptoeing around and let your children in on your intentions. I use the word 'children' figuratively. They're young women, and deserve to be treated so." Reprimand finished, he shut his mouth.

Ethan, still chagrined, stirred first. Glancing at Larissa he said quietly, "I reckon we had that coming, in spite of our reasons for keeping quiet. Whether those excuses are valid isn't the question. We planned to tell the girls, but that's beside the point now, too."

Larissa raised questioning eyes. "I don't understand why she's so upset, why she's withdrawn from me like this. She couldn't be dearer to me if she were my flesh and blood child. I always assumed she felt the same way."

Doc's tired eyes took in her grief and confusion. "She admitted her feelings for you are as a child for its mother."

Ethan's perplexity matched hers. "So what's the problem?"

"The problem," Doc said slowly, "is that she cares for Mac."

"Of course she cares for Mac!" Ethan stared at Doc as if he had suddenly grown simple in the head. "He's been her big brother for years now."

Ethan's impatient explanation drowned Larissa's quick-drawn breath, but Doc saw her sudden comprehension. *She realizes. She understands the consequences.* He couldn't honestly name his gut reaction as relief or foreboding. "Listen. You're thinking of her and treating her like a child without a brain in her head. Now hear me out," he continued doggedly over Ethan's vehement protest. "Call it puppy love or whatever name you choose. But ignoring it, denying it or calling it something else won't make it go away."

Larissa shivered. "No wonder she's upset. But how did she see us? She was in bed when I came out to ... talk ... to Ethan."

Behind the snowy beard, Doc's lips showed the ghost of a smile. "You got caught fair and square. She needed to use the outhouse. She didn't notice you on her way out back, but she passed right by you on the return trip. Apparently, you were so involved in your ... talk, you never saw or heard her." Larissa blushed scarlet and Ethan turned red as a rooster's comb. "Must have been quite an education for her," Doc observed dryly.

"Doc." Ethan tried to come to grips with what he'd heard. "You make it sound like she's in love with Mac. It's absurd. How can she possibly know about that kind of love?"

Exasperation crept into Doc's words. "You must stop thinking of her as a child. Go back a bit in your own romantic career. When did you know with absolute certainty you were in love with your wife? Did it take you a hundred years? When did you know with Larissa, for that matter?"

His shot hit home. Ethan opened his mouth for a furious reply, but closed it again. The heat beat in his face with a vengeance, and he wouldn't meet Doc's or Larissa's eyes. Having scored a direct hit, Doc moved in for the kill. "Another point you obviously haven't considered is the recipient of all this emotion. Remember, she's talking about Mac. Having worked with him for the past several years, I can truthfully say, with the exception of his mother, I probably know him better than anyone else does. In the two of you, and in Zane, he's had the finest of examples to follow in his upbringing. He's grown to maturity facing and handling situations critical enough to make a full-fledged adult question his own abilities. And he's handled them well."

He glared at Ethan. "You ask, 'Why Mac?' My question is, why not Mac? I'm not saying I stowed a pair of angel wings in the medical bag I gave him before he left. But he's as fine a specimen of young manhood as I've encountered in many a blue moon. If anyone's to blame, you're the ones." Seeing their amazement, he paused before delivering his irrefutable medical conclusion. "Charity's just choosing to follow the example set for her by you two."

"Doc, we've never...."

He sliced off Ethan's protest with an impatient chop of his hand. "You have! Every day of your lives since you came to this farm." He watched them glance at each other, and away, in a gesture sealing his private observations, and his words. He rolled down his sleeves. "I best be getting back to the office. No telling what disaster's waiting on the front step." He tipped his head toward the cabin. "Be sure she gets adequate rest tonight. With all her churning around today, she'll probably resist going to school tomorrow. Whether you send her is up to you, but medically speaking, I see no reason to keep her home."

"Doc, you can't leave without supper. I won't take no for an answer." Larissa's bossy tone startled her as much as it did Doc and Ethan. "Rose and Charity believe it's family policy never to send a guest away hungry at mealtime," she added brightly. "You don't want me to set a bad example by implying such neglect is acceptable?" She smiled wickedly. Ethan put his hand to his mouth to cover his sudden coughing spasm.

Doc's brows drew together, but he already knew arguing with her to be a lost cause. Ethan raised his hand in warning. "Better do it. Trying to win an argument with her is like trying to catch the wind. Especially when she's right."

To cover his agreement, Doc cleared his throat noisily. "There you go again. Each backing up the other. Only a blamed fool would go up against the two of you, so I accept your invitation. But one of these evenings you're to come to supper at the hotel, as my guests."

"We'd like that." As Larissa spoke their acceptance of the invitation, Ethan nodded. Doc threw up his hands in defeat.

The logistics of serving a meal in the house, with Ethan and Charity in the cabin, presented Larissa with a predicament. She told Ethan she would bring a basket of food to them, but he adamantly refused. "Doc says Charity is perfectly healthy. I will not reward her for throwing a spectacular temper tantrum, and for her incredible rudeness to you, by pampering her. You go ahead with Doc and Rose. Charity and I will be along in a few minutes." His tone suggested those few minutes would prove to be quite memorable for his daughter.

Over the years, Larissa had seen him stern with Charity. He'd nipped in the bud her pouting because she disliked a particular barn chore he assigned her. He also cured her of sticking out her tongue when liver and onions appeared on the supper table. Only once before, Larissa saw him really angry with Charity. She flinched, remembering how, as now, she'd been the unwitting cause of that particular disciplinary action.

Charity had sassed her.

The incident had evolved innocently enough. One evening after supper Larissa, washing the girls' pantalettes for school the next day, asked Charity to please fetch a bucket of water from the well for an extra rinse. Charity, her nose in a book, mumbled she would go in a minute. Larissa waited and asked her again. Charity, eyes still glued to her story, protested she was busy and Rose could just as well get it.

Unfortunately, with her attention so focused on the book, she'd paid no heed to Ethan filling his pipe at the table. His hands froze in their tamping of the tobacco into the bowl. In one swift motion, he dropped the pipe and shot to his feet, his eyes more angry than Larissa had ever seen them. She put her hand out in a quick gesture, but he shook his head and muttered something about "… to show proper respect."

He advanced on Charity, who still had her head down. His shadow, falling over the page, caused his daughter to look up, rather like a field mouse at a swooping hawk, and realize, much too late, disaster was descending.

"Charity, stand up, please. Didn't Mrs. Edwards ask you to do something?" He didn't speak loudly. His tone could even be considered pleasantly mild. However, he enunciated his words with precise clarity, a small but vital clue Charity should have heeded, and didn't.

"I was going to in a minute, Pa." Her bland assumption that he was getting worked up over such a trivial matter did nothing to shore up her already wobbly position.

"I don't think I heard you correctly, Charity Annetta. What did you say?" Larissa had never heard him use Charity's middle name in such a manner. Neither had she ever heard him slice off his words so distinctly. Apparently, Charity hadn't either, for her defiance clearly tottered in the breeze as she industriously searched for a tactful answer to grab onto.

As Larissa pushed out a silent, hasty prayer of relief for the girl's change of heart, Charity stiffened. "I said I would in a minute, Pa. Why don't you believe me?" Her tone, of bitter injustice heaped upon her by the world, numbered second on her program of the evening's mistakes. Regrettably, it failed to be her last. "I'll get the dumb water." She threw the book onto the chair, completing her list of fatal errors. She'd started to brush carelessly past Ethan, but somehow, without even twitching a muscle, he'd become a looming presence. Mouse to hawk, she looked up, astonished. If she'd possessed whiskers, they would have quivered.

"First, you will go to Mrs. Edwards and apologize. Second, you will bring in the water. Third, you will go to the cabin and wait for me. Is this clear?"

If not before, it was abundantly so now.

Eyes on her shiny black shoe buttons, she dragged her feet over to Larissa. "I'm sorry, Mrs. Edwards."

"I'm sorry, too. Thank you for bringing the water now." She sidled past her father and they heard her cross the porch.

Ethan put out his hand to Larissa, but dropped it back to his side. "I'm very sorry. It will never happen again."

"Forgive me. I didn't mean to cause trouble."

"You didn't cause any trouble. She started it all by herself. And she'll finish it, with a little assistance from me, when we get back to the cabin."

"Ethan, please don't."

"I'll not have her defying you." The words were so low, Larissa scarcely heard them. His tone, however, left no doubt whatsoever of his resolve. Before she could answer, Charity lugged in the bucket of water and set it on the wash bench.

"Go to the cabin. I'll be there in a minute."

"Yes, Pa." The door shut behind her.

He reached for his hat on the peg above the bench. "I'll be back."

She'd listened to his footsteps fade. Finally, squaring her shoulders, she'd returned to the neglected pantalettes. Dutifully putting her hands in the now cool water, she'd made no attempt to rinse the lacy material but stood motionless, staring down at the pan. *Please guide him in understanding how to handle this situation wisely.* Her plea was no less heartfelt for directing her gaze at the sudsy water.

She'd completely forgotten about Rose who, before the ruckus erupted, was sitting beside the stove busily sketching the ordinary, after-supper kitchen scene. Larissa jumped and squeaked as the girl materialized beside her. Seeing her child's woebegone expression, she abandoned the undergarments once more to put her damp arm around her daughter. "It'll be all right, Rose." At the time, she had had no clue whether she intended her words to comfort herself or Rose, or as reassurance for Charity.

Now, standing on the front step of the cabin these many months later, she saw clearly how the anger lighting Ethan's eyes equaled his fury during that earlier time. She put her hand on his arm. "Be understanding."

He set his jaw. "Despite Doc's 'young woman' opinion, I'd like to understand her right out to the woodshed."

"Ethan...."

"She must learn she can't use other folks for punching bags when something goes wrong in her life. I also won't allow her to show disrespect to her elders. Especially you."

Perhaps because of the intense gravity of the situation, a sudden tremor of laughter tickled Larissa's interior. With effort, she kept her face straight as she murmured, "Her elders? I hope you're not planning to have Charity buy me a walking stick for my birthday."

He opened his mouth to refute her query, did a double take as he realized what he'd said, and clamped his jaw shut. He finally spoke, his voice strangely strangled. "I wasn't implying you—Larissa Edwards, how can I properly discipline my daughter to be respectful to you if I can't stay mad at her?"

As she watched anxiously, Larissa saw, in spite of his intimidating growl, the blazing anger in his eyes bank to smoldering coals. Correctly reading her concern, he said stiffly, "I'm still furious. I won't beat around the bush. But you've reminded me of the question I always ask before I discipline her. Am I doing this out of anger, or because she needs to be reprimanded? No matter how justified, if it's 'because I'm angry', I back off. If it's 'she needs to be disciplined', then woe unto her, because I proceed with the program. And, yes, I have answered 'because I'm angry' before."

At this somewhat less than graciously given admission, a wave of relief swamped Larissa. "Far be it from me to interfere with your parental program," she said airily. "Especially since those are the very two questions I ask myself when the need arises. We better not tell Doc, though, about our newest thinking-alike discovery. I'm not so sure his crabbiness level could handle it. Come along, Rose. We'd better start supper, or we'll have to deal with two really cranky gentlemen." She held out her hand to her daughter.

At Larissa's call, Rose slipped past Ethan. Her wary expression, coupled with Larissa's tactful but clear admonition, gave him pause as he turned to his daughter. Leave it to Larissa to bring him down to size. *All without raising her voice or even suggesting I need to think very carefully before acting.*

As he eased into the chair beside her bed, the waves of rebellion rolling from Charity might have been molten lava. "Sit up on the side of the bed, with your feet on the floor." This opening surprised her so, she obeyed without thinking. "It's been a memorable afternoon." Again, he caught her off guard, although she tried to hide her startled wriggle. "I want to hear what happened today, and your explanation for it."

Wariness, much like Rose's, crept into her expression and she stuck out her lower lip. "Charity, we are going to talk about this, make no mistake. I much prefer it to be with your cooperation." He kept his voice mild, but the firmness behind the words came through loud and clear.

Defiance edged out wariness. "You wouldn't understand."

He squelched his impatience at this sweeping observation. "I certainly won't understand if you don't tell me. It's only fair you give me a few clues. Why don't you start with what happened at school today?"

"You already know," she mumbled. "Rose tattled."

"Rose told us because it was the right thing to do. Same as you would if the situation were reversed and something deeply troubled her. Wouldn't you?"

Charity studied her stockinged toes. "I guess so."

"Good. Now I want to hear the story from you."

Sniffling, and skimming over several of the more incriminating details, she told him about failing the test. The sniffles became louder as she reached the after-school session with Miss Sullivan. "She wrote a note for me to give you and bring back to class, signed, tomorrow." There was no mistaking her indignation at this dirty trick.

"Where's the note?"

"With my books." She indicated the corner where Rose had stacked them neatly.

"Go get it."

She slid off the bed, fumbled with the books and returned with a folded white paper.

Ethan studied the note, refolded it, and tucked it in his shirt pocket. "She says she's deeply disappointed with your behavior. I sincerely hope the occasion never arises again for her to write this. She's not going to, is she?"

Charity stared at her clenched hands. "No."

"All right, then. You fully understand your actions were wrong?" She gave the barest of nods. "I'll sign the note for you. I expect you to apologize to Miss Sullivan. You will also tell her you want to take the history test."

"She already told me I failed. Why do I have to take it?"

Her voice, pitched perilously close to a whine, neatly cemented his wavering resolve. "You will not receive a grade for taking it. Your grade today will stand. You will take the test so you and she will know you really were prepared."

"In front of the class?" The horror in her voice suggested being boiled in oil would be preferable.

"Whatever Miss Sullivan deems best, you will respect her decision." Her renewed molten-lava rebellion nearly scorched him at this ultimatum. "We discussed what you did and what you are going to do. Now we'll discuss *why*."

Her lips set stubbornly and wariness crept back to mingle with the defiance. *Strange you haven't yet figured out how contrariness only prolongs the inevitable.* Her balking also jabbed him with the incentive necessary to wade into the next part of the discussion. Heaven knew he needed all the help he could get. He still couldn't give full credibility to Doc's diagnosis that Charity, only thirteen after all, loved Mac.

Nevertheless, he knew he needed to poke around the subject, if only to prove Doc wrong. *How often is Doc wrong?* Ethan's common sense slithered away from the answer to this perfectly reasonable question. *And Larissa? Are you going to doubt her perceptiveness, too, while you're at it?*

With a silent, swift prayer for the right words, he plunged in. "What happened the other night to make you so angry?" She pressed her lips more tightly together and wouldn't look at him. *I don't much want to look at you, either, when it comes down to it.* "Charity, I asked you a question. I expect an answer."

"It's all *her* fault!" The words burst from her, dumfounding him into silence as the pent up lament poured out. "Acting so sugary sweet and hanging onto you every chance she gets. She's trying to make you love her better than you love me, so she can have you all to herself! I saw her with you. She *kissed* you. The way married people kiss. She's not supposed to kiss you that way. You're not married."

And just where did your knowledge of kissing come from? Not particularly eager to unearth the answer to this question, he broke hastily into the stream of grievances. "Charity, I'm going to set a few facts straight for you, and you will listen." His voice brooked no nonsense. "You must understand you didn't see just Mrs. Edwards kissing me." He willed his face not to turn beet red but suspected he would have to settle for the shade of Larissa's cherry jam. "Putting it so makes the view too one sided. We kissed each other. A most important difference." Her lower lip now stuck out like a buggy step.

For one eternal moment, his mind went blank. He opened his mouth without a clue what would fall out, and heard a voice speaking calmly. His voice, he realized numbly. "We're not married, it's true. We would like to be. But we want our children to want it, too. Despite what you think, if it's just Mrs. Edwards and me, it's not enough. Our happiness is not complete if our children don't feel happy, too. Neither Mrs. Edwards nor anyone else can ever take the place in my heart that belongs to you alone, and always will. You've always liked Rose's Ma. I hope you would like it if she and I married. She thinks of you as her daughter, just like Rose."

"No!" The word leaped from her, shocking him with its intensity. Apparently, it shocked her, too, for her next words came in a squeaky rush. "No, Pa. She can't. Please, no."

"Whatever do you mean?" He couldn't have hidden his astonishment even if he wanted to.

"She can't be my Ma! If she is, I can't marry Mac."

CHAPTER SEVEN

Larissa shifted pans around the top of the stove, sliced bread, and filled the coffeepot. Her mind was not on her tasks, but on Ethan and Charity in the cabin. Rose, too, worked silently, setting the table, filling the milk pitcher, and stirring the pan of fried potatoes while her mother went down cellar for a new jar of dill pickles.

Doc, milk pail in hand, came in as Larissa emerged from the cellar. He handed the bucket to Rose, who took it to the worktable and began straining it. "The chores are done. All critters present and accounted for."

Rose, eyes round as saucers, stared. "You know how to do evening chores?"

Behind the snowy beard, Doc's lips twitched. "Well, *Miss* Rose, I can honestly say I've shucked my share of corn and shoveled my fill of fertilizer in my day. Of course, 'my day' has been a spell. I grew up on a farm. Knew from a right young age I wanted to do something different with my life. Doctoring seemed a good bet. Still does, most days." He winked at Larissa as she eased the lid off the pickle jar.

Entranced by the *Miss* preceding her name, a social courtesy accorded young women, not mere girls, Rose lost part of his explanation. Larissa smiled warmly. "I know a town full of folks who are mighty glad you took that bet and hope you don't ever change your mind."

"Too many years behind me now to change," he growled. "Besides, doing the chores tonight reminded me why I skedaddled off the farm when I was a pup. It's hard work!"

Rose, hands laced in front of her, head tipped to one side, gazed at Doc through half-closed lids. Try as she might, she couldn't picture him as a freckle-faced, barefoot boy milking a cow. She summoned up only a shrunken version of him, bending over the cow's flank, constantly pushing his beard away from the bucket.

"Rose, what are you doing?" Larissa's voice recalled her sharply to the fragrant kitchen, and to her mother and Doc, watching her curiously.

"Just imagining, Ma. He should have tied up his beard to keep it out of the pail." She turned to the milk strainer, blissfully unaware of the stunned looks the adults exchanged. Fortunately, Ethan and Charity's entrance distracted their confusion over the dubious change in her mental status.

Doc, drying his face at the wash basin, straightened and peered from under the flour sack towel at father and daughter. Ethan looked like he'd been dragged through the corn-sheller backward. Charity's smoldering resentment threatened to ignite into an inferno of magnificent proportions.

Larissa's questioning eyes met Ethan's haggard ones. He tipped his head a fraction toward Charity, who stared at the floor, fascinated by the knothole between her feet. Her arms were crossed in a statement of shutting out the world if Larissa had ever seen one. She drew a silent breath. "Charity." Eyes still fastened on the knothole in the oak floor, the girl turned her neck slightly. Larissa saw embarrassment and misery flit through her resentment. "I'm glad you're feeling well enough to come to supper. If you and your Pa want to get washed up, we can eat in just a couple of minutes."

Unprepared for this mild suggestion, Charity darted a look at her father, whose fixed expression clearly indicated he expected something from her. Placing her stare in the region of Larissa's apron waistband, she said in a flat, single-sentence rush, "I'm very sorry for being rude to you it won't ever happen again I promise."

Larissa reached, both instinctively and out of habit, to put her hand on Charity's shoulder. Catching herself in time, she squeezed her hands in her apron front. "I'm sorry, too. I never intended to cause you hurt."

Charity's gaze moved to the button on Larissa's dress above the waistband, and froze. "May I get washed up now, Pa?"

Doc, watching intently, saw Ethan's eyes meet Larissa's and a silent message pass between them. Ethan set his jaw at her pleading, glanced at his daughter's blond head, and sighed. "Yes. As soon as Doc's done."

As she headed for the wash bench, Doc stepped aside and handed her the towel. She took it without a word, then apparently thought better of it. "Thank you."

Muttered as it was, Doc didn't push it. Turning to the table, he asked, "My usual place, Larissa?"

Supper conversation limped along, aided by Doc's gruff attempts to keep the dialogue from sinking like a rock-weighted elephant. As soon as they finished, he stood. "Forgive me for leaving so soon, but I must get back to the office and see what disasters the good citizens have cooked up in my absence."

"I'll help you hitch up." Ethan shot out of his chair and headed for the door with more haste than dignity.

Left with the girls, Larissa began clearing the table. They completed the washing up in total silence, so different from Charity's usual chatter about anything and everything of the day's events. *Even if she avoids looking at me or speaking to me, at least she's helping.* Larissa took as much comfort as she could from the meager knowledge.

The dishes done, Rose picked up her schoolbooks. Ethan hadn't returned. While giving her time to talk to Charity, Larissa suspected he was also seeking comfort at the barn, providing the horses extra attention as he did in moments of deep stress. *It's now or never.* With the thought,

54

she squared her shoulders. "Charity, I'd like to talk to you." She hid her dismay as the sullen mask stiffened the girl's face.

"I'll do my homework in my room." Rose clutched the books and began backing up.

Larissa waited until she no longer heard her daughter's footsteps on the stairs, then pulled out a chair and motioned Charity to do the same. Unmistakably reluctant, she obeyed. With more assurance than she felt, Larissa began. "I won't sidestep this issue with you. You're a young woman, and deserve to be treated as such." Charity blinked, again thrown off by the direct approach.

Snatching at this small advantage, Larissa continued as calmly as she could. "I'm sure your Pa spoke to you about last Thursday night, so I'm not going to discuss it, except to say I'm very glad you know how your Pa and I feel about each other. I've wanted to talk with you so many times, and now I can. It's a very good feeling." In response to this confession, Charity pressed her lips firmly together. Larissa's good feeling was sinking rapidly, with no lifeboat in sight, but she splashed on. "I've been thinking about the day you first came here to the farm. Do you remember?"

"Not much."

"Some big boys at school pushed you into a mud puddle and Mac fished you out. Unfortunately, before it was all over, he landed in the same puddle and ended up just as wet and muddy as you. I'll never forget when he showed up with you on the doorstep. You were so covered with muck, I thought at first you were Rose. And that's how it's been ever since," she said softly. "You've been in my heart right alongside Rose. I didn't carry you under my heart before you were born, but I've carried you in my heart all these years."

Charity, blinking rapidly, refused to let the tears fall. "If you marry Pa, I can't marry Mac," she said stiffly.

So here we are and no escaping or putting it off. With a swift prayer for guidance, Larissa said quietly, "I told you we're going to talk as adults." *But I definitely did not want to hear this from you.* She continued hastily, "When adults talk, they speak honestly with each other, not to hurt, but for each to come to an awareness of the other's feelings. I won't say 'I know exactly how you feel' because I don't. However, I do have understanding of your emotions. They're valid and you shouldn't have to keep them a secret. Now I must ask you something, and I know you'll answer me honestly."

The sullen mask had slipped, letting the old Charity peer through. Now it shadowed her face once more, obviously warring with her interior struggle to discuss matters "as an adult." Larissa waited, showing none of her own inward conflict. Finally, Charity said awkwardly, "Yes'm."

"Does Mac know your feelings? Has he given any indication of returning them?"

Despair overrode sullenness. After another sharp tussle with herself, she stared at the floor. "No." The single word, devoid of all hope, almost broke Larissa's heart. "He treats me the same as when we were little, like he treats Rose. He calls me Speck even though I've been saying 'expect' for years." Larissa couldn't tell if disgust or pride were uppermost. Mac gave her the nickname when she was very young and, thanks to Ethan's extensive vocabulary, used words almost as big as herself. She had used *expect* often, in spite of her difficulty getting her tongue around the first and last letters. Mac, in a moment of teasing, christened her Speck. The name had stuck.

Relief darted through Larissa at confirming Mac was not entangled in a love situation. *He has so much schooling to complete.* On the other hand, if she searched the world for a daughter-in-law, she wouldn't find a finer one than Charity. *Even now, grumpiness and all, you're my first and last choice.* Whether Mac would, eventually, reach the same decision, only time could tell. *Just don't let him come to it, or any other one, until he finishes school.*

She knew better than to voice these wayward thoughts to Charity. Considering the past months of hiding her feelings for Ethan, she certainly possessed personal acquaintance with Charity's dejection. But in light of the girl's obvious annoyance with her, she didn't see any necessity in pointing it out. "As I said earlier, your feelings are valid. I hope you can come to your Pa or me when you need to talk about them, or anything else. Just as you've always done, I want to make sure you understand you can continue to do so. No matter what the problem. We might yowl first, like a cat with its tail caught under a rocking chair, but then we'll set about finding a solution."

Charity stared at her shoe, her fingers working at a piece of her skirt, pinching and smoothing it, and pinching it again. Larissa, having said everything that mattered, left it to her to make a decision. She seemed so mesmerized with the pleating and smoothing, Larissa, too, stared fascinated at the lavender-striped material.

She caught herself and looked up just as Charity raised her head. Her blue eyes held none of their usual sparkle, and sullen resentment still smudged her expression. "I understand. May I go now?"

Larissa didn't know if she'd just won the battle and lost the war, or whether the battle, too, should be listed as a casualty. *Please God, let us salvage something from all this.* Keeping her voice level, she gripped her hands tightly in her lap to keep from reaching out to Charity. "Yes, you may."

Charity edged past her and out the door before Larissa could say good night. Heavy hearted, she sat at the table and waited for Ethan to come. Some time passed before he knocked lightly and pushed the door open. She stood as he strode across the space separating them. Wordlessly, he drew her into his arms and held her tightly. She buried her face against his chest and felt his love encircle her. He said brokenly, "I'm sorry. I'm so sorry."

She raised her head and saw his stark grief and guilt. She pressed her fingers gently across his mouth. "You have nothing to be sorry for."

He shook his head in anguished negation. "My child turning against you! After all the love you've given her. She's been crabby this past week. I thought she was experiencing one of those 'becoming a woman' times you warned me about. But she truly believes she's in love with Mac and if you and I marry, it will destroy everything for them. I never even saw this coming."

"I didn't, either," she confessed. "With being so wrapped up in Mac leaving, I missed it, too. What shall we do, now?"

He inhaled deeply, kissed the top of her head, and drew her to the table. "Come, sit down. As for what we're going to do, I know what I'm *not* going to do. Give you up."

In spite of the gravity of the situation, Larissa's lips curved up. "Afraid you'd have two crabby women to contend with?"

He looked startled, then smiled wryly. "One seems to be more than I can handle at the moment." He covered her hand with his. "This doesn't change anything between us. You know that, don't you?"

She put her other hand over his, curling her fingers around its warm strength. "I know."

***

The next days passed relatively smoothly. Charity returned to school, under strict orders to apologize to Miss Sullivan and to take the history test. She came home lacking her usual bounce but, at least for the time being, the sulkiness had retreated to its cubbyhole. She dutifully reported to Ethan that she had apologized as directed and given Miss Sullivan the signed note.

"Did she ask why you acted that way?"

Pink stained Charity's cheeks and she shook her head. "No, Pa. Honest. She just looked at me kind of funny and thanked me for coming to her."

He studied her. "Did you take the history test?"

"Yes."

"In front of the whole class?"

"No. Miss Sullivan made me stay in at lunchtime. Then she asked me the same question as yesterday. She said I received one hundred percent today."

"Did you tell her yesterday's grade stands?"

"Yes."

How she could manage to look so relieved, and yet so woebegone at the same time, he had no idea. "Did she agree?"

This time, she only ducked her head in assent.

"I'm sorry it came to this. Everything we do in life is because we make a choice, and whatever you choose to do or not do, the outcome is your responsibility, no one else's. You do understand why you didn't earn today's grade?"

"Yes."

"Since you gave her the note, and since yesterday's grade stands, and Miss Sullivan didn't ask you what provoked all this, I see no reason to discuss it further with her. Unless something like this happens again. It won't, will it?"

She shook her head.

"I can't hear you, Charity."

"No, Pa, it won't happen again, I promise."

"All right, then." He held out his arms. Woebegone, elbowed out by relief, skittered away without a backward look as she scooted into his embrace.

CHAPTER EIGHT

A few evenings after Charity's temper tantrum Larissa, finished with the supper dishes, put on her dark blue wool shawl and slipped down to the apple orchard. Although not in the habit of venturing so far from the house at night, something within her, far older than herself, tugged at her to view September's harvest moon in all its glory before it started to wane.

Prickles of starlight outlined the path ahead of her, and she proceeded without tripping over stones, grass clumps or her own feet. Stopping at the edge of the orchard, she lifted her face to the dazzling panorama of the just-rising moon. As she did each evening, she sent up a prayer for Mac, for the success of his venture and for his safety and well-being in a large city so far from home. *I know you'll take care of my son, God. I shouldn't fret. But I'm sure Your Son's mother worried about Him, too.*

Her thoughts turned to Charity, and a smoke wisp of uneasiness curled within her. After her fit of temper at Mac's departure, Charity had become quiet to the point that, beside her, Rose seemed a veritable chatterbox. Under Ethan's edict that he would tolerate no more such behavior, Charity obeyed, not belligerently, but with forlorn compliance. She didn't actively avoid Larissa, but neither did she seek her out for motherly advice and affection. In its own way, this stung more painfully than her outright rejection. Larissa took no comfort from the knowledge Charity's attitude toward Ethan also exhibited restraint.

With their relationship revealed, Larissa and Ethan didn't flaunt it, but they also didn't, as Doc Rawley had so colorfully put it, tiptoe around. Although instinctively reticent about publicly displaying affection, they no longer sharply schooled themselves to conceal their emotions. Through smiles, gestures, and shared laughter, they made evident their delight in each other and in their new openness. *Does seeing this affect Charity for good or ill? Does it fuel her withdrawal or allow her to see a strong relationship between a man and a woman is a wondrous bond and a strong foundation for a healthy family life?*

She wondered if Charity remembered anything at all about the interaction between Ethan and Nettie. She had been so young and nine years had intervened. Now, undoubtedly for the first time in her memory, she observed her father in a relationship with a woman, a coming together in which he freely gave and received love. *Charity's been around other married couples, of course, including Zane and me.* She drew a shaky breath as the ache that would be in her heart as long as she lived awoke, stretched and went back to sleep.

Determinedly, she pushed on with her musing. Charity's father, her security in life, hadn't been involved in any such giving and receiving. *Until now, she hasn't had to share him.* Would all the affection she and Larissa had achieved over these last seven years buffer them through this change in their lives? With no answer to the question, she shivered and suddenly realized how much cooler the night air had grown.

"Lizzie?"

Intent upon her thoughts, she jumped with fright even as she recognized Ethan's voice behind her. The heel of her shoe skidded off a grass-hidden rock, and, for a long second, she teetered precariously between heaven and earth. Only his quick grasp of her arm saved her from an ignominious tumble.

"Lizzie, I'm sorry! I didn't mean to scare the stuffing out of you. You started to turn and I thought you heard me."

She gave a wobbly laugh. "I was concentrating on thinking, not on your finding me." She buried her nose against his jacket front as his arms drew her close.

"You're cold." Her shawl had slipped down her arms and he drew it up snugly around her shoulders. She burrowed into its welcome warmth. "Are you all right?" He couldn't hide his concern.

She gave another, not quite so shaky, laugh. "I'm fine. I didn't realize how long I've been here. I just came to watch the harvest moon and started thinking. Until you spoke, I didn't consider how isolated it really is out here at night."

"Must have been some dandy thoughts to make you concentrate so hard." At her mischievous smile, he raised his eyebrows. "That good, were they now? If you'd like to share, I'd be most happy to listen." He tucked her head against his shoulder.

Her laughter stilled. "I've been thinking about Charity." She felt his breath leave his lungs in a discouraged sigh.

"Did a brilliant thought strike you in this long pondering session? I'm open to all suggestions."

She shook her head. "I think it's just going to take time for her to accept the idea. We can't force her to feel something she doesn't. We also can't force her to discard the emotion she's experiencing."

With her cheek still against his shoulder, she felt him stiffen as he clenched his jaw. "She also can't force us out of doing what we know is right for us. I love my daughter dearly. But after everything you and I have been through in our lives to reach this time of *together here and now,* forsaking what we have between us is not an option. It's that simple."

And that complicated. "I've been doing some thinking, too."

"I hope yours is more productive than mine."

"Productive, yes. But for whom, I'm not certain." She waited while he gathered the words to explain with as little awkwardness as possible. "I assure you with my word of honor, I haven't and I don't intend to belittle Charity's feelings. What Doc said about my knowing for sure when I fell in love with Nettie, I've been turning it over in my mind, trying to get a better grasp of Charity's emotions. Nettie's folks had the farm next to us and our parents were good friends. Naturally, we were in and out of each other's houses all our growing-up years. Since neither of us had brothers or sisters, we had to help with a large share of the farm work. We didn't have much free time, but we spent most of it together." He grinned.

"She was a great companion to get into trouble with. She'd never let me take more than my fair share of blame when we got into mischief. She could climb a tree faster than a cat, and certainly faster than I. She wasn't afraid of bugs or snakes." His voice caught momentarily as he realized what he'd said. "She greatly respected snakes, but she didn't fear them. Maybe if she had...."

Larissa knew Nettie had died from a rattlesnake bite, but she knew no words of comfort to give him. He continued hastily, "When Doc asked when I first loved her, I didn't have a clear answer. But I'll never forget the first time I saw her dressed up at a barn dance. She wore a blue dress, with her hair caught back from her face with a blue ribbon. I recall staring at her with my mouth hanging open. She'd turned into a girl!" Remembering the awed amazement that had washed over him, he shook his head with a wry chuckle. He quickly sobered, though, as he turned Larissa's face up to his. "Only twice in my life have I experienced such a sense of wonder. The first time, in my youth and ignorance, I accepted it as life's way, and the way life was naturally going to be. This time, I'm taking nothing for granted or simply as my due. That's why I want to write to Mac."

Now Larissa's mouth fell open at the sudden switch from romantic reminiscence to reality. She managed a confused, "Write Mac?"

"Yes," he said firmly. "I haven't a clue if he's aware of our feelings for each other. Strictly speaking, we don't need to consult him. He's now an adult with plans for making his own way in the world. But you're his mother. He's Zane's son. It just seems proper to allow him to validate his feelings."

"What if he says 'No!'?"

"Then we'll have Charity *and* Mac mad at us. An interesting combination, under the circumstances. In which case, I guess we'll just have to forego getting married and turn old and gray while allowing our children to dictate to us. You don't think he'll object, do you?" For all his bantering, he finished on a note of anxiety.

Teasing forgotten, she said quietly, "No. I don't think he'll object. But if he approves, in writing, Charity's hopes will be dashed beyond redeeming. What will this do to her and, ultimately, to us?"

"Seems we've gone full circle," he said dolefully. "I don't know the answer. I guess we'll take it one step at a time, and the next step is to write Mac. We must make our own decision, regardless of what he or Charity or anyone else says."

***

On a frosty October afternoon, Mac Edwards, hurrying up the steps of the dignified old brick house that had been converted to a dormitory, paused at the mail desk in the parlor. The student working the desk today stood with his back to the room, poking envelopes into the appropriate boxes fastened to the wall. Juggling the armload of books threatening to cascade to the floor, Mac attempted to keep his tone casual. "Say, Jeff, anything for me?"

Jeff Kinsley glanced over his shoulder and grinned. Almost all their free time the past month had been consumed by adjustment to the medical program, homework, and merely trying to keep their heads above water in their alien surroundings. Sharing most of their classes, they knew each other enough to nod in recognition as they passed in the hallway while hurrying to the next item on their crammed-full schedules. Perhaps part of the awareness came from the fact that Jeff Kinsley's hair was, if possible, even redder than Mac's. From long years of teasing, however, each tactfully refrained from any comparisons.

"I'm surprised the whole mailbag isn't for Edwards. You seem to collect mail like horses collect flies! Some fellows never receive any, and here you are with at least two every week. What's your secret?"

Mac smiled modestly. "Guess I just know the right people."

Jeff turned to Mac's pigeonhole. "Looks like I was wrong," he said apologetically. "Hope no one's sick." He held out a single letter.

Mac took the thin offering and suppressed a twinge of unease. His mother and Rose each wrote a weekly letter, and sent it in the same envelope. Similarly, Ethan and Charity wrote separate messages but made it a joint offering. This envelope felt flatter than usual, as if it held a single sheet of paper instead of the always-before two sheets or more. With Charity, it was always more. He could count on her contribution running to at least three pages as she told all about the farm and school, and how she and Rose had definitely decided to become teachers. "But not like Miss Sullivan!" she'd proclaimed last week. He could just see her sticking out her tongue as she wrote the last bit. To him, her adventures seemed like little-girl exploits, but cheered by any news from home, he read everything eagerly. So far, Charity and Rose had written the address on each envelope. This time, he recognized the careful script as Ethan Michaels'.

"If I can be any help, let me know." Mac had forgotten Jeff standing behind the desk, his green eyes now solemn.

Mac, intent upon the envelope, nodded. "Thanks." As he stepped aside, another student craving word from home took his place. He turned toward the stairs to go to his room, but suddenly changed his mind and veered toward the outer door. If it turned out to be bad news, he didn't want to read it in front of his roommate.

With his crowded schedule and people constantly around him, Mac had by chance discovered a quiet spot where he could think his own thoughts without fear of interruption. It lacked the satisfaction of his old Sitting Seat rock jutting out over Mill Creek back home, but in all these strange surroundings, he'd take what he could get.

He'd come upon it by accident one afternoon. As he hurried across the University grounds, a duck-drowner rainstorm caught him mid way. Since no lightning accompanied the downpour, he'd veered off the path and headed for a group of venerable cedar trees. Once under the sheltering branches, he discovered three of the tree trunks grew so close together he couldn't distinguish where they started and ended. Some whim of nature had curved the trunks and roots into a roughly u-shaped form. Sitting with his back to the tree under the spreading branches, he could look out upon the world passing by, without anyone taking notice of him. He felt a little foolish, like a small boy in a hideaway, but not foolish enough to stop using it as a retreat.

Now he ducked under the branches and settled in his usual hollowed-out spot. All the way over, he'd kept so busy balancing his load of books he didn't have time to worry about the contents of the letter. Now, in his hurry to find out what it said, he dropped the books haphazardly on a flat topped root that formed a perfect shelf. Slitting the envelope with his pocketknife, he drew out the paper. He'd been right. The letter consisted of a single sheet, written on both sides.

Dear Mac,

You will be wondering, so let me immediately assure you everything is fine here. Your mother, Rose, and Charity all miss you, as do I, but we know you are fulfilling your life's dream, so we wouldn't have it any other way. I'm sending my letter only, this time, and next time will forward Charity's (several!) pages. Rose and your mother wrote, but because of what I want to say, I asked your mother to hold off sending her envelope until you received mine. I hope you don't feel it highhanded of me. If you were here, we would talk face to face, but "letter to face" must suffice. I am writing to formally request your mother's hand in marriage.

Mac's heart gave a peculiar thump and his eyes shot back over Ethan's words, confirming he hadn't read them wrong in his haste.

I know it's not strictly necessary to ask your permission, but because you are the head of your family, I would like to do so. Your mother and I care deeply for each other, but we also care very much how our children feel about our relationship. As I explained to Charity, the happiness we share is not complete if our children don't feel happy, too. Each of us is a package deal, so to speak.

Your father was the finest man I've ever known. I could never, and do not ever want to, take his place. But I would be happy and proud to call you the son of my heart.

Mac swallowed around the sudden tightening in his throat.

I give you my word. I will love and cherish her all our days together. I'm still not quite certain how I came to be the recipient of such a miracle, but I am thankful to the depths of my soul.

Ethan Michaels.

Finished, Mac stared at the paper without seeing the words. He'd long suspected the affection between his mother and Ethan, but they'd never come right out into the open with it. For a long time he sat under the tree, thinking about his father's physical strength, and his quiet ways and, as his son, of the security of knowing, absolutely, how much Zane Edwards loved his children.

He thought of his mother and her grief after word came of Pa's death. Finally, he thought of Ethan Michaels who, having endured the anguish of his wife's death, had understanding of Larissa's agony of loss.

He recalled Doc Rawley asking once how he'd feel if his mother and Ethan ever wanted to marry. He also recalled his answer. Now with *maybe someday in the future* actually coming to pass, should he, would he, give the same reply? He stared across the darkening lawn, as if to find the answer written in the last reflected rays of the setting sun. From his tumbling thoughts, Ethan's words came as clearly to Mac as if they were, indeed, talking face to face. *I'm still not quite certain how I came to be the recipient of such a miracle, but I am thankful to the depths of my soul.* Spoken or written, the quiet promise of those words defined the man who wanted to marry Mac's mother.

He folded the letter, carefully replaced it in the envelope and, with no more hesitation, knew his answer to Doc to be his answer to Ethan. *If they can find happiness together, I'll be happy for them.*

***

On a morning with October's glorious colors fading into November's gray dullness, Larissa shut the chicken yard gate. She secured the latch, but her thoughts remained on the night Ethan had told her he wanted to write to Mac. Absentmindedly setting down the chicken-feed pan, she leaned against the gate. The last weeks had passed with all the speed of a turtle out for a Sunday stroll. An elderly turtle. With a sore foot.

There had been no letter last week. Perhaps one would come today. Once more, she enumerated the litany of facts. Waiting for Ethan's letter to leave the Fairvale post office on mail day. A week for it to reach Mac. A week, logically, for him to write and send his response. A week for his letter to reach Fairvale. *And how long for Ethan to ride to town and back?* He'd taken the girls to school in the buckboard and mentioned, casually, he would check at the post office for mail. In spite of his nonchalance, she knew without doubt that he was as tightly wound as she, waiting for a response.

Well aware the weekly mail delivery didn't arrive in town until late morning, she couldn't expect him back for some time. The knowledge, however, didn't keep her from glancing, with increasing frequency, at the curve in the drive where he would come into view. She admitted ruefully that if she intended to exercise patience, she'd better concentrate on another topic. The subject immediately veering into her mind, however, proved more unsettling than the one she was attempting to avoid. The issue had lurked in her consciousness, half-acknowledged, for days.

Once again, memory taunted her with the night she'd sought out Ethan, when Charity, in Doc's words, "caught them fair and square" as they stood on the path, kissing. *Charity stumbled upon us because I dragged my feet about going inside the cabin.* Past time, now, to meet head on her deep reluctance to even set foot inside the building if Ethan was there.

You're always admonishing Mac and Rose to face the truth. It's your turn now. How do you like taking your own medicine? All too familiar heat burned her cheeks, but before she should lose her courage, she squarely confronted the past.

Her behavior alone had catapulted them into the events of the day they learned of Zane's death. There was no denying she had led Ethan to the cabin. But now over and done, it would not be changed. In the time since then, Ethan had been patience itself with her jittery behavior. *You have no right to expect him to be so forever.* If she now continued out of acute embarrassment to sidestep those facts, no matter how well self-justified, such conduct didn't bode well for the future intimacy of their relationship.

Are you willing to risk this? You can admit your part in it to yourself 'til the cows come home, but you know it's not enough. Only by speaking of it to him, could she begin to conquer her aversion. True, opportunities to broach such a subject didn't pop up at a penny a dozen. *I can hardly slide it into one of our discussions of hog butchering time or next spring's wheat planting.* In spite of her emotional turmoil, she managed a faint smile at Ethan's probable reaction to such a maneuver.

She shifted her foot, and the toe of her shoe rapped against the chicken-feed pan. Startled, she realized she'd been out here far longer than she'd intended. With a firm admonition to get busy with her sadly neglected work, she returned to the house. Once there, however, she merely poked around at aimless kitchen tasks of polishing the stove and checking her pantry supplies, all the while keeping within hearing distance of Ethan's return. Disgusted with such transparent stalling, she gave herself a sharp mental shake and headed upstairs to tidy her bedroom.

As always, upon rising she'd pulled the sheet and blankets back to air. Still listening for the buckboard, she made the bed, venting her keyed up emotions by giving the pillows an extra plumping whack or three. Dusting the top of the dressing table, she paused and picked up her bottle of glycerin and rosewater. With their many-times-a-day dunking into various liquid solutions, the lotion kept her hands from feeling—and sounding—like dried corn husks rubbing together. As she unscrewed the cap, the top went flying and landed under the bed.

On hands and knees, she stuck her head under the frame, squinted into the confined space and spied the lid crouching at the head of the bed, naturally just out of reach of her fingertips. In this ungainly position, she heard Ethan calling her. Scooting backward with a decided lack of elegance, she banged her head against the bottom rail. She extricated herself, without the cap and so frustrated she kicked the bed frame. The action didn't faze the wooden rail, but the pain shooting from her toes to her hip caused her to mutter an extremely derogatory observation about furniture in general and bed frames in particular.

As Ethan called again, she threw up her hands in ungracious defeat and fled the room. Rounding the corner at the head of the stairs, she found him standing at the foot, holding two envelopes. As he took in her red face and frankly disheveled appearance, curiosity replaced his air of anticipation. "Lizzie?"

She rolled her eyes as she hurried down the staircase. "Don't even ask!"

Registering the unmistakable hint of doom in her voice, he needed no further incentive to drop the subject, whatever it was. A last cautious scrutiny of her grumpiness convinced him his hasty decision was indeed the correct one. Warily, he held out the letters.

"Two?" Her ill humor faded as she focused all her attention on the white envelopes.

"Only one's from Mac. The other's from Anne Clayton."

Delighted as this news would make her any other time, she scarcely heeded the information. "What does he say?"

"I haven't opened it."

"But I never expected you to wait!"

"I know. Didn't seem fair, though, for you not to be included. Can we look now?" he finished plaintively.

She passed back Mac's envelope and a pin from her hair. "It's addressed to you." He'd watched her open Zane's letters with a hairpin, but his big hands and the small tool refused to cooperate. Finally, taking pity, and wanting to know her son's response, she expertly slit the envelope. He grinned sheepishly. Slipping one arm about her, he drew her down onto the bottom step, where they could both read Mac's reply.

CHAPTER NINE

One arm holding Larissa close beside him on the bottom step, her chin resting against his shoulder so she, too, could read the letter, Ethan slid the folded sheets from the envelope. "Two pages, written on both sides. Whatever he feels inclined to say must be a real gully-washer." Her quick breath of anticipation stirred warmly against his ear as he began reading aloud.

"Dear Mr. Michaels,

"I received your letter asking my feelings about you and my mother marrying. I'm fully aware you aren't obligated to seek my opinion, but I appreciate your giving me an opportunity to speak, even if only by letter to face. You were direct and honest with me, so I shall be the same with you.

"I must admit, seeing your request in writing really startled me. I'm not sure exactly why, because I've sensed for a long time your affection for each other."

Ethan broke off reading to meet Larissa's disconcerted gaze. "After all the care we took because he's so observant. Maybe it's a good thing we didn't know just how observant." He reached a gentle hand to brush her suddenly pink cheek and returned to the letter. "In case you're wondering, there was never anything I could put my finger on. It came more as recognition you enjoyed each other's company as friends, and so naturally had regard for each other." Larissa's sigh of gratitude spoke for both of them.

"Reading your intention point blank, however, I'm afraid my reaction was not what you undoubtedly hoped." Ethan's voice thinned and Larissa moved closer under his arm. "I thought about it for a long time and remembered, and realized, many things I had forgotten or not understood. I thought about Pa and his sense of duty that made him do things he didn't want to, but which must be done. I realize now he never enjoyed hunting, and the killing it required, but he did it to provide food for his family. I knew at the time he did not want to leave us to go to war. But he went, because for him it was, ultimately, the only option for protecting his family and his country. I can only begin to guess how torn he must have been."

Still tucked against his side, Ethan felt Larissa's shudder. He put both arms around her and held her tightly. She bowed her head against his chest. "Go on." Her voice caught, but she shed no tears.

"Are you sure?" The impact on Ethan, reliving those days of anguish, staggered him. He could not conceive what it must be for her.

"I'm sure." Her chin lifted.

After a last uncertain glance at her chalky face, he kissed her temple and turned back to the letter. "I don't wish to paint him as a sugar-coated angel striding the earth. Very much a human being, his temper rose to the surface when occasion demanded. Fortunately, occasion didn't demand too often! Rose and I witnessed strong evidence of his authority on our infrequent trips with him to the woodshed. I know now, of course, he didn't take any more pleasure in punishing us than we did in receiving it.

"I've thought a lot about Ma and her strength and courage for Rose and me after Pa died." This time Larissa's tears flowed, accompanied by a radiant, if watery, smile. "I've also thought a lot about you, Mr. Michaels."

Ethan cleared his throat and Larissa nudged him. "Your turn, now."

Straightening his shoulders, he plunged on. "I've never forgotten the first time I saw you, after Charity and I ended up wearing a large portion of the school mud puddle. I tried to explain, but you looked so furious, I thought you thought I'd caused the whole mess. Only later, I came to realize you reacted so because of your fierce protective love for your daughter. Through the years, you extended that same instinctive love to Rose and me, although I'm certain at times we really tried your patience and you probably wished you could sweep us out the door."

Ethan interjected gruffly, "Only a time or two." Firmly ignoring Larissa's silent quiver of mirth, he continued.

"This, because of all three of you, is the atmosphere Rose and I have grown up in, with the certainty of being loved and cared about, always. This is the foundation you and my mother would bring to your marriage. With such an enduring framework, I must tell you, if you and Ma choose to marry, I will be proud to be the son of your heart.

"Mac."

Both sat for several moments, absorbing the words. Finally, Ethan stirred. "I knew he'd matured this past year. I just had no idea how much. Your heart must be overflowing with pride. Zane's would be, too."

"The 'son of your heart,'" she murmured. "I suspect your heart is heaped up and brimming over, also."

"More than words can say," he confessed. "I missed his first cry and his first tooth, but I'll certainly accept what he's offering now."

They studied the letter again. "With those observant qualities, we better never plan to rob a bank. He'd have us in jail before we even made up our minds whether to actually do it or not! Was he always this way?"

"Even at a young age, he noticed changes. If we moved an object from its normal spot, he fussed until we corrected the error. Woe unto us when we couldn't fix the situation."

"What did you do?"

Her eyes danced with laughter. "When all else failed, we distracted him by moving a different object. By the time he put the new one back in place, he'd forgotten the original problem. As soon as he learned how, we put him in charge of repairing all such negligence."

"Did it work?"

"He plugged away diligently for a while. His fervor tapered off as he grew older and learned some things can't be made right again, no matter how much trying goes into the effort. I must say, I enjoyed his zeal while it lasted. Everything stayed in its proper spot and saved me countless steps."

"Too bad Charity didn't pay closer attention around our place. She could have learned a thing or two from him." He stopped abruptly. She'd learned a thing or two, just not what her father had intended.

Larissa touched the letter. "What about Charity? Mac clearly indicates his feelings. Or lack of them."

Ethan tugged at his lip. "Receiving his blessing presents a problem. We concentrated so intensely on a positive response for us, we pretty much ignored the other side of the coin. Charity feels low enough. The last thing we want is to send her back into another tantrum."

"But we can't keep Mac's opinion from her. Can we?"

Ethan slumped against the stair rail. "I don't really know why we must tell her. She already believes Mac to be more distant than the moon as far as his interest in her goes. Besides, as I said, the last time I looked, we're the adults and are in charge of making the decisions. I've always tried to be honest with her about matters truly concerning her. Since Nettie died, I guess I've felt a greater need for her to know she can trust me."

"If children can't rely on a parent, who can they trust in life?" She knotted her hands in her lap. "I also know sometimes it would serve no good reason to tell them something, so I've kept quiet." She bent her head, studying her tightly laced fingers, and her voice came muted. "For instance, they don't know the whole story of the day we found out about Zane dying."

Even with her head bent, he saw a painful flush sweep her face. "Lizzie." He couldn't manage more. Only once since it happened had she initiated a discussion of the events of the afternoon that was seared into their hearts forever. He finally reached over and tipped her chin up. The lashes of her tightly closed lids trembled against her cheeks.

"Larissa, look at me." He waited, not at all sure she would, but at last she opened her eyes. His gaze locked with hers and he saw the distress she could not conceal. His heart felt like it was being squeezed in a vise. Useless phrases of comfort pushed against his throat. The one day they had talked about what happened, he'd tried desperately to assure her she had done absolutely nothing to be ashamed of. Apparently, he'd failed miserably. He said now the only words that made any difference. "I love you, Larissa." For an instant, he thought he saw a resolute spark overshadow the distress in her eyes. He didn't have much chance to identify it, because she leaned forward and buried her face against his shoulder.

"I love you, too, Ethan." With the faint admission, he sighed heartily at the abrupt release of tension. Her next words, too, came so low he scarcely heard them. "As we said, our children do not need to know some things, no matter how honest we are with them otherwise." She raised her head and, in spite of her still-crimson cheeks, her mouth quirked upward ever so slightly. "If I'm not mistaken, since we don't intend to inform Charity of Mac's feelings, and we plan to keep quiet about our cabin adventure, our present underhanded plotting doubles our extensive list of subterfuge to two items. Guess I'd better be careful. You might throw me out on my ear as a bad influence on you."

Knowledge she could make a joke, however small, about their time in the cabin flooded him with such relief he could only respond with a weak, "I can't throw you out. I've given you my heart, so I have to keep you around. I certainly don't want the neighbors saying I'm completely heartless."

"They'd better not!" Her indignant protest broke off as she saw his quick amusement. The slight upward curve of her mouth gained momentum. "They wouldn't dare," she retorted in her best mother-authority voice, achieved from years of practice. "If anyone thinks you're heartless, they better rethink it really quick or they'll answer to me!"

Thinking of five-foot one-inch Larissa taking on all comers, he felt a stab of pity for the individuals dumb enough to cross her. Even with his height of six feet, he'd rather rouse a sleeping beehive than stir up her ire. And he held no misgivings about admitting it.

After he departed for the barn, Larissa slumped onto a kitchen chair. She'd never expected the opportunity to come so swiftly to keep her promise about discussing her cabin qualms. She'd almost lost her courage before the words trickled out. Now, her promise fulfilled, and remembering his undisguised shock, she wondered fleetingly why she'd balked for so long. The answer came as swiftly as the question. In spite of his acceptance of her for herself, baring her soul's flaws wilted something inside her. *Will it be easier the next time? Or the one after?* She only knew she'd done her best, and memory of Ethan's response warmed the chilly spot lurking in her heart these many months.

These many months. She sat up straight, remembering the second envelope he'd brought home. Ordinarily, she dropped everything to read a letter from Anne Clayton. For all their anticipation of each week's mail day, they didn't receive many letters. Ethan kept contact with friends in Michigan, but the spaces between the arrival of those letters had lengthened over time. She secretly wondered if at some point the correspondence would cease entirely. She hoped not. He obviously cared deeply about these people, and they him, to still be in contact after seven years. But she well knew how distance, time, and a branching out of interests loosened the ties people shared.

Anne Clayton's envelope lay on the stairs where Larissa had set it in her eagerness to hear Mac's news. Stooping to pick it up, she mulled the irony of few-and-far-between letters and then two in one day. *Not that I'm complaining about receiving either one.* She supposed some folks considered the women's correspondence odd. *If so, it's the other person's problem.* Anne evidently agreed, because they'd been writing for two years now.

Anne's first letter, over a year after Zane's death, had caught Larissa unaware. The Army had assigned Anne's husband Ben and his friend Steve Jamison to the 6th Ohio Volunteer Cavalry during the Civil War. They'd served alongside Zane at Fort Laramie and fought in the Indian attack in which he died. Their enlistments up, on their way back to their families in Marietta, they stopped by the farm to return Zane's Morgan horse Deneb to Larissa. Their arrival caught her taking a peach pie, made from the last of her canned fruit, out of the oven. They told her about army life with Zane, and about his death. After large helpings of peach pie and coffee, they'd continued to Marietta and their waiting families. Larissa never expected to hear from them again.

Ironically, she was peeling peaches for a pie the afternoon Ethan brought home Anne's first letter. She'd stared, puzzled, at the Marietta postmark and with trembling fingers unfolded the paper. Anne explained she wanted to let Larissa know she had been in Anne's thoughts. Since their husbands served their enlistment time together, and Ben spoke so highly of Zane, and of her from their brief meeting, Anne wished she and Larissa could meet. If Larissa cared to answer, Anne would be delighted.

Larissa wavered for several days. On one hand, the contact resurrected the pain of Zane's death. On the other, it offered a link to people who knew him, had lived with him, and were with him in his final moments, as she could not be. She replied tentatively, as if feeling her way through a dark room, seeking light that, so far, had proved to be on the other side of a set of firmly closed shutters. Anne's swift, warm response opened those shutters a slit, providing Larissa assurance this unlikely-begun friendship would blossom into one to cherish.

Through the ensuing months, they'd shared their ongoing joys and griefs. Larissa told of their lives on the farm. She wrote about Rose and Charity, of their sometimes backward-sliding ascent into young womanhood, and each one's growing ambition to become a teacher. She wrote of Mac, and her hopes and dreams for all the children's futures.

Anne confided her pregnancy following speedily on the heels of Ben's arrival back in Marietta, and Amanda Jamison's almost as swift one after her husband Steve's return. Her next letter told how Ben and Steve had decided to move their families to Nebraska Territory to take up cattle ranching.

In February, a terse, clumsily written note had arrived from Ben, telling of the premature birth and immediate death of their baby daughter, Elizabeth, and assuring her Anne would write when she could. Months of silence followed, while Larissa waited frantically for news.

In late September, she finally received Anne's letter. Her joyous relief had twisted into deep sorrow at the bitter news Steve and Amanda Jamison had been killed in an Indian raid. Larissa had let the letter fall onto her lap as she remembered the warm gray eyes and quiet ways of the tall young man who sat at her kitchen table eating peach pie. He'd told her of the Indian attack resulting in Zane's death, never dreaming he and his wife would soon suffer the same fate. Tears had flooded Larissa's eyes as she'd resumed reading. Anne and Ben were raising the Jamison children, Matt, three years old, and Catty, only a few months old.

Early on, Larissa had mentioned how Ethan proved such a blessing around the place, and how she never would have managed without him. At first, she easily kept her tone friendship grateful for his presence, because she felt exactly so. Since the June morning she and Ethan revealed their feelings to each other, but to no one else, frustration seeped into her pleasure each time she wrote. She and Anne had shared so many other muddy spots in the road of life. Hard put to keep silent, she nevertheless took care not to inject anything more than simple gratitude into her descriptions of Ethan. She had, she thought, been studiously vigilant in writing any news of him.

After Charity's escapade brought their relationship to light, Larissa had shared her new-found joy. Undoubtedly, today's letter held Anne's response. Larissa sank onto the bottom step, sharply vexed about delaying so long to open it. Reading, reassurance replaced her fretting. Anne admitted she'd wondered but left the decision to Larissa whether to speak up. Knowing for sure, she wholeheartedly shared her friend's delight and wished her a lifetime and a home full of joy.

She confided how, after two years, she still couldn't think of the plains as home. She'd lived in bustling, tree-shaded Marietta most of her life. In sharp contrast now, their nearest neighbors ranched miles away, and trees grew only along the creeks and streams. The grasslands felt vast and empty with neither human life nor foliage between here and there to break the monotony. So both Larissa's letter itself, and her happy news, became joyful occasions in Anne's life.

For a long time, Larissa sat with the letter in her lap and thought about Anne going from city life in Marietta to those lonely, windswept plains. Faced with the same hardships, how would Larissa fare? With a sinking feeling, she suspected her own performance would not shine spectacularly. She thought of the patience and humor marking Anne's letters. *Against baby Elizabeth's death, however, she had had no defenses....*

CHAPTER TEN

On a drizzly afternoon two days after receiving Mac's letter, Larissa bent over her ironing board, carefully pressing tiny tucks into Charity's pinafore. She planned to finish in good time to make cornbread for supper, to go with the bean soup simmering on the stove. Her plan, however, possessed a mind of its own. Instead of shrinking, the unironed pile appeared to grow larger with every piece she removed. She had the sneaky suspicion that, as soon as she turned her back, two pieces jumped onto the stack from some mysterious space, taking the place of the one she'd just picked up. Assured no one lurked nearby to observe such mature behavior, she stuck her tongue out at the uncooperative heap, which produced no effect whatsoever on the height of the pile.

Exchanging her cooling flatiron for a hot one from the back of the stove, she heard a rig on the drive. Ethan, in the sheep shed tending an ailing ewe, probably wouldn't hear the visitor's arrival.

Setting her iron back on the stove, she rubbed a clear spot in the steam-fogged window over the sink, and took a quick look through the now earnestly splattering rain. Her lips curved into a smile. Ears laid back, Doc Rawley's ornery mare jerked to a halt so suddenly the buggy swayed. *If a horse could scowl, Bella would certainly take the first prize.* Two bonneted heads popped out from around the buggy hood. Rose and Charity scrambled to the ground and made a mad dash up the path to the shelter of the porch.

Doc clambered down and lifted out the weight stone to fasten to Bella's bridle to keep her from wandering. Larissa had heard him mutter more than once that, dang fool lazy as she was, chances were slim she'd meander off. Well acquainted with her stubborn temperament, however, he allowed, just in case she took such a notion, his bones could find better things to do than chase her all over creation.

Hastily checking her hair in the mirror above the wash bench, and her apron for spots, Larissa stood back as the girls tumbled in and headed for the warm stove. Giggling at their plight, they began shedding drenched coats and bonnets. Larissa shook her head in sympathetic amusement. Leaving them to it, she stepped onto the porch to find Doc already halfway along the path in his rush to get up the steps and out of the now driving rain. "Why don't you take Bella on over to the barn and get her out of this wet?"

At her call, not missing a beat, Doc pulled his hat brim down and about faced toward a soggy, sulky Bella. As he unfastened the weight rope, Ethan hailed him from the barn doorway. The mare didn't need to be told twice. Doc barely managed to scramble under the negligible shelter of the dripping buggy top before, weight stone and orders from her master to the contrary, Bella complied with Ethan's invitation by dragging the rig over to him.

Larissa covered her mouth with her fingers, but her laughter trickled out, anyway. Assured Ethan would tend to everything necessary, including Doc's sputtering and colorful indignation, she shivered in the coolness and turned back to the warm kitchen with its scent of ironing in progress. Rose and Charity had hung their coats on the pegs behind the stove and now stood with their backsides bent as perilously close to the radiating heat as their skirts would allow without inconveniently catching fire.

Never knowing these days just what kind of reception to expect, Larissa smiled and stretched her hands to the warmth. "You're home early. Charity's Pa planned to fetch you from school so you wouldn't have to walk in all this wet. Looks like Doc beat him to it."

"Miss Sullivan dismissed us early. She said a colossal storm was brewing, and everyone better get home before it broke. Just as we crossed Mill Creek bridge, Doc drove by and said he planned to stop here. So he brought us, too."

Larissa still couldn't get used to Rose's chattiness, any more than she could Charity's subdued behavior. At mention of Doc, Charity's cheeks turned pinker than her proximity to the fire warranted. Larissa knew she felt mortified around him, but Ethan had decreed flatly that unacceptable behavior reaped unpleasant aftereffects.

Careful not to put his parental authority in question, Larissa said brightly, "How lucky for all of us. Would hot chocolate warm your chilly bones?" Charity added her restrained assent to Rose's enthusiastic one, and the girls clattered down cellar to retrieve the milk from its cool earthen nook.

Larissa reached for a pan and the cocoa powder tin. *If Charity doesn't accept Doc's presence gracefully, Ethan will…* This unproductive brooding flapped back into its pigeonhole at the girls' triumphant return with the milk pitcher. The business of measuring, simmering, and taste-testing the hot chocolate concoction quickly occupied them. Larissa scooped up the rebellious laundry pile, stuffed the heaping basket into the woodshed adjoining the kitchen, and shut the door firmly. Without even a pinch of token guilt, she removed her ironing board from the two chair backs upon which it rested.

With one last taste test, just to be sure, the girls pronounced the chocolate mixture done to perfection. With admirable timing, Ethan and Doc blew into the room on a gust of cold, wet air. Charity edged backward, but the look Ethan shot her speedily edged her forward again. Having made his point, he sniffed appreciatively as he and Doc sloughed off their dripping coats and hats. "Something smells mighty good." Even Doc looked interested.

"Hot chocolate!" Suddenly mysteriously animated, Charity joined her voice to Rose's. "Do you want some?"

"We also have hot coffee," Larissa interjected. The glance between Ethan and Doc was pure little-boy. Her lips twitched. "It's a good thing you made plenty," she acknowledged teasingly to the girls as they hurried to set out cups and saucers. She added a platter of fresh-that-morning doughnuts and stealthily held out her own cup for a chocolate fill before gathering the cornbread ingredients.

She turned the batter into the pan as Doc reached for the last doughnut. "Got a letter from Mac," he announced casually. "Thought you might be interested in what he has to say."

Larissa's hands stopped their scraping motion. Ethan set his cup into the saucer with an audible clink. Rose's eyes widened with delight. Embarrassment forgotten, a different flush stained Charity's cheeks, and she stared as if Doc just claimed he could pull a rabbit, long ears and all, out of his black medical bag.

Seemingly oblivious to the lighted firecracker he had tossed into their midst, Doc finished the doughnut, then patted his rumpled black suit coat until he discovered the envelope sticking out of an inside pocket. A prolonged search for his glasses followed. He finally fished them from an outer pocket. At last he held up the letter. "Shall I read it?" His innocent query earned him four vigorous nods that caused his lips to turn upward behind his bushy beard.

"The first part's just medical talk about his classes. I told him to keep me updated on everything they're teaching him. But I thought you might be interested in the last page." He cleared his throat and suddenly thrust the paper at Larissa. "Here, you're better at reading out loud than I am." She wiped her cornbread-batter hands on her apron and caught the gruffness in his tone that all his blustering couldn't hide.

Her own voice shook a little as she began. "Please say hello for me to everyone at home. I hope this won't sound disgustingly dramatic, but I am eternally grateful for the opportunity they, and you, have given me in sending me here.

"If you see Rose, tell her I'd like a pair of those socks she's so good at knitting. That way, I won't ever get cold feet because I came here." Larissa smiled at his wording, Ethan chuckled, and Doc gave forth a rusty grunt, his equivalent of wild laughter. At the backhanded praise, Rose's cheeks turned as pink as Charity's, but the two girls looked equally puzzled over Mac's strange reference to "cold feet."

"I must close for now but will send you another update at the end of the month.

"Mac."

Larissa held the paper several heartbeats more before slowly handing it back to Doc. As he took it, their eyes met for a fleeting moment, his touching hers with an unutterably gentle expression. Even as it formed, he turned away to Rose. "Well, young lady, are you going to knit those socks your brother requested?" he asked brusquely.

Rose beamed. "He asked me to draw a picture of the house. I never thought he'd ask me on purpose for socks!" Sudden mischief sparked her eyes. "I believe I'll make him a pansy purple pair, to cheer him up, you see, just in case he gets to feeling gloomy. Do you think he'll wear them?"

Doc tugged at his ear. "Rose, I believe he'd wear ones colored ripe-pumpkin orange." He tapped the letter thoughtfully against his palm. "I suspect, as a part of home, he'll wear your pansy-purple ones. Maybe just not in front of anyone!"

***

The dreary November days slogged past, and Larissa's attention turned to planning Thanksgiving dinner. She truly enjoyed the holiday, but it always meant much more work and fuss than usual in getting a meal. She for one had been glad when Abraham Lincoln, back in October 1863, specifically proclaimed the last Thursday in November as a day of "thanksgiving and praise to our beneficent Father."

Before that, the day had been erratically chosen. *Probably by someone who didn't have to organize a big dinner and so didn't care if the date jumped around from year to year. Rather like a leaping frog wanting to go in all directions at once and unable to decide which lily pad to plop down on.* Through President Lincoln's wisdom, the frog had landed, with only a quiet splash to mark its presence. Now she could prepare her menu in a much more orderly manner. For this, she gave genuine thanks.

Her thoughts ran in this fashion on a morning that was, miraculously, neither pelting icy rain nor so windy the chill blew into her bones as soon as she stepped out the door. It was cold, to be sure, but a drier cold than they had seen in days. Ethan's prediction of snow before tomorrow had prompted her to go to town to complete some errands before the tiresome winter storms tied her to the house.

Pegasus and Andromeda, hitched to the buggy, stepped briskly as if they, too, enjoyed the chance to get out on this rare-fine day. She guided the buggy into a spot in front of Morey's Cabinets and Furniture and checked out the hats in the millinery shop next door before entering the dry goods store that was her goal. As she fingered the quality of a bolt of blue-checked flannel for a new shirt for Ethan, a lilting voice behind her spoke her name. Turning, she saw Martha Gallaway threading her way through the clustered merchandise.

Before and after church the last few Sundays, Martha had been surrounded by a group of women delightedly wishing her well on her and Reverend Gallaway's recent marriage. Larissa had had no opportunity to do more than smile and wave. Now, after glad greetings at today's unexpected encounter, Martha put her hand on Larissa's arm. "I hoped to talk to you Sunday after church, but this is even better."

"Is everything all right?"

Martha's swift smile promptly shooed away Larissa's concern. "Oh, yes! Shawn and I wanted to ask if you and Ethan, and the girls, of course, would join us at the parsonage for Thanksgiving dinner."

"We'd love to." Impulsively, Larissa responded warmly before she caught herself. "But you're only just married. This is your first Thanksgiving as a family. Surely you want to spend it privately, just the two of you and the children."

Martha laughed and gave her friend an ecstatic hug. "Thank you for thinking it, but that's exactly why we want to have you over, to help us celebrate our happiness."

Larissa returned the hug, then gazed at her friend thoughtfully. "You really are happy, aren't you?"

Joy leaping into Martha's eyes gave its own answer. "Yes," she said softly, "we really are." It had not been an easy road for Martha to travel. Her first husband, Ross, died in 1861, at the First Battle of Bull Run in the Civil War. He left Martha a widow with four young children to raise and a farm to manage as best she could alone.

Shawn Gallaway, the minister of one of Fairvale's four churches, which just happened to be the one Martha attended, counseled her during the first months of her insupportable grief. Only gradually he came to the realization he cared for her in definitely more than a ministerial way. Not wanting to influence or take advantage of her, he had stepped back. It was then, Martha had confessed to Larissa, she understood how, much as Ross had left her alone, and lonely, she felt alone, and lonely, without Shawn.

Upon hearing of the marriage plans, the church superiors had issued their decree that Martha's farm, left to her after Ross's death, not be a source of income to Shawn. Their inability to find a way around or over the brick wall thus raised, had precipitated Martha's anxiety-filled visit to Larissa just after Mac's departure for Philadelphia. That brainstorming session, as with all of their previous attempts, had yielded no flash-of-brilliant-light results. With all their careful pondering, in the end, it was Larissa who came up with the solution.

It hit her, as such things do, at three o'clock in the morning of the Sunday after Martha's visit in September. With the wind howling outside her window, she lay staring at the patterns of moonlight wavering across the ceiling. She had been awake for some time, putting the problem before a Higher Authority. As she stared upward, the answer came with the almost physical jolt she always experienced when something she was deliberating became as clear to her as if a candle suddenly glowed in a dark room.

Her thrill over the solution, and the simplicity of it after all their thrashing about, sorely tempted her, in spite of the hour, to dash to the cabin to tell Ethan. Before she could do so, her imagination painted two vivid pictures of this excursion. She, running along the leaf-strewn path in her white nightgown, barefoot, hair flying every which way in the wind, pounding on the door to waken him. And his open-mouthed shock at seeing such a spectacle. However reluctantly, her sanity retained some outraged semblance of dignity. She stayed dutifully in her warm bed, but sleep eluded her for the rest of the night.

At breakfast, properly dressed and hair neatly pinned, she had broached her idea to Ethan. "Why can't she simply rent out the farm and contribute any proceeds to the district church for distribution wherever needed?"

Ethan looked distinctly embarrassed for not having thought of it himself, but speedily agreed they should put it to Martha and Shawn. They did so after church services that same morning.

Shawn's expression of incredulity and his prolonged, vigorous pumping of Ethan's hand, along with Martha's radiant smile, sufficiently confirmed their approval of the plan. Disregarding the fact it was Sunday, Shawn persuaded Miles Painter to open the railroad depot and send a telegram to the church superiors who had handed down their edict. The church office responded with silence, until a letter came requesting Shawn's presence at a meeting with the Church Session over in Delaware County.

On the evening of the third interminable day after Shawn's departure, Larissa and the girls put the finishing touches to the supper table. Ethan came from the chores and washed up at the basin. The clatter of a horse and buggy took them all to the door. Martha close beside him, Shawn pulled the mare to a halt beside the path. One look, and Larissa and Ethan didn't need their ecstatic announcement. "They said yes!"

With the four children gathered close around them, they had married the following Sunday.

In the dry goods store this November afternoon, Larissa thrilled to her friend's new-found happiness. With no further protest, barring checking with Ethan, she accepted the invitation to Thanksgiving dinner, with the stipulation she be allowed to contribute to the menu. Over the bolts of flannel, they worked out a satisfactory plan of nourishment for the big occasion.

The next evening, the aroma of Larissa's New England pot roast having lured the family to the supper table, discussion meandered from one subject to another. Somehow, it landed on favorite Thanksgiving dishes. They debated the merits of turkey as opposed to goose, sage dressing over chestnut, and cranberry relish with walnuts or without. The hot rolls Larissa made only on holidays unanimously fell into a category all to themselves, with no rival in sight.

The bickering eventually turned to selecting the best of all desserts. Plum pudding, from Larissa. Pumpkin pie, with lots of sweet whipped cream, from Ethan. Apple pie with lots of *ice* cream, from Charity. Her preposterous choice drew a laugh from the others, as well as herself, because she knew perfectly well ice cream was an indulgence for a hot summer day, not a cold winter night. All choices were tossed into the ring for heated discussion.

After several moments of laughter and extremely biased bids for their own candidates, Larissa realized Rose hadn't revealed her choice. Her puzzled glance touched her daughter's face and the gravity there startled her. She'd certainly been lively enough during the earlier squabbling. "Rose? Do you have something you'd like to add to the commotion?"

She spoke lightly, but Ethan and Charity broke off their wrangling and swiveled toward Rose. She seemed not to notice their scrutiny but sat, hands clasped tightly in her lap. Eyes on her mother's face, she said softly, "Rhubarb cobbler."

Larissa's heart gave a painful jerk and for a moment she simply couldn't answer. Rhubarb cobbler had been Zane's hands-down favorite dessert.

"Ma?" A sudden pleading note crept into Rose's voice.

Awareness of Ethan and Charity watching touched Larissa, but they seemed a long way off as she focused her attention on her daughter. She never afterward knew for certain from where she unearthed a smile, but she felt her lips curve appropriately. "You've made an excellent choice. I know someone who would be very pleased with it."

Rose slipped off her chair and threw herself against Larissa's shoulder. Arms tight around her mother's neck, she whispered, "You're not sad?"

Over the duck-egg-sized lump in her throat, Larissa smoothed her daughter's soft blond hair. "No, I'm not sad. You mustn't be, either. I think you just won our contest and left the rest of us behind in the rhubarb patch!"

Charity started to utter her opinion, but Ethan's hand on her arm silenced her. She tried again and his hand pressed more firmly. She subsided, lower lip protruding, rather like a sulky pup that has just been scolded for chasing the chickens. Rose raised her head from Larissa's shoulder and flushed as she saw them watching her.

Ethan cleared his throat. "Well, Charity, it looks like you and I better re-think our priorities. I'd say Rose's choice, with or without whipped cream, tops them all!"

***

Accordingly, the day before Thanksgiving, Larissa finished baking an apple pie and prepared to slide a pumpkin pie into the oven. Spicy odors of cinnamon and nutmeg hung tantalizingly in the air. Ethan had gone hunting that morning and a plump turkey, plucked and cleaned, was now on its way to the Gallaway doorstep in plenty of time for it to make its personal contribution to the day.

Closing the oven door, she turned to inspect the apple pie. As she bent over the golden brown pastry, a Mason jar of rhubarb on the far side of the worktable winked as the glass container caught the light. Although she'd brought it up from the cellar with the pumpkin and apples, Larissa had not yet decided whether she would use it. Even now, remembering Rose's selection, tears blurred her vision.

When the children were small, any time rhubarb cobbler made its appearance at the Edwards' table, Zane had unabashedly voiced his pleasure. It was, as he expressed it, his "most favoritest" dessert, which appalling grammatical destruction always brought shouts of glee from Rose and Mac.

Each Thanksgiving since his death, Larissa had included the dish on her holiday table. She did it mainly for the children. She wanted to give them a sense that their father remained a part of their lives, even though the demolishment of the English language, and the laughter following, would not ever again be more than a wistful echo in their hearts.

She admitted to herself that a small portion of the ritual had been for her sake, as well as the children's. Until this year, serving the cobbler hadn't posed a problem. Before the war took Zane away, Ethan and Charity often ate with the Edwards family, including many times when rhubarb cobbler made its appearance. Now, however, since she and Ethan were to be married, was such an inclusion fair to him? He could not fail to be aware of its significance. As with her earlier cabin qualms, she faced the awareness that, if the future were to have a chance, the past must be let go.

Except for his one "topping them all" remark to Charity, Ethan hadn't mentioned anything, either last night or this morning, about Rose's dessert selection. Larissa knew he was leaving the decision up to her and would express an opinion only if she asked him.

Facing the question squarely, she acknowledged honestly that her heart ached not for herself, but for her daughter. *Have I been wrong in keeping this ritual intact?* Rose and Mac had so few ways they could keep their father a part of their daily lives without being distastefully sentimental about it. *But has the time come for Rose, too, to acknowledge that the past must be let go, if the future is ever to have a chance?*

Larissa shook her head impatiently. *You couldn't let go yourself. Look how long it took you! And you expect a twelve-year-old to have that kind of maturity?*

Thoroughly vexed with herself, she set about tidying the worktable and picked up the sugar canister to return it to the pantry. Once again, however, her eyes strayed to the rhubarb, and she absently set the canister down. Slowly circling the table, she lifted the glass container. With Mr. John Mason's invention a few years ago, she could can her produce in a jar fitted with a zinc lid that screwed tightly, sealing in the contents and keeping them from spoiling. She remembered her reluctance to try this improbable method of preserving the fruits and vegetables she had grown with such care and hard work. Zane, however, neatly sidestepped her objections by triumphantly bearing a box of the jars home from town. Highly skeptical, but unwilling to hurt his feelings, she had experimented with a panful of peas from the garden. Now she wondered how she'd ever managed her preserving any other way.

She ran her fingers over the raised "Mason Jar" lettering and the star resting between the words. The batch of jars became the last gift Zane surprised her with before he went to war. Inside the one she held, the neatly cut rhubarb portions, whose fate she must soon decide, glowed like jewels.

Fate. Fate had put so much heart-hurt in her life these past years. And what had it done to Rose's life? Once more she blinked back tears as she thought of her daughter, of the hurt her child had already suffered and the pain that would, inevitably, come to her in the future. The hurt that all Larissa's mother love could not prevent, if her daughter were to be guided in learning to face life courageously.

She was so intent upon her thoughts that when Ethan, back from taking the turkey to the Gallaways, banged open the back door, bringing a gust of cold air in with him, she jumped. "Sorry, Lizzie! I didn't mean to startle you." His laughing apology broke off as he caught sight of the jar clutched in her hands. At the same instant, the light of greeting in his eyes vanished, to be replaced by a shuttered look she had never seen before. She caught only a glimpse as he heeled back around to the door. "The girls went to the cabin. They'll be along in a minute. Only came in to tell you I'm back. I have to tend the team." He flung the last words over his shoulder as he—there was no other word for it—bolted out the door and yanked it shut behind him.

"Ethan!" Her heart wrenched as sharply as if someone had kicked it. She took an instinctive step toward the door and reached her hand to the space where he had been standing.

Only then she realized she still held the jar of rhubarb. She had a sudden vivid remembrance of how Ethan had come out from town and been present in the kitchen the day Zane presented her with the box of jars. Unwittingly, he had witnessed Zane's tenderness and shy pride at surprising her.

She stared a long moment at the jar in her hands, then raised her eyes to the empty space in front of the door. Very carefully, she set the jar on the table, before she sank onto the nearest chair and buried her face in her hands.

CHAPTER ELEVEN

Yanking the kitchen door shut, Ethan faced into the rising wind. In spite of his ill humor, he glanced toward the cabin path to check for the girls. Through the flurrying snow, falling much more thickly than just minutes ago, he glimpsed the two figures hurrying toward the house. Foregoing the path, they cut across the lawn. Heads down, they gained the shelter of the porch, almost mowing him down.

"Pa?" Charity's gasp came partly from surprise as he materialized from the ghostly gloom and partly because the storm had snatched her breath.

"Go inside. I have to get to the chores." They needed no further urging, but pitched through the doorway, and he heard Larissa's exclamation. *Larissa… No! Just get yourself out there and tend the stock before this storm becomes a blinding blizzard.* He shook his head to clear it. No time now to think about her or the scene he'd just scurried from, tail tucked between his legs. Grabbing the guide rope, he secured the safety line around his waist. One end of the rope fastened to a porch post and the other to a hefty pole sunk into the earth directly beside the barn door. He could see the barn through the shifting flakes, but he refused to take any chances, now or later. Every winter, stories circulated about men confident they knew their way to the barn, even in a blizzard, and who didn't make it. He certainly didn't need to pretend courage he didn't feel.

Not after your cowardly dash from Larissa's sight. He gave the rope a savage tug, as if so doing would transfer to it all his pent up frustration. Testing the strength of the line against the rising storm, he slowly crossed the road. He heaved a sigh of relief upon reaching the smaller barn door they used in the winter to avoid letting in the weather through the larger one. Assured the line would hold in a time of real necessity, he shucked the waist rope, secured it to the post, and pushed into the dusky haven of the building.

Retrieving a pair of coveralls from a peg by the door, he pulled them on over his town clothes. Working quickly, but carefully as always, he tended the animals now safely gathered under the sheltering roof. All exhibited good health, even the ewe that had needed a potion earlier in the month. He gave all of them extra rations in case he should be longer than he expected in returning, although he thought he could get through with the help of the guide rope.

He finally finished, except for bringing the unneeded skimmed milk back from the house for the pigs. Since he'd be returning to the barn, he shrugged his heavy coat on over his coveralls. Carrying the foaming bucket of fresh milk, he pushed open the smaller door. He caught sight of the house, candle-lit bright at the windows but outline-blurred behind the falling snow. Reluctance to step out butted him as forcefully as a riled-up billy goat.

Fierce concentration on his chores had kept at bay the realities he would face when he returned to the kitchen. Now, with no thoughts to crouch behind, all his scrupulously tamped down emotions surged up, grinning maliciously. Carefully, he set the milk bucket where he wouldn't accidentally kick it over. He scrubbed his hand across the back of his neck and, nose to nose as it were, glared at his problem.

With knowledge born of bitter experience, he'd stood quietly by Larissa in her grief as she came to terms with Zane's death. He'd said nothing of his own love until he was certain both of them could leave their past married lives to the past and look to the future. Not that he'd forgotten Nettie or their shared joy, and not that Larissa should forget Zane, as though the happiness she'd had with him could be put up on a high shelf to collect dust.

He'd never worried about competing with Zane's memory. Larissa had certainly never given him cause. At sight of her distress as he entered the kitchen, his first instinct had been to go to her. Instead, glimpsing the jar clutched in her hand, he'd bolted like a jackrabbit. *If, after three years, a canning jar holds such power to affect her, what hope do we have to walk together in a joyful marriage?* He tried to smile over a jar of dessert makings causing such woe, but it wouldn't stick. He slammed his clenched fist into his palm. *This matters, damn it!* Last night when Rose chose rhubarb cobbler, Larissa seemed shaken with the unexpected selection, as well she might. *But tears twenty-four hours later? As a delayed reaction, it must set a record.* He admitted he couldn't always comprehend women, especially in moments like this. Even with Nettie, sometimes their minds seemed miles apart, and only later they discovered they'd been working to get the same point across, but from very different angles. He supposed all couples experienced a similar gulf now and then.

Remembering the mess he'd made talking to Larissa about his continuing to live on the farm after Mac departed, he grimaced. He'd heard how as a man advanced in years, Nature bestowed maturity and wisdom upon his graying head. He suspected, with him, Nature had fallen a tad behind in her job. *I certainly can't claim a whopping lot more luck with Larissa than I had with Nettie.* He sighed. He'd skidded all around the problem. Obviously, his reluctance to face it hadn't helped him skid very far from his starting point.

Thrown together by chance, war, and Zane's death, he and Larissa, from the awkward beginnings of mutual respect, to their companionship as friends, and into their relationship of love, had been able to talk things out. He'd never had any suspicion they wouldn't always continue to do so. He knew last night's episode with Rose troubled Larissa more than she let on, even though she hadn't spoken of it since. And therein lay his problem. He ached to help her, but in this matter he couldn't aid her in finding a solution.

He couldn't even offer her a comforting shoulder.

This time differed from discussing the children and the farm. Those problems always involved both of them and so could be jointly considered and solved. *Not this one. Not this time.* While he sure as Heaven didn't know everything, he knew this much for truth.

No matter how deep their love, her heart contained, as did his and every other human being's, a small, sheltered space belonging to no one else. Breaching the boundaries of that shielded place would trample upon the attributes that made Larissa uniquely and wholly herself.

He would not rob her of that essence.

Larissa had been Zane's wife and was the mother of Zane's children. Rose was Zane's daughter in a matter concerning Zane. That left no room for Ethan, standing on the outside of that precisely formed circle, to elbow in, spouting words of wisdom and dispensing perfect solutions galore. *Even if I had any to spout or dispense.*

He realized with surprise the early dusk brought on by the storm was deepening and the interior of the barn had become much darker. The wind had died down and the snow curtain didn't seem as heavy as earlier. *Maybe we won't have a blizzard tonight, after all.* This suited him fine, with their trip to town tomorrow to visit the Gallaways.

Stooping, he picked up the pail of milk and once again pushed at the small door. A flicker of movement near the house caught his eye. He peered through the still-falling snow and saw Larissa, shawl over her hair, trudging toward the barn. One hand grasped the guide rope. The other held up her long skirts in a futile effort to avoid their becoming soaked from trailing in the accumulating drifts. Head down to watch her steps, she didn't see him in the doorway. Again abandoning the milk pail, he hurried to her. "What are you doing out here?"

Astonishment roughened his tone and she raised her head, startled. "I came to find you." Uncertainty crept into her voice. "I wanted to make sure you're all right. You've been gone a long time."

"With the snow coming on, I switched the buckboard wheels for runners for tomorrow's ride. It took me longer than I realized. I'm almost done. Come inside out of the direct cold while I finish up."

Her shoe slid on an icy spot and he grasped her hand to steady her. Her chilly palm shocked him. "Just a shawl and no gloves? You'll catch your death coming out this way." Aware of the gruffness still in his voice, he said nothing more until he'd shut the door against the outer chill. "Wait here. I'll light the lantern so we don't kick over the milk bucket."

As the soft light chased back the dark, he hung the tin lantern on its peg. "I'll just make one last check of everything." He escaped into the dimness at the rear of the barn, stopped, and drew a deep breath. In spite of his earlier turbulent quarrel with himself, or perhaps because of it, he must not let emotion weaken his resolve to allow her to come to her own terms, in her own time, with her dilemma. *Sounds sensible—and cold-hearted.*

Even without the self-mockery, he entertained strong doubts about his success in performing such a feat. Catching her unmistakable hesitation as she'd raised her head to meet him on the path, he'd wanted nothing more for himself than to put his arms around her and absorb the healing comfort of her touch. Only by speaking abruptly, he'd fended off this unfair-to-her notion and made good his escape to the shadows. *Do you honestly think you can shut her, and her problems, out of your life for any reason? You've been the dazzling star of this little performance a full three minutes and you're already making a mess of your lines. It'll be one or the other, but make up your mind, screw your courage to the sticking place, and do it!*

Fists knotted at his sides, he slowly straightened his shoulders before returning to her. She hadn't moved from the spot, but now stood in profile to him. She'd lowered the shawl from her head to her upper arms and gripped it as she would a lifeline. He tightened his jaw. "We'd best get back. I'll shuck these coveralls and be ready."

She turned slowly. "Ethan, I'm sorry if I've caused you any distress. I would never do it intentionally." She faltered, but her eyes held his steadily. "I know what it looked like, but I wasn't crying for Zane." He flinched at her bluntness, but she hurried on. "I was thinking what to do about Rose. She's so young. I'm well aware this is by no means the end of the pain she'll suffer during her life. I'd take it from her in a breath if I could. But I can't. And it hurts so much to think of her hurting and to know I can't help her." Her voice trailed off and she looked away from him.

He stood rigid as her words pelted him with sharper edges than she could realize. He would take her pain in a breath, to spare her, but he couldn't, any more than she could take Rose's. He'd been so sure their minds were a mile apart in their thinking, and the whole time they'd just been viewing the problem from very different angles. *I've done it again,* he realized bitterly. *I'm getting to be quite an expert at building a gulf where none exists.* So where did that leave him and all his fancy notions about doing the right thing by her and staying out of her private decisions?

He had no brilliant answer to this query. He walked slowly toward her, anyway. "Larissa." His voice once again came gruffly as he put his hand under her chin and turned her face to his. The distress in her eyes slapped his heart, knowing as he did that he had put a large part of it there. He brushed the back of his fingers across her cheek.

"Lizzie." His voice came roughly this time because his throat had tightened so much he could scarcely speak. He knew, suddenly and surely, words weren't necessary after all. Drawing her to him, he held her tightly, his cheek resting against her soft hair. He felt the breath go out of her and she curved even more closely into his arms. This, then, was his answer. He could not solve her anguished problem with Rose. He could not offer her a comforting shoulder while she worked through to the decision that must come only from that sheltered spot in her own heart.

But, out of everything they were to each other, he could offer his love and comfort, and his shoulder, for several very good reasons. Because of the past they shared. Because of the present which, for good or ill, shaped their future relationship even as they stood close together and the seconds scurried past. He could offer them to her just … because.

As he felt her lips come to his with joy and urgency, he knew it to be a very good reason, indeed.

CHAPTER TWELVE

Thanksgiving morning, the buckboard now sturdy and serviceable on runners, Ethan halted the team beside the newly shoveled path where Larissa and the girls waited. With more sliding and surreptitious jostling than the slippery track actually demanded, the girls finally bounced into the back of the buckboard, now heaped with straw and quilts for them to snuggle under.

Ethan gave Larissa an assist onto the seat. "Strange, I didn't slide around nearly so much," she murmured. She tucked her feet against the hot stones he had wrapped in old carpet pieces and propped against the dashboard. "Seems to me they're making a lot of work out of it."

Ethan grinned. "You mean, at the ripe old age of thirteen, or in Rose's case, with her birthday next month, the near side, you always walked slowly and carefully? You never ended up in a drift and, of course, had to throw an unholy amount of snow around in your struggle to get out?"

"Well, maybe once."

Her reluctance to answer intrigued him. "Did you? I can just see you, skating on icy patches without benefit of skates and having a glorious time."

"Are you laughing at me?" Her suspicion would have done credit to a fox sniffing at a meat-baited trap. His eyes widened in surprised innocence. She continued resignedly, "When I was in second grade, after a particularly big storm, the teacher allowed us at recess to play in the snow. I had great fun until one of the boys slipped and fell against me and I ended up face-first in a drift tall as a haystack."

"Were you hurt?"

"Just my pride. My head may have been covered, but the rest of me stuck out rather prominently."

"With your head in the drift, how did you know what the other end was doing?" He wasn't certain she would answer. He waited patiently, anyway. She fiddled with a button on her coat sleeve. He waited some more.

"Oh, all right! Obviously, I won't have any peace until I tell you." She directed her next comment to her gloved hands clutched tightly in her lap. "When the others dug me out, they had no hesitation whatsoever in describing in great detail, then and for days afterward, just how prominently one portion of me had been on view for all to see."

"Young ones can be mean, but I think a lot of it comes from their being glad because they aren't in the same," he hesitated visibly, "position."

"They could afford to be glad. Pa ran the livery. Ma practiced thrift by making my drawers from grain sacking."

He suspected what was coming and struggled to maintain his solemnity as she paused. "You might as well know," she sighed. "Everyone else in town and for miles around did, after that. Ma had tried to get the printing out of the material, but I still advertised in bright red letters that Pa used 'Allegheny Falls' Finest Oats'."

Before he could say anything, giggles erupted behind them. Too late, they realized the exceptional quiet in back resulted from Charity and Rose's sneaking up directly behind the seat to listen avidly. Ethan struggled for a composed breath as Larissa turned scarlet as sunburn. Another quarter mile wound behind them before he could speak over his shoulder with any degree of firmness to the still giggling girls. "This is not to be spread among your friends. We will pursue the path known as 'keeping it in the family.' That goes for both of you. Understood?"

"Mr. Michaels, we would *never*—"

"Oh, Pa!" Charity's indignant protest of innocence blended with Rose's shocked denial.

He cut them off. "I remember another young lady, once upon a time, who gained a healthy respect for mud puddles after having been shoved into one."

"At least your drawers didn't advertise 'Allegheny Falls' Finest Oats'!" The words bubbled from behind the mittened hand clapped over Rose's mouth.

An injured frown puckered Charity's forehead. "That happened a long time ago when I was little."

"But you remember?" Ethan decided not to pursue the fact that Larissa, too, had been small when she and the snowdrift collided. *For Charity, of course, the incident happened to Larissa clear back in the Dark Ages.*

"A little. The mud felt cold and gooey and squishy." She screwed up her face and shuddered dramatically before she suddenly brightened. "I remember Mac helped me out."

You would. Ethan halted the team, arranged his features into a properly stern expression, and faced his daughter. "He helped you, and he didn't tease you. Shouldn't you extend the same courtesy to Mrs. Edwards?"

"I guess." At sight of her father's raised eyebrows, she hastily amended her less than enthusiastic response. "Sir." When the eyebrows didn't lower, she heaved a martyred sigh. "I'm sorry, Mrs. Edwards. I won't tell anyone." Ethan's brows finally resumed their normal position. She rolled her eyes and sank back beside Rose, who leaned over and whispered a comment that started both girls shaking with laughter once more.

Ethan flicked the lines and spoke to the horses, but he retained a strong suspicion that while Charity and Rose wouldn't speak of it to anyone else, it would be their favorite topic for many days to come.

In spite of the disciplinary delay, they soon swished into town and pulled up in front of the small parsonage next to the white church that Shawn Gallaway ministered. The day held simple, comfortable plans. Shawn had scheduled Thanksgiving church services for mid-morning, with Ethan, Larissa and the girls to accompany Martha and the children. Afterward, they would return to the parsonage for a day of shared friendship and thanksgiving.

They arrived just as fourteen-year-old Garth finished shoveling the front path. He bore a strong resemblance to his father, who had died during the first major battle of the Civil War. Along with his dark curly hair and tall sturdy build, Garth had inherited Ross Van Ellis's pleasant manner. Even five years later, the likeness of features and mannerisms startled Larissa when she encountered him after any length of time. *What must it do to Martha?*

In the side yard, the six-year-old twins, Noah and Mara, were busy producing a snow family. Waving, they resumed their task. Garth hoisted the snow shovel to his shoulder. "Morning, Mrs. Edwards, Mr. Michaels. Hi, Rose." Apparently, his tongue stuck in his throat. His "Hello, Charity," emerged between a squawk and a growl as his adolescent voice cracked.

He leaned the shovel against the picket fence, and Ethan's casual attention sharpened as he caught a momentary view of the boy's face beneath his blue knit cap. *Garth's shoveling exertions shouldn't make him turn that red. Surely, neither would self-consciousness over his traitorous voice.* With a strange twist in his heart, he watched Garth speak to Charity. He couldn't hear the words, but they brought a smile to her lips. When Garth reached a mittened hand to give her assistance in descending from the buckboard, all of Ethan's fatherly protection instincts rose up squealing and pointing.

Charity, who had earlier bounced into the vehicle without any help whatsoever, gracefully accepted Garth's arm to steady her as she stepped to the ground. Neither of the young people noticed Ethan observing their interplay. With no hint of embarrassment or flippant behavior, Charity thanked Garth for his assistance.

"Your little girl is growing up." It came as the barest whisper against his ear. Ethan felt Larissa's hand press his arm in unspoken support, but he kept his eyes on his daughter, and on the young man attracted to her.

One pin-sharp thought stuck itself onto his frozen brain. *Rambunctious as she is at home, she knows how to behave politely in social situations. This,* unfortunately, failed to be one of the social situations he had fondly contemplated.

Charity having reached the ground without mishap, Garth turned and politely offered his hand to Rose. She accepted his gesture with simple grace. Like a wave leaving the shore, Ethan's numbness receded. "It appears your little girl isn't too far behind." Larissa's expression held the same bewilderment he felt.

His disbelief melted into a bit of amusement and much sympathy for Garth. *I wouldn't be his age again for anything.* With Ethan's mannerly aid, Larissa, too, safely stepped to the ground.

Garth retrieved the shovel and once more settled it on his shoulder. "This sure is a fine team, Mr. Michaels." Recalling his manners, he added, "Reverend said after I see you to the house, I'm to take your team around to the barn and tend them, with your permission." He made a valiant effort to appear casual, to give the impression he had done it all a million times. His voice cracked again in his eagerness, but this time, with his rapt attention focused on the horses, he didn't even flinch.

His stalwart effort completely failed to deceive the adults, but they showed no hint. Larissa gave Ethan a faint nod when he turned to her. "You have our permission, but only if you really wish to tend them."

Garth's deep brown eyes widened, and he couldn't disguise his jubilation. "Yes, sir. I'd like it fine."

Ethan couldn't blame him a bit. A young man didn't often receive the opportunity to drive such a magnificent team. Garth escorted his guests along the newly shoveled path to the front door, but as soon as Shawn and Martha came forward to greet them, he slipped quietly back to the horses.

The day for giving thanks sped by with friendship and laughter, cooking and conversation. With everyone seated at the laden table, heads bowed, Shawn expressed gratitude for their being together, for "friends who have become family" and for the many gifts of happiness they had received during the year.

Larissa, her left hand in Ethan's, and her right clasped by Gretta, Martha's ten-year-old daughter, realized Shawn had neatly included his guests in his thanks. He and Martha had married and become, with her children, a true family. Now, with Ethan and herself free to speak of their feelings for each other, she realized their own circle of four had become a family in heart and spirit. *Mac, too,* she amended to include the son who was far from her physically, but always near in her heart.

Following dinner, Martha, the girls, and Larissa conducted a lengthy dishwashing session. Shawn, Ethan, and the boys tackled the barn tasks. Once all the chores they must complete, even on Thanksgiving Day, were duly discharged, the young people gathered in the sitting room to play charades. The adults retired to the parlor to sit before the fireplace and enjoy those after-moments of relaxation and contentment which follow a special day of visiting, meal preparation, and eating.

The conversation drifted from one topic to another until Shawn said quietly, "I don't believe we ever thanked you properly for helping us come to a decision about the farm. It literally made all the difference in our lives. If Martha and I hadn't been able to marry...." The look he gave his wife spoke volumes.

Surprised, Larissa realized that the dark time of which Shawn spoke had occurred less than three months before. Her existence as it was then might have taken place in another world entirely. Mac had not yet left for Philadelphia, Charity had not confounded them with her undeniably spectacular fit of rage, nor had she and Ethan yet openly declared their love. *Amazing how just a few days or hours can change the direction of one's life forever.*

"... such a simple resolution." She blinked now as Shawn's words recalled her to the cozy, candlelit room. "I told my superiors your suggestion that Martha rent out the farm and contribute any proceeds to the district church to be distributed wherever needed. They ruled that as long as Martha and I realized no personal gain or profit, the church had no objection to her keeping the farm 'in the family' and no objection to our marrying. A most wise decision, because I knew a host of good reasons why we should marry."

"And more reasons to add to the list, now," Martha said softly. She confirmed Larissa's suspicions a short time later as they made fresh coffee to serve with the pumpkin and apple pies. "I couldn't mention the baby while we were in the other room, but Doc Rawley's confirmed it, and I've been wishing so much to tell you. It couldn't have happened without you."

Larissa's eyes danced with an unholy twinkle. "I suspect you and Shawn had the most to do with it. Speaking of Shawn, what does he think?"

Martha laughed. "He's certain no one else ever thought of the idea. I'm not just about to tell him anything different!"

CHAPTER THIRTEEN

During the drive home on Thanksgiving evening, Rose and Charity, curled under the quilts in the back of the buckboard, whispered for only a few moments before falling silent. Neither Larissa nor Ethan knew why they acted so quiet. Wrapped in their own languid haze from the pleasant day, they simply accepted the silence as a blessing.

Ethan didn't say much, either, in response to Larissa's remarks, but he drew her close and she rested her head against his shoulder in peaceful drowsiness. He halted the team beside the porch path. It hadn't snowed today, but with the dark came a sharp drop in temperature and the drive and walkway sparkled with ice crystals. "Looks mighty slippery. If you don't mind staying put for a bit, I'll help the girls, then come back for you."

Snuggling more deeply into her coat, Larissa buried her nose in the fur collar. Vaguely, she heard him rouse the girls. He assisted them along the treacherous path and returned for her. She skidded once or twice as they progressed, but his heavier-soled boots allowed him, with reasonable caution, to maneuver without falling on his backside or dumping Larissa on hers. Safely on the porch, he gestured to the door. "I'll build up the fire, then get to the chores." In the faint light, he caught her smile.

"Why don't I fix the fire and have hot coffee waiting when you finish?"

"I don't have to weigh such an offer twice. I'll be back quick as I can." But first he drew her into his arms for a lingering kiss. "If we keep this up, we won't need to build up the kitchen fire. I feel much warmer already." He kissed the tip of her nose and released her.

Prepared to deal with a chilly kitchen, wonderment stopped her in the doorway. Flames danced behind the glass door of the pot-bellied stove, positioned for the winter between the kitchen and sitting room, and tendrils of warmth already reached into the cool room. The banked fire in the range stove had been prodded to life, too. She only needed to fill the coffeepot with water from the stove reservoir and grind the beans. *Bless Rose and Charity. Our little girls are growing up, and perhaps it isn't such a bad process, after all.*

Setting a plate of cherry turnovers on the table, she marveled yet again at the handiness of Mr. Mason's canning jars. *Eating cherries on Thanksgiving Day. What other wonders can someone possibly dream up?* An illustration in her *Godey's Lady's Book* showed a modern invention she secretly coveted. For some years now, eastern city housewives had used a kitchen contraption called an "ice box" to keep dairy products cold even in the summer. How timesaving not to traipse down to the springhouse on a hot July day for a quart of milk or a pound of butter. She smiled at the outlandish notion. *Might as well ask to fly to the moon while you're at it!*

The unopened jar of rhubarb winked at her from the worktable. She was glad, now, she hadn't used it. Rose had made no comment on its absence from the desserts they took to the Gallaways. Had she enough maturity, after all, to make the necessary emotional adjustment? *Perhaps more maturity than her mother, if it comes down to it.*

Resolutely, she grabbed the jar of rhubarb by the scruff of its neck and banished it to the cellar. She'd just reached the top of the stairs again when Ethan, carrying an armload of firewood, thumped through the woodshed door adjoining the kitchen. He hastily pulled the door shut and deposited his burden in the box beside the range. "It's downright cold out there. Sure glad the barn's so sturdy and tight."

"The coffee's ready." She poured a cup as she spoke, and he yanked off his gloves and took a grateful sip. "Merciful heavens, be careful! It just finished boiling."

He grinned. "Hot feels so good going down, I didn't even notice."

With biting-her-tongue effort, she held back an outraged reply. *After all, it's his mouth.* Still peeved, she joined him at the table for the cherry turnovers and coffee.

Apparently, he received the message, because he praised the turnovers several times. He also ate three. The conversation skipped around the day's events and she unbent enough to tell him how the girls had tended the fires, pleasantly surprising him, too. Plates in hand, she started to rise, but he suddenly reached out and caught her free hand. "Lizzie, let's not wait until spring. Let's get married now."

She sank into her chair and searched his face for a hint of joking. She found none. "Now?"

"Soon," he amended earnestly. "We've waited so long. Things keep happening, and we keep putting it off. It'll never be a perfect world, no matter how long we wait."

The thoughts scampering through her brain finally arranged themselves into a slightly more coherent form. "Is it because of seeing the Gallaways so happy?"

"Partly. It brought home what we're missing. We have so much, right now, but we could have so much more if we were married. I want that. Not just for myself, but for us."

His hand still clasped hers. She maneuvered until her fingers covered his. "I want it, too. For both of us. I don't think 'soon' can get here fast enough, to be honest."

For an instant, he looked certain his ears had heard wrong. Then his mouth and his eyes smiled. He rounded the table and drew her up into his arms. His kiss sent sweet fire from her heart to the tips of her toes.

"Thank you," he murmured against her hair.

"For what?" she asked hazily. His breath, somewhere in the region of her right earlobe, thoroughly distracted her as she circled her arms around his neck.

"I can't remember," he confessed. At her soft breath of laughter, he drew her closer.

Joy flooded her soul as once more he bent his mouth to hers. The barriers they initially had set so carefully, to protect them both, were crumbling as a sand figure crumbles when stroked by a feather-light touch of wind.

Raising his head, he brushed her cheek with the back of his hand and inhaled deeply, a long steadying breath that didn't quite succeed in doing its job. "I seem to recall saying our relationship is missing something," he said huskily. "But I must admit, we're certainly pointed in the right direction." Arms about her waist, obviously reluctant to break their embrace, he stood her back a bit.

She saw he, too, had felt the feather-light touch of that wondrous moment. Felt it and came as perilously close as she to brushing away the restraints they had set for themselves. She could not—would not—let him take upon himself the full burden of accountability in drawing away from their mutual feelings. With every fiber of her heart protesting the delay, she reached to cup her hand against the curve of his beard. "'Soon' better hurry up."

"Please, Lord, give me patience and hurry up about it!" He kissed her once more, lightly. "If I heard right, 'soon' has been ordered to hurry up. If I were 'soon' I'd hop to it, because I wouldn't want to face a certain woman's wrath if I disobeyed orders. She's fierce when she's crossed." The intensity of the moment passed. It did not ebb entirely, but the remnant became, at least, manageable. "I reckon we have some discussing to do, to hammer out a few pesky details that will undoubtedly crop up." He seated himself across from her and again reached for her hand.

She cupped her fingers over his. "If 'soon' hops to it, as you strongly suggest, I expect we should pick a date."

"Tomorrow?"

"Ethan!" It came out a squawk.

"Too far away?" he asked innocently.

"It is better than your earlier, 'Now, right this minute'," she admitted grudgingly, "but I was thinking of even a few hours farther away than tomorrow. For instance, a month or so from now."

"We've waited this long. I guess a few more weeks don't even compare with the stretch of time behind us. A month brings us to Christmas, or mighty close."

"Not Christmas." She was no longer joking. "It's Rose's day. It's enough she already has to share it. I won't take even more from her."

"I was teasing," he said contritely. "I wouldn't take more away from her, either. But before Christmas is always hectic. How about New Year's Day?"

"A new year and a new life for us. A wonderful day to begin the rest of our living."

"New Year's Day it is, then." He hesitated. "We need to decide about the children."

Pure mischief lit her eyes. "I think children are a wonderful idea. How many shall we decide on?"

"Lizzie!" It was his turn to squawk. She rarely shocked him, but this time made up for several lost opportunities.

"It has been known to happen," she said demurely. "The Gallaways prove that."

He finally untangled his tongue. "I didn't mean potential children," he said sternly. "Seems to me we have enough trouble on our hands with the current ones, without adding to it before we're even officially married." He sobered. "There's Charity's attitude to consider."

"Do you think she's still brooding? I thought she'd worked her way rather well past that."

"I think she's had time to come, if not completely, at least to speaking terms with it. I suspect she and Rose have discussed it thoroughly. Anyhow, I'm wagering she'll accept the situation. We may owe young Garth Van Ellis our thanks, if today indicates anything. I'm also thinking of Mac. One reason to wait for spring was the hope he could be here. I know it's extremely important to you. And it should be."

She hesitated, praying the words would stumble out properly. "It is so very important to me. I'll not pretend otherwise. But, as you with Charity, we must go ahead with our lives and do what's right for us. Mac may or may not be able to come in the spring." Her lips curved up. "I'd hate to waste all that time and then not have him here after all."

His hand tightened over hers. "You're sure?"

"If he's not here in person, he'll be here in my heart."

He cleared his throat roughly. "There's one more consideration to stir into our pot of plans. We've already talked about adding a downstairs bedroom onto the east side of the house. We originally set the wedding for early spring because I can't do any building until the snow clears off and the ground settles. At this point, the room is still a pile of lumber waiting to happen. Now we've just plunked our wedding date firmly into the middle of winter, with the ground frozen solid where I plan to dig the foundation. I think this poses a bit of a problem."

During their discussion weeks earlier, each one, unknown to the other, had discovered an unslain personal dragon. Ethan had been in Larissa's bedroom only once, the day they learned of Zane's death. Coming from town in a driving rainstorm, he had been unable to find her anywhere around the yard, outbuildings or kitchen area. Frantic, he'd checked all the upstairs bedrooms, including hers.

He had not been in her bedroom, or even upstairs, since that day. In all the time after, however, he had not lost the memory of the discomfort he experienced, knowing he had intruded into the most intimate area of Larissa's life with Zane. Loving her, he'd never felt any necessity to measure himself against Zane. He had no intention of doing so after their marriage, either. Larissa accepted that he had memories of moments with Nettie that were his alone, just as she certainly had with Zane. Without elaborating, he had told her he didn't want to take Zane's place, in her bedroom or any other area. She'd agreed with his pronouncement so quickly he suspected her uneasiness matched his.

They'd discussed using the cabin but, as with their mutual discomfort concerning her bedroom, they jointly and hastily concluded the plan wouldn't work with the inevitable necessity of constant travel back and forth to the house.

They touched on the possibility of taking one of the bedrooms belonging to the children, but quickly dismissed the idea as unfair to the present occupants. Charity had, for all intents and purposes, moved into Mac's room, at least a large portion of her possessions had, and the girls spent a lot of energy going back and forth between that room and Rose's.

Adding a downstairs bedroom quickly became the best solution. When Larissa had worried where the money was to come from for the building materials, Ethan quietly but firmly told her he still had funds from the sale of the farm in Michigan. The room would be his wedding gift to her. He insisted he'd always intended to spend the money only on dire emergencies, and if this didn't rate as a dire emergency, then he for sure didn't know what would. They had both laughed, although tears weren't far behind her stunned thankfulness.

Thus, the addition of the bedroom became the ideal solution. Until tonight. She possessed no answer for his "a bit of a problem" revelation that their ideal solution had just jumped the tracks because the ground was frozen solid three feet deep. He shifted his feet restlessly, a sure sign he was mulling how to speak whatever weighed on his mind. She waited, a little impatient and a whole lot curious, until he raised his head from staring at the two remaining cherry turnovers.

"I have a temporary solution, if you're agreeable. We could use the woodshed."

Of all the solutions she had mulled, this was not on the list. "The woodshed?" she repeated weakly. "Next to the kitchen here?"

"It'll work. I think. The room's not a woodshed in the strictest sense. It's enclosed weather tight and has board flooring. It won't take much to finish the walls and smooth the floor. I could do it even with our new schedule, in plenty of time for New Year's Day. I know you hang your laundry in there to dry on stormy days, and we use the room to store extra wood for bad weather. Surely we can manage those difficulties. What do you think?"

As he talked, her stupefaction lessened with each solution possibility. Now he looked at her with a pleading in his eyes not unlike a young boy asking for his first pony. "I think," she said softly, "it's a wonderful idea."

It took him a second to realize she agreed with his plan. Grinning from ear to ear, he once more rounded the table and drew her up into his arms. "It won't be forever, Lizzie, I promise. Soon as the weather allows, I'll start on the addition. But for now...." He stopped speaking for the simple reason his mouth found something better to do. Standing on tiptoe, she drew his head down to hers. Her kiss held all the joy, wonder, and gladness she felt at this forging ahead step in their lives.

He eased her head onto his shoulder and pressed his cheek to her soft chestnut hair. His voice, shaky but distinct, floated above her. "Jumping jackrabbits, woman! I'll start on the room first thing in the morning."

***

True to his word, the next morning Ethan took the girls to school in the buckboard. After he dropped them off, he stopped by the hardware store and Paxton's steam sawmill. He returned to the farm with the back of the buckboard filled with a lumpy mound covered by a canvas tarp.

Larissa hurried out to meet him, but he shook his head when she asked what he'd bought. "I want this to be a true wedding gift to you, Lizzie, a genuine surprise. I ask that you don't see or know anything about it, except of course, the obvious fact I'm doing this, until the right time. I know it's a lot to expect, but can we just try it this way?"

She considered briefly, then her understandable disappointment melted into happy anticipation. "I'll try. But I'm not promising!" She touched the tarp and he made an instinctive move to stop her. "No touching, either?"

"No touching, either," he said sternly.

She stuck out her lower lip and tried to look pathetic, but couldn't carry it through as he swung to the snowy ground. "All right. I promise."

Seeing relief and pleasure dart across his features, she knew she couldn't spoil his plans. It would certainly take patience. But if she had learned anything from the war years with Zane's letters coming in exasperatingly irregular intervals, she had learned how to wait.

She retreated to the kitchen and tried to ignore the banging, thumping, and spirited, even if one-sided, remarks occasionally drifting to her as he passed back and forth through the outside woodshed door carrying his plunder into the adjoining room. She rolled her eyes.

At the supper table that evening, Charity began casting suspicious glances at her father. He noticed, but could hardly object with Rose doing the same to her mother. Finally, he decided enough was enough. "Charity, do I have a snowball on my head? You seem to have discovered something more fascinating than usual in my appearance. Would you like to share with us?"

"You, too, Rose." Larissa firmly included her daughter in the deliberations. "I thought I combed my hair this morning, but the way you keep inspecting me, I'm not so certain."

Silence greeted these feeble adult attempts at humor as the girls exchanged "I-told-you-so" looks. Rose squirmed a bit at being the one ordered to volunteer, but said gamely enough, "You look different, Ma. It's not your hair," she added reassuringly as she tilted her head and scrutinized her mother. "I can't tell exactly what it is, but the last three times you picked up your coffee cup to drink, it's been empty and you haven't refilled it even once."

"You, too, Pa," Charity chimed in. "You've been acting really goofy." Suddenly, she sat up straight in her chair, stroked her chin thoughtfully, and intoned, "What mischief have you two children been up to?" She favored each adult with an impartial glare as she folded her arms on her chest.

Her mimicry of Ethan was so telling, his jaw dropped, and Larissa slapped her hand up to cover her mouth. "Well, *Miss* Charity, I see you've listened attentively to my detailed instructions about behaving properly and improperly. Evidently, you absorbed half the lesson. The *wrong* half," he added gloomily. "Surely, I shouldn't be the only one so honored by your talents."

"Charity, do one of Ma." Only Rose's intervention saved him from the fate-worse-than-death promise Larissa was silently transmitting down the table.

"Go ahead," Larissa sighed. "I'm curious, now." Charity turned to Ethan, who was busy avoiding his future wife's eyes.

He stroked his beard, realized what he was doing, and guiltily tried to look as if he hadn't been doing it. "I want to see this, too," he confessed.

Taking his statement as parental permission, Charity hopped out of her chair. She patted her hair and smoothed an imaginary apron. Hand on hip, she became a woman stirring a pot on the stove. Spoon to lips, she tasted carefully, frowned and reached up. Moving her finger sideways, lips pursed, she selected an imaginary container and sprinkled some of the contents into the pot. She stirred, raised the spoon, tasted thoughtfully, and beamed as she snapped her fingers in a *That's perfect!* gesture. Curtseying, she sat down. Larissa stared at her in disbelief, but joined the hearty applause.

"With encouragement such as that, Lizzie, should we tell them about our mischief?" Receiving her consent, Ethan turned to the girls. "You know we've planned for a while now to marry." They abruptly sobered. Unnerved by two sets of unblinking blue eyes fastened upon him, his carefully planned words vanished like early morning mist over Mill Pond.

"We've felt like a family for a long time," Larissa added, "and we've been acting like one, just like tonight. We love you so much. With all our hearts and spirits, we want to become a true family, for always, in every way. We want it for us, and we want it for our children. We hope so much that our children want it, too. Charity, I told you once, I've carried you in my heart, even if I never carried you under it."

Ethan smiled. "Rose, I've learned from Charity how wonderful it is to have a daughter. It seems to me two daughters can only double my happiness and pride. I would be very proud and happy for you to become my daughter."

They'd earlier agreed to offer the facts simply and calmly, with the unstated but clear message it was not a matter of the girls choosing for or against their decision. Rather, it was an invitation for them to take the steps they alone could to accept and bind five into one.

Having spoken, Larissa and Ethan fell silent. For a moment seeming to encompass two eternities, neither girl said anything. They exchanged another glance unreadable to their parents, but obviously a clear message to each other. "Does it mean we'll be really and truly sisters?" Charity asked earnestly.

Larissa wondered if she was secretly weighing the fact that it also meant that she and Mac would be "really and truly" brother and sister. "Yes, it does." As if seeking any shade of doubt or untruth in her answer, Charity studied Larissa's face but said nothing more.

"No one can change that, ever?" Rose persisted.

"No one can change that, ever." Ethan's breath snagged. *Please trust me enough to take the chance.*

One more glance between the girls, and each one walked to her parent. Larissa held her daughter close and knew that joy came in many forms, but for a parent, it would take something truly incredible to match this moment.

Ethan hugged Charity and she whispered something to him before she stepped away as Rose moved back from Larissa. Neither adult knew for certain how it happened, but suddenly Rose dove into Ethan's arms and Charity stood in front of Larissa. Guilt, uncertainty, and shame flicked across her young features. Larissa's movement was instinctive, no matter how many times previously she had sternly schooled herself not to do it. She held out her arms. With one more search of the face above her, Charity, guilt, pleading, uncertainty and all, stepped into Larissa's embrace.

The eyes of the parents met over the heads of their daughters, and Ethan said remorsefully, "I don't really look as stern as all that. Do I?" As three heads nodded emphatically, he straightened his shoulders. "I knew practice would make perfect," he said proudly and stroked his beard.

CHAPTER FOURTEEN

Over the next days, Larissa felt remarkably like a conspiracy victim. The morning after they revealed their marriage intentions, Ethan took the girls aside. Confiding his plans about the woodshed, he asked their aid in keeping the secret. Totally entranced with conniving against an adult, they promised not to reveal anything. "Even if she threatens to dunk us in the horse trough," Rose added staunchly.

Ethan accepted this as the most solemn oath the girls could produce. It came from the days when Mac was pestered, annoyed, and frazzled by two giggling little girls following him around and whispering mysteriously. He took his revenge by threatening to dunk them in the horse trough if they didn't come forth with whatever information they possessed and he didn't. They always stood their ground, and he never actually carried out his threat, but at times he came perilously close.

With those days long past and Mac no longer available for them to harass, the spirit of the threat lingered. The family used it during times calling for an absolute guarantee. Thus, Ethan could be sure the girls wouldn't spill the beans.

The first day, they ignored the sawing and banging. Inevitably, their natural curiosity—Mac would have termed it downright snoopiness—emerged. They badgered Ethan about the details, causing him to feel large sympathy for Mac and affinity for his horse trough. They started doing little things, such as fetching the saw or tape measure he needed but had, naturally, left just out of reach.

By week's end, they had entered so fully into the project that, aided and abetted by Ethan, they teased Larissa with sly hints and broken-off sentences as they "suddenly remembered" her presence. Exasperated, as they fully intended, Larissa nevertheless rejoiced at this endeavor uniting them in a common cause, in spite of her position of dubious honor as the object of their entertainment. To worsen matters, Ethan sought Martha Gallaway's advice on feminine-frill details, and she joined the tormentors. Shawn and Garth volunteered to assist in the heavier tasks needing six hands.

Martha and Shawn came to the farm with increasing frequency as the design took actual form. Larissa's persecutors then increased by four, including ten-year-old Gretta, who was so taken with the romance of the situation that she too gravely promised not to tell. Larissa breathed a prayer of thanks because six-year-old Noah and Mara couldn't have cared less about the commotion their elders made, and so didn't join in the pestering.

Once, Larissa picked up a sketchpad Rose had left on the table. Normally, she tried not to pry into her daughter's artwork, but Rose had left the cover turned back. The top drawing showed a room Larissa didn't recognize. Possibly the woodshed, it lacked adequate form to supply her with any clues, but offered sufficient suggestion to prod her carefully banked curiosity into flame.

Periodically, Ethan graciously provided her with a cheerful report such as "progressing right on schedule" to assure her his accomplishments kept pace with his purpose. Maddeningly, he provided no hints in these wordy bulletins about *what* progressed, but at least they freed Larissa of any qualms about the shortness of their imposed time frame. This particularly benefited Ethan. She had enough jitters over all the other tasks to be accomplished, and he served as the hapless recipient of the bulk of her panic-stricken woe.

Martha, delighted beyond words at the happy turn of events, assisted in the ever-lengthening list of details to be accomplished before the wedding. Having so recently been there herself, she proved an invaluable source of information and practical advice for her increasingly flustered friend.

Simultaneously planning Christmas, Rose's birthday, and the wedding, the bride-to-be put pepper in the cornbread and mixed pieces of her own gown with the dresses she was sewing for Charity and Rose. Finally, Martha threw up her hands in defeat, removed the girls' gowns from a feebly protesting Larissa, and bore them home to finish herself.

All went well, if chaotically, for ten days, until the morning Ethan burst into the kitchen as Larissa actually remembered to grind the beans and add water before setting the coffeepot on the stove to boil. Her mental cheers at her success snapped off as she saw his face. "Something's wrong with Charity," he blurted. "She doesn't want to get out of bed and she's covered with spots."

Larissa thrust the coffeepot at Rose, who had been refilling the toast rack. "Can you tend everything here?"

"Sure, Ma." In her haste, Larissa dismissed the worried catch in her daughter's voice as natural concern for Charity.

"It's pretty rough out," Ethan warned as they left the porch. "It snowed last night and I haven't shoveled the paths."

"Just what have you been doing in your spare time?"

At her attempt to make light of the situation, Ethan's mouth smiled but his eyes remained sober. Head down, he tramped through the drifted snow, following the boot tracks he'd made going to the house. It simplified his progress, but caused Larissa behind him to struggle as she attempted to fit her steps to his longer stride. Her skirts also hampered her by threatening to trip her up at every sliding hop.

He turned to make certain she was all right, and loosed a muffled exclamation. Immediately shortening his steps, he reached his hand back for her to grip. With the added assistance, she plowed through to the cabin steps.

Catching their breath, stamping their feet to dislodge the clinging snow clumps, she saw his worry had intensified. Putting her hand on his arm, she spoke urgently. "Ethan, listen to me. You can't go tearing inside looking scared to death. She's going to take her cue from you how sick she actually is. If you give her the impression you're on your way to a funeral, she'll panic. And rightfully so."

She wasn't certain her words made any impression, but after a moment his shoulders straightened. "My ears know you're right, but my head is lagging a little behind." He gave one last stomp of his boots and stepped back to follow her through the doorway.

With none of her usual bounce, Charity lay watching the door. She raised up, her eyes going to her father's face, then to Larissa's. Apparently finding whatever she sought, she let out her breath and sank onto the pillow.

While Ethan murmured to his daughter, Larissa pulled off her gloves and briskly rubbed her hands together. Once the chill subsided, she bent over Charity and saw the mottled red rash on her face and neck. "You've certainly done a fine job of cultivating this," she said admiringly. Charity gave her a wilted grin. She asked a few questions and weighed the replies. "Will you let me take a look under your gown to see what's growing there? You just might have a cash crop by now."

Ethan retreated to the fireplace, stoked the flames, and fiddled with the logs until Larissa called him over. He was doing an admirable job of hiding his anxiety, and her heart contracted in sympathy as he waited for her verdict. "I think it's the measles. You have the cough, the spots inside your cheeks, and all the other symptoms." He couldn't hide his relief, and his daughter looked at him curiously.

"The measles?" Larissa suspected Ethan's incredulity wasn't all faked. "For a bit, you had me convinced you were trying to give me some kind of crawly disease. But I've already had the measles, so I fooled you there. Guess you'll just have to think of something else to torment me."

"Oh, Pa." Charity wrinkled her nose at him. She had, evidently, not heard the faint ragged edge to his voice.

Larissa recognized it, however, and sprang briskly into action to distract both father and daughter. "I think we should send your Pa for Doc Rawley. I suspect he'll have the same diagnosis." She cupped her hand to her mouth and whispered loudly to Charity, "But this way, we'll have him out from underfoot for a while, and we can get on with helping you feel better. All right?"

Charity dipped her chin in assent and Ethan raised his hands in defeat. "I can see when I'm being told, very subtly, of course, to get the blazes out of here."

"Before you 'get', if we take Charity to the house, she'll be more comfortable and closer for me to help her."

"Maybe she shouldn't be out in the cold when she—"

Larissa smoothly overrode his protest. "She's not going to be out in the cold." He stared, as puzzled as Charity. "We're going to wrap you so snugly in a blanket, you won't feel any chilly air. Then, so your toes won't even twinge, your Pa will carry you over to the house. If you'll get the blanket off your bed, Ethan, we'll start there." She began explaining her intentions to Charity, completely unaware of the turmoil into which she had just thrust him.

Dutifully, he picked up the wool blanket, with an anguished sense of doing this before. Not just with Larissa, the day he brought her, drenched to the skin, here to the cabin and wrapped her in the blanket from his bed. Memory struck with venomous fangs. He had done this for Nettie, too. When she shook with chills from the rattlesnake bite, he had tried desperately to warm her....

"Ethan?" Larissa's voice held a perplexed note. She knew nothing about the details of those hours here in the cabin, other than that they had happened and he had taken care of her. Of Nettie, she knew still less. He had never spoken to Larissa, or anyone, beyond the necessary facts about the day he found Nettie in the sheep pasture. He straightened his shoulders, set his jaw, and handed her the blanket.

Absorbed with Charity's needs, she took it with an absent "Thank you," and explained they were going to bundle her like Baby Bunting from the nursery rhyme. However, since she had no brother handy "to purchase a skin to wrap you in," she would have to settle for a plain old wool blanket.

Larissa's flowing banter distracted Charity from the reality and indignation of being handled like a squirming infant who lacked the sense to care for herself. By the time she lay snugly wrapped, the expression on Ethan's face as he beheld his child bundled like a newborn sent Charity into painful laughter.

Following Larissa's instructions, he picked his daughter up carefully to avoid rubbing the rash. Once he settled her in his arms, Larissa draped a quilt over them. She secured it under Ethan's chin with a large darning needle from Charity's sewing box, thus completely hiding the girl. Only Ethan's face peered out from the middle, much like an inquisitive squirrel poking out of its hole.

His arms full of daughter, Ethan couldn't assist Larissa on the way back to the house. Fortunately, their prior crossings had pushed the snow into something resembling a path, and she puffed her way behind him with less difficulty than on her earlier trip.

Rose, wide-eyed, held the door as they stumbled in. She had the heater stove glowing red. The kitchen range, too, radiated welcome heat. Ethan deposited his daughter on a chair near the heater and flexed his taut shoulders. Rose poured steaming cups of coffee, which the adults accepted gratefully. They loosened Charity's protective blanketing but, at Larissa's suggestion, did not remove it completely, to avoid giving her a possible chill from the sharp temperature change.

Rose started to dish up the waiting breakfast, but Larissa stopped her. "I'll eat later. Right now I'm going to light the fireplace and fix the bed in Mac's room for you, Charity, so we can get you settled in. While I'm doing that, please heat the flatirons, Rose, so we can warm the sheets."

"I don't need any breakfast, either," Ethan put in. "I'll just head for town to get Doc." It was a nice plan, but he reckoned without Larissa's opinion.

"Ethan Michaels, you sit and eat breakfast before you go rushing out on such a cold trip. You won't be a help to any of us if you come down with an attack of the wheezing sneezes. So sit and eat."

Stunned by this outburst, he studied her warily and decided he'd better do as she told him. "Yes ma'am," he said meekly, and sat.

After filling his plate and refilling his cup, Rose edged over to Charity. Larissa knew she should keep the girls apart, but reasoned how, with their being together so much, Rose was probably already exposed. Heads together, they conversed too low for the adults to catch the words, but a reassuring spurt of laughter drifted through the room.

Charity looked distinctly wan by the time Larissa came back for the flatirons. Wrapping the bases in pieces of old quilting, she directed Ethan to carry his daughter as she led the way. She tucked the hot irons at the foot of the blankets as he more slowly bore his burden up the stairs. With a subdued Rose trailing behind, he deposited Charity gently on the bed. Larissa bent over her, talking soothingly.

"I'll go for Doc." At Larissa's preoccupied nod, he backed into the hallway, keeping his eyes averted from the closed door of Larissa's room at the far end. The sudden gust of loneliness that pushed through him came as a shock. Setting his jaw, he descended the stairs.

Larissa hurried down behind him. "Ethan, did you eat?"

"I didn't dare not to, after I received orders from a very determined woman." He touched her cheek. "You eat, too. Or else you'll have to answer to me. Promise?"

At the stern echo of her earlier bossiness, she bowed her head meekly. "I promise."

113

"Good. I don't want to marry someone who is fainting weak because she's so busy caring for other people she forgets to take care of herself. I want you strong when I send you out to plow those fields, woman."

He put his finger under her chin to tip it up. As her lips curved, he kissed her, briefly but heartily. "I'll be back as soon as I can."

She watched out the window as he tramped to the barn. It was beginning to snow again.

CHAPTER FIFTEEN

Larissa's measles diagnosis proved correct, but Charity convalesced rapidly. Her fever eased after the first couple of days, and although her rash itched unmercifully, her buoyant spirits also seemed on the road to recovery. Out of his daughter's hearing, Ethan confessed to Larissa he was so glad she no longer resembled the droopy, ashen young girl he'd carried to the house, that even her chatter sounded good. He made no promises how long this mood would last, however.

She recovered so quickly that, although still quarantined, Doc allowed her to come down to the sitting room. The first afternoon, bundled in quilts with pillows at her back, she lay on the high-backed bench facing the fire, supervising while Larissa and Rose stitched the wedding dress.

They discussed odds and ends, including the school's closing. Doc had issued the drastic decree after diagnosing Charity. He'd already made calls to two other homes for the same purpose, one to a farm just outside of town, the other to the parsonage, where the twins were fevered and fretful. Martha, still in the early stages of pregnancy and not feeling well, was having a rough time. With Charity on the mend, Larissa wanted to go at once to help Martha, but Doc squelched the plan. Larissa had had the measles as a child, but Charity remained contagious so long as she remained feverish. Doc refused to chance it being carried to anyone else.

From her bench, Charity basked in the happy supposition of the students' gratitude to her for shutting down the school. For several weeks now, her plans to teach had perched high on her list of favorite topics. Larissa felt sorely tempted to ask how she would react if someone closed *her* school. With admirable tact, she merely observed how, although the children might be thrilled, the parents probably weren't overjoyed. The current crop of snowstorms would keep their offspring confined to the house and underfoot all day. Charity dutifully looked repentant at this distressing consequence. Unfortunately, knowledge the adults had been foiled again severely thwarted her attempt to maintain a remorseful attitude.

As Charity chirped on about one topic after another, Larissa nodded in the proper places. *She's more vocal than at any time since her tantrum. Because she accepts the marriage will take place and fighting against it is useless? Or because she realizes the affection between us is too precious to lose?* Larissa's heart hoped it could be for both reasons. Although she probably would never know the answer for certain, she was deeply grateful.

Charity switched the subject to Garth Van Ellis and was enumerating his many wonderful qualities when Rose dropped her sewing to her lap and leaned her head back against the chair. "Ma, I feel awful," she said in a small voice that still carried over Charity's description of Garth's good looks.

Larissa thrust aside her sewing and bent over her daughter. "Rose, you're burning up! How long have you been feeling this way?"

"A couple of days."

The admission jolted Larissa. What with concentrating on Charity, she'd not seen any trouble brewing with Rose. She'd simply assumed her daughter would speak up if she started feeling ill. "Why didn't you say something?"

"It just felt like I was catching a cold. It didn't seem very bad. Honest." Rose made an unsuccessful effort to look healthy.

"It must be the measles. We'll get you to bed right now." Larissa hoped her voice betrayed none of her anxiety, for under her supporting hands Rose already felt warmer than Charity had been at the height of her rashy episode. One arm about her daughter's waist, she helped her up the stairs and into bed. On her way down to the kitchen with a pitcher for fresh water, she saw Ethan standing by the bottom step.

"Charity came to the woodshed and told me." He gestured to his daughter's top half, the only part visible as, all ears, she bent around the edge of the bench. "How's Rose?"

"She feels really warm to the touch. I'm going to bathe her and see if I can get her temperature down."

"Should I go for Doc?" In the face of her concern, he deliberately kept his voice calm. Tempting as it was, he made no reference to her scolding him about his worry over Charity. He was fully aware she wouldn't favor her daughter over his. If she looked troubled, she had a reason.

She bit her lip as her heart and common sense clashed. "No, don't go yet. I'll try a couple of things first. If she's no better in an hour, you should go, before it gets dark and the temperature drops."

Instinctively, he glanced toward the front window. "We still have a few hours of daylight. I'll go whenever you say. In the meantime, whatever you need done, just tell me. I'm a handy fellow to have around for running up and down stairs."

"You're a handy fellow to have around for a lot of reasons, Ethan Michaels."

He raised his eyebrows. "Thank you for the vote of confidence. I fully intend that always, in all ways, it will be so." He took the pitcher from her and disappeared into the kitchen, leaving her standing with her hand raised to her mouth to conceal the smile she could not quell.

Unknown to either of them, those were their last moments of levity for many hours to come.

At the end of the allotted time, Rose showed no improvement. In spite of the cooling rubdown Larissa ministered so carefully, she seemed even hotter than before. Larissa again found Ethan waiting at the foot of the stairs. "I think you should go for Doc. Her temperature still seems to be going up, and she's coughing quite a bit. She hasn't broken out very much. Just a little rash in her hair and behind her ears." She hesitated.

"Lizzie?"

"She says she hurts all over, inside."

"I'll tell him."

He turned away, but her hand on his arm stopped him. "Just one thing more before you go." She moved into his arms.

Although she had scooted back around the far side of the bench, a conspicuous rustling reminded them Charity remained well within seeing and hearing distance. Nevertheless, he drew Larissa close and pressed his cheek against her hair. He kissed her and set her gently back from him. "If you need anything while I'm gone, Charity can fetch it for you." His daughter's face popped back into sight around the bench. "It won't hurt her a bit, and it'll save you a few trips up and down the stairs." Over Larissa's head, he gave Charity a look suggesting she obey without argument. Her top half once more disappeared. "I'll be back with Doc just as soon as I can," he murmured. "Try not to worry. You know Doc. He'll get her fixed up just fine."

***

After an interminable time, Larissa heard Doc, just behind Ethan, swish up the drive in his cutter, the runners slipping easily over the drifted snow. Awkwardly, he climbed out of the deep enclosure formed by the large top that protected him from the worst of the elements. With a prolonged snort, Bella, his cantankerous mare, voiced her view of the proceedings. He grabbed his bag and sketched a salute to Larissa standing on the porch. His other arm similarly waved acknowledgment to Ethan's call that he would take care of Bella.

Once in the house, Doc paused only long enough to thaw out his hands before he went up to Rose. As always when he entered a sickroom, the gruffness and bluster vanished. He took a long time with his examination, asking questions he had not put to Charity's illness. Finally, tipping his head for Larissa to follow him into the hallway, he pulled the door shut behind her and moved toward the head of the stairs.

Ethan, sitting on the bottom step, stood when he saw them. At Doc's grave expression, he took the stairs two at a time, and drew Larissa into the curve of his arm.

Doc tugged at his beard. "I won't beat around the bush. She's a very sick young lady. I suspect she's been feeling bad for more than 'a couple of days.' You know for yourselves, she has a high fever and it will probably go higher. We're going to have to work to get it down. I've a few tricks up my sleeve for that." His reluctance to continue showed clearly.

"To put it simply, her measles have 'gone inside.' That's why she's hurting so much, and why the visible rash is so slight. I'm giving you straight fact about this, so you'll know what we're up against." Larissa's deep blue eyes seemed to bore into his very soul.

"She is going to get better, isn't she?" At Ethan's question that Larissa could not ask, she stiffened and waited for Doc's answer.

He looked at Ethan, because he could no longer face her with the truth. "I'm going to do everything in my power to see that she does. I'm going to need help, though."

"Of course." Larissa's voice quivered. "Just tell me what to do."

"Good." Doc touched her arm. "She's an Edwards. She has spunk, just like her mother. Don't forget that." Behind the fear in her eyes, he glimpsed a determined spark that made him glad she was on his side. He wasn't dumb enough to want to oppose her under any circumstances.

***

Doc was right. That night, Rose's fever climbed. At times she slipped into delirium, crying out words they couldn't understand. After his initial examination and diagnosis, Doc, as a matter of course, recruited Larissa's help. When he attempted to kick Ethan out of the room, also as a matter of course, Ethan balked and informed Doc he was staying put to do whatever he could to help.

"But—"

"But nothing. I won't get in the way. I can tend the bedroom fireplace and spell you and Larissa the times you need to be out of the room. I do know a little about fevers." The simply spoken, utterly truthful statement dried up Doc's outraged sputter. His glare, however, spoke volumes about the inadvisability of opposing his orders.

Ethan crossed his arms on his chest and returned the glare, with interest. When Doc, for once in his medical career and probably for the first time in his whole life, couldn't get his tongue to work, Ethan calmly added the clincher. "Besides, she's my daughter, too."

Doc knew defeat when he saw it. He just wasn't used to it coming from his side of the argument. After one glance at Larissa's equally solid obstinacy, he threw out his hands. "There you go, again. The two of you taking on the world. I don't know why I even bothered with such an idiotic attempt to use common sense. Far be it from me to beat my head against a stone wall. Or in this case, two of them." Crossly, he started to push between them to go back to Rose. Stopping in his tracks, he shook his head in disgust and veered around them.

The endless night following finally blurred into dawn. With gray light creeping into the room, Doc urged Larissa to rest. She stared at him as if he'd told her to go up on the barn roof and flap like a chicken, but he said firmly, "You've been up all night. She's made it this far, and that's a positive sign. I think she'll crisis by tonight. She and I will need you physically strong when it happens." She turned as white as the sheet tucked under Rose's chin. Other times through the years, he had watched her face unbearable facts that must be borne. Now, as then, the necessity to endure, emerging from deep within, made her seem much taller than her actual height.

Ethan had just come from the morning chores, bringing the fresh scent of the snowy outdoors with him into the darkened room. Walking in on Larissa's worried reluctance to leave her daughter, and Doc's rock-hard determination that she should, he said a swift prayer that she would forgive him for his brazen interference. Before she could dig her heels in, he grabbed her arm and propelled her out the door. With a quiet but decisive thump, Doc closed it behind them.

She protested indignantly, but her willpower deserted her in one sudden puff of breath, and she wearily yielded to the warm comfort of his shoulder under her cheek.

As his arms encircled her, shock jolted him. In spite of her outward show of strength, she seemed so fragile, as if, since yesterday afternoon, she had shrunk inside. New fear zipped through him. "Lizzie, you're cold as ice!"

Under his hands, she stiffened, pushing away the weakness. "Except for being mad as a wet hen at Doc, I'm all right. But I'm not so sure I feel like obeying his demand to get some sleep. Of all the high handed—"

As if on cue, the bedroom door opened a crack and a hairy arm, sleeve rolled to the elbow, shot out. The hand at the end of the arm held a glass of some indeterminate liquid. "Drink this." Doc's disembodied voice intoned the command. "It'll help you sleep for three or four hours."

Her mutinous expression warned Ethan she had no intention of obeying, and his suddenly empty brain could think of no way to talk her into it. Holding her nose and forcing her didn't strike him as much of an option. For no reason he could guess, except as an answer to prayer, she abruptly plucked the glass from Doc's hand. Taking a sip, she wrinkled her nose.

"All of it."

She stuck out her tongue in the general direction of the bedroom door before following orders. Her deep shudder as she drank made Ethan highly happy not to be the recipient of Doc's generosity. She plopped the empty glass back into the still outstretched hand. Hand and glass disappeared through the narrow opening. The door shut with an uncompromising click.

"Bad as that stuff tasted, it better work," she muttered.

"It will." The door muffled the voice, but not the inflexibility of the command.

Ethan hastily pulled her across the hallway. "Along with an extra pair of eyes, the old codger really does have ears in the back of his head, just like he's always boasted. You'd better do what he says."

"Between the two of you, I don't have much choice." Her grousing now out of her system, she put her hand on his arm. "You'll wake me up in three hours, if I'm asleep?"

"I'll wake you."

She took it for the promise it was. At her doorway, she paused with her hand on the knob, gave him a small smile, and slipped into her room.

He gazed at the closed panel for a long moment before turning back to Rose's room.

***

Three hours trudged by. Doc pulled out his watch to check Rose's pulse and glanced over at Ethan, pouring fresh water into the basin. "Your time's up."

A distant part of Ethan's brain noted how Doc said *his* time was up, not Larissa's. He carefully set the pitcher on the dresser. "What'll I tell her when she asks?"

Doc returned the watch to his pocket. "Same as I would. The truth."

Ethan nodded, once. His numb hand fumbled with the knob before he stepped into the hallway. He approached Larissa's door and his mind, too, fumbled with what he shortly must do.

He paused on the threshold as his eyes adjusted to the dim light of the winter midmorning. On the bed across the room, he made out a curved bump, covered with a knitted spread, lying on top of the patchwork quilt. The uncomfortable sensation of intruding upon her in a private moment did not lessen when he stumbled over one of her shoes on the floor beside the bed. The resulting clatter sounded as loud as shelled corn rattling into a metal pail. Clenching his teeth at the unholy

120

racket, he bent over her. His hand, brushing against the top of the bedside table, met air. Zane's picture—the one he remembered only too clearly from his other time in this room—was gone.

The implications drifted away as he discovered that, beneath the coverlet, she lay curled into a tight ball. He placed a tentative hand on what he hoped to God was her shoulder. "Lizzie?"

At his voice and touch, her eyes opened. She had been so deeply asleep that she simply looked at him in bewilderment. He repeated her name and comprehension wiped away the relaxed softness. She stiffened. "Oh. Three hours?" Already throwing off the knitted covering, she struggled to sit, but in her half-asleep confusion, she became tangled in her rumpled skirt and apron. "Rose?"

As her feet touched the floor, he took her sleep-warm hands. "There's no change." Before his courage fled, he added quietly, "Doc thinks now that she'll crisis this afternoon."

***

Doc's four decades of experience once more proved him right. A short time after Larissa's return to the sickroom, Rose's tossing and delirious murmuring ceased, so that her breath fluttered audibly in the otherwise silent room. Over the next hours, Doc checked and rechecked her pulse. Each time he finished, he tucked the small hand carefully under the covers, turned to face Larissa's silent torment, and slowly shook his head.

Faintly from downstairs, the Seth Thomas clock chimed four times. As if it were a cue or a portent, Rose sighed and became very still.

An overwhelming rush of anguish suddenly swamped the terror that had lurked in Larissa's heart for so many hours. *So strangely the same, yet not, as when Ethan told me that Zane was dead.* Eyes closed against the onslaught … Ethan's arm around her … Doc saying something … waves roaring in her head blocking his words....

"Larissa." Ethan spoke urgently against her ear. "Did you hear Doc? Her fever's turned. She's going to live!"

CHAPTER SIXTEEN

She's going to live! The joyous pronouncement bounced in Larissa's heart. *She's going to live.* The words echoed eerily from the past and, for an instant, she returned to Rose's Christmas Day birth. Over time, the memory of the seemingly endless hours of struggle to bring her child into the world and the gravity of Doc's expression in contrast to his usual just-bit-into-a sour-apple glumness had blurred.

But memory of the silence following her daughter's delayed arrival, Doc's adamant refusal to give up, and, finally, the first piercing wail, remained undimmed in Larissa's heart. Those moments, and Doc's exultant words. "She's going to live!"

Now, nearly thirteen years later, by God's mercy and Doc's skill, Rose had survived again. *Does he remember? Or is Rose simply one of many he's pulled from death's grasp?*

Doc stepped aside so she could take Rose's hand, could brush gentle fingers against her cheek, assure herself her daughter was, indeed, alive. He murmured, "She's fallen into natural sleep. I wager she'll stay so for several hours. It's the best thing in the world for her right now." Seeing the tears sliding down her cheeks, he said gruffly, "It's always a wonder to me how you women do it. Stay strong as iron during the ruckus, and break down after it's all over."

She gave him a radiant, if soggy, smile. "I guess God gives us lots of opportunities to practice."

"Too many, seems like, sometimes. I don't know about this young lady. It's thirteen years since she scared the spit out of us. I hope she doesn't plan to do it again in another thirteen years. I'm too old for it now, let alone for any future repetition."

So he remembered.

He smoothed the already smooth coverlet. "She was a scrapper then, and she is now. Anyone sells her short, they're making a big mistake." To cover this unwonted lapse into emotion, he said briskly, "We'll have to keep an eye on her to make sure this doesn't go into her chest. I'll write out instructions on what to watch for. The main thing now is lots of rest and liquids. She'll be up and sketching the barn owls again before you know it."

Ethan stood at the foot of the bed to allow Larissa the wondrous moment of absorbing the full rapture of the miracle. Doc glanced his way. "I'd better be getting back to town. I have sick folks who require my attention. Unlike here, where no one needs me."

"You're always needed here, Doc," Larissa said softly. "I don't know what we'd ever do without you." He cleared his throat and became very busy returning his instruments to the worn, scarred black bag.

In the hallway, they almost tripped over Charity, huddled beside the door. "Charity, what are you doing up here? Are you feeling sick?" Ethan did his best not to sound like the over-anxious parent Larissa had chided him for all those days ago, but everything considered, he didn't entirely succeed.

"I'm all well. How's Rose? May I see her?"

"She's going to be fine. But it would be better if you don't have any contact for a day or so. Besides, she's sleeping and mustn't be disturbed."

At Doc's pronouncement, Charity's face fell. "I promise I won't disturb her. Please?"

Doc possessed a crusty heart, but not one that impervious. "All right. Just for a second. And no nonsense about it."

Charity edged into the room and tiptoed to the bedside. She reached a tentative finger, very gently touched the end of Rose's braid, and bowed her head. True to her promise, she immediately turned. In her white nightgown, she seemed to float back across the room. "I just wanted to tell God thank You. I thought He'd hear it better and know exactly who I meant if I stood next to Rose when I said it."

Larissa's eyes misted. Ethan pulled his daughter close in a warm hug, and Doc fumbled with the clasp of his medical bag. "Pesky thing doesn't want to close properly. One fine day I'm going to end up spilling everything onto the floor." He finally got the uncooperative latch fastened to his satisfaction. He raised his head, and the moist glint in his hazel eyes belied his grumbling explanation.

At the foot of the stairs, he pounced on Charity. "So you think you're all well. What medical expertise leads you to such a conclusion?"

She grinned proudly. "My throat isn't sore anymore, I'm not coughing, and I'm almost all unrashy." She stuck out her tongue for Doc to peer at her throat, and provided an almost unrashy foot for his inspection.

"It appears your medical expertise is correct. But I still want you to take it easy for a few days. I don't think now it'll go into your lungs, but we'll have to watch it. I suggest you hike over to that bench and cover up. Now."

She hastened to obey, and the adults turned toward the kitchen. Ethan pulled on his coat and went out to hitch Bella to Doc's cutter. Larissa suggested he have a cup of hot coffee before starting back to town, but he refused.

"I'll just get on back. I want to stop by the parsonage and check on Noah and Mara. And Martha."

"Just a minute, now," she broke in sternly. "I think it would be best if you went back to your office and got some sleep. We'll want you to be physically strong for the next crisis."

Doc's jaw dropped at her bossy tone, then his lips twitched. He emitted the rusty gate-hinge creaking that conveyed his version of a full-blown laugh. "Yes, ma'am," he said meekly. "Just don't make me drink that vile medicine!"

Larissa's look strongly suggested the thought had occurred to her. All teasing aside, she touched his sleeve. "Thank you. More than words can ever say."

He met her eyes for an instant before fumbling for the doorknob. "I must be going. Where's Ethan and that fool mare?"

Ethan and the fool mare chose that moment to emerge from the buggy shed, and Doc plodded down the path to meet them. Before he disappeared into the cavern of the cutter's hood, Ethan grasped his hand, then waved as doctor and mare were lost to view around the curve of the drive. Turning, he bounded up the path to Larissa waiting on the porch. She clasped his hands and tugged him into the blessedly warm kitchen, where he promptly shed his heavy coat.

In gratitude beyond words, they clung together. Dizzy with happiness, Larissa nestled her head against his shoulder. He tightened his arms about her waist and lifted her clear of the floor. Executing an unrhythmic but energetic dance step, he swung her around the limited confines of the kitchen in unabashed exuberance.

***

Rose did not recover as rapidly as Charity. Becoming more unrashy daily, Charity refused to be exiled to the high-backed bench with so many exciting things happening around her. Appointing herself official messenger, she saved Larissa precious time and hundreds of steps by relaying everything from meal trays to verbal reports between Rose's room and the rest of the house.

With Christmas and Rose's birthday rapidly approaching, to say nothing of the wedding, Larissa thanked heaven for the assistance. Their carefully prepared schedule had been torn to shreds, leaving them standing in the midst of the fluttering pieces. Strangely enough, she ceased to worry about each tiny detail. What could be accomplished, would be. The rest could, quite frankly, go to the devil, because her daughter lived, gaining in health every day. The day before Christmas, Doc even decreed her improved enough to lie on the bench before the fireplace, well bundled against any stray draft.

Because most of their activities took place in the kitchen, Larissa cheated a bit and had Ethan set the bench beside the cook stove. Cocooned in quilts, Rose once again filled her place in the family circle as Larissa and Charity planned the dinner, baked, and decorated cookies. In Ethan's case, he shelled walnuts, kept the wood box full, and taste-tested the results of their efforts.

For Larissa, Christmas Day held an odd mixture of sensations. Joy for Rose's improving health; the small, steady ache that had resided in her heart since Mac's departure, sharpening today because he could not be with them; and the bliss that persisted in welling up within her at the knowledge she and Ethan would marry in just one more week.

Laughter, too, curled in and around the other emotions. They saved the gifts from Mac for last. Shawls for the girls, a green plaid for Rose and a blue plaid for Charity, with sweeping fringe, had them both exclaiming in delight. Ethan unwrapped his new pipe and inhaled deeply the rich aroma of the tobacco accompanying it.

Finally, Larissa's turn came. The others watched closely and jokingly provided endless possibilities about the contents of her package as she slowly unwrapped it. It proved to be a cherry-red shawl of the softest yarn Larissa had ever touched. Heart full to bursting for the son she could not embrace, she pressed his gift to her cheek for a long moment before she settled it around her shoulders. Admiring murmurs from the girls and a wordless clearing of Ethan's throat signified their approval.

In the afternoon, they celebrated Rose's birthday, providing her with enough sketchpads and colored pencils to stock a small store. They also flooded her with a wealth of wise suggestions concerning cutting and serving her cake, so that the day ended with thankfulness, love, and laughter.

***

The next morning Rose settled onto the bench near the cook stove, not yet allowed to help, but her presence a warm contentment in the room. Snuggled into the green plaid shawl from Mac, head bent over one of her new sketchpads, she didn't contribute much to the fragments of conversation passing between her mother and Charity.

Charity stood at the worktable, salvaging the meat from yesterday's turkey bones for soup. Larissa at the stove heated the milk, butter, and yeast made from hops, for the prized rolls she baked each Christmas. She had made a batch for the family's dinner yesterday, but with Doc's lifting of the no visiting edict, she wanted to go see Martha and thought she'd take a basket of rolls to the children.

After admitting he couldn't be sure now he would finish in time, Ethan had returned to his secretive carpentry activities in the woodshed. By virtue of her blissful state, even this confession didn't stir any anxiety in Larissa. Whatever the outcome, she knew it would be the best he could achieve.

He'd been thumping around in there since shortly after breakfast, whistling various Christmas tunes as he worked, obviously at peace with the world. Larissa whirled at a sudden horrendous crash. Muffled somewhat by the intervening wall, a few salty comments directed at the cause of the calamity drifted out, followed immediately by Ethan's call. "I'm all right! Everything still moves. No blood."

Larissa heaved a sigh of relief. At the start of the project, she had requested he let her know he remained alive and uninjured in these frightful-sounding mishaps. Since he didn't allow her in the room, she informed him haughtily, if he killed himself, she would much appreciate it if he would tell her right away. "It's a good thing!" she called back now at his reassuring report.

Once more facing the stove and her neglected mixture, she stirred it briskly. "I don't know what we're going to do with him," she said laughingly, with a half glance at Rose. "He...." The words died in her throat as a hard fist punched her in the lungs. "Rose?"

Rose, still swathed in the green plaid shawl, head bent over her drawing, gave no indication of hearing her mother.

"Rose!"

Unfazed by the sharp tone, she raised her head and said teasingly, "Are you going to yell at Mr. Michaels for dropping the hammer on his toe again? He's not going to have any feet left if he...." Her voice trailed off at the dismay on her mother's face. "What's wrong?"

The world around Larissa—the overheated mixture boiling in the pan, Charity, knife in hand, standing motionless, staring at them—suddenly had no shape or meaning. She felt as if she were engulfed in a huge void. She couldn't take her eyes off her daughter's face as puzzlement slipped over the earlier animation. "Ma?"

With no awareness of her feet moving, somehow she was standing in front of her daughter, was kneeling to her level. With a frantic "Please, God, when I open my mouth, let the right words fall out" plea which every parent, at some point in their child's life, sends upward, she took Rose's hand. "Rose, did you hear me call you?"

"Sure." Her matter-of-fact tone indicated she had no idea why her mother asked such an odd question. "But it was only the one time, and I answered. Are you mad at me?"

Larissa's stomach knotted and her mouth suddenly felt too dry to form the words. "Of course not. When Mr. Michaels dropped something, it really startled me."

"It did? It didn't make much noise."

Larissa asked her daughter, then, the hardest question she had ever had to put into words. "Can you hear me all right now?"

Rose's expression indicated she thought her mother had drunk too much of Dr. Watson's cure-all elixir. "You are talking kind of whispery low, but I can hear you."

The knot in Larissa's stomach tightened with such force she almost cried out in pain. She cupped her hand around Rose's cheek and, from somewhere, dragged up a smile. She stood at the same moment the woodshed door opened and Ethan stuck his head through. "Everything all right in here? Smells like something's burning."

With an exclamation of dismay, Larissa grabbed the pan of thoroughly charred milk and stood staring at it.

"Lizzie?"

The perplexed concern in Ethan's voice did nothing to help her struggle to hang on to her composure. The knot twisted tighter. She whirled on him and the voice in her ears, echoing hollowly, seemed to come from someplace other than her throat. "Ethan Michaels, you're going to give me a heart attack! I keep imagining the hammer falling on your head instead of your foot, and I'm getting tired of it! We'd better go in the other room and discuss this once and for all."

She made certain to face away from Rose as she flung this criticism at him. *Please, God, let him not question.* Her sole bit of fortune lay in her carping at him all those days ago, when she'd felt so pressured to finish everything on time. She prayed he would discount this bout of crankiness as another round of wedding jitters. His swift glance took in Rose's confusion and Charity's stunned silence. She couldn't begin to imagine what he must be reading in her face.

"Well," he drawled, "I suppose we could. Would you like to set your culinary creation down first?" He tipped his chin toward the pan of burned milk in her hand. She stared at it blankly, then plopped it onto the worktable. Brown milk splashed, but she took no notice as, head held high, she pompously gestured toward the sitting room. Passing Charity, Ethan muttered, "You stay here. And no eavesdropping."

Throwing a half glance back, ensuring he followed her, Larissa retreated to the corner farthest from the kitchen. She didn't immediately face him, and he put his hand on her shoulder. "Lizzie, what is this? Are you that worried about my getting hurt?"

Gathering the shreds of her strength and courage, she turned. "Larissa!" Unknown to him, his tone held much the same horror as hers when she spoke Rose's name so sharply at the stove. "*What is it?* Talk to me."

"It's Rose. I … I think … she's losing her hearing."

He stared at her as if he'd suddenly gone deaf, himself. "Dear God." The shock in his voice mirrored that in her heart. "Tell me. What happened?"

In brief, broken words, she described calling to Rose. "She thought I was whispering. I spoke louder than I normally do." His face began to register stunned comprehension. "That crash you made in the woodshed. She thought you dropped your hammer again. It was only that loud to her."

"God in Heaven." He pulled her to him. She came stiffly, then buried her face against his chest as shudders racked her. His breath fell harshly against her hair. "I'll go get Doc. He'll know what to do. You must keep your courage, Larissa. She'll need you to be strong, stronger than you've ever been in your life before. Do you understand what I'm saying?"

"My own words coming back to haunt me," she said dully.

"She's an intelligent young woman. She knows you're upset and that it's about her. You'll have to tell her something."

"No. Ethan, I can't!"

"You can and you will." His flat conviction left no room for argument.

Fighting panic, she bit her lip so hard it bled. "I really don't have any choice, do I?"

His arms tightened, then released her. "I'll go for Doc. I'll be back as soon as I can."

At the kitchen doorway Rose, dry eyed, flung herself at her mother. "Charity thinks you think I'm going deaf! I'm not, am I?" Larissa didn't see the murderous look Ethan flung Charity, but the frantic pleading in her daughter's voice would remain forever in her heart. She held Rose, much as earlier Ethan had held her.

"We just don't know. Mr. Michaels will fetch Doc. He'll tell us what's happening. It may not be serious at all. Maybe it's just wax in your ears." She tried to say it lightly, talking against the violent trembling now gripping her daughter's body from head to foot.

"Come, let's sit beside the fire until Mr. Michaels gets back with Doc." Arm about her daughter's shoulders, Larissa led her to the rocking chair close by the sitting room fireplace. She pulled her onto her lap and held her tightly. Rose didn't resist the offer. She curled into the comforting arms and buried her face in Larissa's apron front.

Ethan swiftly built up the fire, yanked the knitted afghan off the other chair and tucked it snugly around them. On the way out, he put his hand on Larissa's shoulder and squeezed, hard. She leaned her head against his wrist and he touched her cheek before vanishing into the kitchen. He spoke sharply to Charity. Rose gave no sign of awareness of his voice. Eventually, the outer door thumped shut, leaving Larissa in the sudden, vast emptiness of the sitting room.

She cradled Rose, much as she had all those years ago. Time slipped backward and, scarcely aware she did so, simply because it felt so instinctively right, she began to sing softly as she rocked.

"Sleep, my child, and peace attend thee …
Guardian angels God will send thee …
Soft the drowsy hours are creeping …
I my loved one's watch am keeping,
All through the night."

A corner of her mind pointed out that Rose probably couldn't hear her. Her heart answered back how, for the moment, anyway, going through the motions soothed the frantic, helpless screaming within her that she didn't dare let escape. Rose must have felt her calmness, for the tearing shudders slowly eased. After a long time, she relaxed and slept.

Only then Larissa slumped back in the chair and closed her eyes. The tears she had, by force, kept in check burned her tightly shut lids. *No! Don't you dare get all weepy, now. Rose is scared enough already. That's all she needs, to wake up because of a full-blown flashflood in her face!* Her reckless attempt at humor didn't succeed completely, but at least the threatening downpour subsided into a silent trickle down her cheeks.

CHAPTER SEVENTEEN

Time dragged its feet, much as a child reluctantly entering the schoolroom before a big test. Larissa held her sleeping daughter, and rocked her, and softly sang the lullaby that had soothed her to sleep when she was so small she fit neatly in her mother's arms with no hanging-over edges.

The Seth Thomas clock chimed eleven and twelve o'clock. It seemed a much longer time as she fought to stem the thoughts that kept jumping out, jeering at her. *What if ...? What will happen ...? How can we ...?*

At last she heard the bells Ethan had fastened to the horses' harness to warn other vehicles coming toward them through the snow. The bells that normally rang so cheerfully, today clanked dismally. Rose must have felt Larissa's muscles tighten, for she stirred and woke. She looked blank, clearly not remembering why she lay curled on her mother's lap. Too soon, memory came, and terror swamped the drowsy softness. She burrowed her head into Larissa's neck, clutched and re-clutched the now rumpled apron beneath her fingers. But she shed no tears.

Unable to smother her own sorrow, Larissa held her close, rocked her with her body, and willed her own faltering strength into her child. Seemingly at a great distance, she heard the noise she knew would come, the back door opening and Doc's and Ethan's voices as they stamped into the kitchen. Again, Rose gave no indication of awareness.

Ethan—heavy coat, gloves, snowy boots and all—crossed to Larissa. "Soon as Doc gets his hands warm around a cup of coffee, he'll be in." His voice spoke the words, but his eyes, looking directly into Larissa's, asked their own question.

She shook her head slightly and Rose, feeling the motion under her cheek, looked up. Following her mother's glance past her shoulder, she turned to see Ethan pull off his gloves and bend to rekindle the fire. Realizing she hadn't heard him come in, her eyes asked their own terrible question.

Gathering her battered courage, Larissa spoke close to her ear, as matter-of-factly as possible. "Doc's here. Let's wait and keep warm until we know what he wants." She couldn't tell how much Rose caught, because she didn't turn as Doc strode toward them. However, she must have seen the slightest shake of Larissa's head, for she twisted to look behind her.

"Well, young lady, it appears you're up to mischief again." Doc spoke in the exasperated tone he had used with her all her life. "Did you put candle wax in your ears?"

She heard him, for her lip quivered. "I didn't. Honest."

That stopped him. It had never occurred to him she'd take his reproachful bantering seriously. *How did you think she'd react? By bursting into song?* He turned and set his bag on the walnut table. "It's a good thing, since I didn't bring my candle-wax retrieving tool." He faced back, tipped her chin up and began assessing her physical signs, but the sinking feeling in his stomach already told him what he didn't want to know. He'd purposely turned so she couldn't see his lips move, and he'd spoken at a normal volume. She gave no sign that he'd said anything. She trembled violently in spite of the warm afghan tucked about her. Her eyes had turned so deep a blue they were almost black. He bent to her. "I need more light to examine you properly. The kitchen would be best. Will you come with me?"

She held fast to her mother, but slid down obediently when Larissa gave her a gentle nudge. She was shivering so hard, however, her legs wouldn't hold her up. Ethan caught her before she fell. Her arms clamped around his neck and stuck tightly as he carried her to the kitchen and eased her onto the chair Doc placed under the window.

Seeking extra candles, Larissa yanked open the door to the pantry built into the space under the stairs and Charity toppled out, further frazzling Larissa's already-depleted supply of wits. "What on earth are you doing?" she squeaked.

Regaining her balance, Charity hastily backed deeper into the pantry. "Nothing."

At this informative answer, Larissa set her jaw and moved the girl aside to continue her quest. "Please do it someplace else. I need to get to the shelf behind you."

Startled at this weird response, Charity scrunched aside. Locating the elusive candles, Larissa brushed absently past her out of the pantry. Halfway over to Doc waiting at the window, she glanced back in puzzlement, shrugged, and continued on her way.

Doc's painstaking examination took a long time. He asked Rose questions in tones varying from light and high to deep and heavy. At last, as if reluctant to finish, he slowly stood and removed the light reflector from his forehead. Scrubbing his hand across the back of his neck, he glanced at Larissa and Ethan, sitting at the table. He couldn't tell for sure, but he suspected they were holding hands under the hanging edge of the tablecloth. He sent up a swift word of gratitude for her having Ethan to turn to. *In the next minutes, she's going to need every bit of strength she can beg, borrow, or steal.*

Normally, he sent his young patients out of the room while he talked to the adults. This time he couldn't bring himself to do it. Rose knew why he examined her so carefully. He wasn't prepared to inflict the cruelty of prolonging her anguish. He held out his hand. "I'd like you to come over by me while I talk to your folks. A person your age deserves to know exactly what's happening and shouldn't have to wait to learn it second-hand."

He enunciated slowly and clearly and she slipped off the chair. At the table, he stood her beside his knee. Speaking simply and directly, leaning close to her ear, he paused at intervals to make certain she understood.

"Hard as this is for you, Rose, for all of you, I'm going to be totally honest. I give you my word I'm not going to hide anything that can sneak up on you later when you're not expecting it. Can you accept my promise?" His glance included Larissa in the query, and he saw her affirmation coming from his long years of conscientiously facing facts. He turned back to the young woman beside him and, for a fleeting instant, cursed the ingrained scruples bringing him to this moment.

"Right now, Rose, you hear someone if they're close and facing you, and speak clearly. You hear noises if they're loud and close, but not farther away. Is this correct?" The relief sweeping her features at his understanding of the newly hushed world around her forced him to clear his throat before he could continue.

"We don't know why it happens, but your high fever damaged the auditory nerves, the ones that relay sound signals to the brain." He stopped, seeking words to soften the blow. There were none. "That damage is permanent. We cannot know at this point whether this is as much hearing as you will lose or if the nerve function will continue to deteriorate until all hearing is gone. We simply have to wait and see."

At the irrevocable verdict, Rose jerked violently, and Doc saw Larissa flinch as surely as if her daughter's pain embedded itself in her own heart. She held out her arms and Rose fled to their strength and comfort, tucking her head against Larissa's shoulder. Leaning against her mother that way, she reminded Doc of a chick gathered safely under a protecting wing.

His examination complete, and the first harsh truth conveyed, he turned his back, fumbled his instruments into his bag, and pinched out the candles that had provided the extra light he needed to assess the damage to her ears. His deliberate movements gave the shell-shocked people behind him a few moments to absorb the impact of the blow he had just dealt them. Squaring his shoulders, he faced them. "I want you to hear this, too, Rose. Will you come back over here?"

Larissa spoke into her ear and Rose slowly uncurled from her mother's arm. Her fierce trembling had eased during the testing, as her sharply protesting body came to terms with terrible reality. Now her eyes, shadowed in her pale face, reflected the betrayal her heart and soul had yet to conquer.

Doc waited until she was standing beside him once more, then said gruffly, "I've given you the medical facts. Now I'm going to give you suggestions for coping with those facts." He talked on for a time, mixing practical advice and quiet confidence in their innate strength, in about equal measure.

When Doc stood to leave, he did a rare thing. He bent to her and lightly touched her temple. "You are a courageous young woman. To have a daughter like you would be a privilege." Her eyes widened and the faintest touch of color brushed her cheeks. He grabbed his bag and bolted for the door.

Ethan hurried to bring Bella and the cutter around, and Larissa followed Doc onto the porch. Carefully shutting the door behind her, she drew a trembling breath. "Would this have happened if I'd realized sooner that she was feeling sick?"

He turned sharply. Their eyes met. "It wouldn't have made any difference," he said at last. "We can use medical skills to command a fever not to go any higher, but we can't force it to obey."

They stood silently for a time, looking out over the snowy landscape while he fidgeted with the brim of the hat he had not yet put on. "I'm sorry, Larissa."

"I know you did the very best you could." Tears clogged her throat. "You saved her life. Again."

"Someday, someone will find a way to prevent this happening. I hope to God I'm around to see it." Catching sight of Ethan, Doc jammed on his hat and stomped down the steps. She watched him go, medical bag in hand, a weary old man traveling the slippery path. In saving Rose's life, twice, he had produced two miracles, and now berated himself because he had not produced a third one to save her hearing.

Returning to the kitchen, Larissa took Rose upstairs to rest. Thumping wood chunks into the box beside the stove, Ethan figured it was past time Charity returned from wherever she had dragged her injured feelings. Undoubtedly, she was smarting from his reprimand about blabbing before Larissa had a chance to talk to Rose, but she hadn't even sat with them during Doc's examination and discussion. What kind of support did such an attitude show Rose? The thought fanned the sparks of his smoldering anger. *Enough is enough! For certain, the earlier scolding will pale in comparison to my next little chat with her.*

She wasn't outside—her coat and bonnet still hung on their peg. He didn't find her in the sitting room or woodshed. *Maybe she's upstairs.* Normally, he wouldn't barge up there, but a flicker of concern poked up beside the embers of displeasure. Before he could search further, a muffled sound slid from the pantry. He yanked open the door to find

Charity huddled against the back shelves. "What are you doing in here? Are you hurt?"

"N-n-n-o-o."

In spite of her drawn out moan, he eyed her sharply. No blood. Everything still moved. His alarm flipped swiftly to impatience. "What, then?" His present mood contained no desire to cope with one of her hysterical scenes. With the thought, his anxiety again focused on the two upstairs, causing Charity's tearful explanation to waver past him.

"... because of me."

The words were truly dramatic but her anguished tone veered his attention back to her. "What is?"

"I heard Doc say Rose's go-going deaf because of the m-measles. And I gave them to h-her-r!" The stammered confession ended in a wail of misery.

He stared at her, thunderstruck. "You can't be thinking this is your fault?"

"She caught them from me!"

His rock-heavy impatience dropped with a dull thud and shattered into a thousand pieces around his feet. "No. Charity, she didn't."

"But I had them first!"

"No. Listen to me. You were sick first, yes. But Doc said it takes about ten days to show symptoms. Rose came down with them too soon to catch them from you."

She smeared her wet cheeks with the backs of her hands while she studied his face minutely. She must have decided he told the truth, for this time, her pleading held no trace of drama or hysterics. "You're sure?"

"I'm sure."

She could not possibly feign such enormous relief. "I was so scared!"

He hugged her hard. When he stepped back, the lump in his throat almost strangled his words. "Go wash your face with cold water. Unless you plan to hide in the pantry and eavesdrop on other people's conversations a while longer?" Her face still red and swollen from weeping, he could only suspect she flushed at his words. She hunched her shoulders and gave him a shame-faced grin. "I take it, young lady, that's a 'no'." He propelled her out of the pantry. "I could use a cup of strong coffee. Would a cup of strong tea be beneficial to your spirits?"

"I'd like coffee, too, please."

He blinked and hid his refusal behind a parental tactic Adam and Eve had undoubtedly used. "You probably wouldn't enjoy it. The taste is rather bitter."

"Rose and I drink lots of coffee."

This didn't startle him as much as she intended. He said sternly, anyway, "When?"

"If you and Mrs. Edwards are someplace else when we clean up the kitchen, we drink what's left in the pot."

Knowing how strong bottom-of-the-pot coffee could be, he felt a twinge of sympathy. But only a twinge. "Do you drink it black?" he asked conversationally.

"We tried at first, then we put in lots of cream and sugar. Rose can drink hers almost straight black, now, but I still like some sugar in mine."

He touched the pot steaming on the stove. "Why don't you get some cups?" They sat at the table and he managed to remain properly grave as she took a sip and her lips puckered in spite of herself. Silently, he pushed the sugar bowl toward her and watched as "some" sugar became several heaped teaspoons full. He sampled his own portion and had a hard time not reaching for the sweetener, too. He'd give them credit. *If they've practiced on this stuff, they'll be shocked to discover how enjoyable the real thing can be.*

She stirred the sugar into the coffee, her spoon making little clinking sounds against the inside of the cup. "Pa, have you ever done something wrong, but you haven't, but you still feel like you did?"

He didn't need to untangle that one. The question rammed into him and slammed the breath out of his lungs. The clinking of her spoon against the cup sounded loud in the sudden stillness. *You were so sure you were prepared. You knew it was coming. Just not at this particular moment, please God.* With utter disregard for his careful planning, this particular moment crashed into him while his daughter watched curiously. "Yes, I have."

Her interest immediately perked up. "When?"

His tongue was so dry, he took a swallow of coffee, then heartily wished he hadn't. The stopover in the cup certainly hadn't improved the delicacy of the flavor. He braced himself against the pull of memory and reeled in his floundering mind. "How much do you remember about the day your Ma died?"

She stared at him in perplexity. "Not very much. I have one memory from when I'm little that I'm cold, shivery to the bones cold. I'm running as fast as I can. And I'm scared, so scared. I never can remember why I'm running or why I'm scared. But it feels connected to Ma, somehow."

Her words hurtled him into the past, blown there by gusts of memory he had long thought stilled.

"Pa?"

Wrenching himself into the present, to his daughter watching him in puzzlement, he landed with a bone jarring clunk. "I've always promised myself when the time came for you to know, I'd tell you."

"You don't have to talk about it, if you don't want to."

Coming from his little girl, this mature recognition of his distress gave him another wrench. His smile became both rueful and pensive. "I turned my head for just a second and now you're a young woman. It's time for you to know. I'm just not sure where to start." He absently stroked his beard.

"It happened in October, as you know. It turned cold early that year, and this particular Saturday felt like we were on the far side of fall instead of not even to the middle. I worked around the barn most of the morning, getting the stock ready to winter over. I hadn't expected the weather to turn quite so fast, so there were a hundred things left to do." She listened intently, cheeks propped on her hands.

"Back then, it didn't take much of an excuse for folks to throw a party and invite the whole neighborhood. A birthday, a wedding, Fourth of July, a barn raising. Someone, somewhere was sure to come up with an event worth celebrating. October being the hunter's moon, our friends on the far county line figured it as good a reason as any to throw a shindig. They'd set it for that night and your Ma'd been lit up like a candle for days ahead, anticipating it. For the dance, she sewed a new dress, then made a matching one for you, because naturally you'd go, same as all the other youngsters. She was so proud of those dresses." He shook his head, remembering her delight.

"We planned to go in time for the potluck supper, but snow threatened, and I needed to finish the barn work. She came out a couple of times to nudge me along. I got on my high horse and let her know in no uncertain terms we weren't going to any party until I felt good and ready to go, and I wouldn't be good and ready until I'd tended to all the animals. Among the other chores, I planned to bring the sheep down from the high pasture, but it came on toward late afternoon and I was still plugging away in the barn. Apparently to surprise me, and probably to hurry things along, she decided to go after the sheep herself. Rather than ask me to keep an eye on you and spoil her plan, she took you with her. I'd crabbed at her thoroughly, and I didn't even realize she was gone." The old regret swirled through him.

"I finally finished at the barn and headed for the house to tell her that when I got back with the sheep, we could go to the party. Then I saw you running down the path to the barn. You were shaking with cold, and crying so hard I couldn't make out your words, other than 'Mama' over and over. You grabbed my hand and tried to pull me back the way you came. You were in an absolute frenzy for me to go with you. That's how I found your Ma. The rattlesnake had struck her upper arm." His voice rasped as he spilled out the words he'd kept locked within himself for so long.

"It was late in the year for rattlers, but near as I could figure, she'd surprised one in a rocky patch at the high end of the pasture, and he struck before she could back off. Her coat sleeve wasn't thick enough to blunt it. By the time we got there, she'd already become lightheaded. She kept insisting the snake was attacking you. I couldn't make her understand you were safe." As fresh as if it were yesterday, memory of those piercing screams chilled his blood.

"She was shaking so hard her words weren't all clear. I got as much venom out as I could, wrapped her in my coat and carried her to the house. I couldn't take her in the wagon to get help. The jolting would only have speeded the venom along. You were still crying, and you stuck to me like a burr. I could have taken you with me to go for help, but I couldn't leave her. I rang the bell to signal the neighbors, but by that time, they'd already gone to the dance. No one came for a long time. I did everything I could, but it was already too late by the time I found her." His breath sighed out. "If I hadn't stiffened my heart against her, she wouldn't have gone without telling me. She wouldn't have gone at all."

Charity listened, transfixed by the revelation of events long puzzling to her. As he fell silent, she started to speak, but hesitated before the words burst from her. "I remember you told me there are always two ways—to do or not do—and whatever we choose is our own responsibility, no one else's. Ma went because she wanted to." She jumped to her feet and threw herself against his shoulder.

Astonished, he patted her on the back, then grasped her by the arms so he could look directly at her. "She was beautiful, inside and out. Not a day goes by that I don't see her, every time I look at you. It would give her great joy to know the daughter she cherished is becoming a beautiful young woman, inside and out."

With her face once more buried against his neck, he barely heard her choked whisper. "I won't be sad anymore if you won't be."

***

He shrugged into his coat before going out to the evening chores, while Charity set out the leftovers from yesterday's lifetime-ago Christmas dinner. Turning to tell her he'd be back, he saw Larissa framed in the sitting room doorway. She looked utterly drained. Ethan started toward her, but his arm caught in his coat sleeve and delayed him so that Charity reached her first. She flung her arms about Larissa, almost knocking her off her feet. "May I go see Rose?"

"Not now. She's asleep, and I think it's best for her if you don't."

Crestfallen, Charity gestured to the pans on the stove. "Don't worry about fixing supper. I've already started."

Since her mind had not been on fixing supper, Larissa looked blank. "Thank you," she managed belatedly.

Ethan finally untangled himself from his sleeve. "I'm heading out to the chores, Lizzie. Would you like to come along and get some fresh air?"

His casual tone didn't deceive her. "Yes." She bundled up and stepped out onto the porch where she discovered it was snowing again. She walked to the railing and held her hands out to the noiseless drift. The flakes touched her gloves, clinging for a moment without melting. She raised her hands to her face and rubbed the cold remnants against her cheeks. She felt him beside her, not intruding, but very much there. As silently as the drifting flakes, she rested her head against his bulky coat as his arms went around her.

Neither spoke. Of what use were words against the heart-tearing reality they must confront? Finally, she lifted her face. "I suppose I better let you get to the chores. At this rate, before you finish, it'll be morning and you'll have to turn right around and do them again."

He touched her snowflake-damp cheek. "I'm here for you. For however long you need me to be. You know that."

"I know. I've always known. You've propped me up so many times when I've been sagging, I feel selfish taking so much from you and not returning it."

He brushed at a wisp of hair escaping her hood. "Never fear on that account. If we were keeping score, I'm sure you'd be three fish in the frying pan ahead of me, day or night." His amused, if doleful, confession brought to her lips her first smile in many hours. "I'd better get to the barn or else you'll be four fish ahead before I know it. Can't be having that! Will you come with me?"

"Not this time. I'll stay here and sort things out."

"Don't stay so long you get chilled," he said gruffly.

She watched him stride along the path until he reached the barn. Only then she moved to the porch steps. She rested her head against the support post and watched the soundless world in front of her for a long time.

***

In the kitchen, she found Charity at the sink and Rose huddled on the bench by the stove. Vague realization touched Larissa that, at some point in the day, the turkey carcass and the burned milk mess she had abandoned in her terror for Rose had been cleaned up. By Charity, presumably. *I didn't even notice.* The thought that had nudged her on Thanksgiving Day fluttered past. *Such a few hours for our lives never again to be the same.*

Rose faced toward the door enough that she could see her mother's entrance. Vast relief mingled with the anxiety in her features. Larissa hung up her coat and hood and knelt in front of her child. "I couldn't sleep, Ma. I just wanted to be down here with all of you."

Larissa rubbed Rose's cold hands in hers. "We're so very glad to have you with us." Charity nodded vigorous assent.

"Shall I set the table?"

Doc had advised that they keep everything as ordinary as possible. "Watch she doesn't get chilled these next few days. We still don't want to take a chance with lung fever. Otherwise, let her set her own pace, as long as she doesn't withdraw into herself. She's going to be making one of the most difficult transitions of her life. Knowing she's loved and needed will be the best medicine I could prescribe."

So now Larissa nodded and smiled. "Yes. Please."

The meal became the strangest one Larissa had ever taken part in, as they attempted to make normal conversation when life, and conversation, were no longer normal. Rose sat quietly, eyes darting from face to face as their lips moved. Charity, beside her, repeated their comments. *What will happen if she can no longer hear even that?* Larissa caught Ethan's eye and realized his thoughts were very close to hers.

CHAPTER EIGHTEEN

That night, when Rose was ready for bed, Larissa went up to tuck her in. Putting the candlestick on the dresser, she sat on the edge of the bed and bent close so Rose could hear. "I'm so very proud of you. You've been enormously brave about all this, especially when Doc kept asking so many pesky questions."

Pale and woebegone, Rose stared up at her mother and silently took in this praise. Larissa hesitated over her next vitally important words. "This is a very difficult experience for you, and I know that. It's all right to be sad, and scared, and mad, too."

"Are you sad and scared and mad, Ma?"

"Yes, I am."

"Are you mad at me?" she asked in a bare whisper.

Cruel hands grabbed at the knot in Larissa's stomach and yanked the trailing ends fiercely in opposite directions. *Just when you thought it couldn't possibly be tied any tighter.* "This isn't your fault. It just happened. I'd make it go away, if I could. But I can't. I can only try to help you bear it."

She tucked the quilt around Rose's shoulders. "To do that, we need to share our happy or sad feelings. Charity, Mr. Michaels, you, Mac, and I, we're a family, and families are there for each other, no matter what. We love and trust one other enough to be honest." She smoothed a wisp of hair behind Rose's ear. "It's all right to cry."

Rose sat up and buried her face in Larissa's apron front, so that her words came muffled. "I was so scared you'd be mad at me. I can't cry, Ma. It feels like all my tears are stuck in one big lump in my stomach, and I don't know how to unstick them."

Relief at this confession washed through Larissa and she laid her cheek against her daughter's. "Don't be afraid for that. They'll figure it out pretty soon, all by themselves. Just remember when they do, there's nothing wrong with crying. You're being honest, that's all." She sat Rose back so she could look directly at her. "Do you think you can sleep?"

"Will you stay here?"

"Yes, my Christmas Rose."

She lay down with her lips close to her daughter's ear and Rose snuggled into the comforting arms. "Pa used to call me his Christmas Rose," she said shyly. She hadn't mentioned Zane since the rhubarb cobbler episode at Thanksgiving.

"I remember."

"Do you think Pa knows what's happened to me?"

"I'm sure he knows. And I'm absolutely certain he's very proud of you, just as I am."

A long sigh escaped Rose. She said nothing more, and after a while, her fluttering breath told Larissa she slept. She stayed with her long enough to ensure she would not wake, before carefully edging off the bed. Bending, she pressed a kiss against her daughter's forehead before she picked up the candlestick and slipped into the hallway. Her hands shook so she blew out the candle before the hot melted wax spilled onto the floor. *And mine is only a small part of what Rose must be enduring.*

As her heart had known, Ethan waited at the foot of the stairs. Wordlessly, he took the candlestick from her and set it on the bottom step. Still wordlessly, he held out his arms and she slipped into the haven of his quiet strength.

Hard as she tried, she couldn't stop shivering. Before she realized his intentions, Ethan lifted her into his arms. Carrying her to the fireplace, he settled back in the leather-covered chair and stretched his long legs out on the hassock. Pulling the afghan over them, he cupped her head against his shoulder. *Ethan never sits in this chair.* Her first chaotic thought slid into the next. *Zane held me very much like this the day he came home from town after signing up to go to war.* Remembrance flickered and faded in the reality of Ethan's love.

They sat for a long time. The pulled-taut strings within her slowly loosened and began to coil into an untidy heap. *Is it really only the space of a few hours since I laughed at Ethan's mishap in the woodshed?* Surely, years had passed. She heard the far-off echo of her own lighthearted amusement and could only wonder at such carefree happiness. At the moment, bone-deep weariness and a wish never to have to move again dragged at her. Of tomorrow and the heartache waiting for them, she dared not give even fleeting thought.

Finally, reluctantly, she forced herself to stir. Ethan's arms tightened, then eased. "Did you sleep?" he murmured. She shook her head and his arms again tightened, then relaxed.

She straightened. "Where's Charity?"

"Off to bed upstairs. She wanted to sleep with Rose, but I explained how important it was for the two of you to be alone, how if Rose wants her to be there, she'll tell her."

"Thank you for understanding, Ethan."

"I'm not so sure Charity did, but I told her she'd have to take my word for it."

"I suspect there's going to be lots of that for our daughters in the next few days. I just pray the words we give them are the right ones."

***

Hours later, Larissa lay staring into the blackness engulfing her bedroom. There wasn't enough moonlight to relieve the dark about her, and pray as she might, there weren't enough words to penetrate the midnight blackness swamping her spirit. Once again, she turned restlessly, then the sound she waited for pierced the darkness about her and the gloom in her soul. Rose was crying.

Without pausing to find her shawl or slippers, she hurried to her daughter's room. A corner of her mind registered how the glow from the banked fireplace in the sitting room lit the stairway more strongly than it should at this hour. In spite of her need to reach Rose, the never-ceasing danger of fire propelled her to the top of the stairs. She peered down into the sitting room. The logs in the fireplace were no longer banked, but burning steadily. Reassured by a lack of foul smoke and ugly flames, she found her way to Rose's bed by instinct as much as by the almost non-existent moonlight.

She put out her hand, hoping she wouldn't scare the wits out of Rose, who had buried her head in the pillow, evidently attempting to muffle the sobs coming from deep within her. At the touch on her shoulder, she jerked up and threw herself against her mother. Face buried in Larissa's nightgown, her anguished tears soaked the material.

Larissa held her and rocked her and murmured into her ear, while her own tears fell onto the silky braids beneath her cheek. The painful knowledge of *been here, done this*, made it no easier to bear now than it had been after Zane's death. Night after night during that time, Rose, stoic enough during the day, had cried herself to sleep in her mother's arms.

She waited until Rose relaxed and slept before she edged to the door. The glow she noticed earlier still threw shadows at the end of the hallway, and caution forced her to drag her weary self downstairs to investigate. In the fitful light, she saw a dark shape in the leather chair beside the fireplace. At her approach, the shape moved and became Ethan as he sat up and pushed aside the afghan covering him. She stopped, hands on her hips. "Why ever are you keeping the fire stirred up at this hour?" Her wobbly attempt at humor, to avoid the question she knew was coming, fell flatter than her prize rolls would if she forgot to add the hop yeast.

"How's Rose?"

"Confused. Frightened. And I don't know how to help her understand why this is happening. How can I reassure her when I can't make any sense of it, either?" Her voice caught jaggedly. "She cried herself to sleep. She finally just wore herself out."

"I'm betting she's not the only one." He wrapped the tossed-aside afghan around her shoulders. "Would you like a cup of reasonably fresh coffee and some company, or would it end all hope of your getting any sleep?"

A quavery breath escaped her. "The roof falling in wouldn't keep me from sleeping now, so I expect one small cup won't. Especially with the company I'll have."

"Your company will take that as a compliment." He cleared his throat. "I think."

Her exhaustion-clogged brain didn't immediately realize what she'd said. Before she could scramble enough thoughts together to stammer an apology, she found herself at the kitchen table. He set a cup of the reasonably fresh coffee in front of her and waved aside her sputtering attempt to make amends. "Been there a time or three, myself." He raised his eyebrows as she took a sip and hastily set down the cup. "You think this brew is strong, wait 'til you hear what our daughters have been doing." He relayed Charity's proud confession of learning to acquire a taste for coffee by drinking the dregs of the pot. "Apparently, Rose can drink hers almost black, now."

Realization of what the girls had put themselves through to achieve their desired goal penetrated even Larissa's foggy brain. "They've been learning on leftovers even worse than this? And Rose can actually stand to drink it black?"

"Practice makes perfect. Charity let slip they've been practicing for quite some time."

"Obviously, a mule isn't even in the same category with them when it comes to stubborn," she said dryly. "Heaven help us if we interfere with either one when she's set her mind to doing something. But it staggers the imagination to picture them tackling this stuff just to prove how mature and adult they are." She curled her lip as she eyed the black liquid lurking in the bottom of her cup.

Ethan didn't respond to her brilliant observation. Looking up, she caught him watching her intently. Her mouth fell open as she realized what she'd said. "'… when she's set her mind to doing something,'" she repeated, dazed. "It really will be all right, won't it? Rose really is going to come through all this." She would have sworn she had no tears left to shed after holding Rose and weeping as her daughter cried herself to sleep. Now, as Ethan squeezed her hand tightly, once more her eyes misted. This time, the tears were ones of comfort and release, and so were warm and sweet with thanksgiving.

***

The morning following these nocturnal activities did not get off to a merry start. Larissa, finally falling into a deep sleep, failed to waken at her usual hour. When at last she surfaced, gray light filtering into the room clearly proclaimed she'd overslept. Guiltily scrambling out of bed, she threw her clothes on. Of course, her hair refused to cooperate with her hasty efforts to corral it into the usual neat knot at the back of her head.

In the kitchen, with Rose and Charity obeying her crisp orders and gestures, they had breakfast on the table in record time. After their joint effort, however, they ended up waiting for Ethan to come from the barn. He finally appeared, apologetic because he, too, had overslept and so was late getting to the chores.

The only good thing, Larissa reflected, Doc's decree that school remain closed until after New Year's effectively eliminated the usual hassle to get the girls out the door on time. *Will Rose ever again be a participant in the morning flurry that so often annoyed me?* Her mind twisted away from the probable answer. The thoughts replacing it, however, didn't bring her any comfort, either. *New Year's Day ... the wedding ... postponing the ceremony ... again.* She glanced at Ethan. He'd said nothing, given no indication, but he must know as surely as she that another delay stared them in the face.

Nevertheless, after breakfast he once more retreated to the woodshed. His hammering, never before a nuisance, now pounded in Larissa's ears, and the half-headache she'd acquired from lack of sleep leaped into full-blooming glory. Abandoning the girls to the dishes and the muddy remains in the coffeepot, she fled up the stairs to her room. Shutting the door helped muffle the rhythmic hammering, even if it didn't dispose of it completely. With every intention of tidying her room, she actually started to make her bed.

Her head thumped in time to Ethan's ringing strokes and it occurred to her that if she lay down for just a few minutes, the pain might go away. Five minutes, no more, she promised before her head touched the pillow and she sank into oblivion. She dreamed that Doc kept tapping his reflex hammer against Rose's head and asking if she could hear it. The panic in Rose's expression increased as the tapping and Doc's questioning became more vehement. Larissa jerked awake and realized the tapping and the voice weren't a dream, after all. The rapping at her closed bedroom door proved unmistakably real. Charity's insistent voice, unmistakably tinged with impatience, called to her.

"I'm coming!" Still half asleep, she leaped off the bed, promptly twisted her ankle, and fell with a graceless thud onto the braided rug. Pain lanced through her, but it also woke her up in a hurry.

"Mrs. Edwards?" The alarm in Charity's voice crumpled Larissa's faint hope of not looking completely foolish.

"Come in," she called resignedly.

The door banged open before she had the words out. Charity's impatience melted into fright as she flew to Larissa and dropped to her knees beside her. "What's wrong?"

Larissa gave what she hoped passed for a silly smile. "I'm all right. I must have tripped on the rug. How's that for the ultimate in ridiculousness?"

Charity's face betrayed her personal conclusion. With surprising discretion, however, she forbore to voice it as she took Larissa's hand to help her up. When she put her weight on the twisted ankle and winced, Charity burst out worriedly, "You're hurt! I'll get Pa."

"No!" That was all she needed, for Ethan to come and rescue her from such a humiliating predicament. "No," she said more calmly as Charity stared. "There's no need to get your Pa away from his work. My ankle just twinges a bit. It'll pass." Charity looked doubtful, but before she could argue, Larissa said hastily, "Why were you looking for me? Is Rose all right?"

"I forgot I was going to tell you Mrs. Gallaway is here."

"Martha? In this weather? I hope nothing's wrong." In her anxiety, she ignored her still-protesting ankle and hurried down the stairs. Rose had shown Martha to the sitting room and ensconced her in the rocking chair beside the cheerfully crackling fire.

Larissa vaguely noted the girls' disappearance into the kitchen. Mysterious noises began to float from that direction, but she focused her attention on Martha, who stood up at sight of her. They embraced, holding tightly to each other in a mutual giving and receiving of support and affection. Martha grasped her friend's hand. "I had to come see you. Doc told us about Rose. I'm so sorry."

The coiled knot in Larissa's stomach stirred and raised its fanged head. Only remembrance of last night's healing assurance that Rose would find the strength to deal with this dumped-in-her-lap calamity gave Larissa the ability to withstand her own heartbreak.

"Doc didn't break your confidence when he told us," Martha assured her anxiously. "He actually didn't give us very many details except, because of the high fever, she's losing her hearing. I suspect he knew I'd come right out if he said even such a little bit. So I had Shawn bring me as soon as he could. He's in the woodshed with Ethan."

"I'm very glad you're here." Impulsively, Larissa hugged her again before motioning Martha back to the rocker and dropping down onto the hassock in front of the leather chair.

"You don't have to talk about it unless you want to."

Martha's sympathetic understanding slipped like balm into Larissa's battered heart. *Ethan is so very good to me, but sometimes a woman needs another woman to truly comprehend.* "I want to tell you. It just seems it's happened so fast, and I'm so mixed up I'm not sure I'd make sense."

"Tell me whatever you want, and leave the rest."

As so many times before, Larissa thanked God for Martha's friendship. Haltingly, and somewhat disjointedly as she moved back and forth in time with bits of the story, she spilled out the basic details, the uncertainty, and the anguish. Martha listened quietly, asking no questions, letting her tell it her own way. She finally stumbled to a stop, feeling as floppy as the rag doll Rose had cherished as a toddler. A sense of peace seeped into her soul. A peace different from last night's brief illumination of Rose's innate strength. For the first time since this nightmare began, tendrils of resolve pushed out from her own soul, the first frail indicators she, too, would find the innate strength to surmount this tragedy.

Martha jumped up, as much, anyhow, as the unborn baby allowed her to jump, and crossed to the hassock. Taking Larissa's limp hands in both of hers, Martha squeezed them comfortingly. "How awful for you," she said simply. "I've always admired your courage, but never more than now."

Courage? It was not a word Larissa would have used to describe the confused mess of emotions she'd experienced since her initial discovery of Rose's measles. Before she could respond, Charity and Rose emerged from the kitchen. Charity carried a tray with Larissa's blue willowware teapot and cups. Behind her, Rose's tray held dessert plates, linen napkins, and a platter of Christmas cookies. Clearly thrilled by the women's surprise, both girls made stalwart attempts to appear properly solemn and poised as they served the tea and cookies.

Gratified as she was by their gracious behavior, Larissa paid more attention to Rose's attitude. The bruised bewilderment in her eyes had receded to a shadowed knowledge of sorrow beyond her years. For the moment, flickers of animation at the success of their surprise party chased away the pinched, fragile expression that had torn so at Larissa's heart.

"Would you like anything else, Mrs. Gallaway?"

Rose asked the question so naturally, Martha replied without thinking. "No, thank you. I must say, I don't know when I've felt so elegant, being served this way."

Rose turned to Charity and watched her intently. Her face lit up, and she and Charity politely retired to the kitchen.

Puzzlement poked Larissa, then fled as Shawn and Ethan sauntered through the doorway. "May we join you ladies?" Shawn sketched a bow.

Ethan was more direct. "We knew we smelled something good all the way back in the woodshed."

Larissa stood as she and Martha exchanged amused glances. After Ethan directed Shawn to the high-backed bench, he headed toward the leather chair. Larissa moved aside for him, but as he sank onto the cushioned seat, he took her hand and pulled her back down to the hassock. Her cheeks warmed at this display of affection in front of the Gallaways, and her heart tapped its own little song of joy.

Charity and Rose brought cookies and freshly perked coffee for the men, then once more disappeared into the kitchen. The adults spent the next hour in conversation no more serious than the antics of the twins, now recovered from the measles. Martha told how Mara decided Noah needed a haircut, "So she proceeded to give him one."

"When she finished, he looked like he'd backed into a mowing machine," Shawn confessed.

Martha refused to smile at her husband's picturesque contribution. "Unfortunately, he decided what was good for him was good for her. She didn't take kindly to the idea at all. Fortunately, I heard her howl fit to wake the dead, and I caught him just as he was about to take the first whack, right off the crown of her head."

"Sort of a biblical 'parting of the ways', one might say." Shawn coughed behind his hand. "Martha was a tad upset."

Clearly, Martha was still a tad upset, but their joint vivid description made it impossible for Larissa and Ethan, knowing the children as they did, to hold back their laughter. Fortunately for the future of their friendship, Shawn promptly added his merriment to theirs and Martha joined in, although with notably less enthusiasm.

Shawn wiped his eyes. "That quiet spell while they were sick provided a nice break, but honestly, I'd a hundred times rather have them this way."

The look Martha gave him strongly hinted she suspected he'd been dipping into the church's communion wine. Shawn prudently avoided her eyes and said hastily, "Speaking of our little angels, we probably should be getting back. Garth and Gretta volunteered to watch them, so we don't want to use up too much of their willingness."

Ethan and Shawn picked up their own conversation as they wandered toward the kitchen ahead of the two women. Martha took advantage of the separation to murmur to Larissa, "Shawn's so good with Mara and Noah. He spoils them in little ways and jokes about their misadventures, but he's right there when they need him. For Garth and Gretta, too."

"It really has worked out for all of you, then?"

The joy lighting Martha's face was its own answer. "What we had before we were married, wonderful as it was, doesn't hold a candle to what we've had since. It's a new closeness, a new understanding, when we were so sure it couldn't possibly increase." She laughed. "But I don't need to tell you about that. You'll know for yourself on Tuesday. Just think, only five more days." She broke off, alarmed. "What's wrong?"

She followed Larissa's misery-filled glance toward the two men nonchalantly involved in their own discussion. Comprehension struck and, clearly shocked, Martha swiveled back to her friend. "You *can't* be thinking of postponing the wedding?"

"What else can we do?" Larissa protested despairingly.

When Martha spoke, her low voice didn't carry to the men, but Larissa had never heard her so furious. "Don't you dare get such an idea into your head," she hissed. "You and Ethan have been through so much. It's your turn, now. What good will it do to put it off? What's done is done, and it won't be undone by delaying your own happiness." Larissa opened her mouth, but no words came. Martha promptly took advantage of her silence. "Besides, have you thought about Rose? With everything else being thrown at her, how will she feel, knowing she caused this newest delay? All because of something that's not her fault and that she's already sorrowing over. Can you really put such a burden on her?"

The two friends glared at each other.

"Martha—"

"Are you coming, Wife?" Shawn's voice slid across Larissa's reply.

"Right away. We're just discussing an important detail concerning a certain wedding coming up on Tuesday." Martha's eyes locked with Larissa's. "No matter how many details get worked out, unexpected ones keep cropping up."

"I remember some exasperating moments before we were married." Shawn turned to Ethan. "Strange as it seems, the important details get settled and the unimportant ones just kind of fade away." He laughed. "I've done a fair share of weddings, and I promise you, all my brides and grooms have survived the procedure."

Martha put her hand on his arm and they strolled toward the kitchen. A moment later, their voices, thanking Rose and Charity for the tea party, drifted back to the sitting room. Ethan chuckled. "Mara and Noah are going to run Martha and Shawn ragged yet." He added more soberly, "Shawn's a good listener. He knows how to cut right to the heart of a problem." He snapped his fingers. "I knew I wanted to ask him one more thing before they leave." He turned to Larissa, who hadn't moved.

He does look different, she realized with a start. The grave pensiveness shadowing him these past days had faded, replaced by the quiet confidence normally so much a part of him. *Maybe a man, too, has moments when only another man can truly comprehend.*

He smiled and held out his palm to her. "Coming with me, Lizzie?"

For one more moment, she stood there, before she straightened her shoulders and reached for his waiting hand. "Always, Ethan," she murmured. "Always."

CHAPTER NINETEEN

After waving goodbye to the Gallaways, Ethan headed for the barn to catch up on some odds and ends of tasks he had been putting off. Sunlight striking the snowdrifts ignited flashes of color, making Larissa scrunch up her eyes as she watched him follow the path he'd shoveled earlier.

A black-winged feeling of restlessness suddenly swooped down on her. Whether it was the bright afternoon or the realization of her first opportunity in days to be outside taking in the fresh air and sunlight, she couldn't determine and didn't care. Her heart emphatically rebelled at returning to the confining kitchen, and her head agreed.

She had not let on to Martha just how deep her distress ran, because she knew if she did, she would begin moaning like a panicked screech owl and never stop. *So much has happened, so fast.* If only she could be alone for a few minutes, she could sort through the past days and try to put them into something resembling a tidy arrangement. *Martha's accusations, too?* She flinched away from the thought. *There's more than enough to think about without adding her preposterous observations to the blend.*

She longed to go to the Sitting Seat at Mill Creek, her sure and certain refuge when she wanted to be alone. Common sense squashed the idea almost before it formed. Ethan, vigilant about keeping the paths from house and barn shoveled and walkable, didn't bother making access to those areas they didn't use in the winter. Now the snow had drifted far too deep for her even to attempt venturing out to the creek. The springhouse bench? Closer, true, but just as inaccessible. *I'm restless, not foolhardy.*

She squinted toward the cabin. Ethan had roughed out a track wide enough for Charity and him to come and go, but it sadly lacked the qualifications needed to call it a level, inviting walkway. In a field of no other options, however, it won her vote. She picked up her skirts and edged down the porch steps.

The path proved to be rougher, and more slippery, than she had anticipated as she made her precarious way over the humps and chunks of uncleared snow. I'll only go as far as the cabin, she assured the finicky inner voice nagging about the wisdom of this venture. Her decision turned out to be highly sensible, because the cleared portion ended in the walkway leading up to the cabin.

She knew, even leaf-stripped, the intervening trees screened her from direct sight of anyone at the house. Beyond the cabin, the piled snow extended as far as she could see. *Not the Sitting Seat, by any stretch of the imagination. Actually, not even a seat to sit on.* But at least here, alone, she could think things through.

Pacing back and forth along the narrow confines of the snowy walkway, she kept swatting at the hard truths that buzzed uncomfortably near. Finally, realization penetrated. Just as her trips back and forth along the path led her nowhere, evading the reality of Rose's situation didn't take her any place, either. She stopped and looked around at the leafless, black-branched trees. *It's just how I feel at the moment. Stark, battered by the elements, with my feet planted in a snowdrift.*

Her lips twitched at the pathos of the comparison. However small, the bit of lightness creaked open the firmly closed door of her obstinate refusal to voice, even in thought, the grim realities facing Rose. Her footsteps quickened, but truth stubbornly kept pace with her.

Will Rose lose the small amount of hearing she now retains? Doc, sticking by his promise of honesty, admitted he had no way to tell. The initial loss had progressed rapidly. Larissa breathed a prayer of thanks that, if they spoke slowly and clearly and close to her ear, she could still hear them. All well and good at home, but what would happen when others spoke to her on a simple shopping trip to town? Or at school? *School.* An excellent student, Rose enjoyed learning, but how could Miss Sullivan possibly convey the work to her?

Beyond school, what will happen as she matures? It's not a far-fetched question. Adulthood is galloping toward her with frightening speed. Both girls remained determined to teach, but they resoundingly agreed they would never be as fierce as Miss Sullivan. They would instruct *their* students with kindness and understanding. Larissa and Ethan had been hard put to solemnly agree how always using tact and reasoning definitely demonstrated the best course of action. *Has this bright future now been thrust beyond her reach?*

What of marriage? Jumping the gun there, too, maybe, but she must reckon with reality. Rose had just turned thirteen. Most young women married at seventeen or eighteen. How could Rose marry if she and her husband couldn't communicate? If they couldn't talk to each other, how could she, and this as yet unproduced young man, get to know each other well enough to want to marry? *The cart is definitely before the horse with this worry.* Larissa smiled weakly and felt slightly better. She didn't know the answers, yet, but at least she now had a grip on the questions, instead of cringing away from their painfully sharp edges. Long ago, she had come to the awareness she couldn't fight shadows, but she could face the truth.

This line of reasoning brought her face to face with her next set of uncertainties. *"What good will it do to postpone the wedding?"* Martha's voice hurled the question at her. She jumped a foot and whirled, fully expecting to find an infuriated Martha glaring at her. She blinked in confusion at the empty path behind her.

"But you've never been in the position of your child going deaf!" Larissa flung her protest to the empty air as though Martha actually stood there. "How can you even begin to comprehend?" Undeniably, the paths of the two women had paralleled each other through many of life's hurts and disappointments. Obviously, however, Martha had no concept of Larissa's guilt at the thought of abandoning her child's needs to follow her own happiness.

Honesty forced her to admit Martha had not once uttered that most useless of phrases, "I know exactly how you feel." She had simply been there for Larissa. She now worked hard to maintain her fury at Martha's presumptuous interference. However, somewhere along the line, the white-hot flame of anger had subsided to a red ember.

Part of her mind even suggested quietly how, quite possibly, Martha might be right. Like an old biddy refusing to be shooed into the hen house, the other portion squawked that Martha was hands-down wrong. The quiet suggestion fragment staunchly refused to allow the squawking section to override it. Softly, insistently, it persevered. *Martha would never deliberately say anything rude or hurtful.* Their friendship had endured too long for her to be anything less than sincerely honest in her opinions.

Martha, you said the past is past and no undoing it in the future. But tell me what happens when past and future join forces, create another obstacle, and dump it squarely in the path between past and future, making travel either forward or backward equally impossible?

While Rose lay fighting for her life, Larissa had blotted out all lesser concerns. Now with the wedding only five days away, she harbored grave misgivings whether she could quickly and easily shut the door on her daughter, turn right around, and open the other one leading to Ethan. After this past worry and heartache and using up all her energy, she now felt capable of generating only one emotion: exhaustion.

Not just bodily fatigue dragged at her. More than once over the years, household duties and backbreaking chores had caused her such bone-deep tiredness she could have curled up and died. She had survived those bouts by putting one foot in front of the other, and doing what she must to get herself and her family through them. Each time, eventually, she revived.

Exhaustion of the mind and spirit presently compounded her bodily weariness. She had kept herself tightly strung all these past days. Now, assured her daughter would live, and the first great grief and rebellion about Rose's hearing loss having been absorbed, she had loosened her vigilance. But easing the tightly wound tension left her feeling empty and listless, and she didn't know how to retrieve her gladness in everyday living. *You're just like a pump.* The odd comparison leaped at her as clearly as if Martha once more stood at her shoulder, handing out unsought advice.

"Now that's really elegant," Larissa muttered. But her mind ignored the sarcasm and relentlessly worked toward the truth of the words. *The stream of water doesn't shut off simply because someone ceases to work the handle. Water always spills for a time before the flow ends.*

Unfortunately, this lassitude of mind and spirit wouldn't magically shut off, either, simply by wishing it away. Could she, in five more days, fully share her heart and willingly give Ethan the time, attention, and consideration that were such a vital part of marriage? She well knew married life was not a fifty-fifty proposition. Inevitably, situations arose when one spouse gave, and one received, more than the other. *However, one percent can scarcely be considered an equitable contribution, particularly on one's wedding day ... or night....*

She walked slowly back to the house. Shawn's last words bobbed to the surface. "Remember, things that are important to us are important to God, too." She pictured God, turkey-feather pen in hand. The paper He was checking was so long that it curled around His feet. He scratched His head as He studied the list of everyone's problems, sorting the really big issues from the lesser ones.

Dear God, I hope this catches Your attention. This is so very important to me. Please let it be important to You, too.

***

Unknown to Larissa, Ethan directed his questions to Pegasus and Andromeda, the bay horses. After seeing the Gallaways off, he'd tramped to the barn. As he'd claimed, plenty of snowy-day odds and ends needed attention, but he did not finish any tasks. Instead, seeking the familiar solitude of the stalls, with the horses munching oats nearby, he hoped some answers would appear from out of the blue and fall into his brain.

He didn't hear everything Martha said to Larissa, but he'd caught enough of the conversation to realize she might put off the wedding again. He doubted he could cheerfully embrace another postponement, even one of necessity. He'd meant every word when he informed Doc during Rose's illness that he had a right to be with her because she was his daughter, too.

During those dark days, his anguish and dread couldn't have been stronger if it were Charity lying there. That was just the way it was. He had given his strength and caring to Larissa, even as she gave hers to Rose. That, too, was just the way it was. Given a hundred choices, he would do the same a hundred times over.

In spite of all his efforts, however, Larissa had not taken the complete measure of support within him that he would have given her. Even during the afternoon she first discovered Rose's measles, he perceived a hesitation in her, as if no matter how deeply each of them had settled into the other's heart over the past months, she could not share with him the full extent of the lonely burden she carried.

He had no sense that it came from distrust or fear. She might not even know it existed. They were as the pieces of wood he had shaped to make a picture frame for Rose's birthday, separate sections fitting together into one complete piece. He had no qualms about their melding together quite agreeably after they married. *But how are we to come to this melding if the wedding continues to be postponed?*

He had read how cavemen eons ago simply grabbed their women by the hair and dragged them home to meet the folks. The method earned merit for simplicity, but he had to concede how Larissa might take a dim view of the procedure.

He'd talked to Shawn earlier, out in the woodshed. Shawn had possessed no divine solution, but he presented a possible explanation which hadn't occurred to Ethan. "Perhaps, unconsciously, she feared by sharing all her burden with you, she would have nothing left with which to wage her fight for Rose's life. Make no mistake. That is exactly what she was doing." He'd cautioned Ethan against displaying his sense of inadequacy to Larissa. "I don't normally advise couples to keep their thoughts from each other. But showing frustration on your part is only going to add guilt to all the other emotions swamping her right now."

Remembering Shawn's warning, Ethan slumped onto a seat made from an old flour barrel. *Guilt is the last thing I want to give you, Larissa.* He dropped his head into his hands. *God, I expect You have it all figured out. I surely would appreciate it, though, if You'd let me in on the secret.*

***

He left the barn, a dozen thoughts still stirring up his mind. A cold gust of air smacked him in the face and he sneezed vigorously, four times. He fumbled in his coat pocket for his handkerchief. When he pulled it out, a folded piece of paper fell to the ground, his to-do list and the items he still needed to get from town to finish the woodshed. *Only five more days.* How could five days be such a short time to finish a project, and yet seem to be so many before he and Larissa were actually married? With the thought, he stooped, but before he could grab the paper with his clumsy gloves, the breeze lifted it and fluttered it onto the top of a snowdrift off the path. It moved gently with the air, rather like a smug butterfly waving its wings.

Without thinking, he lunged forward and his boot promptly disappeared into the crusty drift. This morning, as always, he'd rolled his pant legs up, to keep them out of the many substances a farmer walked over, around, and through in the course of a day. Unfortunately, this precaution did not help him now as his leg sank deeper than the top of his boot—much deeper. The icy particles cascaded down his sock and settled cozily around his toes and the sole of his foot. He stopped so fast he hadn't put his other foot down, and thus stood suspended on one leg in the middle of the drift. Such a position might be dandy for a stork, but for him it presented definite drawbacks.

Two choices smirked at him. Return to the path, leaving his carefully itemized list and knowing he'd be hard put to recreate it. Or plunge his other boot into the snow for the step he needed to reach the paper still swaying lightly in the breeze, just beyond his reach.

With a rude comment, he gritted his teeth and swung his free leg forward. As the snow filled his boot top and slid merrily down his shin, too late he reversed his opinion about the necessity of retrieving the list. With another comment, one Shawn definitely would not include in next Sunday's sermon, he leaned forward and snatched the paper just as it lifted to take skittering flight.

Clutching the list, he waded out of the drift. Back on dry land, he shook first one foot, then the other before jamming the paper deep into his pocket. He knew he'd better get dry socks fast or he and his feet would be in big trouble. Already the soggy yarn was chilling his skin. Squishing along the path to the cabin, trying to divert his attention from the biting cold now nipping at his feet, he concentrated on his vast relief that Larissa and the girls hadn't witnessed his stellar performance. *Storks really sleep in such a position?* He shook his head in disbelief, and came to almost as abrupt a halt as in the snowdrift.

He heard voices—a voice, he realized—coming from somewhere ahead. *Lizzie?* As he quietly drew nearer, he saw her pacing back and forth on the path in front of the cabin. She was arguing, but no one else was around. At that distance, he couldn't make out more than a few words. The tone of her voice, however, told him with perfect clarity he'd better head for the hills before she saw him. He backed carefully away, wondering why she was squabbling with herself. And who would win.

***

That evening, for the first time in many nights, they gathered in the kitchen after supper and the dishes were done. Doc had urged them to resume their family activities as soon as possible to help bring a sense of normality to their lives. Charity had promptly curled up on the bench with her book. Rose, at the table, bent her head over her sketchpad. Larissa, sorting rice kernels for tomorrow's pudding, cast a sidelong glance at Ethan. Pipe close at hand, he appeared to be lost in the book he held. *I'm so glad he and Shawn talked today.* Her thoughts bumped against her earlier heated discussion with the invisible Martha. After returning to the house, she'd decided not to say anything to Ethan. *Am I wrong in not speaking to him about it? Is there any need for him to know, when he knows nothing of my dilemma?*

The next morning, Larissa arose and didn't cringe from facing whatever the day might bring. She still felt deep-into-her-bones tired, but somewhere between her quarrel with herself yesterday and waking this morning, the anxiety and defiance had retreated to a dusky corner. She didn't know if it was because she'd dumped all her troubles back into God's lap or because she'd slept the night through for the first time since this tragic situation began.

Resolving to take full advantage while she could, she announced at breakfast it was time they gave the house a good cleaning. Charity passed the information to Rose, and three questioning faces turned Larissa's way. "It's been days since everything has had a thorough turning out," she reminded them, as if this explained everything. Acutely aware of Ethan's perplexed gaze, she carefully avoided his eyes. He asked no questions. He simply started eating with more enthusiasm than he had in many days.

When Larissa reached to clear away his plate, he stood and pushed his chair aside. Instead of moving out of her way, he put his hands on her arms. He studied her intently, pulling her to him for a hearty kiss, at which Rose and Charity rolled their eyes, before he disappeared into the woodshed. He began such a vigorous hammering and thumping, Larissa fully expected the wall to come crashing into the kitchen.

Doc's initial edict for Rose to stay bundled up and quiet had crumbled under the sledgehammer events of the past days. He'd checked her lungs and pronounced them in good working order, in spite of the upheaval she had been subjected to. He'd told her she might as well be up and around, as long as she didn't overdo.

Under those terms, Larissa set her to helping with the housework, with the strict admonition for her to pace herself and not get out of breath. Leaving the girls to wash the dishes, she went upstairs to make her bed. With the three of them working at dusting and scrubbing, they restored the house to its normal fresh and shining appearance by the time they sat down for the noon dinner.

Larissa watched Rose covertly, but she appeared no more fatigued than would be natural after a morning spent tackling household chores. Taking no chances, however, she decreed Rose should rest for a while after they finished eating. Rose protested, but Larissa held firm. "Just for an hour. I want to make more cookies this afternoon. Those big batches we made before Christmas, someone must have been pilfering them between meals, because they're almost gone." She looked meaningfully at Ethan.

"I didn't think I ate that many," he protested, then brightened. "They were so good I just couldn't help myself."

Having neatly pulled himself out of the quicksand, he winked at Rose, who, after Charity translated, burst into laughter. "Maybe I better rest, Ma. I expect you're going to need lots of help if Mr. Michaels eats them as fast as we bake them." Ethan squirmed guiltily, but didn't deny his intentions.

After her nap, Rose rejoined them downstairs, and she and Charity helped Larissa process three large batches of cookies. Ethan swore he was up to his ears in secrets out in the woodshed, but, with uncanny timing, he managed to need something from the kitchen at the precise moment another full pan emerged from the oven.

He had just appeared for his third drink of water in a half hour, and Larissa had just swatted his fingers away for the umpteenth time. "You'll burn yourself!" she admonished, also for the umpteenth time. Charity maneuvered the hot sheet onto the worktable, across from Rose, who was carefully cutting dough into shapes for a new batch of sugar cookies.

Larissa picked up the spatula and happened to glance out the window over the sink. "Why, Doc's here." Her startled tone caught Ethan and Charity's attention. Rose, watching Charity intently across the table, suddenly looked up and smiled.

The same thing happened yesterday, when she and Charity served tea. Larissa lost the thought as she pulled open the door to greet their visitor.

CHAPTER TWENTY

"Doc, we didn't expect to see you back so soon. Come in."

He dutifully stomped the snow off his boots before venturing onto Larissa's clean floor. "I hope I haven't come at an inconvenient time."

Ethan hung his coat behind the stove to dry. "No time's inconvenient when it's you."

Larissa cut in. "I'm so glad you stopped by. I need your expert advice about a situation we have here."

Doc turned quickly. "Rose?"

After all his concern and caring, Larissa could have bitten her tongue off for such a thoughtless remark. "No, not this time, thankfully. I'm sorry. I didn't mean to sound alarming. We need you, as an impartial observer, to give us your opinion about Ethan's judgment skills."

The relief on Doc's face gave way to solemnity. "I don't know the question, but I can tell you with complete assurance Ethan has excellent judgment." He looked at Larissa as he said it, so that she couldn't mistake his meaning. She blushed.

Ethan chuckled. "Thanks for the vote of approval." He reached for his coat. "I'll exercise some of that excellent judgment and take care of Bella. Be back in half a shake." Passing Larissa, he gave her a quick kiss on the cheek. "As the lone male in a horde of womenfolk, my unsurpassed wisdom isn't always treated with proper respect." He sighed. "Even though I keep telling them I've never been wrong, yet. Women!" The door shut firmly behind him.

Larissa felt a sudden urge to yank the door open and throw a snowball at him, but catching the hint of a gleam in Doc's eye, smiled reluctantly. "He'd best be careful or he'll use up all that excellent judgment. Then he'll be sorry."

"I expect he's got enough to spare without having to worry about that."

"Men!" Larissa sniffed.

"Now that we've sorted out that matter," Doc said pompously, "why do you require my impartial opinion?"

"The girls and I have spent the afternoon baking cookies. Ethan has spent the afternoon eating them. He says they taste so good, he just can't resist. Would you please do us a favor and try some so you can give us your viewpoint?"

"That's a pretty serious obligation, but I'll do my best." On his way to the table, he passed Rose, arranging cookies on a platter while Charity set out cups and plates. He bent toward her ear. "How are you doing, Miss Rose?"

At the formal address, she blushed almost as thoroughly as Larissa had. "I'm doing just fine," she said cheerfully.

Doc had been around too many bends in the road to be fooled by this bright assertion. He frowned and started to speak, but Larissa interrupted, urging him to sit and warm up with some coffee. As he hesitated, Rose darted away to help Charity. For the moment, he clamped his mouth shut on his misgivings and joined them at the table.

He sampled a cookie, scowled, and reached for another one. "Can't judge them fairly if I only try one," he explained gravely. His justification so precisely matched Ethan's excuse that Charity and Rose, after Charity's translation, shook with silent merriment. Larissa pressed her lips tightly together, but a sliver of laughter escaped, anyway.

Ethan returned to find them munching cookies and chatting about the latest town events. Doc waved a gingerbread man at him. "I must once again concur with your unsurpassed wisdom, Ethan. I can't choose the one kind I like best. Every one of them is mighty fine. Maybe I should try just one more." He plucked the last cookie from the platter.

Ethan took the chair beside Larissa. "You can't blame the empty plate on me this time," he crowed. Rose and Charity, red faced from stifling yet another fit of giggles, jumped up to refill the platter to overflowing and bring more coffee.

During the momentary pause, Doc's lightness fell away. "I haven't been ignoring you the last day or so." He brushed aside their quick reassurance. "Actually, I've been burning up the telegraph wires between here and Philadelphia." They looked at him blankly and he added, "To the medical school."

Larissa's breath caught. "Where Mac is?"

"Yes. I've maintained friendships with some of the doctors there. Over the years we've corresponded regularly. They've advised me on difficult cases, and they've also informed me of new methods and procedures that have helped me keep up with modern advancements in medical techniques." Rose and Charity, all levity stilled, slipped quietly into their seats as he continued.

"I've telegraphed them about Rose's situation, and they are most interested in her case. Particularly my friend Lawrence Cornell, a brilliant doctor who specializes in ear, nose, and throat abnormalities. He and his colleagues have conducted extensive research on the cause and prevention of deafness, as well as on treatment. Knowing their expertise to be far superior to mine, I presented Rose's case history, including the fact that she has retained some of her hearing."

Doc spoke to all of them, while carefully remaining turned in Rose's direction to allow her to catch the flow of words. Now he leaned closer and spoke to her alone. "The upshot is they would like you and your Ma to come to Philadelphia so they can examine you." At the sudden leap of hope in her eyes, he said hastily, "They can't restore the hearing you've lost. I want you to clearly understand that. But by studying your situation, perhaps they will be able to learn more about what happened and why and, maybe, gain information that will help someone else, someday. They will also have more knowledge than I about the hearing you've retained."

Her airy composure wavered. "They can't help me hear again?"

"No. I'm sorry." The once-leaping fire of his youthful idealism, the confidence that he would be a positive force in people's lives, flickered fitfully in the cold breeze of despairing knowledge. In the face of her need, his medical skill was worthless. "They can't. I wish to God they could."

At his uncompromising words, her bright cheerfulness, up to now stubbornly maintained in front of the others, faded into undisguised grief. She leaped up from the table and her eyes swept the kitchen, frantically seeking escape. She fled through the door to the sitting room and they heard her running footsteps. Both Larissa and Ethan jumped up, but Doc roughly waved them back. "I'll go." He disappeared into the sitting room, shutting their stricken faces from his sight.

He followed Rose's anguished sobbing over to the fireplace. She had flung herself into the leather chair and was huddled in a corner as if she had run out of room to retreat from the inescapable. Tears poured down her cheeks.

His normally piercing glare softened into compassion at her sharp struggle to accept that, however hard she might strive to conceal her feelings from the world, she could not conceal them from herself. He sat on the hassock. "Rose."

Tears still flowing heavily, she moved her head from side to side in rejection of any consolation he might offer. Silently, he cursed his own inadequacy, acutely aware that these next moments would determine her future physical and emotional well being. She could not go back. She alone could determine if she would go forward.

He bent close to make certain she heard him. She pulled back as far as the limited confines of the leather chair allowed. "Rose, you must listen. Sometimes I don't know the answers, either. But I've always strived to be honest with you. Have I ever done anything to make you wonder whether I was telling you the truth?"

He waited until a single reluctant shake of her head answered him.

"I've always wanted you to know, that no matter what, you can trust me. Have I ever done anything to give you cause to doubt me?"

Her head moved against the back of the chair in another barely perceptible denial.

"I know this is God-awful for you. I'm not so sure, if it happened to me, I could handle it with the courage you've shown. Now I'm going to ask you to trust me one more time. If you can, I have plans I think will interest you and your Ma, something even she doesn't know, yet. Will you come to the kitchen with me so I can explain everything all at one time?"

With the soothing flow of words, her frantic sobbing eased, although tears still slid down her cheeks. She shuddered and smeared at the dampness with her fists. He silently extended a large white handkerchief. She mopped her cheeks and chin and, just as silently, returned the cloth to him. Tucking the square into his coat pocket, he solemnly extended his hand to her. She regarded him searchingly, inched forward, and put her palm in his. He closed his eyes in huge inward relief and helped her to her feet. Her hand still clasped in his, they re-entered the kitchen.

His first appraising glance took in Larissa sitting rigidly, eyes fixed on the door, the anxiety for her daughter's anguish printed plainly on her features. Ethan, beside her, had his hand on her arm and, as she started to rise, warningly pulled her back. She flicked a sharply protesting glance at him before sinking slowly into her seat. Charity slumped, hands gripped tightly on the tablecloth. She was, for once, utterly silent.

Doc motioned Rose to sit and eased down onto the chair beside her. As he groped for words, Ethan's voice dropped into the stillness. "How long should this testing take, once Rose gets there?"

Doc drew a grateful breath and replied with all the old orneriness he could muster. "They don't know, exactly. They also mentioned, very briefly, something about teaching you and your Ma signs for talking with your hands, Rose. Telegrams aren't the best devices for lengthy discussions, so I'm not sure just what they intend. It would probably mean a longer stay, but if they can pull it off, that alone—"

Rose had been sitting, shoulders bowed and chin drooping near her chest. At his words, her mouth opened in surprise. She and Charity stared at each other. Rose nodded vigorously and Charity gasped, "Rose and I—"

"Not now, Charity," Ethan said firmly. "You are interrupting."

"But Pa—"

"I said not now." His stern voice told his daughter quite plainly that, even though he'd just interrupted her, twice, she'd better heed him or face unpleasant consequences. She subsided, but her mutinous expression boded ill for a future amicable parent-child relationship. With one last silent but clear warning to her, Ethan turned to Doc. "I apologize. You were saying?"

"I just wanted to point out, whatever happens with the testing, checking out this communication method is another reason to go, if there's any way it can be managed."

The change in Rose's expression from dark despair to pleading was too much for Larissa. Having taken her daughter's burden of grief into her own heart, she had listened with more and more of a sense of unreality to Doc unfold his various pieces of news. Now four faces, obviously expecting her to respond, swung her way. The room buzzed with silence, and, sieve-like, her mind emptied of all intelligent thought.

"Rose, I don't—I have to—" Panic kicking her, she stood abruptly and tried to drag some air into her lungs. "I have to think. I can't—" She turned to Ethan, who looked as dazed as she felt. "Will you come with me?"

Wordlessly, he rose and slipped his arm around her.

"While you're considering," Doc interjected, "I'm authorized to tell you, if you make the trip, the hospital will cover any expenses involved in the examination and teaching her to work with her hands. That would leave travel expenses, hotel arrangements and such, for you to cover."

Larissa tried to speak, but nothing came out. She tried again. "I—we'll be back." She shook so badly she fumbled with the doorknob. Ethan shrugged into his coat and grabbed hers before she could escape without it. As she lunged out the door, she glimpsed the three faces turned toward her, Rose's pleading, Doc's musing, and Charity's sulky. Yanking the door shut, Ethan caught her by the arm as, in her haste, she skidded on the ice-slick porch.

"Careful," he said gruffly. "Put your coat on. You can't stand here in the cold and reach any reasonable conclusion." Scarcely aware of it, she slid her arms into the sleeves. When she failed to pull the hood up over her hair, he did it for her. "Why don't we go to the cabin? I'll stir up the fire and we can consider everything without freezing."

As they navigated the slippery steps, she tried to pin down at least one of the hundred thoughts suddenly buzzing through her brain. On the path to the cabin, however, Ethan kept just fast enough a pace that, instead of thinking, she devoted her attention to forcing air into her lungs. Standing on the cabin porch while he fiddled with the uncooperative latch, her struggle for a coherent thought finally produced one. It was, of all things, the unsavory memory of the night last fall when she'd sought him out, and of her embarrassment and refusal to come inside with him. She preceded him into the room and sat at the table. Watching him kindle the fire, she thought about that long-gone humiliation. *It's so strange. Things we once believed to be crucial to our very existence are so foolish later on.*

The flames, tentative at first, licked higher. Dusting ash from his palms, he pulled out the chair across from her. "Probably be a good idea to keep your coat and hood on for a bit, until the fire really catches hold." He reached for her hand across the table. "I'm here for you, Lizzie."

She smiled weakly. "For always?"

His clear gaze met hers unflinchingly. "For always."

"Even with the hospital covering the medical costs, there simply isn't money for such a journey. The war's been over almost two years, and we're still not back on our feet with expenses. Buying seed for the spring planting will set us back. And what about our plans to start raising blooded horses again, as we did before the war? It's a necessity, not a luxury, if we're to succeed financially with the farm."

He started to speak. Staring at their joined hands as her words spilled out, she didn't see. "The part about learning to talk with hand signs. I presume it's for us to talk to her if she isn't standing close by. It'll take time to learn, which means more expense."

"Would you go, if the money weren't a consideration?"

She didn't hesitate. "Yes. It's like Doc said. It's a chance for her to feel that all of this isn't just for nothing. Maybe they can learn something to help someone else, someday. And this hand-talking idea. If it works…."

Knowing it was now or never if he were going to speak up, he tightened his fingers around hers. "There is a way."

"Go to work in a saloon?" she said brightly. "I've heard the pay is —"

"There isn't one in town," he said crushingly. "You'd have to go at least forty miles."

"Oh. That is a bit impractical."

"I have a much better idea and you wouldn't have to go such a long distance." From past experience justifiably wary of her reaction, he spoke quickly to get his plan out before she could start objecting. "I told you before, I have money left from the sale of the farm in Michigan. We can use some of it to get you and Rose to Philadelphia."

"But—"

"Larissa, for years Charity and I have taken from you without putting back. Now, it's our turn to return to you a little of what you've shared with us."

"You've more than given back. If not for you, we would never have kept the farm going during the war years."

"This is what families do, Lizzie. They help each other in whatever way comes up. This isn't a luxury trip. Rose needs to do this. Remember I said I've been saving the farm money for important things? Well, the woodshed qualified, so these circumstances should, too. Besides," he gave her a lopsided smile, "I want to do it. Does that count for anything?"

Her throat closed so tightly, no words came. He swiftly rounded the table and drew her up into his arms. "We have to try," he said quietly. "We have to give her a chance to know if something can help. She can't go through the rest of her life wondering. We can't, either."

"I guess maybe I can give up the saloon idea," she murmured against his shoulder. She felt his breath sigh out.

"It probably would be for the best. I hear the hours are awful. Besides, I've gotten used to knowing you're close by. I'll be waiting for this trip to be successfully completed, so you can be close by again." Reluctantly, he stood her back a bit. "We should probably go let them know. They must be wondering what's keeping us." Releasing her, he bent to bank the coals so he could restart the fire when he returned.

Leaving the warm shelter of the cabin, they discovered the wind had risen sharply. On the walk back to the house, neither one spoke, but she kept her fingers clasped tightly in his. When he reached around her to open the kitchen door, she put her hand on his arm. He tipped his head questioningly.

"Thank you, Ethan." She stood on tiptoe, pulled his head down, and kissed him.

He didn't waste any time in joining wholeheartedly in the activity. They finally stepped apart, and his lips twitched. "With a thank you like this, I'll have to see what else I can do to merit such appreciation!"

Entering the warm kitchen, Larissa was acutely aware, as when she had left, of the three faces turned toward them as if pulled by one string. Doc's now grim, Rose's hopeful, and Charity's cantankerous. Ethan hung their coats near the stove while Larissa sat at the table beside Rose, still flushed and swollen from her earlier violent weeping. Bracing herself against renewed hurt for her daughter, she bent close and spoke slowly and clearly. "Rose, do you want to go to Philadelphia?"

"Yes, Ma." Rose clasped her hands tightly together.

"Will you do whatever the doctors tell you, even if it seems strange or a little uncomfortable?"

Rose's chin bobbed.

"Then, yes. We'll go."

Rose simply stared at her mother as if assuring herself she had heard correctly.

Doc stood. "I'll be going. There are arrangements to make with the hospital. I'll let them know you're leaving here on the Monday train. That should get you to Philadelphia sometime Tuesday night. They'll probably want to meet with you first thing Wednesday morning." He studied his watch. "I'll go roust out Miles Painter and have him send another telegram. I'll also put together Rose's records for you to take. I've kept track of everything, so maybe it'll give them a better idea where all this is coming from."

Ethan went out to hitch up Bella, and Larissa started moving pans around on the stove. "Won't you stay for supper, Doc? It won't be fancy, but it should be filling."

Doc wavered, but finally said reluctantly, "Thank you, but not this time. The sooner I get back to town, the sooner we can start all the necessary arrangements."

"If you won't stay, at least let us pack you some supper. We'll have it ready by the time Ethan gets back, and this way you won't have to stop and fix something."

Doc's firm resolve wavered under Larissa's won't-take-no-for-an-answer attitude. When Ethan returned and announced that Bella was ready, Larissa and the girls were putting the final touches on a packet of food, in spite of the fact Doc was still arguing the matter with her.

Charity and Rose each handed Doc a parcel. "Turkey sandwiches and pumpkin pie in this one," Charity explained.

"And cookies in this one. Since you haven't made up your mind about which ones are best," Rose added.

Doc caved in, more because of this first hint of Rose's old mischievousness than for the cookies themselves. "I shall do my utmost to remedy the oversight. Thank you for the added opportunity to do so."

"Are you sure you should go back to town?" Ethan asked, concerned. "The wind's rising, and all the signs indicate another storm's on the way. Maybe you shouldn't try to head back right now. We'd be more than happy to put you up here." He looked to Larissa for confirmation, and, receiving it, added, "You can stay in the cabin with me. I assure you, I don't snore. Very loud, anyway."

"Charity can stay the night with Rose. This way, you two men won't have to endure a horde of women pestering you."

Ethan grandly ignored her on-target shot. "Sounds like a plan. For sure, Doc, you don't want to be caught in a storm."

Doc had crumbled under Larissa's determination about supper and Rose's offer of cookies. Now, he looked wishful but held firm and reached for his coat and hat. "I've been out in worse weather than this, and Bella knows the road better than I do. Sorry to leave you to your horde of womenfolk, Ethan, but I have to get back and see who's done what in the frostbite department, or broken a bone falling on the ice. I'm sure there'll be something."

Hand on the knob, he turned back to frown at a startled Ethan. "Rose and Charity have something to tell you that will add merit to our earlier discussion. I strongly suggest you listen to them, this time." He gave the girls what from anyone else would have been a wink and stomped out the door.

CHAPTER TWENTY-ONE

As soon as the door slammed shut on Doc's unsubtle recommendation, Ethan turned to the girls. Rose and Charity stood side by side, but it was his daughter, looking remarkably like a cat with canary feathers stuck to its chin, who received the full force of his glare. "What have you been up to, now?"

"Nothing. We just told Doc what we were trying to tell you and Mrs. Edwards. He listened to us."

Ethan opened his mouth, but before he could deliver his fatherly opinion of her last pointed observation, Larissa cut in. "We do want to hear what you have to say. Before, there was just too much confusion, and too many people thinking and talking at one time."

Slightly mollified, Charity looked at Rose, who nodded urgently. "We wanted to tell you we already do, about teaching Rose like Doc was saying."

"Do what?" Ethan's difficulty in following this speech was apparent.

"Talk with our hands." She sounded like a teacher whose patience has been exhausted explaining a basic fact to a dim-witted student.

Larissa, as bewildered as Ethan, hastily suggested, "Why don't we all sit down and you start at the beginning, so we can hear the whole story?"

Charity took a deep breath. "Years ago, when Rose and I were little, we found it in a book at school."

Under the table, Larissa poked Ethan with her foot before he could ask what *it* was. Fortunately, Charity, ever the talker, warmed to her subject and didn't notice. "Miss Sullivan had a big book with all kinds of information in it. It had a funny name, something like 'Cyclops.' Rose remembered her Pa reading out loud at night from his Greek history book about the Cyclopes. They were huge men with only one eye, and they made thunderbolts for Zeus. But we couldn't figure out what that had to do with Miss Sullivan's book." For a whole second or two, she paused to ponder the problem.

Larissa kicked Ethan again. He coughed raggedly before he asked, a little hoarsely, "Did she call it an 'encyclopedia'?"

"I remember, now, she did." His daughter stared at him in amazement. "How did you know?"

Ethan prudently shifted his foot from reach of Larissa's shoe. "I heard it somewhere," he said vaguely. "But go on with your story about the book with all the information."

"She didn't have it very long before she gave it to a student who was moving west all the way to Indiana with his family. Afterward, we never saw another book that told about so many different things all at one time.

It was on a stand in the schoolroom. If we finished our work before time was up, she allowed us to read from it. I was looking at it one day and found a page with pictures of funny hand shapes. The story explained it was the alphabet. I remember how it said a bunch of men, who weren't allowed to talk out loud to each other for some reason, invented it so they could talk without breaking the rules."

Larissa had been patiently following the twists and curves of Charity's long-winded explanation. Realization suddenly dawned, with all the force of a fist punching her in the stomach. *This is why Rose and Charity have been acting so mysteriously.* The thought stunned her so, she missed the next part of Charity's narrative.

"… I showed Rose, and we decided it would be a good way to talk in front of Mac and he wouldn't know what we were saying. So we learned it and Mac never figured it out. Even when he threatened to dunk us in the horse trough, we didn't tell." Having run out of words, she finally noticed Larissa's disbelief, heard the ringing silence around her, and warily waited for lightning to strike because of their deception.

"Why didn't you tell us what you were doing?"

Rose didn't hear her mother's question, but Charity squirmed. "It was our secret." Larissa discreetly ignored the touch of defiance in the words, and Charity continued, "We could pay Mac back for being mean to us. But after a while, he was hardly ever around. It wasn't nearly as much fun when we couldn't make him mad. So we used it around you and Pa, because you're always making us be quiet when you're talking." She answered Larissa, but clearly directed the words to her father.

Ethan started to protest indignantly, thought better of it, and wisely stayed silent.

Too busy trying to grasp the implications of Charity's story, Larissa missed this exchange. "You each can actually understand what the other one is saying?"

"Not as much now as when we were little. We even made up a bunch of shapes to use for words because it took so long to spell everything, but we don't remember them all now."

Larissa sat forward in her chair. "Can you say 'Rose'?"

Charity picked an imaginary flower, held it to her nose and sniffed. Larissa and Ethan watched, fascinated. "Can you make, 'I love you, Rose'?"

Charity pointed to Larissa, crossed her fingers over her own heart, and pointed to Rose. Rose watched intently, then slid out of her chair and flung her arms around her mother's neck. "I love you, too, Ma."

After so much bleakness, true hope for her daughter's future danced in Larissa's heart. Holding Rose tightly, she gently swayed their bodies, just as she had done a million times when Rose was small. For the first time in days, Larissa didn't fight to hold back her tears. Happiness, warm and sweet, filled her soul and spilled over into a joyous smile.

***

That night, Larissa lay long awake, sorting the events of the day. Doc's news of the trip to Philadelphia and the positive implications for Rose's future. Ethan's generosity in making the trip possible. *God must have decided my problems were important, after all.* She closed her eyes in humble gratitude for the answers He had provided, and for His speed in providing them.

The wonder with which she had watched Rose and Charity demonstrate their coded language still pulsed within her. Rose had explained Charity's sign was a slight dip of the knees, as if she were preparing to sit in a chair. Intrigued, and unable to hide it, Ethan asked if they had a sign for him. As soon Charity spoke into Rose's ear, both girls reached up, pulled on their chins, and assumed a thoughtful, far away expression. The image of Ethan stroking his beard while he pondered something was too plain to be missed, and he'd joined in the laughter at his expense.

"Guess who this is." Rose put her hands to the back of her head, pretending to tuck a hairpin into a bun at the nape of her neck, which illustration caused a full round of teasing aimed toward Larissa. Doc was a fierce scrunching together of the eyebrows. It was an image Doc, if he learned of it, might not find quite as humorous as they did.

As she lay in bed, Larissa recalled Charity's talent for pantomime. Learning the finger alphabet and inventing those signs had all the earmarks of her creative imagination. *But who would have dreamed how a game played by two little girls would ever assume the importance displayed by its use today?*

Larissa started to drift off. The knowledge that had been biding its time in her heart during all the hours since Doc's announcement now skipped forth.

In four more days, I'll see Mac.

***

Waking the next morning, Larissa couldn't remember why her heart felt so light. Then it came bounding back to her. On its heels came realization the day would be crowded with pre-departure projects.

In the kitchen, Rose and Charity flew about, helping her put breakfast on the table. Even in the midst of baking biscuits and scrambling eggs, she watched Rose carefully. The fixed-in-place cheerful smile had been replaced with Rose's usual serenity. The last traces of the bruised, pinched look that had torn at Larissa's heart had faded. A soft pink tinted her cheeks. *My Christmas Rose is blooming once more.*

During breakfast, they discussed the various tasks they must accomplish. The most time-consuming one would be going to town to buy the train tickets. "I'll do that, Lizzie."

Ethan had been rather quiet through the meal, but she'd put it down to their coming separation. For her, too, it was the one cloud hovering over this trip. In her day-in and day-out pattern of living, she drew immeasurable contentment just from knowing he was somewhere about the farm. Now, facing a separation of many weeks, her heart quailed. *Stop it! You're doing what you must by making this trip. He knows that. He's doing what he must by staying here and keeping the farm going. He hasn't even mentioned the wedding. But, then, neither have you.*

In the midst of her disappointed resignation because the wedding must once again be postponed, a picture popped into her head. The friends who had been invited to the marriage ceremony were starting for the church, reversing direction, starting forth again, once more turning back, until they were literally coming and going, very much like the confused inhabitants of a disturbed anthill.

"Thank you, Ethan." Her belated response to his offer to go to town was nonetheless grateful.

"I'd like you to come with me, Charity. If you can spare her, Lizzie."

"Of course. Well, not really." She winked at Charity. "You do so much to help, but I guess Rose and I can struggle along without you this once." Charity, accompanied by Rose, raced upstairs to get ready.

"Anything you need from town, while we're there?"

It had been weeks since she'd been able to undertake a proper shopping trip. She snatched at the opportunity. "I'll make a list while you're hitching up."

Before they left, Ethan, still subdued, held her close. "We'll be back as soon as we can, but it may take a while, depending on the road. So don't look for us until you see us coming." He kissed the top of her head and turned to collect Charity, who was busily discussing something with Rose that made both girls giggle. He directed his eyes heavenward, but made no other comment.

Larissa trailed them to the porch. Rose, her face stuck through the narrow space of the ajar door, hopped out to wave vigorously, then scooted back into the kitchen before her mother could admonish her for being out in the cold.

Larissa dutifully performed the morning chores, but her mind was only half on them. Caught up in speculation of the future, she glanced often at Rose, who was completing her portion of the work in similar silence. The unexpected coming departure necessitated doing a tub of laundry, definitely not one of Larissa's favorite household activities, especially in wintertime, when she must hang the wash inside to dry.

The washtub and wringer normally lived in the woodshed. Ethan, however, had been diligent in his determination that she be surprised when she finally viewed his carpentry efforts. His first action had been to run a partition across the woodshed. Thus she had full access to her laundry supplies, brooms, and mops, but the barrier rudely prevented her from spying on his mysterious activities. It was a sharp source of frustration for her on wash days, but it was also handy in that she transferred her annoyance into getting the laundry clean. *I'm not looking for any prizes, but we must wear the cleanest clothes in Fairvale. I just hope they don't also end up with the most holes from rubbing too hard on the washboard!*

She pulled the tub into the warm kitchen, and she and Rose set to work. Ethan had strung lines on Larissa's side of the partition, so most of the laundry could dry in there. She habitually hung only the soonest-needed items on a line near the stove. Thus, in crossing the kitchen, a family member who forgot to duck didn't get slapped in the face with a clammy sheet or towel. For the most part, it worked, although Larissa was always fervently happy when, the onerous chore completed, she washed her hands of it for another few days.

Intent on her thoughts, and her anticipation of seeing Mac after all these weeks, she and Rose finished before she realized it. As she straightened her aching back and handed Rose the last garment to wring and hang up, the Seth Thomas clock struck. Out of long habit, she counted the chimes, startled to realize it was noon.

She had no clue when Ethan and Charity would return, but fixed enough dinner that it could be put aside and reheated. They had not yet come by two o'clock. In spite of Ethan's admonition not to worry because he and Charity might be quite some time in getting back, she felt a poke of concern. *They wouldn't have gotten stuck in a snowbank. Would they?*

By three o'clock, they still hadn't returned. Her imagination plucked them from the snowbank and deposited them in a blizzard where they were wandering lost and frozen, although there was not even the hint of a snowstorm on the horizon between the farm and town. In spite of her efforts not to let Rose see her anxiety, she knew her daughter, too, was concerned. During the next half hour, one or the other was edging to the window over the sink to sneak a peek.

By three-thirty, she had them safely out of the blizzard, but trampled under the hooves of a runaway horse..."Ma, they're back!" Rose's cry brought Larissa to the window almost before the sentence was completed.

They were starting up the path, arms full of bundles, and not a frostbite, frozen limb, or horse hoof-shaped bruise in sight. She was so relieved that she flew to the door, with Rose right behind. Somewhere in the brief space between the window and the door, however, rational thought kicked in. "Rose," she said urgently, "now we know they're all right, we mustn't let them see how anxious we were. It would be embarrassing for us because it'd sound really silly to them. Not that I'd blame them, especially after Mr. Michaels assured us we needn't worry. But it'd become a big joke, and we'd never hear the end of it."

Rose must have caught most of the hasty words, and Larissa's intention, because her apprehensive expression melted into a frown. "Can we be mad, instead?" she hissed back, "now we know they're safe?"

The amusement that streaked through Larissa was sheer relief after all the fretting. "Shall we try 'mildly concerned'? It wouldn't be a lie." She heard their feet on the porch steps. "We just won't tell them the degree of 'mildly.'"

Rose's chin bobbed in agreement. Larissa pulled open the door and stuck her hands on her hips. "Here you are! We were starting to think you'd decided never to come back." She felt Rose crowding behind her and a sudden squeeze on her right hand.

She squeezed back and shifted slightly so Rose could stick her head out the door in time to witness the "what are you talking about?" surprise flashing across Ethan's face. Luckily for him, he'd been around this particular horde of women long enough to pick out the proper response. "We didn't mean to be so long, did we, Charity?"

His daughter gave an exaggerated sigh. "I thought we'd never finish. Look at all the stuff we bought."

"We promise to be good. May we come in now?" Ethan asked pathetically.

"All right." She stepped aside as Rose retreated. "Wipe your feet first," she added sternly. As they edged around her and dumped their packages on the table, Larissa inwardly relaxed. Silly as the exchange sounded, the message had been received and dutifully filed for future reference. The incident was closed, although Rose couldn't resist giving her mother a knowing grin.

Ethan hung up his hat and coat beside Charity's and patted his outside pockets. "I think I left my pipe in the sitting room. Could you get it, please, Charity?"

"Sure, Pa. Come on, Rose. I have lots to tell you."

"Charity." She turned from the doorway inquiringly, and read his silent message.

"I know, Pa. Get your pipe!" she finished hastily and disappeared with Rose into the sitting room.

"Did you get the tickets?" Larissa whirled back to the stove. "Whatever am I thinking? You must be half frozen. I'll make fresh coffee."

"That's all right. I don't need any right now. I'd like you to sit down with me."

"It'll only take a minute." She began pushing pans around.

"Please come and sit down. We need to discuss some thoughts I had about the trip."

She reached for the bag of coffee beans.

"Larissa, please!"

She finally focused her concentration on him. She'd never seen such an odd expression on his face. Pleading, determination, uncertainty, and desperation mingled there in about equal parts. She abandoned the coffee and smoothed her apron. "Ethan, is something wrong? You got the tickets, didn't you?"

Now that he had her attention, some of his desperation eased, but not much. "Come sit here. Yes, I have them," he assured her, dropping onto his own chair.

Mystified, she waited. He reached inside his sweater-vest, pulled out the tickets, and handed them to her. "My, it certainly is a thick bunch. I didn't realize we'd need...." She stopped abruptly. "Ethan, there are four sets of tickets."

"Yes." He reached for her free hand. "Charity and I are going with you and Rose to Philadelphia."

"But—"

"No buts. No way in this world am I going to make you take this trip by yourself. It'll be hard enough on you as it is. I want to be with you to ease some of that hardship."

As he spoke, the desperation in his eyes faded, only to be replaced by something else she couldn't immediately identify. Her thoughts scattered like blueberries spilling out of an overturned pail. She tried, unsuccessfully, to collect them. "Ethan, I don't quite know what to say. There's so much to consider."

His hand tightened on hers. "If you want me to go, say yes. We'll work everything else out."

"Yes." One simple word to convey so much appreciation, relief and gladness.

The something in his eyes became a spark of light, but he only said, "Good. With that question settled, we can tackle the other matters." He leaned back slightly, but kept his hand around hers. "I wasn't just loitering around town, I assure you. I went to the parsonage, first. I talked to Shawn and Martha and laid it all out for them."

"What did they say?"

He squinted toward the ceiling. "I remember now. Shawn said something to the effect he thought it entirely appropriate that I go with you to assist, of course, but for moral support, as well."

"What did Martha say?"

"Martha told me in no uncertain terms if I didn't go with you, she would personally come to the farm and explain to me the error of my ways. Her explanation involved hanging me from the nearest tree by my toenails until I came to my senses." He shot a sudden smile at Larissa. "I assured her such drastic measures would not be necessary."

"Sounds like Martha, for certain."

"For keeping the farm tended, they suggested I talk to Dolf Hyatt. You remember, he's renting Martha's farm so the Gallaways don't realize any profit from the place." At her affirmation, he continued. "Shawn went with me to see him. The upshot is that Dolf's two near-grown sons can come do the chores and stay on in the cabin if the weather gets bad. I said of course we'd pay them, but no one would hear of it. I was informed the Hyatts and the Gallaways would work it out among themselves, and I was to keep my nose out of it. Martha threatened me with something about finding the largest stick she could carry and hunting me down. The hunting part didn't sound so bad, but the catching up with me part sounded rather grim, so I agreed to do as they said."

Larissa didn't know whether to laugh or wince at Ethan's narrative. She did neither as she said hesitantly, "And Charity? I suspect she wants to come along."

He looked directly into her eyes. "That's my doing. The Gallaways assured me, several times, she would be most welcome to stay with them. But it just didn't sound right, leaving her behind and the rest of us going and, yes, meeting up with Mac." He reached to cup her chin as she blushed. "It's all right to let seeing him be part of this trip. Seems to me it's only natural."

She blinked. "You're starting to know me only too well."

His lips quirked upward. "I'm looking forward to seeing him, myself. And I'm not even his mother."

She maneuvered her hand to cover his where it lay on the table. He studied their joined fingers. "You don't mind, then, including Charity in this trip?"

She shook her head. "It would be cruel to leave her out. She needs to know what's happening, just as much as the rest of us. Besides, she'll be companionship for Rose."

The light in his eyes sparked brighter. "You're starting to know me only too well. I was thinking along those very lines, with one slight deviation." He reached inside his sweater-vest again and drew out a folded paper. When she didn't ask the obvious question, only waited for him to continue, it was his turn to experience difficulty in getting his words out in the proper order.

"You haven't said anything, but I know you well enough to realize you're wondering. It is possible for us to go on this trip without being married. But that's not the way I want it. I don't think it's the way you want it, either. When I talked to Shawn, he filled this out." He slid the still-folded paper across to her and watched intently as she opened it. Her eyes widened.

"A marriage license." She tried to continue, only to have the words come out in a gasp. "But when? There isn't time before we leave on Monday!" The paper fluttered in the breeze of her wildly waving hands.

He rescued the license and laid it carefully on the table between them. "Tonight?" he asked brightly.

The absurdity of his response shocked some sanity back into her. "Ethan, you can't mean it."

Uncertain whether she was hopeful or distressed, he cautiously reached for her hand again. She didn't pull hers away, which he considered an encouraging sign. All levity gone, he laid his plans before her. "Shawn said he can marry us tomorrow, right after church. This way, most of the folks we'd want to invite will already be right there in town. I don't know much about putting together a fancy party afterward, but Martha said she'd take care of it. I expect the rest of the day will pretty much sort itself out."

"Martha said so, did she? Seems to me a lot of folks are taking a mighty lot for granted, when the bride hasn't even said yes."

Ethan stood, but made no move toward her. "The groom is hoping with all his might she will."

She eased from her chair and rested her head against his chest. "Yes." She whispered it against his heart, and the arms enfolding her drew her closer still. He put his cheek against her hair, and she felt his breath sigh out. He tipped her face up to his. Their lips had barely touched when the rush of feet and Charity's joyful squeal thoroughly startled them.

"She must have said *yes*!"

Larissa pulled back but his arms firmly drew her close again. Calmly ignoring the interruption, he once more bent his mouth to hers. Only after a long, magical moment, he raised his head enough to murmur, "Nothing in this world was going to make me miss out on an opportunity like that." Resignedly, his arm still holding Larissa close to his side, he turned to deal with his suddenly-silent daughter.

She and Rose had retreated through the doorway to the sitting room and were standing, one on each side. Only their heads were visible as they peered around the frame. Both were staring, clearly weighing a heretofore unimaginable concept. *Could people as old as their parents possibly know anything about romance?*

CHAPTER TWENTY-TWO

The next morning, Larissa woke earlier than usual, and lay quietly for a time, sorting out her thoughts. With awareness this was the last time she would sleep in the bed she and Zane had shared each night of their marriage until he went to war, she touched the pillow beside her. Weeks past, knowing Ethan must, then and in the future, come first, she had put her wedding ring and Zane's picture away in the small trunk where she kept the various treasures of her life. She intended to pass the sketch on to Mac, just as the quarter-eagle pendant and chain Zane had given her before their marriage would become Rose's.

It was not guilt or even sadness that came to her at this parting from Zane. He would have been the first one to urge her to live to the fullest and embrace the happiness Ethan was offering. She felt, rather, wistfulness, and deep thankfulness for the years she and Zane had shared. Because he had shown her what it is to truly love, she knew she had nothing to fear in loving Ethan.

It was still early, but she decided to begin her breakfast preparations. She suspected time would fly by this morning, and she'd better get ahead while she could. Since she'd never finished the gown she intended to wear for her marriage, she'd decided on the violet-blue dress Ethan liked because, he said, it matched her eyes. She wore it only on special occasions. *If this isn't a special occasion, then I don't know what is!* Ethan's words came so clearly, she turned to see if he was standing behind her. He wasn't, so she continued musing as she chose an old red calico she could spill as much as she wanted down the front of while fixing breakfast, straining milk, and doing sundry other messy morning chores. In her dressing table mirror, she surveyed the much-washed material. *It's a bride's prerogative to wear what she wants on her wedding day.*

Hurrying down the hall, she roused the girls, who hopped out of bed on her first call, forcing her to stifle a motherly urge to check their foreheads for fever. At the kitchen door, she was greeted by a clanging and banging that turned out to be Ethan lowering the cook stove lid over a snapping fire.

Catching sight of her, he abandoned lid and flames. "I woke up a while ago and decided I might as well make an early start getting the chores out of the way." He followed her gaze to the contents of the milk pail sitting on the bench. "It was a great idea until I decided to milk Bluebell." He smiled guiltily. "I don't know if it was the early hour or my cold hands, but she didn't take kindly at all to my inspired plan."

"I don't blame her," Larissa said crisply. "Men just don't understand how important it is for us women to get a full night's rest."

He'd been walking toward her during this admittedly peculiar discussion. Now he drew her into his arms. "Why are you up so early, then?"

"I couldn't sleep, either."

She raised her mouth to his. Their lips had barely touched when a voice chirped behind them. "Do all married people spend so much time kissing?"

Ethan's mouth hovered above Larissa's. "Please tell me I didn't hear what I just heard."

"You didn't hear what you just heard."

"Thank you. Excuse me a moment while I strangle my offspring. Charity, have you gathered the eggs this morning?"

"Oh, Pa, there aren't any eggs! You know the hens aren't laying this time of year."

"Go look anyway. You might be surprised."

"He's trying to get rid of us," she said indignantly to Rose. "All right, Pa. We'll look for your pipe some more." Her voice drifted back from the sitting room. "I think we're going to be doing an awful lot of pipe hunting from now on."

"Come to think of it, Martha's hanging by the toenails idea just might have some merit, after all." Larissa ducked her head to hide her laughter as he turned back to her. "Where were we?" he murmured. "I remember, now." He bent to her once again.

"Do they?"

He raised his head in confusion. "Do they who?"

"Do all married people kiss this much?"

His lips touched hers. "Only if they're very, very lucky."

***

True to Larissa's prediction, the hands on the mantle clock circled so fast, she was amazed the numbers weren't one big blur. On the way upstairs to change, she shooed the girls ahead of her and warned them not to dawdle. Once in her room, however, she didn't follow her own advice. She dressed quickly, but lingered before the mirror, fretting over her hair. Twisting the heavy chestnut mass into a figure-eight coil at the back of her neck, she pulled a few strands free in front of her ears and curled them to frame her face. The young woman she had been twenty years ago looked out at her from the mirror. She would have redone it immediately, but had no more time to fuss. *At least it's not my usual boring bun stuck on the back of my head.*

Leaving the room, she paused to look back for a long moment before quietly shutting the door forever on that part of her life.

Ethan, at the bottom of the stairs, watched her descend, his face giving no doubt of his approval. He took her hand. "I surely do like that color on you. It matches your eyes."

He wore a black wool suit she had never seen. His white shirt with the stiffly starched high collar, and the carefully tied black neck cloth were also new. "You look wonderfully fine, yourself."

"I feel wonderfully fine." He brushed his fingers against her cheek. "I expect knowing I am a most fortunate man has a lot to do with it." He tucked her arm under his, pressing her close to his side on their way to the kitchen. He stood in the center of the room and pivoted with her until they completed a full circle. No offspring in sight. Assured they were alone, he drew her to him. "Lizzie, are you…?"

"Looks like we better go pipe-hunting again, Rose."

He spoke through gritted teeth. "Do you know anyone who wants a thirteen-year old daughter? I have one I'll be happy to sell, cheap."

Larissa truly understood his frustration, but was hard put to hide her amusement. The girls, hanging over the stair banister, obviously had a clear view into the kitchen.

"If you want, Pa, we can go gather the eggs the hens aren't laying this time of year." Charity's totally innocent-of-any-wrongdoing offer didn't improve Ethan's mood.

"That sounds like an extremely wise decision."

"You don't have to go away." Larissa hastily cut across his meant-to-be-obeyed suggestion. "We're not doing anything you shouldn't see." She choked to a stop as she realized what she'd said. Her strategy worked, however. Charity and Rose looked blank, but Ethan's annoyance disappeared as his eyebrows and the corners of his mouth shot upward.

Larissa felt the color rush to her cheeks. It was the first time so far today she had blushed. But she felt a strong premonition that it wouldn't be her last.

***

On the road to town, she was so busy being embarrassed about her slip of the tongue, she didn't notice at first that the usual non-stop chatter from the buggy's backseat was missing. Instead, the girls were quietly discussing the upcoming trip. It took a minute for her to realize the significance of their actions. Earlier, they had showed acceptance of the marriage by their little-girl teasing. Now, on the way to the wedding, they showed their respect by behaving like the mature young women they were rapidly becoming. Uncertain whether Ethan was aware of the phenomenon, she turned her head ever so slightly.

"I noticed. Quite a nice wedding present, isn't it?"

Garth must have been watching for them as they pulled up to the parsonage, because Ethan hadn't even brought the team to a full stop before he hurried down the path.

"Morning, Mr. Michaels, Mrs. Edwards." He halted beside the inhabitants of the backseat. "Hi." He didn't gulp, but he swallowed carefully.

Covertly, Larissa watched Rose's first encounter with the outside world since her hearing loss. Garth raised his voice enough to carry, but he didn't shout or stare at her. Larissa breathed a prayer of thanks that Martha's son was the one to share this experience with Rose. What could have been an awkward situation passed without embarrassment for either one.

He colored slightly as he assisted each girl to the ground, but stuck manfully to his duty. One on each arm, he delivered them safely up the slick path to the porch steps, where his mother waited. Once they were in Martha's care, however, he hustled back to the buggy and casually put one foot up on the near runner. "I'll tend the team, Mr. Michaels." His voice cracked, but when Ethan surrendered the reins, his eyes glowed as no young woman had yet caused them to do.

As Garth stepped to the horses' heads, Ethan's glance met Larissa's. "A fine young man," he murmured. "Any father would be proud to have him for a son, or a son-in-law."

"I would like nothing better, one day. But, please, not for a few years yet."

"Amen," he said fervently.

Shawn and Martha greeted them cheerfully and quickly drew them into the warm hallway. "It's just a little too cold out for comfort. You must be frozen stiff with the long ride."

"I really didn't notice it being cold at all. You know how everything else just flies out the window when you have one thing on your mind." A tiny pool of silence that made her want to jump feet first into its watery depths followed Larissa's sprightly response. For the second time that day, her cheeks flamed. In sheer disbelief that she had done it again, she raised stricken eyes to Ethan.

"I quite have to agree with you." The gravity in his voice was deep and sincere, but he couldn't quench the spark flickering deep in his eyes.

"Come to the kitchen," Martha interjected hastily. "The hot water is all ready for tea." Mortified, Larissa was only too happy to follow her down the hall. Behind her, Shawn, with only a faint catch of laughter in his voice, ushered Ethan into the study. The girls disappeared with Gretta and Mara, who showed no trace either of her recent encounter with the measles, or her twin's short-lived barbering career.

The kitchen door safely shut behind them, Larissa sank into a chair and buried her burning face in her hands. "I don't know what's the matter with me! Everything I say seems to come out wrong."

Martha put a steaming cup of tea in front of her friend. "It'll be all right. Brides are allowed to say all sorts of things that folks wouldn't think twice about any other day. Everyone thinks it's so cute." She curled her lip.

Larissa had raised her head as Martha began her soothing speech. Now the two friends eyed each other and burst into laughter. "Oh, Martha, I needed that. You have such a way of putting things into perspective."

Martha laced her fingers across the newly noticeable roundness of her waistline. "Without a doubt, my perspective of life is expanding rapidly. Remember, not long ago, I was where you are now. I still don't believe some of the things that came out of my mouth sounding one way when I meant them entirely another. Of course, everyone was quick to pick up on the wrong meaning. Then they'd make everything worse by pretending not to be thinking what they thought I was thinking, even when I wasn't thinking it."

She curled her hands around her hot teacup. "Speaking of things coming out wrong, I want to apologize for the other day. I had no right to squawk at you. Can you forgive me?"

"There's nothing to forgive. I tried to be mad, but I just couldn't stay that way when you were so absolutely right. Because you squawked, I'm here today, where I truly want to be. I'm not so sure I would be, otherwise."

"I'm so glad. My big mouth sometimes gets me into big trouble. But the last thing I want is to harm our friendship."

"You couldn't harm our friendship with a sledge hammer," Larissa said inelegantly. "My own big mouth needs your understanding too much."

Shawn popped his head through the doorway. "It's time to go over to the church. The youngsters are rounded up and waiting in the passageway."

"Thank you, Shawn. I'll be right there." His head disappeared. "I hope you don't mind, Larissa. We always walk over to the church with him. This way, we have a little time to be just like any other family going to Sunday services."

"I don't mind. I think it's a wonderful idea."

"We'll take Charity and Rose, if you like. Then you and Ethan won't have to come over just yet. When you're ready, you can go through the passageway to the church instead of going outside." She paused at the door. "I recall how difficult it was on our wedding day for Shawn and me to have even a few moments to ourselves." She smiled impishly. "I suspect you'll find a way to fill the time." She ducked out before Larissa could answer.

"Lizzie?" Ethan poked his head into the room.

"I'm here. Everyone else is on the way to church."

With a hesitation puzzling to her, he sat in Martha's abandoned chair. "Lizzie, I wanted to talk to you earlier, but it didn't work out. Before we go to church, I need to ask you a question."

"I'll do my best to answer."

"I know you've had some doubts about the wedding," he said carefully. "I just want to make certain you really want to go through with it this morning. With the Philadelphia trip and all, I rather railroaded you into the decision, so to speak." He began fiddling with Martha's napkin ring.

"I have had some qualms." At her confession, his fingers stilled on the ring he had been sliding around his thumb, but he didn't speak. "These past days, all my coping and strength have gone into Rose's needs. I'm so worried the little energy I have left won't be enough." She felt the pesky blush rising again, but determinedly ignored it. "You have every right to expect so much more from our marriage."

He closed his eyes and sat perfectly motionless. When he opened them, they held such a mixture of love and tenderness that her breath caught. "Lizzie, I...." He had to back up and begin again. "Believe me, don't ever worry whether you're giving your 'share' in our marriage. What we have together is right and good, no matter what."

Dropping the napkin ring, he moved swiftly around the table and took her in his arms. She rested her head against his chest and heard his heart beat sure and strong under her cheek. He kissed her temple. "We should probably be going over now. Are you all right?"

She gently touched his bearded jaw. "I have to admit, I feel wonderfully fine."

***

Forever afterward, Larissa couldn't remember a word of the church service, until Shawn announced at the conclusion that the wedding would take place in an hour. As the congregation murmured in surprise, everything came sharply into focus. Once again, events happened with whirlwind speed. Martha whisked her away to the parsonage and propelled her upstairs to freshen up.

Larissa went meekly. She didn't bother to argue because no one was listening to her today, anyway, except when she blundered. Martha opened her bedroom door and gestured for her to enter first. Charity and

Rose, standing beside the bed, wore the white, lace-edged dresses tied with red sashes that Martha had offered to finish. Large red bows perched at the crowns of their heads. Larissa blinked. "Girls, you're beautiful. Martha, I didn't realize—"

"Happy wedding day!" they chorused, stepping apart to reveal something spread out on the bed behind them.

The something proved to be her wedding gown, now completed. "Martha." Words failed her as she gazed at the dress of her dreams now become reality.

"You'd better see if it fits."

"Try it on," Rose urged.

Gretta and Mara, who had been standing back watching, now rushed forward with the others to assist her slipping into the dress. "It fits beautifully." The girls sighed with rapture.

Martha tipped up her dressing table mirror. "Come see." Larissa stepped to the glass and looked twice before realizing it was really herself. Against the soft apricot silk, her skin glowed. The ruffled neckline curved gracefully about her throat and shoulders. The sheer overskirt, a shade darker than the underskirt and bodice, looped across the front of the dress and gathered full at the back, beneath the tight-fitting waist that accented her slender figure. Behind her, Martha pinned a matching cascade of tiny roses into the crown of Larissa's hair.

"Oh, Martha," was all she could manage as she embraced her friend.

Martha surveyed the results of her labor and her eyes twinkled. "It would be nice to take all the credit, but I can't. When everything turned completely upside down for you, and I brought the girls' dresses home to finish, I had no idea everything would suddenly turn over sideways for me, and that I wouldn't be able finish them, either. When Ethan and Charity sneaked your dress to me yesterday morning, all the church women got together and sewed the girls' dresses. But I told them I wanted to do yours myself. Then they turned around and took care of things here at the parsonage so I could finish your dress without cooking and cleaning interruptions. So it's really a gift from all of us, a way we can all share our happiness at your happiness."

***

Martha and the four girls went downstairs, leaving Larissa to descend by herself. As earlier, Ethan stood by the bottom step. This time, however, catching his first glimpse of her, he looked quizzically past her up the stairs as if seeking the violet-blue gowned Larissa he had entrusted to Martha's care. His gaze skidded back to her and his mouth moved, shaping her name, but no sound emerged.

She paused on the last step and he took her hand. At the mixture of bewilderment, wonder, and love chasing one another across his features, her heart did a little dance of joy. "Happy wedding day, Ethan."

The low-voiced greeting cleared away some of his dazed confusion, but the wonder and love remained. "I surely do like this color on you."

"Thank you for not saying it matches my eyes."

The corners of his mouth turned upward. "It doesn't match them, but it definitely likes being around them."

Martha had been standing discreetly back. Now she came forward and touched Larissa's arm. "Shawn's just going over to the church. If you come along the passageway again, you can stand outside the church door and he'll let you know when it's time to go in." She hustled off with the girls.

Neither Ethan nor Larissa spoke as they waited in the short hallway, but when they heard someone unlatching the door from the other side, Ethan bent to her ear, murmured, "I love you," and quickly straightened. She had no time to respond as the door swung open to reveal the sea of faces of their waiting guests. Shawn motioned them forward and they took their places before him.

Unlike the church service just past that Larissa would never be able to recall, every word of the simple marriage ceremony etched itself upon her heart. Pronouncing them husband and wife, Shawn advised Ethan that he could kiss his bride. Neither one had given thought to a church full of people watching them carry out this particular instruction, but, one and all, they were obviously waiting.

Ethan brought his mouth close to Larissa's, murmured, "At least we're used to an audience," and kissed her, briefly but enthusiastically, before everyone surged forward to wish them well.

In the ensuing happy confusion, Larissa caught sight of Rose and Charity standing back uncertainly, watching. She touched Ethan's sleeve for him to follow her gaze, then held out her hands. The girls dashed forward, but suddenly stopped short. "We have a wedding present for you."

Exchanging a nod that set their red hair ribbons bobbing, they chorused, "Happy wedding day, Ma!" Then, "Happy wedding day, Pa!" before they flung themselves into their parents' arms. Larissa had thought her heart was stuffed to the top with joy. She realized how mistaken she was as she and Ethan held their daughters close and their eyes met above the girls' heads.

Most of the gathering drifted toward the parsonage to continue the party, but Ethan and Larissa were delayed in the church by the last of the lingerers. Ethan's arm circled Larissa's waist as she talked to Bernadette

Colville, one of the women who had help sew the girls' dresses. Thus, she didn't see the guest who came up on Ethan's other side.

"Lizzie." She turned questioningly to find Ethan shaking hands with Doc.

She reached out to him. "We're so glad to see you. We were hoping you'd be able to come."

He grasped her hands in both of his. "I wouldn't have missed it for anything. Or anyone. The sign on my office door says, 'Until you see me coming back, I'm gone.' And now, Ethan, I'm going to avail myself of an old man's privilege." Very carefully, as if he were afraid she might break, he put his hands on Larissa's shoulders and bent to kiss her. Before he could release her, she slipped her arms about his neck and hugged him tightly.

"Thank you for everything, Doc." She kissed his cheek, and, behind his snowy beard, he turned bright red.

With all the bluster he could manage in a futile effort to hide his unwonted emotion, he growled, "Larissa, if this popping-his-buttons-with-pride fellow gives you any trouble at all, you just let me know. I have a potion or two that'll fix his wagon right up."

"I'll remember," she assured him.

"I'll remember, too." Ethan drew her close to his side. The look he gave her caused Doc to clear his throat noisily.

"I haven't got time to stand around here watching the two of you make the finest couple I've seen in many a year. I'm sure I have ailing folks piled three-deep on my doorstep."

"You can't be leaving already. Aren't you coming to the party?"

"A long time ago, I made it a rule never to attend fancy shindigs." Seeing their unspoken disappointment, he sighed. "Every time I mingle with society, someone gets me in a corner and wants free medical advice that they won't come to my office and pay for. The cheapskates." Since Doc was notorious in Fairvale for dispensing medical assistance with or without payment, oftentimes the latter, Larissa and Ethan saw right past his crankiness.

She touched his sleeve. "We'd really like you to come, but we understand."

He looked at her hand resting affectionately on his arm. "Hell and damnation," he muttered. "Why not? It's either hold consultations here or on my doorstep. At least here, I can eat someone's cooking besides my own while I'm listening."

With Doc in tow, they returned to the parsonage to find the party in full swing. The church women had supplied platters and dishes overflowing with food. Larissa and Ethan wandered from group to group, unfortunately unable to take full advantage of the edibles because every time they took a bite, someone else would come up to wish them well.

At one point Larissa, seeking Ethan, glimpsed Doc boxed into a far corner of the parlor. Plate in hand, he was listening resignedly to Sylvie Mayhew, the town's undisputed hypochondriac, list her woes. Taking pity, Larissa edged to his side. "I'm sorry to interrupt, but I need your help, Doc. Could you please come with me for a minute?"

"Certainly. Please excuse me, Sylvie." Doc backed away so fast, Sylvie didn't realize he was gone and continued her description to the air where he'd been standing. Larissa led him into Martha's blessedly empty-of-people sewing room and shut the door.

"I'm sorry. That wouldn't have happened if we hadn't wanted so much for you to come celebrate with us."

He set his plate on the candle stand beside the door and waved away her apology. "Don't worry about it. You rescued me. If she'd come to the office, I'd have been a dead duck. I think I will be going now, though." He surveyed her intently. "A sight to warm even the most cantankerous doctor's heart. You're the picture of health and happiness. In a hundred years, I couldn't have prescribed a better medication than what's taken place today."

"Thank you. More than words can ever say."

"You'd better go find that husband of yours," he said gruffly. "I'll make my own way out."

Stretching up on tiptoe, she once more brushed her lips against his beard. Hand on the doorknob, she turned back to see him pressing his fingers to the spot she had kissed. "It's a bride's privilege," she said softly, and hurried out.

All the guests had gone. Not seeing Ethan, she made her way to the kitchen, where she found Martha adding the last dried plate to a towering stack. "Martha, isn't anyone helping you? You sit down and let me do that."

Martha looked weary, but she laughed. "Absolutely not! This is one day you are not going to do dishes. Besides, I'm finished. I'll get Shawn to put these away, and a cup of hot tea will fix me right up." Overriding Larissa's anxious protest, she put the kettle on to boil and sank gratefully onto a chair. "I think it was a good party."

"It was a wonderful party. I don't know how we'll ever be able to thank you."

"Just be as happy with Ethan as I am with Shawn. I couldn't ask more than that." As if on cue, Shawn stuck his head through the doorway.

"Larissa, Ethan's looking for you. Are you all right, Martha?" He crossed to his wife and bent anxiously over her. With Martha's reassuring reply, Larissa slipped out into the hallway. Finding all the other rooms empty, she turned the knob of the sewing room door.

Ethan, watching out the window with his back to the room, didn't hear her come in. She shut the door quietly and looked at this man who had been her husband for a little over three hours. As so many times before during this day, her heart gave a little skip of joy. She touched the doorknob, making it rattle slightly, and he turned.

Crossing to her in three strides, he curved his palm against her cheek. "Have I told you today how beautiful you are, Mrs. Michaels?"

Several times since the wedding, she had said her name to herself, getting used to the newness of it. Hearing it this time from Ethan, it still startled her, but her lips curved into a radiant smile. "I think you've brought it up once or twice, but if you want to be absolutely certain, you can mention it again."

He touched a curl in front of her ear. "You are so beautiful, and I love you so very much." For the first time that day, there were no children and no curious onlookers as his mouth found hers.

CHAPTER TWENTY-THREE

Ethan raised his head from Larissa's kiss, and the sewing room slowly settled back into focus. "Over three hours. A mighty long time to have to wait to kiss my wife properly."

"I hope it was worth waiting for."

His slow smile gave its own answer before he said huskily, "It was worth waiting for." He led her toward a well-worn leather chair positioned across from a rocker beside Martha's sewing table. Pausing beside the larger chair, he raised a quizzical eyebrow. "I suspect they don't expect us to appear any time soon. My feet certainly wouldn't mind sitting for a while." He leaned back into the chair, drew her against his chest and exhaled gustily. Beneath her cheek, his heart beat steady and sure as they drowsily shared this first quiet space of their married life.

Finally, he stirred. "You asleep, Lizzie?" She nodded against his coat lapel. He brushed a kiss against the top of her head. "In that case, I hate to wake you, but we should probably let Shawn and Martha know we haven't eloped out the window."

"We can't elope," she murmured contentedly. "We're already married."

"I recall something about 'what God has joined together.' I do have some plans for later that I'm hoping will appeal to you, but keeling over from starvation is definitely not on the list. I understand the hotel serves excellent suppers. So can we please go find something to eat?" he finished piteously.

"Married less than a day and already making demands," she said sadly. "Does this mean the honeymoon is over?"

"Not on your life!" The finality in his voice left no room for argument.

Her eyes crinkled with laughter. "Since you put it that way, I expect we'd better go."

The house was quiet, but light spilled from the study. Shawn, seated at his desk, writing, lifted his head. A warm smile lit his features. "Come in."

"We just came to tell you we're going now."

Martha, feet tucked under her, was curled up on the sofa, a bright-worked afghan covering her lap. "I'd invite you to supper, but I hear you have a better offer. The girls will be fine, so go celebrate."

Larissa bent to hug her. "Thank you for everything."

Martha hugged her back with deep affection. "I'm so happy for you," she whispered. Then, in a normal voice, she shooed them out the door. "I cry easily enough these days. Don't get me started now!"

"Please, Lord, no," Shawn said reverently, so that the Gallaways' delighted-for-them laughter followed Larissa and Ethan into the frosty evening air.

The lamplighter, making his rounds through the drifted snow, melted into the shadows down the street, and they had the starlit sky to themselves as they strolled the block to the hotel. In the dining room, the waitress showed them to a quiet corner and deftly whisked away the "reserved" sign before she seated them. Larissa glanced around at the sea of empty tables and Ethan grinned. "Just wanted to make sure we had the best seats in the house." As they ate, they talked about the day's events, Rose and Charity's "happy wedding day" gift of love, and Doc's transparent gruffness.

Finally, Ethan paid the bill, left the waitress a generous tip, and asked Larissa quietly, "Shall we go?" The brightness of her eyes was evidently a completely satisfactory response, for he wasted no time in gathering their coats and escorting her to the hotel lobby desk.

Larissa beside him, he asked for the room key and signed the book the clerk turned toward him. Once out of earshot of the desk, he said in a low voice, "When I worked here, I passed keys to young couples a hundred times and asked them to sign the register. But I never thought about how it felt to be on their side of the desk—until tonight."

The upstairs hallway, lit by candles flickering along the walls, was deserted as he inserted the key into the door. With a flourish, he tossed their coats inside. Turning, he lifted her into his arms and carried her over the threshold, economically pushing the door shut with his foot.

She slipped her arms about his neck. "Have I mentioned today how very much I love you?" Apparently she had. Also apparently, by his response, he hadn't tired of hearing it.

At last he carefully set her on her feet. She rested her head against his chest and he cradled her against his heart. "Lord a' mercy," he said simply. It took a while before he could breathe without sounding like he'd just finished a five-mile foot race. Keeping one arm around her, he gestured to the two bags on the bed. "The carpetbag's yours. Martha sent over some things for you. My stuff's in this one. I'll go on down the hall and be back in a little while." He kissed her, gently this time, and the door shut behind him.

She listened, but, with the hallway carpeted, couldn't hear his footsteps receding. Turning slowly, she inspected the room and its furnishings. She felt the water pitcher and found it pleasantly hot. The light from the candle on the dresser flashed against the gold ring on her finger, and she bent toward the flame to look more closely at the gleaming circle. The mirror shivered slightly with the movement.

She stepped to the glass and, startled by the woman looking at her, touched the image questioningly. The morning's young woman of twenty years ago was gone. This mirror-woman's eyes glowed with happiness and a radiant smile curved her lips. Larissa watched her for a long moment before turning quickly to the bed and reaching for the carpetbag.

Sitting before the mirror a little later, brushing her hair, Larissa again studied her reflection. She wasn't entirely certain who'd put in an appearance this time, but suspected it was a bit of both the younger woman and the older. Wonderingly, she touched the lace-edged neckline of the nightgown she had found in the carpetbag, a gown bearing no resemblance to the high-necked, serviceable cotton variety. She'd never seen such light, filmy material. *If Martha wore something similar on her wedding night, no wonder her new "perspective of life" is rapidly expanding her waistline!*

The doorknob turned slightly. "Lizzie?" His low voice carried clearly to her waiting heart.

She rose. "Come in."

"It's clouding over again," he reported, shutting the door and setting down his traveling bag. He wore a dark red dressing gown and kidskin slippers. "Hopefully, it won't...." He turned to her, then, and took one sharp-drawn breath. He stood motionless, his silence clearly saying everything that words could not. His eyes smiled and his mouth slowly curved upward. He crossed to her, very lightly brushed the back of his hand across her cheek, and traced her lips with the same feathery touch. "Lizzie."

With her name, he echoed all the wonderment and love filling her own heart to overflowing. Raising her face to his, she saw reflected all the anticipation and desire spilling from her own soul. As his mouth met hers, remembrance of all those months she'd worked so hard to keep her yearning under polite, civilized control skidded past her. Imperceptibly, *some day* had melted into *here* and *now*.

Wild, fierce gladness swept through her.

***

Larissa awoke to sunlight filtering into the room. Accustomed to beginning her day well before sunrise, she couldn't even remember the last time she'd slept this late. During those first seconds of returning consciousness, she was fully aware of Ethan, stretched out beside her, and that she was curled close to his side, her head resting against his shoulder. His quiet, relaxed breathing indicated he still slept. Even in sleep, however, his arms encircled her protectively.

Her heart and her body remembered the night just past, remembered the exultation that swirled through her as she learned the strength of his arms and the strength of his love enfolding her. She closed her eyes at the wave of bliss that engulfed her. Ever so careful not to wake him, she pressed her cheek deeper against his shoulder and settled her body closer to his.

She was sure she'd scarcely moved, but in quick response, his embrace tightened. "Morning, Lizzie."

"I didn't mean to wake you."

His chuckle was only a breath against her hair. "You didn't. I've been lying here, wanting to wake you, but I remembered what you said about women becoming perturbed when their sleep is disturbed. I certainly didn't want to be the cause of my wife falling into such a fate this morning of all mornings."

She raised her head. "Do I look perturbed?"

He brushed a strand of hair back from her temple. "No, Lizzie. You don't look perturbed at all."

She discovered marriage had not cured her of that vexing tendency to blush.

***

Ethan had gone to the men's bathing room. Larissa made a last, hasty check in the mirror to ensure she was put together properly before they went to breakfast. Martha's trusty carpetbag had come through once again. Last evening when she discovered the nightgown, she also found the violet-blue dress she'd intended to wear for the wedding folded carefully into the bag. For perhaps the hundredth time, she blessed Martha. Her thoughtful planning and small touches had freed Larissa of any worries over "women's necessities." Practical matters had, obviously, also occurred to Ethan, who had planned so hastily, yet so mindfully. Between the two of them she hadn't even thought to fret, but had let the day unfold as it would. *It's probably a good thing, too, since I was so rattle-headed.*

She heard the door open and, in the mirror, saw Ethan coming toward her. Standing behind her, he slipped his arms around her waist. She leaned against him and they studied their reflection. "What was it Doc said?" Ethan's breath was warm against her ear. "We 'make the finest couple' he's seen 'in many a year.' I've never known his opinion to be wrong, and I'm certainly glad he agrees with me on this one."

His arms tightened for a moment, then relaxed. "I passed the dining room on the way back here. They're serving breakfast, but I'm not certain for how much longer."

"Does this mean you're hungry again?" she asked in mock disbelief.

"Sorry. I guess the food here just doesn't measure up to the good cooking I'm used to, so I didn't eat as much as I normally do." Having neatly sidestepped his first marital pitfall, he wasted no time in ushering her out the door.

They found the dining room more crowded than last night, but the waitress, a different one, escorted them to "their" table. Larissa raised her eyebrows inquiringly, but Ethan just shrugged, completely mystified. "They must think we're a fine couple, too." She caught the slight upward twitch of his lips, but as if on cue, the waitress materialized with coffee. She eyed the fragrantly steaming pot and, with wifely generosity, decided not to comment further.

Finished eating, they lingered over their coffee. She touched the gleaming gold circle on her finger. "It's beautiful. You knew exactly which one is perfect."

He put his hand over hers on the table. "One other came close, but I kept going back to this one. I think by the time I decided, Enos Gibson was ready to throw me, and the rings, out of his store." His fingers tightened around hers. "We probably should get back to the parsonage. We have a lot to do before the train leaves this afternoon."

"I've been so spoiled not having to make any decisions, I've been trying to avoid admitting it's time to go."

He glanced around the still-crowded dining room. No one paid them any mind. "A room full of people isn't the best place to discuss this, but I suspect once we leave here, life is going to get hectic again, and I want to say this before any more time passes."

"Is something wrong?"

He heard her anxiety and said quickly, "Nothing's wrong. Everything is so right, I keep thinking I'm going to wake up and find it's not real, after all. I knew you were deeply worried about Rose, and utterly exhausted, too, from these last weeks. But I didn't know you were concerned about us. It never even occurred to me. I told you what we have together is right and good, no matter what. I want to say now, and for always, I just hadn't learned how incredibly good our 'right and good together' would be."

"I forgot all about being tired. I'm so glad to know my level of leftover energy has been adequate." She couldn't keep the hint of mischief out of her voice.

He started to speak, but had to try again before the words came out properly. "'Adequate'? Jumping jackrabbits!"

It wasn't the most romantic of responses, but it was eloquent. When he finally got his tongue to cooperate, he said quietly, "I hope you don't mind how I went ahead and planned everything without even asking you. It was pretty highhanded, but you'd had such a bad few weeks, I just wanted to give you a space of time where you wouldn't have to make decisions and have to be there for everyone else. Martha agreed. But now, looking back, maybe it wasn't right."

It was her turn to attempt to put words together in the proper order. So many emotions crossed her face so rapidly he couldn't sure of any of them. "'Right'? Jumping jackrabbits," she said softly.

***

Larissa waited while he left an ample tip for their beaming waitress, paid the bill, and collected their bags. On the walk back to the parsonage, both silently savored these last moments, mindful that the outside world was about to close around them again.

Upon their arrival at the parsonage, events swirled together for Larissa like the white and chocolate in her marble cake batter. Greeting Rose and Charity. Attempting to find words to thank Martha and Shawn. Garth's reluctant return of the rig and team to Ethan. The ride home, and the farm looking strange and new after only one day's absence.

Once home, they plunged into their pre-departure tasks. Everyone tackled a different chore, but Ethan and Larissa passed once in the center of the kitchen and, backing up, held each other for a joyful moment before continuing in opposite directions.

During the return trip to town, Larissa's thoughts continued to somersault. *How many items have we forgotten to bring?* Fairvale's train station came into view. Mac had departed on a gold-and-bronze autumn day. Now, snow blanketed the landscape in all directions, except for the shining tracks that would take them to Philadelphia. *Was it really only a few short months ago that Mac left, all of us so unknowing of the future stretching ahead?* Much as the shining train tracks stretched into the unseeble distance....

They entered the welcome warmth of the small waiting room, and Larissa's muddled musing broke off as events snapped sharply back into focus. Shawn and Martha, with the four children, waved their greetings from one of the wooden benches. Doc stood behind them. Charlotte Sullivan, the schoolteacher, stood rigidly beside Doc.

The Gallaways surged forward, leaving Doc and Miss Sullivan to follow in their wake. It took several moments for everything to straighten itself out.

Martha handed them a box tied with twine. "Just some sandwiches and cake. We had a wonderful party at the parsonage yesterday, as you may remember. Now we have so much food left over, you'll be doing us a huge favor to take some with you."

Garth removed his hat and eyed Ethan imploringly. "Mr. Michaels, Reverend and Ma said if it's all right with you, I can take care of your team and wagon while you're gone. If we stable the horses at the parsonage, I can tend them and make certain they get their exercise." He looked to Shawn and Martha, who both nodded.

Larissa's smile confirmed her opinion and Ethan said, as if greatly relieved, "That's a fine idea. This way I know we won't have to worry about them at all."

Garth looked as if they'd just handed him the moon and the stars, but only said with manly gravity, "I'll take good care. You can depend on it."

Doc cleared his throat. "I came to tell you I'm going to Philadelphia, too. Not today," he blurted, seeing their blank astonishment. "They've asked me to come to the University so we can consult face to face on Rose's case. They want to show me some techniques that lose considerably in telegraphic translation, but that will, hopefully, prove valuable in the future if I'm not too old to learn them. I found out this morning." He scowled as if they'd accused him of purposely planning it. "Unlike some folks, I can't just pick up and leave. It'll take a day or so to turn my practice over to Gustav Ingemar over in Delaware County, so I won't be interfering in any way with your wedding trip."

Ethan swallowed wrong and gave a choking cough. When he got his breath back, he said seriously, "Well, Doc, we certainly wouldn't have cause to worry about it. Rose and Charity are coming with us. A couple who includes their daughters on their wedding trip certainly wouldn't think twice if their doctor joins them, too."

Now Doc choked and turned fiery red. Shawn and Ethan vigorously whacked him on the back until he emitted a squawk that sounded reasonably close to, "Enough already!" He pulled his black coat into place and shook his finger in their faces. "I recall mentioning yesterday to a certain fortunate fellow that I'd mix him a certain potion if he didn't behave. Between the two of you, it appears I'll have to double the dose!"

The younger children stared in awe. Garth's ears turned red and he bent hastily to swat some imaginary dust off the knees of his pants. Larissa and Martha turned their backs, but their shaking shoulders clearly indicated their uphill battle to quell their laughter.

Miss Sullivan, lips pressed into a thin line, wearing her sternest air, failed deplorably to maintain it. She stepped into the breach, her voice strangely breathless. "Rose and Charity, I brought these." She handed them a bulky package wrapped in brown paper. They took it warily, and she said grimly, "School books and lesson plans. We can't have two of my best pupils falling behind in their studies." She looked at both of them as she spoke, but now she turned directly to Rose.

"When you return, we'll work out a way for you to continue your lessons." Rose stared at her, uncertain whether she had heard correctly. "You won't have to give up your schooling. That's a solemn promise." With that, stern Miss Sullivan turned, and, with straight-backed dignity, walked out of the station.

The light on Rose's face mirrored Garth's earlier rapture. She clutched the package of books and wouldn't give it up even in the confusion of final farewells and boarding the train.

With the girls each settled beside a window in the seats directly ahead of their parents, Ethan eased down beside Larissa, who had not taken her eyes from the luminous joy on her daughter's face. His gaze followed hers. "I gather from our daughters' reports on school activities that if Miss Sullivan makes a promise, she sticks to it, and woe unto anything or anyone who attempts to stop her!"

"I've never seen one person's face hold so much happiness all at once. It's as if Miss Sullivan just handed Rose a key to the gates of Heaven and said, 'Enter.'"

His thumb traced the curve of her cheek. "Then I guarantee you haven't looked in a mirror in the last few minutes."

***

The trip proved long and wearisome as the train plowed through the countryside. Twice they were forced to stop while the men and crew went out to shovel snow off the tracks, where the wind had blown it into drifts higher than the locomotive itself. Added to these delays were the necessary stopovers and train changes as they chugged their way east.

Fortunately, the train was not full to capacity. As the evening wore on, Rose and Charity each stretched out on a nearby seat to sleep. Larissa and Ethan didn't fare so well. They attempted to nap sitting up, but every jerking movement of the cars jarred them awake. He had insisted she take the wall corner in the hope that the impact would be less for her with something to brace against.

Sometime before midnight, Larissa was dozing when a particularly hefty jolt caused her to pitch forward. Grabbing for her, Ethan summed up his personal opinion of their situation in one crystal-clear word. After making sure she wasn't hurt, he took her hands. "Slide over this way." Wearily, she did as he instructed. He edged past her, settled against the wall, and pulled her into his arms so that her head rested against his shoulder.

Tired, shaken to the marrow of her bones, she raised up and, in the dim light provided by the candles along the walls, inspected the car. She didn't resist as Ethan pulled her back down and settled his arms firmly around her. His breath stirred the hair at her temple. "It's midnight. No one's watching, and no one cares. Even if they were, and they did, all I have to say is polite society be damned. If they think this is scandalous, it'd boil their bacon for sure if they knew what I'd really like to do."

She clapped her hand over her mouth, but a sputtering laugh escaped her. Firmly removing her hand, he covered her mouth with his. Her eyes glowed in the light of the flickering candles. "It's been so long since you've kissed me, I was afraid I'd forgotten how."

"Believe me, Lizzie, you haven't forgotten. But it certainly never hurts to practice."

***

In the morning, it was evident Charity and Rose had slept better than their bleary-eyed parents. Ethan and Larissa, working the kinks from their stiff muscles, watched their daughters bounce cheerfully from one activity to another, and wondered if they would ever again feel such energy. The girls spent quite a while examining Miss Sullivan's books and papers and disagreeing on who would be the teacher, and who the pupil, of their impromptu school. *Has Rose realized that her plans to teach have faded along with her hearing?* Larissa gave the thought a rude push into the far corner of her heart and slammed the door on it.

The girls also spent considerable time pretending they weren't aware of three young males, apparently traveling with their parents, a dozen seats away. This knowledge necessitated frequent trips to the water bucket on the bench at the far end of the car. Larissa and Ethan observed from the sidelines, but Charity and Rose behaved discreetly each time they sauntered past the young men. Once they arrived at the water bucket, it took them a long time to quench their thirst. Ethan chuckled. "At this rate, they'll become waterlogged before the day is done. If they drink the bucket dry, the conductor won't be very happy. It's forty miles to the next stop."

Morning became mid-day. To Rose and Charity's dismay, the masculine trio left the train at Harrisburg. Luckily for the conductor's peace of mind and for the other passengers' parched throats, the frequent trips to the water bucket tapered off dramatically.

During the ensuing hours, Larissa scanned the bleak world outside the window without seeing it. Deliberately, she tamped down her awareness that, soon now, Mac would be with them. Instead, she concentrated on her daughter's prospects. By cruel circumstance, opportunity had become a windowpane through which Rose might view the world, while forbidden to cross into the sunshine on the other side. Now, unseen hands had raised the sash a few inches, allowing in the sparkling possibility that Rose would, indeed, learn to "hear" the world around her. Remembering Miss Sullivan's uncompromising stand, Larissa's throat tightened. She strongly suspected never again would Rose or Charity complain about their teacher's unbending ways.

Afternoon slowly worked its way to evening as the train equally slowly worked its way across the Pennsylvania countryside. In spite of Larissa's determination, the closer they came to Philadelphia, the more thoughts of Mac elbowed in. He hadn't been at the wedding to see or touch, but he had been in her mind and heart every bit as much as Rose and Charity were physically present. Never one to thrust his emotions upon another, she silently repeated the words of the telegram he'd sent. *Happy Marriage Day to our family.* Brief as it was, the simple phrase confirmed, more than a volume full of words ever could, Mac's acceptance of their two families becoming one.

She was startled out of her reverie by Ethan settling onto the seat beside her. Although the space was sufficient for Larissa and the girls, it was cramped for his greater length. As several times before, he'd stretched his legs by a walk through the other cars. "Ethan, what do you think will happen when Charity sees Mac?"

His jaw tightened. "I've been wondering, too. She seems to be fine with you and me now, but after that tantrum last fall, I'll admit I'm more than a little skittish."

"With so many other emotional crises these past weeks, I wonder if she's even had a chance to sort out how she really feels about him now."

"I dare say she's matured and gotten him out of her system," he said with perfect masculine logic. "There's no denying she has strong emotions. When she's happy, the world knows it; and when she's unhappy, the world knows that, too."

They were supposed to reach Philadelphia by early evening, but another drift blocked the tracks, once again forcing the men to get out and shovel. Larissa was sorely tempted to jump down and do a little snow-flinging herself, just to hustle things along.

An eternity or so after they'd dug their way out of this latest delay, the conductor announced Philadelphia Station. Larissa, ready for the last hour, clutched Ethan's hand as the train slowed.

"Lizzie, it's all right. We're almost there."

His soothing encouragement steadied her, and she even managed an embarrassed laugh. "I know I'm being ridiculous, but it will be so good to see him."

He slipped his arm around her in a comforting hug. "You're not being ridiculous. To tell you the truth, I've been wanting to get out and push the train along faster myself."

CHAPTER TWENTY-FOUR

With Charity lugging their belongings and Rose clutching the package of books, the conductor assisted them down the portable step to the station platform. Such a grown-up gesture caused them to beam with delight, never suspecting, because of their burdens, he probably did it primarily to keep them from falling flat on their noses.

Larissa's feet touched the platform, but after riding in the lurching passenger car for so many hours, on reaching firm ground, she swayed. Descending behind her, Ethan's hand under her elbow steadied her as she looked around, blinking in the brightness. It was close to midnight, but torches fastened on posts gave so much light they had no trouble seeing. Her eyes swept the crowded platform, but with the mix of people, she didn't see Mac.

"Ma!"

She, and half a dozen other women, turned. *Zane.* For one wild moment, her heart stopped, then started with a jerk as Mac reached her and wrapped her in a bear hug. "I'd started to think the train had gone the wrong direction. I'm sure glad you're here!"

Long gone were the days when she had cradled him in her arms. Now his arms circled her easily and her nose didn't even reach his shoulder. The others surrounded them, and he shook Ethan's hand. "Good to see you, Mr. Mich—" The habit of years died hard. His ears turned red.

Ethan's eyes twinkled as he gripped Mac's hand. "'Ethan' will do just fine, son." They exchanged a look Larissa found totally incomprehensible, but which the two men obviously understood perfectly. A message was passed, received, and agreed upon, all in masculine silence.

Before Larissa could sort it out, Rose hurled toward Mac. "Shadow." His name for her when she was small and followed him everywhere slipped out easily.

"You haven't called me that for a long time. I thought you'd forgotten." Her pleased amazement clear, she threw her arms around him in an exuberant hug.

"I'd like to know what you've done with my baby sister." He spoke over her head to Larissa who, when Rose didn't react, touched her ear and tipped her chin toward her daughter. Comprehension and dismay flashed across his features, and were as quickly gone. He swallowed, put his hands on Rose's shoulders and looked down at her joy in seeing him. He bent and said in a puzzled but clear tone, "Excuse me, Miss. I'm looking for my baby sister. Have you seen her?"

Her quick laugh was interrupted by Charity, who had been taking everything in. "Hi, Mac." Her voice held awe. Larissa and Ethan watched intently as she greeted this young man who had not reappeared as the boy she had pined for.

"Speck!" He hugged her, much as he had Rose, and her cheeks turned pink. He dug in his pocket. "See this?" She stared at the shiny buckeye seed she'd given him "from a friend" just before he left last fall. "I've not only kept it, I take it to all my exams for luck."

The pink in her cheeks became a full-blossomed blush, but he didn't notice as he drew forward the young man standing back watching the excitement. "Family, this is Jeff Kinsley. He's taking the medical course, too."

"Pleased to meet you, Mrs. Michaels, Mr. Michaels." His handshake was warm and firm. "You must be Charity, and you're Rose. I'm very glad to make your acquaintance." He tipped his hat to them. Charity translated for Rose, their eyes growing big at this man from the city who greeted them as if they were attending a Philadelphia social event.

Mac gestured toward the station waiting room. "I remember the trip only too well, and I didn't have to contend with snow. Ma, if you'd like, you and the girls can wait inside while we collect your baggage."

Larissa happily complied. Now that the reunion had taken place and anticipation no longer buoyed her up, cold and fatigue were setting in. The next half hour passed in a haze as Mac, Jeff, and Ethan retrieved their luggage and got all of them into a hackney cab. A baggage-piled dray wagon followed close behind.

Leaning her head against Ethan's shoulder, Larissa watched her son in sleepy contentment as he explained he had booked them into a hotel near the University. With several places to choose from, tomorrow they could decide if they wanted to stay there or perhaps take rooms in a boarding house. At the moment, Larissa honestly didn't care, as long as she could have a bed in a room that didn't sway, wasn't coated with wood ashes, and didn't reek of stale cigar smoke.

Jeff glanced out the window. "We're here." While Ethan checked in, with unassuming capability, Jeff helped Mac carry everything upstairs to the third floor and locate their rooms, which proved to be around a corner and midway down a long hall. They deposited the bags in the small sitting room between the bedrooms. Once all the luggage put in an appearance, Jeff stuck his head through the connecting doorway on the right wall of the sitting room. "If Rose and Charity are going to be in here, I suggest you prop a chair under the knob of the hallway door." Without undue drama, he answered Larissa's silent question. "This is a respectable hotel. But you are in the city now. Taking extra precautions never hurts."

"It's sound advice," Ethan said soberly. "We'll heed it." He shook hands with both young men and stepped back.

Mac hugged Larissa goodbye, but his attention strayed to the room beyond the connecting door, where the girls' voices floated out as they arranged their belongings. He flinched. "You telegraphed me. I should have been prepared. But...."

"I know. Everything seems so normal, I forget, until one of us says something and she doesn't respond."

"Has anyone said if they can help her to hear again?"

"Doc said they made it very clear they can't restore what she's lost. He also told us they won't know until they examine her whether she'll retain the hearing she has left." She pressed her lips together to keep them steady. "He's been completely honest with us all along. If he knew of any hope at all, he would have told us."

"There are fine doctors here. Some of the best in the country."

"Doc says so, too. We're holding on to that."

"Ma, I want you to know—" He shifted his feet awkwardly, "I'm glad about you and Ethan." He kissed her cheek, and he and Jeff were gone down the hallway.

She shut the door and rested her forehead against the panel, storing his words in her heart.

***

At their appointed hour of eight thirty the next morning, Oliver Terrell ushered Larissa, Ethan, and the girls into his office at the University Hospital. He turned to a man with graying black hair, whose vivid blue eyes rested calmly on each of them in turn. "This is Lawrence Cornell, the head of our Otolaryngology Department, which, I assure you, is just a fancy name for ear, nose, and throat doctoring." Dr. Cornell shook hands, uttered a quiet greeting, and stepped back, relinquishing the discussion to his colleague.

Dr. Terrill shook hands with Ethan and clasped Larissa's hand in a firm grip. "Mr. Michaels, Mrs. Michaels, I can't tell you how much we appreciate your making the trip here. Please, have a seat."

Larissa was becoming more used to her new name, but it still startled her to hear it when her attention was elsewhere. Ethan, alertly watching her reaction, raised his eyebrows, revealing the unmistakable gleam in his eyes.

Fortunately, Dr. Terrill had turned to the girls and thus missed this exchange. Ethan suddenly developed a frog in his throat, so his voice came out slightly rusty. "Our daughters, Charity and Rose."

Oliver Terrill, having observed Charity speaking into Rose's ear, neatly stepped between them, put out his hand and spoke in a normal tone. "So you're Rose. We've been hearing a lot about you."

Without Charity to translate, uncertainty skittered across her features, but she hazarded a guess from his outstretched hand. "I'm pleased to meet you, sir."

In a natural movement, he faced Charity directly. "We've been hearing about you, too." Charity looked as if she didn't know whether that was good or bad. He returned his attention to Rose, whose unruffled expression indicated she didn't even realize he had spoken to Charity. Resting his hands on his knees, he bent toward her. "I understand from Dr. Rawley that you girls are good friends."

"Even better," Rose said proudly. "We're sisters, now."

"Friends and sisters. An unbeatable combination." A sharp rap on the door caused everyone, except Rose, to glance toward the back of the room. Dr. Cornell, hurrying to answer as the rap came again, returned with a folded slip of paper. Dr. Terrill read it and frowned. "Tell them I'll be right along. I'm most sorry, but an emergency requires my immediate attention. Dr. Cornell teaches a nine o'clock class, but he'll send someone to give you a guided tour of our facilities. Please excuse me." Only the words remained. He was already out the door.

Dr. Cornell resembled a man who has just been handed a screaming infant and told to tend it. "I'll send someone—that is, if you'd like to see the hospital." Taking their nonplused silence for assent, he grasped Ethan's hand and smiled bashfully at Larissa. "We'll talk to you later this morning." He, too, fled.

A few minutes later, Mac poked his head around the door. "I heard some folks would like a tour of the hospital. Do you know where I can find them?"

"Mac!" Larissa's delight was plain, but so was her instant mother-worry. "Don't you have a class?"

"I do. With Dr. Cornell. But he sent me here. When your professor tells you to jump, you jump. Especially when it's something you'd really like to do."

Leading them along the school hallways and hospital corridors, Mac gave them a running commentary, interspersed with stories that brought to life his daily activities as his letters could not. After showing them his dormitory's reception area, he paused. "They've a strict rule about not allowing females upstairs, but I suspect they wouldn't dare banish somebody's mother." He grinned mischievously. "Since sisters aren't really females, I guess you two can tag along."

In a woeful abandonment of her new-found maturity, Charity stuck her tongue out, huffily turned her back, and translated for Rose.

Respecting the rules, they lingered just long enough to glimpse the room he and Jeff Kinsley now shared. He carefully pointed out to Larissa his neatly made bed and the clothes folded and put away. "See, Ma, I did listen all those times you got after me for my messy room."

He pulled out the watch and chain they had given him the first Christmas after he began his studies with Doc Rawley. At the time, the chain had required several loops. It now curved smoothly across the front of his waistcoat. "Sorry, but we'd better head back. I have an exam this next hour I don't dare miss, professor's permission or not."

He returned them safely to Dr. Terrill's office, hugged Larissa and was off to rejoin the medical world. *His world now.* Larissa's heart rejoiced for him, but she couldn't stop the wistfulness accompanying the knowledge. The little boy who had mended broken wings and tended, so it had seemed, all the scrapes and bruises in the animal kingdom, was gone forever. But the man who took his place was fulfilling the promise of that little boy's sure, gentle hands, and she knew she could ask no greater attainment for him.

About the time the girls started squirming in earnest during the protracted wait, Oliver Terrill hurried in, apologizing profusely for the interruption. As Dr. Cornell once more silently stood to the side, Dr. Terrill motioned to the girls. "Did you meet Methuselah? If you'll go with Dr. Cornell, he'll introduce you while I talk to your folks."

Having heard none of this, Rose turned to Charity, who leaned close and explained. Looking to Larissa and Ethan for permission, they followed Dr. Cornell out.

"Methuselah is our resident skeleton," Dr. Terrill confided in a hushed voice. Picking up his pencil in a habitual gesture, he became serious once more. "Dr. Cornell will discuss the technical details with you later. To give you a brief overview, we know that, far too often, deafness follows an illness such as your daughter's, in which a high fever is sustained. Dr. Cornell has been conducting research to shed light on *why* it happens and what we doctors can do to prevent it from happening to other children. That's why we're particularly glad of this opportunity to examine Rose. Her illness is recent, and we know beyond question she received the finest medical care from Dr. Rawley."

Contemplating the pencil, he considered his next words. "I don't know how familiar you are with Abe Rawley's background. As students together, we all worked hard, but we had a run for our money keeping up with him. He could have had a brilliant hospital career, but he chose, as he put it, to 'be of some real use to folks.' We've kept in touch all these years. His perspective on a part of the world we don't see, here in the city, has been invaluable. I tell you this to explain why we hold him, and his work, in the highest esteem."

Several of the instinctive *knowing*, without knowing *why*, puzzle pieces fell into place for Larissa, but she had no time to consider them as the doctor continued. "After receiving Dr. Rawley's report, and the news that you would be bringing Rose here, Dr. Cornell and I discussed her situation at some length. Dr. Rawley has conveyed to you that we cannot restore Rose's hearing. As an alternative, we can offer her the tools she needs to maintain her rightful place as an integral, functioning member of society. Have you heard of Melville Bell or Edward Gallaudet?"

Their responses were equally blank. "These gentlemen have opposite schools of thought concerning the deaf and communication. Even though the deaf person cannot hear his own voice, Mr. Bell, and his son Alexander, teach the deaf to speak and to read the lips of those speaking to them. They believe this is the key for the deaf to succeed in a hearing world. Dr. Gallaudet, conversely, advocates that the deaf should be free to communicate among themselves through a language of hand signs, conveying the thoughts and feelings of the non-hearing person into a visual image." He paused over his next words.

"Following this morning's emergency call, Dr. Cornell and I again conferred about Rose's situation. At this point, our personal observations concur with Dr. Rawley's detailed report. Both confirm Rose's diminished ability to respond to normally pitched conversation or sound. We will conduct thorough tests, of course. In light of these findings, however, we are duty-bound to suggest you send her to the American Asylum for the Deaf. It is an excellent school, I assure you. She would be taught to sign and to live in a deaf world. But realistically, after completing her courses, upon her return home to your small town, she would have no one with whom to sign, and thus would be isolated from both the deaf and the hearing worlds.

"Mr. Bell's method of teaching the deaf to speak and read lips, so that sign language is unnecessary, is also to be commended, particularly because Rose retains her ability to speak. Unfortunately, there is no state-supported school offering this instruction. It is being planned even as we speak, but is not yet a reality. The few private schools that teach this method have long waiting lists."

The beginning glow of hope in Larissa's eyes quenched and she flinched as from a physical blow. Ethan reached over and covered her clenched fingers with his. Neither one spoke, but Dr. Terrill saw clearly that everything that needed to be communicated between them had been said. He gave a mental nod to the unconventional alternative he and Larry Cornell had been debating. "However, by considering both of these options, we are given a third possibility. Weighing Rose's existing abilities and her current circumstances, we believe a combination of sign and speech will be to her best advantage. It will enable her to continue living at home." He paused at Larissa's quick indrawn breath, and the twinkle in his eyes nudged aside his professional demeanor. "A factor which, I gather, would be considered a most welcome benefit. It will, of course, be necessary for you to learn to sign, even though Rose must be encouraged to continue to speak. You will hear her voice. She will read your signs and lips. This combination will enable her to 'see and hear' the world.

"A young man, who can hear but cannot speak, works here at the hospital. A number of us have learned to communicate with him by using a hand alphabet, spelling words by using a different shape of the fingers for each letter. He also knows the sign-word method, a faster means, with practice, of carrying on a conversation. He is willing to instruct Rose. All of this is, of course, subject to your agreement."

Larissa turned to Ethan. "The hand alphabet must be the one the girls were talking about." Neither one noticed Dr. Terrill's quiet smile of affirmation at the catch of excitement in her voice. "I've no doubt Rose will want to learn this method." With this positive commitment to her child's future, after all the uncertainty, such extraordinary lightness filled Larissa that she set her feet firmly, afraid she would float out of her chair.

Now smiling broadly, Dr. Terrill rounded his desk, hand outstretched. He shook with Ethan and clasped Larissa's hand. "That's good to hear. We'll tell Hans Druid and he can get started, perhaps even this afternoon." The door latch clicked. "Excuse me while I have a word with Dr. Cornell."

Larissa opened her mouth to share the happiness of the moment with Ethan. As she shaped them, the words died. He was staring at the carpet, but obviously seeing something much farther away. She put her hand over his on the chair arm. Dragging himself back from that distant place, he slowly turned his head.

Even then, she wasn't completely certain he saw her. Her heart gave a frightened jump, and the earlier lightness vanished as quickly as a burst soap bubble. Before she could say anything, Rose and Charity descended on them, both chirping at once. Her body now felt so weighted, she might have been mired in quicksand. Distracted, she did not at first grasp what either girl was saying.

"—says you want to talk to us."

"—never believe what we saw."

The two doctors stood beside the desk, obviously wanting to get a word in edgewise.

Larissa's motherhood button clicked. Numbly, she heard herself hushing the girls and telling them to sit and let the doctors talk. They actually did so, and she sent up an incoherent prayer of thanks.

Dr. Terrill bent to Rose. "As much as we wish we could, we cannot bring back your hearing. But we can help you to 'hear' by teaching you hand signals for words. Would you like to learn these signs?"

Rose lifted her face to his. A depth of grief too old for her years hovered there. "Doc already told me you can't fix my hearing. May Charity learn the signs, too?"

Sitting beyond Ethan, Charity suddenly found several pairs of eyes riveted on her. Reasonably certain she hadn't done anything wrong, she still fidgeted nervously. "I promise to be good," she squeaked.

Along with the others, Larissa had swung her attention toward Charity, which brought Ethan into her line of vision. She wanted to slump with relief. His focus was on his daughter. Whatever it had been, then, he had put it aside to give himself to the moment at hand.

Dr. Terrill beamed. "An excellent idea. We'll get things started. I believe Dr. Cornell would like to begin examining Rose this morning, if possible?" He turned to his associate.

Dr. Cornell's mouth curved upward, chasing all the solemnity from his features. "The sooner the better. With the nature of some of the tests, this examination will take place over several days. I must work around my teaching schedule, so the times may be a little erratic." Secure in the familiarity of his medical work, he spoke more words than they had yet heard from him. The flow squeezing off as suddenly as it had started, he motioned for Dr. Terrill to take over.

"We'll work up a schedule. For now, Dr. Cornell will show you where he will do the examination, and give you more particulars about what he'll be doing. After that, if you can stop by my office, I'd like to discuss a few more details."

Dr. Cornell took them to his laboratory, introduced his assistant, and proudly showed his modern equipment and explained its purposes. Finally assured that Rose felt comfortable with her surroundings, he leaned down. "If you're ready, we'll begin."

Larissa hugged Rose and retreated with the others to the hallway. Events turned a little hazy for her after that, since her heart was with her daughter, but after they returned to Dr. Terrill's office, his recital of Hans Druid's story settled firmly in her mind.

"Ten years ago, when he was six, he was riding one afternoon with his parents in an open carriage. The horses bolted. He was thrown clear, but hit his head against a rock, rendering him unconscious. His parents were killed instantly." Larissa's horrified exclamation cut across his words.

He recounted how Hans was taken to City Hospital, where they treated his head injury. However, he remained unconscious for several days. When he awoke, they discovered that although he could hear and respond normally in every other way, when he tried to talk, the words came out garbled. In time, his head wound healed, but his ability to speak did not improve.

"The doctors concluded the blow to his head caused permanent injury to the part of his brain controlling speech." Because he was now homeless, with no known relatives, the hospital made arrangements to send him to the state orphan asylum. "One of the doctors who had treated him suggested they send him instead to the American Asylum at Hartford, Connecticut, a school for the deaf."

There, although he was not deaf, he learned to communicate without speech. The plan worked well, until he completed all his courses and was required to leave the school. Once again, his home was pulled from beneath his feet.

"A teacher to whom Hans had confided his dream, hopeless as it was, of becoming a doctor, contacted our medical school to find out if we could cure his speech disorder. During the transfer of information, the teacher let drop Hans' obvious intelligence and his dream of practicing medicine."

Dr. Terrill described how the doctors had examined Hans and determined they could do nothing about his garbled speech. However, because of his deep-seated interest in medicine, they allowed him to stay on, doing odd jobs for his keep and absorbing a surprising amount of the medical knowledge flying around him.

"I know I've given you a rather lengthy recital of Hans' background, but I wanted you to understand the circumstances and the obstacles he has overcome to arrive at the fine young man he is today. We've consulted with him and he is willing to instruct Rose, if you agree. Because Rose retains her speech, in our considered opinion, with her family intending to learn to sign, and by utilizing lip reading, she will not have to wait for the world to come to her. She will be able meet the world on her own terms.

"Subject to your approval, we feel confident Hans Druid is the answer you, and we, are seeking."

CHAPTER TWENTY-FIVE

Late in the afternoon, Larissa and Ethan emerged from the hospital's patient admissions office after slogging through the tangle of paperwork confirming their permission for Rose to participate in Dr. Cornell's research. Dr. Terrill hurried toward them, followed by a young man with curly black hair and deep brown eyes.

"I'm glad we caught you before you left. I'd like you to meet Hans Druid." His tall, slender companion gave Larissa a shy smile, clasped her fingers, and put out his hand to shake Ethan's. She saw the hesitation, so slight as to be barely discernible, with which Ethan responded, and her heart gave the same frightened little jump it had earlier. He did not withdraw to a far place, this time, but his eyes held a shadow that was, in its own way, just as remote.

Hans' fingers moved. Dr. Terrill chuckled. "He says, 'I'm most pleased to meet you, and I'm impressed with your hands.'" They looked at him blankly. Hans turned red and once more flicked his fingers. "'For signing. I assure you I say this with the highest respect. Since signing is a vital part of my life, hands are one of the first things I notice.'"

"Thank you, Hans. It's good to know that we're starting off with an advantage, even if it's a small one."

Hans beamed at Larissa's understanding. Again he motioned and Dr. Terrill interpreted. "'Will I meet Rose soon? I'm looking forward to starting her lessons.'"

"She's finishing with Dr. Cornell, and Charity's waiting there for us to pick them up." Larissa paused for Ethan to make the obvious offer for Hans to accompany them. He hesitated perceptibly before doing so. Hans quickly accepted. Dr. Terrill apologized for not joining them, but explained he had an appointment scheduled.

Hans led them through the maze of hallways, and, to be conversational, in light of Ethan's silence, Larissa asked him about the finger alphabet. He carefully demonstrated, so that by the time they reached Dr. Cornell's laboratory, she could shape the letters of her name. Hans smiled as proudly as if he, personally, had achieved this success.

They collected Rose and Charity. Rose seemed subdued but, distracted by Ethan's odd behavior, Larissa put it down to general weariness and introduced the girls to Hans.

Using paper and pencil, he conveyed that their first lesson would begin the following morning. The arrangements made, he took his leave, unaware of his two young students' admiring glances following him down the hallway. Rose perked up and she and Charity put their heads together for quite a while as they discussed his various charms.

Mac had reluctantly refused Ethan's suggestion to join them for supper. With another big exam scheduled in the morning, he and Jeff needed to spend the evening studying. Protesting that they must eat, regardless, Larissa promised if they joined the family, she would not keep them once they finished the meal. Mac proposed meeting in the hospital dining hall, where the food, he assured them, if not as tasty as Larissa's, was still good.

Mac and Jeff were waiting when they arrived. Jeff apologized for intruding, but Larissa assured him they were delighted he could join them. As the meal and the tales of the doctors-to-be unfolded, Rose shed her quietness and Ethan threw off his gravity. True to her promise, when they finished eating, Larissa shooed Mac and Jeff off to their studies. The long, wearying day finally behind them, she was only too glad to accept Ethan's suggestion to return to the hotel for a quiet evening.

Coming out of Charity and Rose's room, she found him standing by the window. She doubted he was aware of the gauzy curtain or the noises of the city world beyond. She paused beside him, unsure what to say.

He slipped his arm around her. "Tired?"

She nodded against his shoulder and sent up a silent prayer for the words she needed. "Are you all right?"

She felt him tense, but he merely said, "I'm tired, too. It's been a long day for all of us."

She tilted her head. "For most of the day, I've had the feeling that something's bothering you."

The shadow flicked in his eyes. "Am I so obvious?"

"Probably not to the rest of the world, but I'm afraid you're stuck with me. If you want to talk, I'm here."

"I know. It's just hard to arrange the words."

"Is it Hans Druid?"

He sighed. "Married four days, and already you know me so well."

In spite of her uneasiness, her lips twitched. "You think this is bad, just wait until we've been married forty years."

"I hope each of those forty years takes an eternity to pass." He parted the curtain slightly to stare beyond the window. "I told you about Andrew."

Her throat tightened. So rarely did he speak of his and Nettie's son, who had died at four months of age. "I didn't tell you Nettie's nickname for him. At first, we called him 'Drew', after my father, Andrew. But he'd get a look on his face that was so solemn and serious, Nettie said 'Drew' just didn't suit him. So she started calling him 'Druid', because he looked like such a wise little old man."

The tightening in her throat became an unbearable ache. "Oh, Ethan," was all she could manage. On tiptoe, she put her arms around his neck and pulled his head down to rest against hers.

"I've always known I needed to be prepared, because someday I'd meet someone with Nettie's or Andrew's name. We have to take life the way it is. I just never expected life to have such a fiendish sense of humor."

***

Long after Ethan lay sleeping beside her, Larissa remained awake, the day's events tumbling through her mind. The final, searing knowledge … *Rose's hearing loss is undeniable and unchangeable.* The jolt she'd received last night at the train station as Mac hurried toward her. *So much the image of you, Zane, during the young years of our marriage, faded by daylight's reality but not entirely vanished, each time I look at your son.* Ethan's time of reckoning over his own son. *Who could have foreseen it would arrive under such circumstances?*

Her spinning thoughts finally quieted. She curled closer to Ethan and fell into a deep, dreamless sleep.

"Ma." The insistent whisper and a tugging at her shoulder dragged her up from the depths. "Wake up."

She forced her eyes open. As she moved, Ethan stirred, but did not wake. Still fogged with sleep, she saw a white-nightgowned form standing at her side of the bed. In the light from the streetlamp, Charity's face screwed into desperation as she again shook Larissa's shoulder. "Please wake up!"

"Charity, what's wrong?"

"Rose won't get into bed, and she won't tell me why."

The leftover mists of sleep vanished. Larissa eased her feet to the floor and threw a shawl around her shoulders. Charity pulled at her hand and hurriedly led the way across the sitting room to the girls' room. The diluted glow from the streetlamps showed their empty bed. Charity pointed toward the curtain, and Larissa made out the figure huddled on the window seat, arms wrapped around her drawn up knees.

"You go back to bed where it's warm." Protest flitted across Charity's features, but she obeyed. Burrowing under the covers, she lay watching attentively. Larissa touched her daughter's shoulder. "What's wrong, Sprite?"

Rose's only response was to hug her knees more tightly against her chest.

"If you tell me, maybe I can help. Did something happen when Dr. Cornell tested you this afternoon?"

Rose flinched, but still would not look at her mother. A hundred half-thoughts formed and faded in Larissa's brain. *Had Dr. Cornell—?* "Rose, you must tell me what's wrong." She prayed her rising panic was not audible in her voice as she spoke directly into Rose's ear.

As if unable to hold her despair inside any longer, Rose suddenly flung up her head. "When will I lose the rest of my hearing?"

The question was far from Larissa's thoughts, and shock stabbed her with a vicious thrust. "What do you mean?"

Haltingly as the words came, their import was clear. "Dr. Cornell said he was sorry that the tests he was doing wouldn't … help me keep my hearing. He said it was so important to do the tests and … I was so brave to do this to help other people so they wouldn't go completely deaf. Ma, I don't want to be brave. I don't want to take the tests and lose … the rest … of my hearing." The words were a wail as her rigid self-control crumbled. "Please don't make me! I want to be able to hear, even if it's only a little bit, like it is now."

Larissa had thought she'd drunk of all the bitterness and grief possible in Rose's situation. Her daughter's anguish told her quite plainly she had not yet come to the bottom of the cup. Forever afterward, she didn't know how she forced the words past her aching throat. "Sprite, listen. Doing these tests will not make you completely deaf. Dr. Cornell hopes testing you will help him help someone who becomes sick, like you did, not to lose any of their hearing. Actually, he said this afternoon he's very pleased, because he believes your hearing level hasn't decreased since Doc examined you several days ago. You remember Doc is coming to the hospital because Dr. Terrill and Dr. Cornell urged him? He might be here by tomorrow, and they'll compare notes. Dr. Cornell says if his findings are confirmed, the chances are very good you will continue to hear as much as you do now."

Rose's inward struggle with hope, and the fear of hoping too much, showed plainly as she searched her mother's face.

"It'll be all right, my Christmas Rose. It really will be." Larissa pulled her onto her lap and rested her chin on top of her daughter's head. Giving a shudder that seemed to rise from her toes, Rose relaxed and buried her face against her mother's shoulder. With no strength left to do more, Larissa cuddled her and sang softly against her ear.

"Sleep, my child, and peace attend thee …
Hill and dale in slumber sleeping…
I my loved one's watch am keeping,
All through the night."

Rose's ragged breaths gradually eased and Larissa was finally sure she slept. For a long time, she continued to rock her and sing softly against her ear.

***

Ethan blinked his eyes open, not certain what woke him. The room was quiet and peaceful. His slight movements had not disturbed Larissa. *Lizzie.* How right and natural it had become, even after only these few days and nights of marriage, for her to be at his side. Drowsily, he stretched out his hand to her. And came fully awake. Her side of the bed was empty and she was nowhere in the shadows of the room. He thrust aside the covers. Not finding her in the sitting room, either, he padded across to the girls' room. A lump under the blankets turned out to be Charity, sound asleep, and alone in the bed.

The shadows created by the still-glowing coals in the fireplace shifted at a slight movement of the curtains. He realized with a start that the dark shape at the end of the window seat wasn't, after all, Rose and Charity's piled-up belongings. Larissa slumped in the corner, her clasped hands around Rose, curled up on her lap. Both slept. Trying not to scare her, he gently squeezed her shoulder. "Lizzie."

Her eyes opened slowly, before she recognized him and awareness returned. "Rose."

"She's right here. She's asleep. Let me take her." He lifted her unresisting weight and laid her beside Charity. Making certain they were both snugly covered, he bent again to Larissa. "She's out like a light." At this reassurance, she once more slumped into the corner. "It's cold here, Lizzie. Come back to bed."

She stood, but her knees were so stiff from sitting in the same position, with Rose's weight on her lap all that time, they wouldn't hold her up. He swung her up into his arms. "First Rose, then me. Your new family is certainly making you work hard. I wonder if Mac will be next?"

"My new family is worth every ounce of effort, and more. Although I do draw the line at carrying Mac. I rather suspect he could carry me and not lose a breath. Not that I intend to find out any time soon." He eased her down onto their bed and sat beside her. "He's a fine young man. You have every right, and then some, to be proud of him."

She touched his bearded cheek. "I had excellent help. I couldn't have done it without my new family."

"Rose and Charity have certainly taken to married life. I believe Rose's saying this morning that they're 'better than friends, they're sisters' rather neatly sums up their acceptance of our marriage, and their affirmation that they consider both of us their parents." He brushed a stray wisp of hair off her forehead. "I don't want to push, but I know for you to go to Rose this way, something troubled her deeply. If you want to talk about it, I'm here." Her earlier words echoed faintly, and he smiled. "I'll have you know, a beautiful woman made me the same offer a while ago, and I'm certainly glad I took her up on it." In the dim light, he couldn't see her expression clearly, but he felt a shiver go through her as her arms crept around his neck.

"Hold me, Ethan."

Wordlessly, he stroked his fingers against her cheek and lay down beside her. He drew her head against his shoulder, and she curled into his warmth. "It's all right, now, love." Clearly, whatever had happened with Rose, it was still affecting Larissa deeply enough that all her light words couldn't brush it away.

With knowledge born of having done this before, he simply curved his arms around her and pressed his cheek to her hair. Once before, he had lain with her and given her his own body warmth. By events beyond his control, he had been compelled, that time, to draw back, to let her go, alone, to fight her soul-deep torment. His embrace tightened at the bleak memory of that forced-upon-him abandonment. *Nothing this side of hell, or the other side, either, for that matter, will ever again push me into shutting her out of my arms.*

He felt her move slightly. "Ethan?"

"I'm here. I was hoping you were asleep."

"No. Just thinking."

"Thinking is good," he conceded.

"It's strange how the same words can mean something entirely different to two people."

He waited.

"Dr. Cornell said one thing, and Rose literally heard him say something else." A little haltingly, trying to convey Rose's anguish, she told him what had happened.

He gave a low whistle. "That interpretation certainly came out of the northeast."

"We've told her all along to listen carefully and do exactly as the doctor instructed, even if it seemed a little strange or uncomfortable." Her voice quivered. "It appears she did exactly that."

"It also appears you were able to set her straight."

"I think so. But for her to go through that kind of anguish, alone...."

"You didn't know. She didn't tell us. We've seen how our Dr. Cornell tends to talk a little technically. No wonder she got confused. One important fact at this moment is that she understands the truth. The second important fact is that you helped her understand it, so there's no need for you to carry any guilt about it."

She buried her face against his neck. She didn't say anything for so long, he was sure she slept. He was dropping off when her voice came low but clear, close beside his ear. "Remember last fall, the first night after Mac left? You told me you couldn't take away my pain, but you wanted to be there for me. It made you feel so wrong, because the times I needed you the most, you weren't there."

"I remember."

"I said your being with me, right then, was all that mattered. You're here with me now, too." Her last words were little more than a murmured breath as her mouth found his in the darkness. "And I'm so glad."

***

The following morning, Larissa and Ethan accompanied Rose and Charity to their signing lesson. Hans Druid, by pencil and paper, had conveyed the importance of their learning the signs along with the girls. It would enable them to communicate directly, even though spelling each word was more time-consuming. Yesterday, he had showed Rose and Charity the alphabet. Although Rose's preoccupation last night had hindered the girls' progress, this morning they made up for it by practicing almost non-stop. They had argued heatedly over a few of the shapes, only to find they were both wrong, and Hans patiently went over them again. Thus, they were far ahead of Ethan and Larissa, still floundering as they attempted to make their balky fingers obey.

After lunch, Larissa was basking in her success at slowly signing all twenty-six letters without a mistake, when a rap at the door was followed by Doc Rawley sticking his head into the room. "Is this a private party or can anyone attend?" Hans watched in bewilderment as his four pupils abandoned ship without a backward look.

"When did you get in?"

Doc looked resigned as Ethan and Larissa asked together, but otherwise let it whiz harmlessly over his head. "Last night or early this morning. The details are hazy."

"You've been in town all morning and are just getting around to letting us know?"

He scowled at Larissa's indignation. "I told you I wouldn't pester you." He tugged at his beard. "Besides, I've been conferring with Dr. Cornell." He pushed past them and bent to Rose. "I've been hearing very good reports about you, young lady."

Rose beamed. "Did Dr. Cornell tell you he doesn't think I'll lose any more of my hearing?"

"He did. Actually, he and I discussed you at length this morning. That's why I couldn't come sooner." He glared self-righteously at Larissa as Rose grabbed his hand and tugged him toward the table.

"Remember what you said about learning to hand talk? This is Hans. He's teaching Charity and me. Ma and Pa, too. Watch!" She fluttered her fingers. "I can already do the whole alphabet. Charity can, too." She cupped her hand to her mouth. "Ma and Pa aren't doing so good," she stage-whispered. "But they're trying," she added sympathetically.

Oddly, Doc and Ethan suffered a simultaneous coughing attack. Still wheezing, Doc extended his hand to the young man who had been standing back, clearly bemused at this easygoing banter. "Pleased to meet you, Hans. It appears she's taking to these lessons like a squirrel to a tree."

Hans smiled. Grabbing pencil and paper, he wrote hastily. *Pleased to meet you, too, sir.*

Doc eyed him keenly, but merely said, "I've interrupted your lesson long enough, and I've some important matters to tend to." Over their protests, he edged toward the door.

"Will you join us for supper tonight?"

"I can't. I've already accepted Oliver's invitation. He asked me to join him and some of the other men I've maintained friendships with all these years."

"Tomorrow night, then?" Larissa wasn't about to let him escape without making certain he'd spend some time with them.

"As long as I'm not intruding."

Charity swiftly repeated this for Rose, so that she, too, joined the chorus. "How many times have I told you that you couldn't intrude if you tried?"

Doc glowered. "It's bad enough when two of you stand together, but with all of you united against me, I've already lost before I start. So I accept your kind offer. We'll settle the details tomorrow." He clapped his hat on, but before he could depart, Larissa put her hand on his arm.

"Have you seen Mac?"

"Not yet. But I intend to, you can count on it." He opened the door, but turned swiftly back to Larissa. Taking in her soft glow of joy, he said gruffly, "It is my unarguable medical opinion that marriage becomes you, Mrs. Michaels." He was gone before she could respond.

Their day's lesson completed, they were leaving the hospital when Dr. Terrill hailed them. "I'm glad I caught you. I'd be in hot water up to my ears, otherwise." Seeing their puzzlement, he said hastily, "My wife and I are giving a small party Saturday night, in honor of Abe Rawley's return. You will, of course, receive a formal invitation, but she wanted me to ask you informally also, since the time is short. We're having a few friends in from the hospital. They are much interested in meeting you, and Rose particularly."

Larissa finally found her voice. "Thank you. We're pleased you and Mrs. Terrill have asked us. But for an adult party, Rose and Charity are only thirteen."

"I told Matilda—Mrs. Terrill—that I'm not good at this sort of thing," he said glumly, "but here I am, anyway. Our daughter Amity will be receiving at the party with us. Mercy, our younger daughter, is fifteen, and two of the doctors have fourteen-year-old granddaughters. The girls are good friends, and when one of us hosts a party, the girls have their own party, away from the adults, but very much chaperoned, I assure you."

Charity having translated for Rose, both girls looked at Larissa pleadingly. Ethan appeared amenable to the prospect, and her own heartbeat quickened with anticipation. "Thank you. Please tell Mrs. Terrill we accept with pleasure."

He resembled a man who'd just learned he would escape his spouse's pot of boiling water after all. "I'll tell Mrs. Terrill. She'll be in touch with you to make the arrangements." He tipped his hat to Larissa and was off to face his wife and her hot water with a clear conscience.

Anticipation of "a real Philadelphia society party" provided the girls with abundant subject matter for the remainder of the evening. Even while they studied Miss Sullivan's lessons, comments unrelated to history or English grammar slipped in, until a warning movement from Ethan or Larissa turned them back into instant models of studiousness.

The formal invitation came by messenger the next morning as they prepared to leave for the hospital. The girls were in awe of the elegant black script and the heavy creamy paper. Even Ethan, carefully casual about it all, peered over Larissa's shoulder as she read aloud. "Mr. and Mrs. Ethan Michaels, and Daughters. The pleasure of your company is requested...."

***

They made arrangements to meet Mac that evening. Doc Rawley, in settling the supper details, spoke of a restaurant where he'd wanted to dine in his student days, but which had been beyond his student means. He said he intended to make up for the deprivation, now, and informed them in no uncertain terms they would be his guests. Realizing he truly wanted to do this for them, they accepted gracefully. His warm-hearted response was, "Mac better show up, too. I haven't laid eyes on the boy since I got here."

Doc was already seated when they arrived that evening, but Mac had not yet appeared. Minutes later, Larissa, facing the door, saw him following the waiter, threading his way between the tables toward them. For once, she did not watch her son's face, but Doc's as he turned and "laid eyes on the boy." The first startled moment of confusion, as he mentally added several months of maturity to the Mac he had last seen at the Fairvale train station, swiftly became wonder, pleasure and, Larissa saw plainly, immeasurable pride. Speechless, he stood and held out his hand. Which one grasped the other's to initiate their handshake was impossible to tell.

Doc studied him intently, and their eyes met in a long, steady exchange. Once more it came to Larissa, the feeling of a message being passed, received, and agreed upon, all in masculine silence. She took her eyes from them long enough to glance at Ethan. To her frustration, she saw the same intent knowing. Ethan clearly understood, even if she didn't.

Doc's eyes were suspiciously bright as he put his hand on Mac's shoulder and said in the gruffest tone he could manage, "I guess I really better start watching who I call 'boy' now." Mac merely grinned and bent to kiss Larissa's cheek.

The meal was one of the happiest she had ever experienced. She and Ethan let Doc and Mac carry much of the conversation. They had a fine time dredging up some of the more socially acceptable adventures they had encountered during Mac's apprenticeship days. "I'll never forget Ian Hollister and, to quote his mother, his 'most dreadful spots.'" Without doubt, Doc was relishing this trip to the past. "She had him all but dead and buried by the time we got there. I don't know which made him more furious, Mac, your doctoring knowledge, your professional concern, or the fact it was you examining him. When you diagnosed chickenpox—correctly, I might add—I thought he was going to haul off and whack you into next Wednesday. Are you sure you didn't get in a few more medical pokes and jabs than were strictly necessary?"

"I was just doing what you taught me and making sure of my findings." Mac was solemn innocence itself.

"All those pesky questions you kept asking on the way back to the office after we'd treated one patient or another." Doc turned to Larissa and Ethan. "I can't tell you how many nights I sat up searching my medical books for the answers. The idea was for me to teach him. Not the other way around."

Rose and Charity watched this by-play and contributed spirited remarks to the conversation. For once, however, Charity listened more than talked as she tried to fit this man into her memory of the boy she had loved from the day he had dragged her, humiliated and covered with muck, from the mud puddle in the school yard. *How can you be so different?* Vast silence was the only response to her bewildered questioning.

The waiters began to make closing-the-restaurant noises, and they realized all the other diners had gone. On the sidewalk, still talking, they waited for the cabs that would take them their separate ways. Doc planned to accompany Mac to the dormitory, then go on to the Terrills', where he'd been invited to stay. "Going in at this late hour, I hope they don't take me for a burglar and shoot me." This cheerful possibility silenced all of them for a moment.

A hackney cab drew up to the curb. Mac hugged Larissa. "Jeff and I have been invited to the Terrills' party. I have classes in the morning, and some matters to tend to in the afternoon, so I might not see you until tomorrow evening." Turning from her disappointment, he shook Ethan's hand, then stood contemplating Charity and Rose. "I seem to remember a couple of giggling girls driving me crazy with their hand talking. Ever since, I've been plotting my revenge. Just be aware, in case you thought you were going to get away with it, I will get even." He intoned the last words as if the bell of doom swung above them.

Their initial guilt and amazement vanished into lower-lip-sticking-out scowls, and for an instant they became three children having a youthful squabble. Larissa blinked and the image wisped away. As Ethan assisted her into the cab, she knew she would carry the moment with her, in spite of all the times during the years now gone, when such behavior nearly drove her crazy. *Wouldn't mothers take to their hearts even the annoying moments when their children are small, if only they realized how soon that time will be gone forever?*

CHAPTER TWENTY-SIX

The next day proved even busier than Larissa's prediction. Since the length of his teaching time with them was so indefinite, Hans decreed a Saturday lesson. Afterward, with a liberal dose of parental prodding, the girls devoted the rest of the morning to Miss Sullivan's lessons. Following the noon meal, Ethan departed to the men's bathhouse, while Larissa and the girls visited the women's bathing parlor.

Relaxing in a tub full of bubbles in the middle of the day was more luxury than Larissa had ever imagined. Rose and Charity soaked until their skin wrinkled. Only anxiety that the creases wouldn't smooth out before the party persuaded them to abandon their watery habitat and don their wedding dresses, freshly clean and starched from the hotel laundry.

When they'd discussed their plans for the afternoon, Ethan had asked Larissa to wear her wedding dress. She'd protested vigorously that her gown was totally unsuitable for an afternoon shopping trip. Only his reminder that they wouldn't be returning to the hotel before the party caused her to give in. She'd added a silent vow, however, to keep her coat firmly fastened. When he entered the sitting room, Ethan's eyes lit up, proof the results were well worth their efforts. He wore his wedding suit, also cleaned and pressed. "Three beautiful women at once. Whatever I did to earn this, please, Lord, let me do it again!" He winked at the girls. "Wait 'til the world sees you. They'll be jealous as sin at my good fortune." As he helped Larissa on with her coat, the look he slanted her way amply repaid her for giving in to his outrageous request.

They'd planned to stroll along the street and window shop, then have supper at one of the restaurants before taking a cab to the party, but Ethan halted before they'd wandered more than a block. "I'll be hornswoggled!"

Larissa looked around to discover the object of his astonishment, but saw only the crowd hurrying past the stores and shops. Behind her, a quickly stifled giggle indicated Rose and Charity knew more than she did. "Ethan, what is it?"

He maneuvered his horde of women folk across the street, toward one of the shop doorways. Larissa glimpsed a large window displaying framed pictures of people in various family poses. "A photographer's parlor." Her voice held undisguised fascination.

Charity and Rose hopped up and down. "Are you surprised, Ma? See, Pa, we didn't tell."

"You knew about this ahead of time?"

"We helped Pa plan it!" They beamed with pride.

"We decided if we were going to be all dressed up, we might as well put the occasion to good use." The mischief in Ethan's voice belied his thrifty-sounding excuse.

"I've never had my picture taken," Larissa confessed. "I wouldn't even know how to go about it."

With a courtly bow, Ethan held the door for her. "The photographer will take care of everything. You only need to look beautiful, and you already excel in that department."

Her recent solemn-as-death vow gave an exasperated sigh as she unbuttoned her coat in the warm room. "I wish Mac could be here."

"Someone's ahead of us." Ethan's voice betrayed his annoyance.

The young man at the counter turned. "Hi, Ma."

"Mac? You said you had other matters to tend to."

"I said I had things to do. I just didn't mention this being one of them. You really are surprised," he said gleefully. "The tattling twosome didn't give it away after all." Charity, outraged, opened her mouth, but Ethan's glare strongly suggested she become tongue-tied or he would do it for her. Unwillingly, she subsided.

"I missed out seeing you dressed up at the wedding. Now's my chance." Mac gave an appreciative whistle. "You look mighty pretty, Ma. You, too, Ethan."

Ethan's eyes crinkled. "I hope pretty isn't an exact description, but I get the idea, thank you."

Larissa's initial surprise at their plotting turned to indignation. "Ethan Michaels."

"Larissa Michaels," he countered, his scolding tone so much the same as hers the young people burst into laughter. Providentially, the shop's proprietor chose the same moment to emerge from a back room. After introductions and explanations, he seated them in varied poses, and over the course of the next hour, committed them to glass and paper.

By the time they emerged from the shop, dusk had set in. Mac declined their invitation to have supper before the party. "I have errands to run." He raised his right hand at Larissa's skepticism. "Honest. I don't have much chance to get out during the week, so I should take advantage while I can. But I'll see you tonight." He waved and the crowd quickly swallowed him.

Ethan followed her pensive gaze. "He has his own world here, Lizzie. We mustn't begrudge it."

"I'm not. He's worked too long and hard to get here. He's happy in what he's doing. His world, now, isn't ours, but it's comforting to know some of our world is still his."

**

The "small party" turned out to be the most lavish event Larissa or Ethan had ever attended. The cab deposited them in front of the Terrill home, from which light spilled out every visible window and probably from a few not visible. The snow-covered grounds stretching away on either side hinted tantalizingly of sweeping beauty during the full bloom of summer. Even Rose and Charity were temporarily silenced.

A sudden vision of their simple farmhouse plopped beside this magnificence caused Larissa's stomach to give an odd lurch. "Jumping jackrabbits!" Ethan murmured, so that by the time they reached the door and a servant in black announced them, Larissa's queasiness had eased.

We are as we are. We'll be accepted or not, on our own terms.

Matilda Terrill clasped Larissa's hand with genuine sincerity. "I'm so pleased to meet you. We must talk later. I'm looking forward to it." At her touch and voice, a picture fluttered into Larissa's consciousness of her elegantly dressed hostess standing in the kitchen of that earlier plopped-down farmhouse. Flour spattered her calico housedress and apron as she kneaded a mass of bread dough. Larissa blinked, and the image vanished. But it left her wondering which likeness was the true one.

Dr. Terrill welcomed them just as cordially. Seeing Charity and Rose hanging back, frankly overwhelmed, he coaxed them forward to introduce them to his wife. "We're so happy you've come. Mercy and the other girls are in the small parlor. Miss Bradwick, Mercy's governess, will show you."

A tall, slender young woman standing to the side came forward. Matter-of-factly, she took the girls in hand. "What time shall they return, ma'am?" Her rich accent brought a misty breath of England into the room.

"Please bring them to the reception hall at nine o'clock."

"Yes, ma'am."

She led the girls away, and a dart of panic stabbed Larissa. *In this vast house, among so many people, they might become lost and never seen again.*

She and Ethan gave way to the guests behind them, and for a time simply wandered through the rooms, marveling at the possessions that filled other people's lives. In the drawing room, they found a musical quartet tuning their instruments. *Dancing, too?* A gruff voice spoke in her ear, and she found Doc had worked his way to them. "We're so glad to see you." In the house full of strangers, her heartfelt words were doubly sincere.

"You're looking mighty fine, Larissa." His top-to-toe inspection was anything but clinical.

Willing herself not to blush, she almost succeeded. "Thank you. You're looking mighty fine yourself." His hair and beard were trimmed and his suit free of baggy knees and wrinkles for the first time in her memory.

"Say, Doc." Ethan leaned around her. "If this is a small party, where do they hold the big ones?"

Doc's raspy breath equaled someone else's burst of laugher. "I'd forgotten, thankfully, how spruced up these affairs can be."

"And you actually came to this one," Larissa teased. "At least with all the other doctors at this shindig, you won't have a host of hypochondriacs cornering you."

"Maybe it's not so good, comes down to it. Getting rescued from my last corner made it more than worthwhile."

"Here you are." The voice behind them distracted Larissa from the brazen twinkle in Doc's eye.

"Mac!" Her happiness level promptly increased a notch. "And Jeff. It's good to see you again."

He took her hand and gave her an offhand grin, but when Mac introduced Doc, everything except respectful courtesy vanished. "Mac's talked about you so much, sir."

Even crusty Doc wasn't totally immune to sincere admiration. He stroked his beard, but, unable to douse his pleasure completely, he hid it beneath bluster. "I hope he said at least a few good things about me."

Mac must have filled Jeff in on Doc's grumpiness, because he laughed. "More than a few, sir, I assure you."

Somewhere nearby, a clock struck the hour, and a murmur rippled across the room. Feeling sudden pressure against her skirt, Larissa discovered Rose and Charity hovering on either side of her. Mac casually shifted to stand on Charity's far side. Charity blushed deeply, but before Larissa could react, Rose tugged on her hand. "Ma, Mercy's in the blue dress. She's nice. The other one is her big sister, Amity." Dr. Terrill, escorting Mrs. Terrill and two young women, paused before the fireplace. While Dr. Terrill waited for the room to quiet, Larissa took note of the striking similarities between the young women of midnight-black hair and delicate features in heart-shaped faces, although Amity's poise contained a maturity not yet come to the younger sister.

Dr. Terrill's voice snagged Larissa's wandering attention. "Mrs. Terrill and I, and our daughters, Amity and Mercy, are honored to welcome you as our guests. Tonight, I'm pleased to assure you we have an excellent reason for asking you to join us. He left town over thirty years ago, and we've been trying ever since to persuade him to return. We have finally succeeded. It is my great privilege to present to you my esteemed friend and fellow physician, Abraham Rawley."

He gestured for Doc to come forward, and all eyes swung their way. Laughter and applause broke out. Doc looked as if he'd rather stick his head in a grizzly bear's cave than face so many people. Larissa caught his muttered, "I'm going to get you for this one, Oliver," as he marched toward his friend. He listened with unfeigned surprise as Dr. Terrill clarified his innumerable sterling qualities.

Larissa, wondering at the girls' reactions to all this, realized Charity, puzzlement large in her eyes, was watching Mac, with Mac paying no heed whatsoever to her. Curious, Larissa stood on tiptoe to see over the heads of the people in front of her. Her heart gave another of those odd little bumps. Mac's full attention centered upon Amity Terrill, standing beside her father at the front of the room. Larissa pulled her gaze back to her son, and, unaware of it, tightened her fingers on Ethan's arm. At her touch, he turned to her questioningly, then scanned the room, seeking the source of her unease. His start of awareness upon discovering the recipient of Mac's intensity told Larissa she hadn't been wrong. She ducked her chin. A speck of black wool fuzz from Ethan's suit clung to the wrist of her white kid glove and she picked painstakingly at it. Ethan could not know the wonderment now lighting Mac's features had, in the long-gone past, glowed in Zane's eyes the day he asked Larissa to marry him.

Her scurrying thoughts finally slowed, and she studied the young woman more carefully. She stood taller than Larissa, but everyone seemed to stand taller than Larissa. From across the room, she couldn't decide whether Amity's eyes were blue or green, so this particular detail was not beneficial, either. *Mac probably knows.* She swatted the thought away as quickly as it pounced.

"Lizzie?" At the touch of Ethan's hand on her arm, her woolgathering thoughts skidded back to him. Miss Bradwick had appeared to escort Rose and Charity back to their own party. The red sashes on their white dresses had scarcely fluttered from sight before an older couple paused in front of Ethan and Larissa.

During the evening, Larissa had met so many doctors and their wives their features now blurred. But she held out her hand and smiled as warmly as if she hadn't done so a double dozen times already. Ignoring the outstretched hand, the guest looked down her nose, her glare the coldest Larissa had ever encountered. *I've seen dead fish with warmer eyes.*

"So you're the ones from the village back in…" The woman searched her memory. "Oh, yes. Ohio." She said it as if the state were impaled on the highest mountaintop in Siberia. "It must be such a shock, coming to our civilized Philadelphia, so full of culture and social graces." Pointedly examining Larissa, she noted the curls in front of her ears, the depth of her neckline, and the kid slippers encasing her feet. Finished, she arched her eyebrows.

Larissa assumed she was joking, but the disdain in those cold eyes assured her the lady was deadly serious. She drew herself up to her full height, ignoring the fact her adversary still towered over her. "We have enjoyed many breathtaking sights in your beautiful city." At Larissa's admission, the disdain came perilously close to smugness. "However, your vast city and our small town have something very much in common. There, as here, most people are kind and helpful. But unfortunately, here, as there, a few individuals are unforgivably rude." It took the recipient several seconds to decipher this sweetly wrapped observation. She drew back as if Larissa had just confessed to having one of the more annoying diseases, such as leprosy.

Larissa had never seen a glacier, but rather imagined it bore a strong resemblance to this woman's features. Only her eyes were alive. They snapped with outrage. "Come, Harold. We must not neglect our friends."

Harold, chatting with Ethan, obediently stopped in the middle of his sentence, but paused long enough to take Larissa's hand. His eyes held all the admiration his wife's lacked. "A pleasure to meet you, Mrs. Michaels."

"Harold!"

He sighed. "A pleasure, indeed." He scuttled off to join the glacier, but even the warmth of his personality couldn't thaw hers.

Ethan leaned toward Larissa. "You really put old ice-in-her-britches in her place."

"I didn't know you heard."

"I bet it'll take the old girl a while to figure out just how you skunked her so neatly."

Before Larissa could convince herself she hadn't dreamed the whole thing, Mac edged his way toward her, and she caught a glimpse of a cloud of midnight-black hair beside his shoulder.

"Ma, Ethan, I'd like you to meet someone." With unmistakable pleasure, he led the young woman forward. "This is Miss Amity Terrill." To her, nonchalantly, "My folks, Mr. and Mrs. Michaels." Larissa prayed her smile didn't look as pasted on as it felt.

Amity's hands, too, were encased in the short kid gloves dictated by fashion. When Larissa took them into hers, the young woman's grasp was firm and gracefully welcoming. Her eyes, meeting Larissa's without evasion, were neither blue nor green, but a beautiful soft shade of both. "I'm pleased to meet you, Miss Terrill." Her voice startled her, for she heard the words, but they seemed to come from someone other than herself. *I've always known this day would come, Mac. I just hoped it wouldn't be quite so soon.*

During the buffet supper that followed, Ethan and Larissa caught several glimpses of Mac and Amity. As daughter of the hosting couple, she slipped from group to group, greeting, smiling, and clearly enjoying herself. Mac, too, traveled from cluster to cluster, talking, joking, and clearly enjoying himself. Strangely, however, his current group was never far from hers. Eventually, their wandering directions crossed just outside the library, before they were lost to sight.

Larissa's breath went out in a tremulous sigh. Ethan set their empty plates on a nearby table and put his hand over hers. "You did well. He's a very lucky young man."

"She is nice, isn't she?"

"She is, but I was talking about how lucky he is to have a mother brave enough to smile while she lets him go."

"It showed so much? I hope no one noticed."

"Probably no one else did. But remember, you're stuck with me."

"This conversation sounds awfully familiar. Maybe I'm jumping the gun."

"I'd say not so much jumping it as making sure ahead of time your powder is dry. Remember, too, he didn't say anything about marriage. He just introduced her."

This time, his practical male logic gave her the comfort he intended. "He's happy. How can I not be happy for him?"

In answer, he silently tucked her arm snugly under his, pressing hers reassuringly close against his side. Resuming their mingling with the other guests, they passed the parlor. Ethan, glancing in, emitted something between an exclamation and a gurgle. Startled, Larissa peered around him. At the far end of the room, an acre or so away, she saw people conversing. She looked at him in confusion, then followed his eyes. When she glimpsed the object of his wonder, a small squeak escaped her.

What appeared to be a round footstool designed specifically for a giant graced the floor beyond them. "It must be eight feet across!" Ethan managed to keep his flabbergasted voice from carrying to the other guests. "I certainly wouldn't want to meet up with its intended user on a dark road at midnight."

Larissa recovered some of her composure. "I think it's called a circular sofa. The center post is the backrest." No one chanced to be within listening distance, so she pitched her voice to a haughty murmur. "Do you mean to tell me that no one in your farming village has one?" she asked icily. "My dear, they're simply all the rage in civilized Philadelphia." She attempted to look down her nose at him, no mean feat since he stood more than a foot taller. But even at her iciest, she was no match for the guest who had confronted them so rudely.

Ethan's totally unabashed grin at her perfect mimicry banished the still-stinging heart-hurt. She leaned toward him as he reached for her but someone passing by jostled them. He gave her a lopsided smile. "Lizzie."

The strains of a waltz drifted from the drawing room. "Ethan, will you dance with me?"

"With pleasure," he said huskily. Leading her onto the floor, he circled his arm about her waist, holding her closer than strictly necessary for those particular dance steps. They had danced together at Fairvale's community socials and barn-raising get-togethers, but none of those occasions offered a setting such as this. She found herself following his lead so easily she didn't even have to think about what her feet were doing.

Their maneuvering took them to the far end of the room where chairs were arranged for the non-dancers. Larissa caught a glimpse of old ice-in-her-britches staring at them. Her sneering arrogance assured Larissa she was waiting for them to trip over each other's feet and fall flat on their backsides in full view of the rest of the company. Their eyes met. If Larissa had been a raindrop, she would have frozen instantly. Fortunately, her parents had constructed her of a more solid substance. Whirling past, she smiled sweetly, thus putting her tormenter on notice that the candle flame of Larissa's integrity was forever beyond the woman's ability to quench it—or even cause it to flicker.

With the deplorable episode behind them—literally, as they glided away down the room—a feather of curiosity tickled Larissa. "Where did you learn to waltz like this?"

His eyes smiled. "A fellow making a living as a tutor in Virginia has to learn many bits and pieces in order to stay ahead of his enterprising pupils."

"I think the fellow learned far more than bits and pieces when it came to dancing." He simply tightened his arm about her waist, drawing her a little closer.

As they spun in and out among the other dancers, her earlier dejection became a heart-singing joy unlike any she had ever experienced. The superbly rendered music, and the elegantly dressed couples circling beneath the gas-lit chandeliers, wove the moment into a breathtaking experience.

In those minutes, realization as shining as the prisms of the chandeliers above them curled around her soul. In spite of coming from a small farming town lacking the cultural opportunities of this large city, she and Ethan had met, and, in some cases surpassed, high society's edicts concerning proper social graces. *We are as we are.* The earlier truth suddenly took on new awareness. For all the prestige attached to wealth and social advantages, she knew, with absolute certainty, she wouldn't trade her place, or her happiness, with anyone else on earth.

By the time the party ended and they bundled a sleepwalking Charity and Rose into a cab for the ride to the hotel, Larissa's fizzing happiness was hushing into a deep pool of peace. As she and Ethan each supported a limp daughter to keep her from taking a nosedive onto the cab floor, neither one said much. But, wrapped as they were in the evening's lingering enchantment, words were unnecessary.

After guiding the girls to their room, Larissa tried to coax them into undressing and donning their nightgowns. They obediently began whatever gesture she told them, but their staying power was nil. Strongly tempted to dump them into bed, coats and all, she couldn't bring herself to do it.

Ethan had stepped back once they were propped on the bed, but he couldn't desert Larissa in her frustrating task any more than she could abandon the girls. He helped her remove their coats and bonnets, shoes and stockings. He then retreated once more, but at least the jiggling movement brought them closer to the surface of wakefulness, rendering them considerably more helpful. Her task completed at last, she bent and kissed them, but neither one stirred.

Ethan had replenished the coal in the sitting room fireplace. The softly popping blaze was already banishing the chill as she eased the connecting door shut. "Will you dance with me?" He held out his arms. She slipped into them and rested her head against his chest.

"I don't think I have another twirl left in me," she admitted regretfully.

His hand cupped the back of her head. "It's probably just as well. I don't think I do, either."

"Do we sound like a tired old married couple already?"

His laugh whispered against her temple. "Married? Yes, very much so. Old? We don't have time to be old. We have too many other much more interesting things to do. Tired?" The faint teasing in his voice shifted to seriousness. "I know this week has been overwhelming, with all the coming and going and little opportunity to enjoy even a quiet moment or two."

"Overwhelming in so many more ways than one." Her eyes lit impishly. "Do you think that just might have something to do with why, instead of feeling tired, I feel so happy even my toes want to dance for joy?"

"It might," he agreed thoughtfully as he lowered his mouth to hers. "It just might at that."

CHAPTER TWENTY-SEVEN

Ethan didn't mention it, but Larissa realized that their plan to remain in Philadelphia for several weeks would cause a serious drain on his emergency fund if they continued to rent the suite of three rooms. The next morning after church when she brought it up, however, he set his jaw. "Our honeymoon has already been moved from here and there to the next place. This shouldn't be a time of disruption. I want us to enjoy being a family, and it seems to me the best way is by having one settled home, even a temporary one."

She pressed her fingers gently along his rigid jaw. "I remember someone telling me, 'What we have is right and good, no matter what.' I guess we'll just have to add 'or where' to the thought. Besides," her eyes sparked with amusement, "I don't know how much closer to family we can get. The girls are here. And Mac. We even have our doctor. If this combination doesn't make a home, I don't know what will."

"I'm glad you're not a lawyer, Mrs. Michaels. I'd lose my case before the trial ever started." He kissed her palm. "We'll move tomorrow."

With Jeff Kinsley gladly providing his city expertise, they optimistically began their search for a suitable boarding house. He steered them through the intricacies of studying the ads in the Philadelphia *Journal* and meeting with prospective landladies. Nearly all were widows and possessed a range of personalities from cagey and friendly to wary and aloof. They discovered an interesting trend. A few allowed pets. Fewer allowed children.

Late that afternoon, drained of enthusiasm, they declined to rent the premises, with its threadbare carpets, rickety furniture, and exorbitant fees, of their eighth encounter. Insulted, the owner informed them that in the middle of winter they were not going to find lodgings more highly recommended than hers. "When cold weather comes, folks move to town. Rooms are mighty scarce this time of year," she warned.

"I swear I heard two rats bickering in the walls," Ethan muttered as they made their escape. Larissa just shuddered.

With a lamentable lack of optimism, they listened to Jeff's urging to look at one more place located near the University. Discouraged as they were, beneath his cheerful confidence they detected his deep desire to help them, strangers in his big city, and they didn't have the heart to disappoint him. They trudged on, and later thanked heaven for doing so. The rooms were clean, the furniture simple but sturdy, and no rodent domestic disputes resonated behind the walls. Added to this fortunate find, Mrs. Nicholas, the owner, was so delighted to rent two rooms at one time she graciously overlooked the inconvenience of their frequent coming in and going out.

The next days fell into a routine. Mornings, Hans tutored them. Afternoons, Rose and Charity worked on their school lessons. Soaking up Hans' instructions, the girls advanced to signing word shapes. The signs they didn't know, they finger spelled, and thus could communicate with each other for long stretches without using their voices.

Dr. Cornell advised them Rose was now unable to hear her own voice accurately. She needed to practice talking quietly, since the others could hear her clearly, even if she felt she was whispering. He also cautioned, to retain normal vocal function, she must continue to speak. Larissa had wondered if it was her imagination that the lilt was fading from Rose's speech pattern, especially when she was elated. After this warning, she became adamant Rose use her voice, without shouting, and was quick to pounce if Ethan or Charity's cooperation lagged.

Larissa and Ethan weren't as speedy as the girls to pick up the finer techniques of signing, but they limped along, and Hans assured them that they, too, would become proficient. Watching the girls flutter their fingers as if born to it, Larissa harbored a few reservations about Hans' prediction. But she wasn't about to stop trying.

During their fourth week in the city, Ethan and Larissa realized Doc was acting odd. They didn't see much of him, but after a time or two of chance meetings, it dawned on them how, whenever their paths crossed, he was in a hurry and undeniably crabbier than the last time they ran into him. At first they took it in stride, as Doc's way, until they noticed he was always too busy to have supper with them, with no excuse forthcoming. As Ethan put it, Doc had possessed a unique set of peculiarities over the years, but keeping quiet had never been one of them.

Before they could have it out with Doc, Dr. Cornell announced he'd finished his testing with Rose. His usual solemnity was broken by a smile that assured them he was deeply pleased with his results. Now, too, he felt confident in confirming that, barring unforeseen circumstances, Rose would retain her present level of hearing.

Even as they rejoiced, the question swiftly became how much longer they should remain under Hans' tutelage. Their minds knew the most sensible solution was for Larissa and the girls to stay, and for Ethan to return to the farm for spring planting. Thoroughly aware of the separation this entailed, they carefully sidestepped discussing the matter. Whether because of, or in spite of this knowledge, their time together became more than ever a wellspring of contentment.

On a blustery February evening when Mrs. Nicholas was busy in the kitchen and none of the other residents had joined them in the boarding house sitting room, Ethan and Larissa were reading. Charity, who much preferred reading to arithmetic, was frowning over a problem from their homework assignment. Rose, who enjoyed mathematics and had swiftly come up with the correct answer, was happily sketching. A sudden ringing of the front door bell splintered the quiet. Mrs. Nicholas answered and called Ethan to the door. Expecting Mac, he found Doc standing in the hallway.

"Well, are you going to invite me in or am I going to drip snow all over this fancy carpet?" Hearing his fussing, Charity reported to Rose, and Larissa hurried to the doorway.

At Ethan's gesture, Doc shed his coat and hat and warily entered the sitting room. This grouchiness was so much more the Doc they knew, they greeted him with relieved warmth. As usual, he wasted no words. "I've been doing a lot of thinking, and I've come to a decision. It involves you, so I guess I should let you in on it."

Startled, Larissa and Ethan moved to stand together. Behind his beard, Doc pursed his lips at this latest unconscious declaration of unity. "This includes you young women, so you might as well hear me out." The girls simply stared at him. "When Mac studied medicine with me, I got used to him riding along on calls and pestering me six ways to Sunday for information. It's been too danged quiet since he left. So I've decided to try my hand with someone else who has doctoring notions. I want to see if I can still pound some learning into a receptive young head. These past days, I've been working out the details."

"Do you have someone particular in mind?"

Doc pondered Ethan's question before turning to Rose. "I've been spending a lot of time with Hans Druid, getting to know him, to find out if it would work for me to take him on. I wanted to be absolutely sure for him and me both. I've asked him, and he's said yes." The room rang with the silence that followed his words. Bewildered by their sudden statue-stillness, Rose tugged urgently at Charity's sleeve. Recovering, Charity spoke rapidly into her ear. Rose, too, suddenly became statue-still.

Doc continued as casually as if he hadn't just altered the course of their lives forever. "He's bright and he's eager to learn. Reminds me a lot of another young fellow I knew, before he went and grew up on me." The pensiveness in Doc's eyes belied his brusque tone. "Of course, with Hans' lack of speech, it's impossible for him to ever be a full-fledged doctor. But poking around patients with me, I figure he'll come a lot closer than he would otherwise."

Larissa had to try three times before her voice worked. "Do you mean he'll be right there in Fairvale?"

Doc snorted. "Wouldn't work. There's not enough room in my living quarters for me, let alone for two people. We'd be tripping over each other every time we took a step. I need to make other arrangements. I hoped you'd have an idea or two."

The swift glance between Larissa and Ethan settled the matter. Ethan stroked his beard. "We don't know if it'll fit in with your 'other arrangements,' but by the strangest coincidence, there's a cabin back at the farm that no one will be using for the foreseeable future. If he stayed there, he could go to town the same as Mac did. The times you didn't need him, I reckon he could try his hand at farming as well as doctoring, to earn his keep. If he were willing."

Doc snapped his fingers. "Now that's a dandy idea. Why didn't I think of it?"

Sign language had flown out the window under the import of the adults' discussion. Charity had been frantically translating verbally to Rose who, hands tightly clasped, listened as if unable to grasp the reality of the words. Suddenly, she hurtled herself at Doc and buried her face in his once-again-wrinkled coat front. "Thank you, Doc! Thank you." He patted her awkwardly, more embarrassed at having his big-as-a-barn heart caught in an act of kindness than they had ever seen him.

Charity edged up to Ethan. He put one arm around her and the other around Larissa, who was once again glowing as if she had just been handed the key to Heaven's gates. More strongly than she had heard it in many days, the lilt had returned to Rose's voice.

Brushing her hair before bed that night, Larissa sorted through this day's events and tomorrow's promises. The *Song of Solomon* whispered through her mind.

For, lo, the winter is past ... The time of the singing of birds is come, and the voice of the turtle is heard in our land.

She set down the brush and moved her fingers carefully, shaping the words of her heart. "Thank You for showing us the way for the voice of our own little turtledove to continue to be heard in our land."

For Larissa, the next days whirled past in bustling confusion as they prepared to go home. Gathering up their accumulated belongings. *How could we possibly acquire so many extra articles in the short time we've been here?* Carefully packing the pictures from the photographer. *The wonders of this modern age. Out of one's entire lifetime, precise seconds can be captured forever.* Meeting with Hans to ensure he felt comfortable with the plan, and finding him actually walking in a daze at his sudden fortune. *I don't know which he's more excited about, that he's to learn medicine, or that he'll be part of a real family after so many years of loneliness.*

It developed that Hans would not return with them to Fairvale, but follow a day or so later with Doc, who had a few more details to iron out. The delay would also allow time to prepare the cabin.

Ethan sent a telegram to Shawn and Martha, optimistically announcing their arrival time. Suddenly, they were crowded onto the Philadelphia station platform, watching the train wheeze in. At the hospital, all the words of departure had been said, including those by which they attempted to express their profound thankfulness for all the kindness and caring the doctors had shown.

Jeff Kinsley came to the station to see them off, and they bade him farewell, deeply grateful Mac had found a trusted friend. Now, only the final goodbye remained.

Larissa hugged Mac and stepped back to study him one last time. "I am more proud of you than words can ever say."

"Thanks, Ma. For everything you and Pa did to get me where I am." Abashed at his blatant emotion, he turned quickly to Ethan. "Thank you, too. I haven't seen Ma so happy in a mighty long time." He gestured to Larissa, who smiled brightly, while clearly fighting to hide her tears at leaving him. "Well, almost so happy, anyway," he amended ruefully. Ethan chuckled and Larissa managed a liquid-free laugh.

The train blew in on a cloud of steam and dust. Mac pulled one of Charity's curls and put his hand under Rose's chin. "Bye, Speck. Bye, Shadow. You behave yourselves. No making up a secret code to torment Hans. I already told him that if you did, he has my permission to dunk you in the horse trough." Before they could express their indignation, Ethan hurriedly pointed them toward the passenger car.

Mac gave Larissa a final bear hug. She put her fingers lightly against his cheek, and turned toward Ethan, waiting to help her up the step. In the final confusion of boarding and finding their seats, Ethan kept his hand firmly around hers. The train started with a jerk, and she put her palm against the window. Mac raised his own hand in a farewell salute, and he and Jeff were lost to sight down the platform.

For once ignoring the presence of Rose and Charity perched on the opposite seat, she turned to Ethan and buried her face against his shoulder. His arms enfolded her as if there were no watching daughters or even anyone else around within a hundred miles. She trembled, and her words came stiffly. "I tried so hard."

"You did real good." Ethan's battering the English language was such a rarity she jerked her head up and caught his knowing smile. Having absorbed this conversation, Charity busily passed it to Rose. Larissa didn't notice. Ethan did. "I think it would be a good idea for the two of you to find where they've put the drinking water." His tone indicated argument was not on their list of alternatives. "Then, if we get a sudden thirst, we can quench it without wasting any time searching for the bucket."

Clearly provoked by this transparent order, Charity told Rose and they headed toward the back of the car. "Why doesn't he just tell us when he wants to get rid of us?"

"I think they saw through that one," Ethan said dryly. His mouth drifted near her ear. "I'm here for you, love."

"I know. Mac's making his life and there's no need to fret as I did when he went away in September. But now he...." She had not spoken to Ethan about Mac's expression as he gazed at Amity Terrill at the party. How could she even begin to explain her knowledge, because of Zane, of the depth of emotion behind it?

Seeing his puzzlement over her reluctance to continue, she said shakily, "Now there's Amity Terrill. He has so much school left, and to be distracted by a...." Her panicky flow of anxiety threatened to become a full-blown flood.

"I honestly think you don't have to worry about her, for a while, anyway. I didn't get a chance to tell you, but he and I had quite a discussion last night."

She pulled back to search his face. "Ethan?"

He eased her head back to his shoulder. "I tactfully inquired about his intentions. He tactfully assured me there's friendship between them, nothing more, right now. He knows he has too much at stake to get involved with anyone at this point. As he put it, 'Tell Ma I remember my upbringing. I know she'd skin me alive if I went back on it.' He added how, if that sounded too noble and farfetched for words, the woman in question is also the daughter of the head of the teaching department. Since her father just happens to hold the red pencil that will make the final determination of his grades, 'discretion is an excellent incentive.'"

Ethan shaded his recital in such a remarkably close rendition of Mac's ruefulness that, in spite of herself, Larissa's voice caught on a twist of laughter. "I'm so glad the two of you talked. It's a relief to find she's an attraction for him, not a distraction." She smiled wryly. "At least for now. I'm truly grateful we've had this much time with him. But I can't help thinking it would have been nice if we'd had those picture-taking contraptions when he was growing up." Her voice was wistful.

"In my mind's eye, I see him just-born squalling, proud as a peacock at taking his first steps, and the gap in his grin when he lost his first tooth. But the pictures are fuzzy around the edges. Those images are still alive in my heart, but as much as I want to hold them, they're slipping away. When they fade completely, that time will be gone forever."

***

Once they settled into the journey, the trip proved blessedly uneventful. No males of the proper age appeared, which left the contents of the water bucket safe from the onslaught of two thirsty young ladies. The tracks stayed driftless, thus eliminating any delays from the men having to shovel their way through snowbanks higher than their heads. The bone-jarring, sleep-depriving motion of the cars, however, remained hauntingly the same.

Rose and Charity conducted themselves with graceful maturity through all the long hours, carrying on conversations in sign, and finishing the last of the work Miss Sullivan had given them. Unfortunately, during the final stretch of the trip, their graceful maturity wore out. They squirmed in their seats and pestered Ethan and Larissa every five minutes about how much longer before they arrived.

The railroad timetable promised they would reach Fairvale by noon on Friday. The train rolled along so smoothly they were only three hours late, instead of nearly eight, as with their arrival in Philadelphia.

When the Fairvale station finally loomed on the horizon, only a sharp eye could have chosen which of the four was the most grateful. With all their possessions gathered long before, the girls were in danger of exiting the car before the last tooth-rattling jerk of the engine brought them to a full stop. Somehow, they and their belongings descended the steps to the platform all in one piece.

"Ethan!" Shawn waved vigorously and maneuvered past a baggage cart. Ethan's hands were full of luggage, so Shawn clapped him on the shoulder in hearty greeting.

Leaving them to tend to the baggage, Larissa and her full arms edged through the waiting room doorway behind the girls. Martha pounced on her with a glad cry of welcome. The next minutes were a happy blur of greetings and hugs and the retrieval of the luggage by the men. "I know you want to get home, but come over to the parsonage with us. It's a little early, but I have a meal all ready. You might as well help us eat it as to go home and cook when you must be exhausted."

Shawn cleared his throat. "You better do as she says. She's cooked enough to see us through the proverbial forty years of famine, and then some."

Now it was all over, Larissa felt a sudden wave of absolute weariness. "As long as you promise your floors don't sway or bounce, it sounds like a fine idea to me."

"Not a sway or bounce in sight," Shawn promised. "Ethan?"

"A home-cooked meal after all that big-city food? You don't have to ask twice!"

Garth silently helped carry the baggage and get it stowed in the wagon box on runners. Finished, he approached Ethan and stiffened his shoulders. "I took the best care I could of the team. Do they look all right?"

Ethan gravely inspected the burnished coats while Pegasus and Andromeda nuzzled him in greeting. "They look just fine. Actually, they look so good and so content, I'm afraid they'll want to stay with you instead of going home with us."

Garth's anxiety disappeared in a blaze of relief and pride. With masculine restraint, however, he only said, "They're a mighty fine team."

Once at the parsonage, Ethan and Shawn joined Garth and Noah at the chores. In the kitchen, Gretta took a roast from the oven, and Mara laid the last fork on its accompanying napkin. The meal following became a blend of telling about their adventures and of started-but-not-finished sentences as one comment sparked another topic.

Afterward, Shawn took Ethan into the study to catch him up on all the town news. Martha refused Larissa's offer of help with the dishes. "This will be your last chance to relax before you have to do your own work at home."

Larissa rolled up her sleeves. "I'll wash," she said firmly, "if you'll put the leftovers away. I never thought I'd say this, but I'm actually looking forward to washing dishes after being lazy for so long." With the girls drying, the work went quickly as Larissa related more of their adventures. The girls disappeared upstairs and Larissa and Martha settled at the table with a pot of hot, fragrant tea.

Larissa squeezed Martha's hand. "I haven't had a chance to ask. How are you doing?"

Martha gingerly reached over her protruding waistline to pour the tea. "Little Prospect and I are just fine. He's getting ornery, though. I tell you, the way he kicks, he must be wearing army boots."

"I remember well. Especially with Mac. I think he had a full set of horseshoes nailed to the soles!" Larissa paused. "I've been dying to ask you. Where did you find that beautiful nightgown you packed for me?"

"You found it all right, then?" Seeing the pink suffuse Larissa's cheeks, Martha added innocently, "I had a feeling you'd like it."

"I've never seen such fine material. And so beautifully made. But how expensive."

Martha's eyes sparkled. "Actually, it didn't cost me anything. You remember my mother's family lived in New York City. The spring she turned eighteen, Ma's younger sister met an older man who had recently come to town, seemingly out of nowhere. He and Aunt Hester met at a party, and just a month later, he declared his intention to marry her. Everyone was shocked at their speed, but she was adamant. She said she loved him and refused to wait a dozen years or so, to satisfy the social set, before they married. My grandparents were terribly upset, but couldn't talk her out of it. She flat-out threatened to run away with him. It was either let her have her way or lose her, so they gave in.

"Aunt Hester was walking on clouds. She chose a complete new wardrobe. Two seamstresses scurried around like crazy to finish everything in time. She and my mother went shopping one day, and she found the nightgown material and a pattern that had come all the way from Paris. She ordered four gowns made. But three days before the wedding, my grandfather dropped a ton of bricks on everything. He'd had an uneasy feeling about this fellow. Something just didn't seem right. So he checked his background and found he was already married—to two other women from well-to-do families."

At Larissa's gasp, Martha smiled wryly. "Needless to say, the wedding was called off, but, being a thrifty Scot, Aunt Hester couldn't bring herself to dispose of all her wedding outfits. So everything just stayed in the trunks that were already packed for the wedding trip. When Aunt Hester died, everything of hers, including the four gowns, went to my mother, her only sister. Ma gave me one when Ross and I were married, and when she died, all her things came to me, along with the three remaining gowns.

"Aunt Hester never wanted to lay eyes on them again, but they were so beautiful, it just seemed wrong not to use them. When Ethan asked me to pack a bag for you before the wedding, it seemed the perfect solution. I hope you don't mind, after hearing all this." Martha's tone was suddenly anxious.

"Of course not. It was perfect." Remembering Ethan's reaction to that perfection, the pink in Larissa's cheeks became a scarlet flame. She continued hastily, "But it's sad to think of your aunt grieving so much all those years that she couldn't bear to see any of those beautiful things again."

Martha choked on a swallow of tea. "She died when I was ten," she sputtered. "I remember her quite well. She dressed in black from head to foot and always looked like she'd just bitten into a sour green apple. I was scared to death of her."

Now Larissa choked at the vision of young Martha peering fearfully from behind her mother's wide skirts whenever Aunt Hester appeared. She started laughing and Martha joined in.

Shawn poked his head into the room. "What's all this? We heard your hysterics all the way from the study." Larissa and Martha had almost mastered their mirth, but Shawn's innocent question set them off again. Giving them a look indicating he highly suspected the true contents of the teapot, he prudently withdrew.

As they gathered their coats to leave, Martha said casually, "When you get home, check the woodshed. There's a wedding gift in there."

At Larissa and Ethan's protests that they had already done too much, Shawn winked at Martha. "We think you'll like it." Neither one would say anything further.

The drive back to the farm in the winter twilight had a strange quality, as if they were for the first time traveling a road that yet seemed so familiar. Home at last, Ethan stopped the team beside the kitchen path and assisted Larissa down. Aware of their plans to return that day, Dolf Hyatt's sons, who had tended the place, had done the evening chores and departed for their own farm. Stepping ahead of Ethan into the warm, quiet kitchen and the hushed peace that immediately enfolded her, Larissa understood the true meaning of *home*. The girls promptly ran upstairs to become reacquainted with their rooms and their left-behind possessions.

Unable to wait a moment longer, she grabbed a candle and headed for the woodshed. Ethan, apparently forgetting his edict that she was not to enter the room, followed close behind. "I'm curious as a cat, too," he confessed.

Larissa pushed open the door and froze on the threshold. Ethan gave a muffled exclamation. She edged through the doorway, taking in the room with stunned delight. "Ethan, it's beautiful. You certainly fooled me. I didn't think you completed everything before we left." The bewilderment on his face stopped her in mid-praise.

"Lizzie, I didn't finish. I still had a ways to go." He stared, as astonished as she, at the freshly painted and wallpapered room. The furniture stood in place. Braided rugs made miniature islands on the polished floor.

Dazed, she walked to the bed she had never seen, and picked up a piece of paper lying on top of a Double Wedding Ring patterned quilt she'd never seen before, either. "'Happy Marriage.' Ethan, all our friends signed this. They must have realized you didn't have time before we left, so they got together and finished it up." Her voice held hushed awe. "It's your wedding dress." Seeing his thorough confusion, she told him how everyone had pitched in so Martha could finish the dress in time for the wedding.

Standing behind her, Ethan circled her waist. "A gift of true friendship," he murmured. "The best kind of all." Turning to face him, she slipped her arms around his neck. Their lips touched.

Rose and Charity barreled through the doorway and skidded to a halt, mouths hanging open as they stared around the room. "We're home," Ethan said resignedly. "No doubt about it."

CHAPTER TWENTY-EIGHT

They determined to devote the next days to settling back into the routine of home and farm. However, they first returned to Fairvale to thank Martha, Shawn, and their other friends for the "Happy Marriage" gift. Shawn and Martha were casual about it. Shawn said simply, "Everyone wanted to help. We prayed with all our hearts when Rose was so sick, but we could put our hands to this."

Everywhere, the response was the same. "We're just glad we could help."

They stopped to see Miss Sullivan. Caught unaware, she quickly composed her questioning exterior into polite interest. Seating them, she took a straight-backed chair and picked up her crochet hook and an afghan-in-progress. "How was the trip?" She spoke to Larissa, but her eyes sought Rose. She listened intently as they described their adventures, including their meetings with Mac. She tipped her head in satisfaction at their report. "He was an excellent student. I expect him to continue to be so." This was high praise. "And your hearing, Rose?" Never one to tiptoe around issues, she aimed the question point-blank at her pupil, past Charity who had been signing and speaking into Rose's ear.

"Dr. Cornell says I shouldn't lose any more of my hearing." The words were low-pitched, but jubilant.

"They taught you this hand communication?" Reticence forgotten, Miss Sullivan was obviously intrigued.

Having lost her inhibitions about being in Teacher's home, Charity piped up. "We can say lots of things to each other. I don't talk into Rose's ear nearly so much anymore."

"You're learning these hand motions, too?" Miss Sullivan fired this query at Ethan and Larissa, who smiled sheepishly.

"Not nearly so fast as Rose and Charity, but we manage to stumble along."

At Larissa's rueful confession, an odd look skittered across Miss Sullivan's face. "Young people soak up knowledge as if their brains were little sea sponges. I find I no longer absorb information as readily as I did in my youth." She faced Rose directly. "But I would like to try to learn these hand signs."

The girls stared at her as if she had announced she would like to learn to dance a jig. "People tend to regard teachers as the possessors of infinite wisdom, forgetting that we, too, enjoy learning for its own sake, and so that we may pass knowledge on to our young people." Alarmed at having revealed so much emotion, Miss Sullivan drove her crochet hook furiously in and out of the dark blue yarn and once more became the stern instructor. "I shall correct your lessons," she announced in her most no-nonsense voice, "and I expect you to be in school Monday morning."

Charity relayed this information to Rose, who asked hesitantly, "May I come, too?"

"Certainly," Miss Sullivan said crisply. "Be assured, you are not escaping my classroom so easily."

As Charity communicated the verdict, Rose's expression broke into a glow as dazzling as sudden lantern light on a dark night. Impulsively, startling everyone, including herself, she threw her arms around Miss Sullivan. "Thank you! Oh, thank you."

Charlotte Sullivan froze. Awkwardly, as if her upper limbs were unsure how to carry out such a procedure, clutching her forgotten yarn and hook, her arms circled Rose in a return hug. "We'll do it, Rose. We'll make it work."

***

Wrapped in the warmth of friendship and caring, they didn't notice the chill February air as they emerged from Miss Sullivan's rooming house. Ethan stopped at the post office, and the girls dashed inside. Scurrying out again, they handed Larissa a letter from Anne Clayton. She opened it eagerly as he turned the team homeward.

Before learning about the Philadelphia trip, Larissa had scribbled a hasty note to Anne, telling her about Rose. She'd written a more detailed one from their hotel, relating their blossoming hopes for Rose's future, and the news that she and Ethan had married.

Deeply sympathetic over Rose's hearing loss, Anne rejoiced with Larissa that her child had survived such a grave illness. *Tomorrow would be Elizabeth's birthday. Strange as it seems, I can see her now just as she would look if she were turning two.* Anne's unintentional wistfulness caught at Larissa's heart. Weighing Rose's deafness, her life spared, against the devastating death of Anne's new-born daughter, it came sharply to her once again how deeply blessed they were. Anne's next words chased the lingering wisps of sorrow back into the shadows. *I'm so happy for you and Ethan! You've been in my prayers since before we began writing, and I hoped for the two of you to find happiness. I just didn't know it would come in such a romantic way.*

Larissa blinked. *Romantic?* Her lips curved in a smile. She'd been so busy enjoying married life and the heart-deep joy that came from knowledge of Ethan's presence, even when he wasn't with her, she hadn't thought to put it in terms of romance. *What we have, just is. But now that Anne mentions it....*

"Good news?" She'd been so drawn into the letter, Ethan's question startled her. The brightness in her eyes confirmed his guess, and he nodded as if agreeing with himself. "Must be very good news at that."

She realized he had turned into the lane leading to Martha's farm, where they found the Hyatts chopping wood. Ethan expressed his hearty thanks for their excellent care of the place. When he tried to pay them, they looked surprised and firmly folded their arms over their chests because, "We're neighbors."

***

Monday morning contained all the old confusion of preparing breakfast and shooing the girls out the door before they were late for school. Larissa stood on the porch and waved her dishcloth as the team disappeared around the curve in the drive. She clutched the towel to her heart. Never before had she realized how much happiness could come from the typically frustrating morning scene they'd just finished.

She found herself already waiting impatiently for Ethan's return. To keep her mind occupied while she checked the foodstuffs in the pantry and down-cellar for spoilage and bugs after the long absence, she mulled over Anne's letter. Besides sharing her joy at their marriage, Anne had related how the Clark's Valley community was jumping with excitement. The men from the surrounding ranches were jubilant because the Union Pacific Railroad was finally and truly coming into Nebraska Territory. As Ben put it, she wrote, "When it comes through, the whole country will be a market for our beef cattle!"

The most important news by far, however, was that the community was discussing the building of a real schoolhouse. "It isn't much more than talk, just yet," she admitted, "because no one can agree on the site. In this widespread land, everyone, of course, is voting to put it near their own home to be close by for their children. So it will undoubtedly be a while, but the very idea is a dream come true for me."

Anne had once mentioned she taught the children at home. Thinking of her own typically crowded days, Larissa had wondered how Anne could fit teaching into a day already jammed full of work vital to her family's survival. *And I still don't have the answer.*

When she finally heard Ethan's footsteps on the porch, she threw open the door. "How did it go?" she demanded before he even made it inside.

He shrugged. "I don't know. I dropped them off same as usual and let them go in by themselves. We don't want to make things more different for Rose than they already are."

Larissa sighed. *Men! Why do they have to be so infuriatingly right sometimes?*

Time dragged until he left to retrieve the girls. It dragged even more until she saw out the window over the sink that they'd returned. She forced herself to remain in the kitchen. Looking up from grating the potatoes she would use to make laundry starch, she said casually, "You're home already. Did it feel strange—?" Her cheerful words bit off at sight of Rose's bleakness, Charity's fury, and Ethan's downright disgust.

Before Larissa could ask, Charity's outrage exploded. "The big boys teased Rose. When we tried to go inside after lunch, Elias Adler and Orville Hadwin sat on the steps and wouldn't let us by. They pretended to sign to each other, then laughed like crazy."

Larissa's heart fell to the bottom of her shoes. She'd wondered about such a circumstance rearing its ugly head, and had dismissed the thought. *Not in this school. Not in Fairvale.* How wrong she had been.

Her silent question, directed at Ethan, showed large in her eyes. Charity burst out, "I told them to let us by, but they just made dopey faces and waved their hands around some more. Elias was sitting on the bottom step. I was so mad I shoved him as hard as I could. He fell back and hit his head against the railing. He sat up and his nose started bleeding." Deep satisfaction in her voice, Charity accompanied her narrative with vividly descriptive gestures. "He grabbed at me, but before I could whack him again, Garth got between him and me. I tried to go around Garth, but he wouldn't let me.

"He told Orville and Elias if they wanted to fight, to pick on someone their own size. He put his fists up like he was going to punch Orville and make his nose bleed, too. I didn't know Garth could look so mad." Upraised fists theatrically clenched, she gleefully savored the memory. "Orville looked just as mad and grabbed Garth's arm. Everyone kept hollering at them, but Miss Sullivan came out before they hit each other. She asked what happened, so I told her. I've never seen her so furious! Except the day Ian and Bruiser pushed me into the mud puddle," she amended. "I remember how scared of her I was that day. I bet Orville and Elias were, too, today, but they'd sure never admit it."

"What happened next?" Larissa couldn't curb her impatience at Charity's meandering.

"She told Elias and Orville to go home, and that they'd have to bring their parents if they came back. She made the rest of us go inside. She glared at everyone and said while she knew none of us had caused the trouble, she *would not tolerate* such behavior. No one made a sound until she dismissed us. Then Pa came, and we had to wait in the entryway while she talked to him." As she ran out of breath and story, a horse nickered.

Startled, Ethan peered through the robin's-egg blue wool drapes that had replaced the green gingham curtains for wintertime. "It's Miss Sullivan." He hurried to open the door.

Once inside, she wasted no time on small talk. "I presume you've discussed this unfortunate matter. I have come to apologize for the unacceptable behavior that came out of my school today." Back straight and unyielding, she did not spare herself. "I am ultimately responsible for my pupils' actions when they are in my charge. I failed all of you today, but I failed Rose the most. I assure you, it will never happen again." She spoke forcefully, sealing the doom of any student who dared attempt such ill-advised behavior.

Having apologized, she moved to the next topic. "Rose managed very well today, and I determined what she heard, and what she didn't, by her reactions. If you agree, I will come here each Saturday afternoon to instruct her and clear up any confusion." Seeing their shock at such a generous offer, she added tartly, "In exchange, I expect her to teach me this signing method she and Charity used today. I was intrigued by how readily Charity relayed my instructions and how swiftly Rose responded."

Rose had followed Charity's dramatic gestures and her recital of Miss Sullivan's apology and intentions. Now she hunched her shoulders. "Will I still have to go to school?"

Ignoring Larissa's sharp intake of breath at her daughter's distress, Miss Sullivan bent so Rose could hear her clearly. "I thought you might be reluctant. It's for your folks to say, but you should. You can't let those boys think they've won. Which they will if you don't return. I refuse to let one of my best pupils lose out because of a couple of bullies. If they left school, it wouldn't matter so much," she said grimly. "But it matters very much when it comes to you."

The next afternoon, Larissa waited with a nearly equal measure of anxiety and impatience while Ethan went to get the girls. This time, Rose bounced into the room with all the enthusiasm she had lacked yesterday. "Everyone was so nice. Helen Olsen even asked if we would teach her some signs, and Gretta and Mara have been practicing the ones we showed them on Friday."

"Did Elias and Orville come to school today?" Larissa was afraid to ask the question and even more afraid not to.

Rose giggled. "Miss Sullivan went to see their folks before school. They came in late, but they apologized to Miss Sullivan and me. Gretta told us she heard them talking at the noon break, and that their Pas whipped them but good. They sure sat kind of funny, all day!"

On Wednesday morning, Shawn stopped Ethan on his way back from dropping off the girls. He reported that Doc had sent a telegram announcing he and Hans would arrive on the evening train. Larissa and Ethan didn't know whether to pity or admire his optimism, but they and the girls were in the station waiting room, waiting, when the train pulled in, only two hours late. They greeted Doc so warmly that he turned prickly in order to hide his pleasure.

Hans emerged from the car and stood staring at the vast dark beyond the train station. Doc pulled him forward, and they welcomed him with heartfelt appreciation. He looked a little stunned at being greeted so enthusiastically. In the disjointed conversation and bustling confusion of collecting the baggage and sorting out what would go with Doc and what with Hans to the farm, his first awkward minutes of newness slipped past.

After dropping Doc at his office, Ethan guided the team back along Main Street, giving Hans his first shadowy glimpse of Fairvale. When they rattled over the Mill Creek bridge and started on the road home, they quickly left the few lights of the town behind, so that they were guided by starlight, by the lamps hanging off the side of the wagon, and by the good sense of Andromeda and Pegasus as instinct urged them toward their warm stalls and the oats waiting for them.

In the dim light, the girls couldn't see Hans' signs, but it didn't matter. They both talked enough for all three of them as they filled him in on their adventures since leaving Philadelphia. He jumped a foot and ducked as a large owl, disturbed by their passing, swooped above them and delivered its opinion in a long-drawn-out *who-o-o-o-o*.

At the house, they hurried inside to thaw out with hot coffee before Ethan took Hans over to the cabin. Even if he could have spoken, he probably wouldn't have as he gazed in awe and curiosity at the warm, cheerful kitchen and its furnishings. His wonder brought sharp awareness to Larissa and Ethan just how much he had lost in that carriage wreck when he was six. His parents, his speech, and the ordinary marvel of standing in a kitchen in a house that was truly a home.

After coffee, and hot cocoa for Rose and Charity, over their strenuous objections that they were grown up enough to drink the adult brew, Larissa sent them, protesting, to bed. Ethan walked Hans to the cabin, and returned with a pensive smile. He had had quite a time convincing Hans that the cabin, all of it, was his living quarters, and that he wouldn't be sharing it with anyone. Once more they received an unintentional glimpse of the barren existence of his growing-up years.

The next days passed swiftly as Hans settled in to his new life. When he was not riding out with Doc, his farming lessons included shoveling snow, tending the stock, and currying the horses. His bustling city life had, plainly, been so far removed from this quiet rural existence that they feared he would have a difficult time adjusting. He encountered a few bumps in the road, such as assisting at the birth of a calf and giving medicine to a sick hog. Evidently, however, his acceptance into a real family more than adequately compensated for the jolts of reality he received.

Lambing time, melting snow, and warmer days heralded the coming of spring. Ethan discussed plowing and planting plans with Hans as though the two of them had been doing it together for years. Hans frequently looked bewildered at the complexity of the process. Having taken eating for granted, he learned that food on the table came as the result of countless hours of backbreaking work and careful preparation.

Doc reported that Hans was showing an aptitude for his medical training. For Doc, this admission was shouted-from-the rooftop praise. When the family learned that in exchange for medical knowledge, Hans was teaching Doc to sign, Doc merely growled that he couldn't do all the talking all the time—in spite of what some folks thought. How was he supposed to answer Hans' questions if he didn't know what they were?

Not in the least deceived by this blustering, Larissa and Ethan were deeply grateful that Doc, too, would be able to communicate with Rose, one more bridge out of the silent world around her. During this time of turning his whole life inside out, Hans also insisted Ethan and Larissa continue their lessons. He was always polite and cheerful, but they quickly learned that his amiable attitude masked a determination that rivaled Miss Sullivan's.

***

In May, Martha delivered a healthy boy. The church women took care of her and the children, so Larissa and Ethan first visited them the day after baby Camden's birth. Ethan, having "been there, done that" was sympathetically amused by Shawn's fear of the baby squiggling out of his clutching hold.

On the way home, however, Ethan's lightness dropped from him like a coat discarded on a too-warm day. At Larissa's questioning touch, he silently pulled her close to his side.

He halted the buggy at the kitchen path. "I need to do a couple of things. It'll take a few minutes." She prepared the noon dinner and waited for him to come in. His few minutes became almost an hour, and her earlier tension returned. He was always as punctual as the sun and moon. Abandoning the cooling meal, she crossed the drive to the barn and called his name. Receiving no answer, she turned toward the apple orchard, his refuge in times of disquiet. He wasn't there.

She found him down by Mill Creek. He was leaning against the Sitting Seat, one arm resting on the ledge as he gazed out over the water. Her appearance didn't startle him. Rather, he drew her head against his shoulder as if he had been waiting for her. His heart beat under her ear, strong and steady as always, and some of her tension eased. The gusty breath he released could have come from his toes. "After Andrew died, I shied away from any memories of those four months with him. Seeing Shawn with Camden, the memories came anyway. I tried to ignore them, but they wouldn't stay ignored. I thought coming out here, now, would give me a chance to clear my mind. I just lost track of time pondering it, no holds barred. Rather like poking a bruised rib, to find out if it's still sore," he said wryly. "I've thought of Andrew and how it was. So many good-to-remember moments, once I quit fighting them. Lizzie, it doesn't hurt. It's all right this time." His voice vibrating with gratitude, he pressed his cheek to her hair. "It really is all right."

CHAPTER TWENTY-NINE

Framed by the rotating farm seasons, the weeks spun past. A windy September Saturday marked two years to the day Mac had left. "We scarcely turn the calendar to a new month before the next one jumps out, and suddenly it's the next year," Larissa lamented to Ethan. "Or am I the only one who thinks that?"

"Rest assured, you're not alone, Lizzie. Shawn and I have discussed it. We see it in terms of the farm cycle of planting and harvesting. He looks at it in terms of babies' heads." He grinned at her total confusion. "He says it seems he no more than pours water over a howling head to christen it than that mad-as-Moses infant is walking and talking and going to school. He says it's impossible to believe Camden is already past a year old. I told him to wait until his son turns fifteen like Charity and Rose."

"What did he say?"

"Something a hard-working, dedicated minister of the Lord shouldn't."

"Ethan!" A spurt of laughter trickled past her hastily shut lips. "I hope Martha didn't hear him."

His eyes twinkled. "He hopes she didn't, either. I received the distinct impression he was much more worried about earthly wrath than he was about heavenly retribution."

***

On a crisp October morning following this conversation, Larissa stuck her head into the barn. Ethan and Hans were husking corn, sitting on the frame Ethan had devised so that he didn't have to crouch on his knees to strip the ears from the shocks. "Martha's here. Doc says Elsie Damon's feeling poorly, so she and I are going out to help."

Ethan brushed corn silk from his green flannel shirt and put his arms around her for a quick kiss. Hans ducked his head and became very busy plucking a last few shreds of silk from the ear he was stripping. It had taken him a while to get used to seeing the quiet affection Ethan and Larissa displayed. Now, nearly two years later, he apparently accepted it as just one more experience in this new world of family life.

"I hope everything's all right with her." Ethan removed a wayward wisp of corn silk from Larissa's dark blue cape. "With nine young ones, I'm sure she can use some assistance. If they need help with the farm work, we'll be glad to lend a hand."

"I'll tell her. According to Martha, Doc says she has a really nasty cold."

Behind them, Hans cleared his throat, a formless sound that, like a sigh or laughter, he could make to get their attention. Ethan and Larissa understood his signs, provided he didn't go too fast. To their joint chagrin, Rose and Charity followed him easily, and had for many months.

Now he signed that Doc was afraid it would go into lung fever if she didn't rest.

"Sounds like you and Martha have the right idea, Lizzie, but I'm not sure you'll actually be able to get her to stop long enough to rest. She's one determined lady when it comes to taking care of her family." Ethan winked at Hans. "Just like someone else I know."

Larissa wrinkled her nose at him. "I don't hear anyone complaining."

Ethan backed away a step, pretending to fend her off. "Not a peep from either of us. Right, Hans?"

Hans grinned, pointed to his mouth and shook his head. "Not a peep from me," he signed. He had been with them for several months when, in a moment of discouragement, he'd confessed to Ethan that he understood how the ugly duckling must have felt among all those swans. When people spoke to him, if none of the family was handy, he couldn't convey a response unless he used pencil and paper. Evidently, he was no longer so self-conscious about his lack of speech. Lately, sometimes, as now, he even joked about it.

"I should be back by mid-afternoon," Larissa assured Ethan as he handed her up to the buggy seat beside Martha. "Rose and Charity can start supper if I'm late."

"I'll pick them up after school. I need to stop by the blacksmith shop, anyway. Good luck with the Damons." He waved them down the drive and, from ingrained habit, scanned the sky for a potential weather change before returning to the barn.

That afternoon, Hans hitched up the buckboard, proud of his country skill, since city life had afforded him no such opportunity. Ethan invited him to go to town, but he declined, saying he would continue with the corn husking.

Once out on the quiet road, Ethan didn't hurry the team. His mind wandered from thought to thought as he considered the tasks to be done before snowfall. He and Hans had plowed and fertilized the corn and wheat fields, giving the coming freezing and thawing a chance to work the soil. He needed to finish cleaning the farm machinery, and get in more wood for the stoves and fireplaces. *A hundred odd jobs, large and small, to contend with.* He was glad Hans was there to lend a hand. It was always more pleasurable to have company, and Hans had proved a willing worker, even if he didn't understand all the whys and wherefores.

In spite of his musing, he reached town with plenty of time to pick up the girls at school. *Might as well stop by the blacksmith shop first and drop off the rake.* He hoped the Painter brothers could straighten the mangled tines. While raking leaves off the paths yesterday, Hans had stubbed his toe on a half-buried rock beside the walkway. With more enthusiasm than knowledge, he had thought he could dig it out with the rake. He had been deeply embarrassed and apologetic at the results, which was undoubtedly the reason he'd declined to come to town today.

Ethan grinned. The way he saw it, even throwing in the possibility of having to buy a new rake, if that was the worst mistake Hans ever made at farming, he was going to be successful beyond anyone's imagination.

Halting the buckboard near the blacksmith's forge, he swung down and retrieved the rake. Neither Jonas nor Jacob, Miles Painter's twin sons, was at the anvil, nor were they out by the corral. It floated into his mind, and back out again, that such behavior was unusual for them. He wandered over to the office. Propping the rake against the door frame, he peered into the dim interior and caught sight of Shawn standing near Jacob and Jonas. His joking comment, about the minister being seen in such a worldly place as the blacksmith shop, died as their united seriousness jumped out at him.

"Ethan." Shawn put a hand on his arm.

His relaxed contentment swiftly became uneasiness. "What's going on?"

"We figured you'd be coming by on your way to pick up Rose and Charity."

"Rose and Charity? What's wrong?"

"They're fine."

Shawn's hasty reassurance did nothing to ease the anxiety now stabbing Ethan like a hundred needles. "Then what?"

"We wanted to let you know, before anyone else told you. Obadiah Beldane is back."

Ethan froze. *Obadiah Beldane.* The Union Army had sent him and Zane to Nebraska Territory during the Civil War. During an Indian attack on one of the outpost stage stations on the Overland Trail, Zane had saved Obadiah's life at the cost of his own. In quick, haunted flicks, the pictures veered across Ethan's mind. *Fairvale's newspaper office, the sharp odors of ink and newspaper assailing him ... John Shearer, the owner and editor, telling him Zane was dead ... Larissa, caught up in those joyous moments of believing Ethan was Zane, come home to her. Her eyes, drowned in anguish when he told her the truth....*

"... it's been preying on him, ever since." Ethan dragged his awareness back to the dusky blacksmith shop and Shawn's words echoing around him. "We told him you and Larissa are married. He had no idea, of course. He wants to see you, Ethan."

"Why?" The lone word, dredged from his deepest soul, grated harshly in his mouth.

Shawn's hand on his arm tightened. "He wants to apologize."

"Apologize?" Ethan's throat was so thick he didn't even recognize his own voice.

"He wants to—"

"Ethan." The word drifted from the darker shadows at the far end of the room. Behind Shawn's shoulder, the shadows stirred, and Obadiah Beldane emerged.

"What are you doing here?" The words choked in Ethan's throat and he spit them out.

"Ethan, wait a—"

He brushed aside Shawn's warning plea, much as he would brush aside a buzzing fly, annoying but too trivial to merit his focus.

Obadiah had aged severely in the years since he left Fairvale. His shoulders were stooped and his once-bright eyes had become those of a very old man. But he didn't back down from Ethan's hackles-raised challenge. "I've come to say how sorry I am for what happened."

"Sorry?" Ethan repeated disbelievingly. White-hot anger burned in his deliberately spaced words. "You can go straight to—go back to wherever you came from."

"I can't. Not yet."

Ethan didn't ask Obadiah the obvious question, just stood there, eyes scorching him. As if he'd gone over them so many times they were branded on his mind, Obadiah's words spilled out. "It should of been me, not Zane. It's been pullin' at me, ever since. I thought if I could talk about it, maybe it'd ease up some."

Pulling at you? A wild urge to laugh welled up, but the hilarity strangled in Ethan's throat. *A part of every one of us died when Zane did. Now you come stomping around to stir everything up again.* "You came here to apologize." His voice was brittle. "Fine. You apologized. We see how sorry you are. We already know what happened, so there's no point in dragging it all up again. It appears that your business here is finished, and you can go your merry way."

Obadiah blanched at the harsh tone and words, but stood his ground, giving Ethan back stare for stare. Shawn spoke into the pit of silence. "Obadiah and I talked before you came. He's made it very clear to me he intends to leave town, just as soon as he finishes what he came here to do."

"Keeping in mind what he's already done, there can't be anything important enough to hold him here." His stare pinned on Obadiah, Ethan sensed rather than saw Shawn stiffen, and knew with total certainty what he was going to say.

"He wants to apologize to Larissa."

The moment ticked into existence and ticked past. The knowledge had been shaped into words that could not be undone. He stood silent for so long, Obadiah finally shifted uneasily. The slight movement released Ethan and he threw Shawn's restraining hand off his arm. "Like hell you will." He strode out the door into the late afternoon sunshine.

Forgetting about the bent tines and the rake still propped against the wall, he thrust past Jonas and Jacob, who had discreetly retreated when Obadiah first stepped out of the shadows. He vaulted into the buckboard, but before he could flip the lines, Shawn spoke behind him. "Ethan. Wait."

Only his deep respect for Shawn kept Ethan from sending the horses into wild flight. Lines in hand and mouth clamped shut, he waited, knowing that, friendship or not, he would cut out at Shawn's first word attempting to soothe him.

"Should I pick up Rose and Charity and take them to the parsonage?"

Caught off guard, brought sharply back to reality, Ethan floundered. "No. They're expecting me. Best keep it so."

"If you decide different, we're here to help."

Scrambled as his thoughts were, Ethan caught Shawn's deeper meaning. Discarding it, he shook the lines, startling Pegasus and Andromeda. The buckboard lurched away, but without the silent strength of Shawn's friendship, Ethan's hard-held control withered like an uprooted cornstalk.

If Zane's death has "pulled at" Obadiah, what in God's name does he think it's done to Larissa? And what will knowledge of his return do to her after she's finally reached a level of peace she can live with?

Somewhere on his short journey from the blacksmith shop to the school, his entrenched sense of duty kicked in, warning him he couldn't pick up Charity and Rose while he was acting, feeling, and undoubtedly looking, like a man fleeing a nest of unhappy hornets. Several children had already meandered past on their way home from school. Regardless, he pulled to the side of the road and made a dogged effort to squash his visible reaction to the events of the past half hour. When he finally motioned the team forward, he suspected his attempt wouldn't win a prize as a rip-snorting success, but it was the best he could do.

His suspicion proved correct. At sight of him, Rose and Charity broke off their cheerful words of greeting. Settling onto the seat, they exchanged wary glances. After they crossed the rattling bridge over Mill

Creek, Charity couldn't stand it any longer. "Pa, are you mad with us?" Her voice wobbled.

Unable to dredge up even the semblance of a lighthearted response, he said flatly, "No." Miraculously, somewhere in these past months, Charity had learned discretion. Instead of peppering him with a dozen questions, she exchanged another cautious glance with Rose, and moved her hands.

Ethan had neither the energy nor the desire to point out that she was breaking one of the family's basic rules. At the beginning, they had agreed no one would sign in front of someone else without also voicing aloud the discussion, similar to the courtesy of not whispering to one person in a group of hearing individuals. Spared the necessity of explanation, he hunched in the seat and stared without seeing at the horses' manes bobbing rhythmically to their gait. The wave of earlier, half-formed thoughts he hadn't dared to complete crashed over him.

Larissa. True, she had achieved a level of peace she could live with. Now, Obadiah's homecoming would test that level. *Because, for certain, she can't remain unaffected by his return, any more than a cornstalk yanked from the soil by its roots can remain unshriveled.* The fear he had, by sheer desperation, kept at bay washed through him. This time, he forced himself to complete the thought. *How will Obadiah's return from that earlier life, hauling the past forward into the present, affect our marriage?* They'd planted their commitment in the rich soil of shared love, but some of the roots stretched deep into their separate pasts....

Ethan let the girls off at the kitchen path, and Hans ran from the barn to take the team. Ethan put a hand on Charity's shoulder as she hopped down. "I want you and Rose to go straight upstairs. I have something I need to discuss with Ma."

"Pa?"

"Do as I say." He handed the lines to Hans and followed the girls up the path. Having mentally shoved himself this far, only to find that Larissa was not in the kitchen, his already wire-humming-thin tension stretched perilously. The table was neatly set for supper, with Larissa's special touch, a bowl of bronze chrysanthemums, positioned in the center. Steam rose gently from the pans on the stove. Rose and Charity hung up their bonnets and coats and looked to him questioningly.

The cellar door stood ajar. Larissa was singing about the bonny banks of Loch Lomond, the melody floating closer as she came up the steps to the kitchen. He jerked his head toward the sitting room doorway and the stairs. "Go along. And no eavesdropping." Turned away as they were, he couldn't tell for certain, but he suspected both girls rolled their eyes. "I'm trusting you to obey me." He knew he was handling this badly, but he could fix it later. *Right now, only Larissa matters.*

She carried a bowl of unshelled walnuts. Her unconcealed happiness at seeing him sent his resolve flapping away like a gun-shy crow. Was it his acute awareness or was her welcome more joyful than usual?

"Ethan, I didn't realize you were home. I've been waiting for you. I have some news I believe will interest you very much."

With his mind clamped around what he must say, he only half heard her as he set the bowl of unshelled walnuts on the worktable and drew her into his arms. He held her close, her hair soft and fragrant beneath his cheek, while the crow, uninvited, flapped back and ruthlessly took a large bite out of his determination to speak. His courage, already faltering, slunk on its belly to the next lower rung of the ladder. His arms tightened around her.

She leaned back. "What's wrong?"

His breath lodged in his lungs, refusing to go either in or out, so that the words rasped from his throat. "I have to talk to you."

Concern joined, but did not override, that lit-up happiness. "Ethan, are you feeling all right?"

He had no way to soften it for her. "Obadiah Beldane is in town."

She merely looked at him as blankly as if he'd announced it was going to snow next August. He waited, his heart thumping against his chest and hammering in his ears. For a long second, time's rhythm stuck fast in place, unable to go forward to the future—impossible to go back to the past. For that long, frozen second she looked at him.

"Why?" The sound was barely audible.

He set his jaw, willing the words to come out steady and sure. "He came to apologize to you. He wants to tell you how sorry he is for what happened."

The light went out of her, as swiftly and completely as a single puff of wind could extinguish the candle flame in his tin lantern. She stiffened and wrenched backward, but he tightened his arms around her. "Lizzie…."

"No, Ethan. Please let me go." The words were low, clear, and utterly without emotion.

His heart, earlier thumping fiercely against his ribs, was now a leaden weight, draining him of strength. He could not, would not ever, hold her against her wishes. He loosened his arms and she backed away from him. "I have to think about this." Her tone was still lifeless. Her spine plumb-line straight and her chin firmly up, she walked into the bedroom and shut the door.

He could only wish that his heart had stayed a leaden lump. Pain clawed at him, tearing his insides as relentlessly as a wolf at the kill. He stared unseeing at the table neatly set for supper. Suffocating hands gripped his ribs so tightly that the candlelit kitchen darkened. Without retrieving his coat or hat from the hook above the wash bench, he yanked the door open. He stumbled on the porch steps and caught his balance barely in time to avoid pitching forward flat on his face.

Hans, grinning proudly, hurried toward him, signing excitedly. "Mr. Michaels, I did the chores all by myself." His hands froze in mid-air as Ethan rushed past him. "Mr. Michaels?" His throat formed the words, but only a hoarse jumble emerged as Ethan headed for the barn like the devil himself was pursuing him and gaining rapidly.

Once inside the barn, dark though it was, he unerringly reached for the tin lantern and lit the candle. The light bloomed, bringing the farm implements and equipment into focus. He wandered around, his mechanical check of the animals confirming that Hans had done everything neatly and correctly. Eventually, he found himself back where he had started. Even when he was no more than knee-high to a flea, entering a barn, inhaling the mingled odors of animals, saddle leather, and hay had given him a sense of well-being. Always, his satisfaction had run deep, knowing he was carrying out the work he had been born to do. Tonight, he stood in the middle of the room and there was no well-being, no satisfaction.

From the first time he'd walked into this place, he had had a sense of home, of belonging. He'd never thought to question it. Now, the empty silence pushed at him and reality slithered around the corners of his mind, taunting him. *Zane's barn. Zane's farm. Zane's wife.*

His stomach kicked and bile rose in his throat. Dropping onto a seat built out of an old flour barrel, he stuck his head between his knees, willing the nausea away. The impulse finally faded, leaving him sweat-damp but all in one piece. He buried his head in his hands. *No, not all in one piece.* When Larissa backed out of his arms, part of him had gone with her.

His lofty thoughts before their marriage buzzed in his head. He'd been so certain he didn't have to compete with Zane in any area of his relationship with her. He was warm, strong and alive, and so deeply in love with her, he had confidently assumed he could fill her heart with that love. Such arrogance now sent a chill through him. For the second time that day, remorselessly, memory thrust her pictures at him.

Larissa, smiling up at him the first time he had ever seen her, and she completely unaware that, in that moment, the cold, hard knot in his heart loosened for the first time since Nettie's death. A hundred everyday scenes of her tending to her tasks about the farm, giving Charity the same loving care Mac and Rose received. *Her radiant joy on their wedding day—and night.* Savagely, he flung the pictures aside and yanked his thoughts away from the past, back to the present pain, to the future he must soon confront.

A shudder ran through him and he realized the night cold had seeped into his bones. Naturally, because he'd neglected to wear his coat and hat, the temperature had dropped. Returning to the house, he tried to shove aside all thought and emotion. They stubbornly refused to stay shoved, particularly when he found the kitchen empty. The bedroom door remained closed, a barrier that mocked him. With deepening despondency, he turned his back on it. The table settings had been reduced from five to two, one at his place and one at Larissa's.

He ignored the covered dishes holding his supper. Her unused setting could only mean she hadn't eaten, either. His aimless footsteps took him into the sitting room. Crouching in front of the fireplace, he kindled the glowing coals into a snapping blaze. He started to sit in the leather chair but halted abruptly. *Zane's house. Zane's chair.*

He turned on his heel to the high-backed bench facing the fireplace. Sinking down, he clasped his hands loosely between his knees and stared unseeing at the merrily crackling flames. He didn't hear anything, but some sense made him twist toward the stairs.

Charity and Rose, in their nightgowns, stood rigid and silent on the bottom step. *How long have they been there?*

The question scuttled away because both girls looked ready to burst into tears. Charity clasped her hands so tightly in front of her, the knuckles turned as white as her gown. "Pa." Her voice wavered so, he could scarcely understand her. "Are you going to die?"

Shocked out of his dark musing, he wondered if he had heard her correctly. "Of course not."

"If you are, you can tell us the truth."

His brain suddenly numb, he held out his arms. They scurried to him and, one on either side, shaking uncontrollably, threw themselves at him. He wrapped an arm around each and spoke near Rose's ear. "I'm not dying, I promise you." He forced the words past the sudden swelling in his throat. "I would never lie to you about that."

At this reassurance, they started bawling. Each one buried her face against the shoulder nearest her. Never having done double duty before, he held them awkwardly. Both shoulders on his shirt were wet and cold by the time the downpour eased. Ignoring the clamminess, he pulled them around to face him. "Why ever did you think such a thing?"

"You looked so sad, Pa. Like you did when my other Ma and Rose's other Pa died. We thought at first it was Ma, because you acted so sad when you picked us up from school. But when we got home and heard Ma singing, and she sounded so happy, we decided it must be you. But you're sad, and now Ma's sad, too. We were so scared!"

Guilt punched him with an iron-hard fist. He'd promised himself to straighten it out with them later, but he never intended it to be this much later. "I didn't mean to frighten you. Someone who left town a long time ago came back today and wants to see Ma. But I know Ma doesn't want to see him. So I was worried about telling her."

Relief flooded both tear-splotched faces. "Do you think Ma'll change her mind, and see him, and not be sad anymore?"

He drew them close again. "I don't know, Rose. I just don't know."

After he'd sent them to bed, he returned to the kitchen and picked up a candle from the table. The closed bedroom door loomed before him. He knocked softly and went in.

She stood beside the window, still dressed, and didn't turn as he set the candlestick on the commode. "Lizzie, it's cold in here. Why don't you come to bed?" She shook her head. In the reflection created by the candle glow against the window glass, he saw her lips press together and wondered what she wasn't saying. *If only you would talk to me.* "Larissa. If you stand here in the cold, you'll make yourself ill, for certain." She turned her head in time for him to see something flick across her features, but it vanished before he could identify it.

Once more he did his best to make his words steady and sure. "I won't do anything you don't want me to. I just don't want you to get sick. I'm not telling you what to do. But I am asking you. Please."

Again, that faint spark touched her eyes and was gone. "All right, Ethan." Her voice still uncompromisingly flat, she turned stiffly, not looking at him.

"I'll go bank the fires." He left hurriedly, lest she change her mind. He tended the ashes, blew out the candles, did all the small things of putting a house to bed.

When he returned, she was huddled under the covers, facing his side of the bed. His initial spurt of hope pinched off with the realization she was curled into a tight ball. With fumbling hands he undressed, blew out the candle, and slid in beside her. Careful not to touch her, he stretched out on his side, facing her, with his hand resting in the gulf of space between them.

It had become part of their private, lighthearted ritual that the second one to get into bed would extend a hand for the other to take, a mutual joining before she lay in his arms. His heart hammering, he waited. Hesitantly her fingers, ice-cold, touched his hand. Her body remained tightly curled, warning him that she had not yet fully crossed the distance between them. Carefully, he moved his hand until his warm fingers covered her chilly ones. Slowly, stiffly, she slid toward him until she lay against his chest in the position that had become natural to them. She remained rigid, however, clearly signaling that the problem had not been solved.

Unable to keep silent, he murmured against her ear, "Lizzie, can't you tell me what it is you need that I'm not giving you?" Against his chest, her head moved from side to side, her only response.

Cut to the bone by her withdrawal, he, too, lay stiffly for a long while, before he dozed fitfully, coming awake each time she moved. At last, worn out physically and mentally, he fell deeply asleep. He woke with complete awareness that she was no longer in his arms. Even before he reached out, he knew her side of the bed was empty. In the shifting moonlight, he saw her standing at the window.

Frustrated, he pushed back the covers. The cold floorboards stung his feet, but he ignored the discomfort. "Come back to bed." He put his hand on her shoulder, half expecting her to flinch away from his touch. This time he couldn't keep the desperation out of his voice. "Lizzie, don't do this to yourself. Don't do this to us."

Beneath his hand, a tremor ran through her. "I just need time. Please. Give me that time."

In the faint light, her eyes were wide and dark. He thought she might have been crying earlier, but she wasn't now. The optimism he had clutched throughout these past hours, the belief that everything would be all right, now clenched into a tight fist of hopelessness and lodged like a rock in the pit of his stomach. "All right, Larissa. I can't keep fighting the decision you've so obviously made. You'll have your time." His voice cracked with anger and she flinched, silencing him.

Hand on the doorknob, he turned to face her once more. "When you're ready to talk, let me know. Until then, I won't bother you." He walked out and the door shut between them.

CHAPTER THIRTY

The door snapping shut cracked like a rifle shot in Ethan's ears, and the bitter thoughts he could no longer hold back snarled through his mind. He started toward the leather chair beside the fireplace, but caught himself and veered to the bench instead.

He stared at the banked coals that were no hotter than his burning anger. Why had she thrown up a barrier so rock-hard neither his love nor his words could penetrate it? Why couldn't he get through to her? *Why in God's name hadn't Obadiah just stayed away?* Trying to kick away the memories that insisted on intruding, he lost track of time, until the mantle clock above his head whirred and chimed.

Sometime during the past hours, the coals in the fireplace had faded to embers, still glowing, but without the white-hot heat they had earlier radiated. Sometime, too, during those hours, his burning anger had dulled to sparks among the gray ashes of his fury.

Larissa. Bleakly, he clamped his mind shut at the thought of her. *Better get out to the barn.* He'd never felt less like moving in his life. Only hard knowledge that the animals under his care were depending on him forced him to stir. Last night, Hans did all the work by himself. *Correctly, too. But I can't do that again to the boy.*

With dreariness permeating every fiber of his being, he moved slowly and stiffly, doggedly forcing his mind away from the only thoughts that mattered. *Time to get the girls stirring.* He had no clue if he was supposed to take charge of the breakfast preparations. He'd better allow more time than usual, just in case.

Larissa didn't answer his rap on the bedroom door. He'd assured her he wouldn't bother her, but he needed his work clothes. Grimly determined, he turned the knob. The room was empty. With no idea where she'd gone, he had to assume she was all right. Her ultimatum, for it amounted to nothing less, spelled out plainly he was to keep his distance. Apparently, this distance entailed getting the girls fed and off to school on time, not to mention the waiting chores. He also owed Hans an apology. Daunted even before he finished compiling the list, he retrieved his clothes. Brutally slamming shut the door of his mind to that other written list he'd fished out of the snowbank for finishing this room before their wedding, he waded into the day.

Hans appeared promptly, as always, to help with the chores, but he didn't initiate a conversation, and didn't ask a million questions about the farm work as he usually did. While they milked, Ethan gathered up his discouragement and his embarrassment and related, as he had to Rose and Charity, how it had been yesterday. The boy listened without comment until Ethan ran out of explanation and simply said he was sorry.

Hans had concentrated on milking while Ethan talked. Now he shifted, and his hands moved slowly, as if his mind were shaping the words carefully. "I might understand a little of her thoughts. I was so angry after the accident. I'd never see my parents again. I couldn't talk. For a long time, I hated the people whose pig had run into the street and caused the horses to bolt. Maybe that's how it is with her. She knows it wasn't Mr. Beldane's fault, but blaming him gives her a reason for Mr. Edwards' death. Thinking he died for nothing at all would be unbearable. I know, now, no one deliberately caused the accident, and I don't hate those people anymore. My life is very different from how it started. Because of that accident, I met Doc, and I'm here with all of you. But I still get angry, sometimes, when people assume because I don't talk, I must be stupid, too. Or because I can't talk, I must not be able to hear, either, and they say all kinds of things."

Ethan, diverted from his own trouble by this confession, demanded, "Here in Fairvale?"

Hans shrugged. "Only one or two. Almost everyone has been very kind to me, here. Not like Philadelphia. People ask me, sometimes, how to sign a word. And Ellen Damon has learned lots of the signs, so we can talk." His fingers fumbled, then, and he turned dark red.

For the first time in hours, something besides anger and frustration stirred in Ethan. *Ellen Damon?* One of Elsie Damon's daughters. A nice young girl. Shy, but not repressed, as she and all the other children had been while under Theo Damon's thumb. *Another benefit to Theo's forgetting to come home after the Civil War ended?* He sighed and rubbed his forehead with his sleeve. "You've given me a bushel of ideas to consider, Hans. It does put things in a different light. But for now, we better get to the house and see what the girls have fixed for breakfast. Just promise me one thing. No matter how it's come out, let's do our best to put a good face on it."

Hans looked doubtful. "If we praise it, do we really have to eat it, too?"

"Let's not open the trap until we're sure we haven't bagged a cranky skunk, then we'll decide."

In the kitchen, the girls, surprisingly enough, had everything ready. Ethan, watching them absently, didn't detect any of their previous night's worry. Was it because, reassured that neither parent was dying, they were getting on with normal living and leaving the other problems for the adults to settle? His swallow of coffee suddenly tasted like brass. He set down his cup. "This is a great meal," he said, signing the compliment with all the enthusiasm he could dredge up. Hans slanted a skeptical look at him, which he carefully ignored.

The girls ducked their chins guiltily before Rose confessed. "We found everything ready to fix when we came downstairs. We just needed to finish cooking it."

"You still did a fine job." Ethan's relief at this announcement took a pound or two of worry off his heart. Unsure how she'd managed it without his knowing, if Larissa put everything together, she hadn't deserted the family. She was just … away.

Hans agreed to take the girls to school on his way to Doc's office, thus further easing Ethan's mind. He didn't want to be off the place if Larissa—he stomped down on the thought, lest it bring false optimism. Anyway, plenty of chores needed doing around the barn.

Hans and the girls set off in the buckboard. Ethan decided to start cleaning and oiling the farm machinery. At least he'd keep his hands busy. Hopefully, too, it would stifle the growing demand within him to go find her *now*, and force her to talk to him, regardless of the promise to her he now fervently wished he hadn't made.

His hands stilled on the harrow's sharp teeth. Some lines Larissa once read to him from a poem in the Fairvale *Tribune*, about being unable to erase the past, ran through his mind.

… nor all your Piety nor Wit
Shall lure it back to cancel half a Line,
Nor all your Tears wash out a Word of it.…

At the time she read it to him, neither one said much, for, about their own lives, those few words seemed to say it all. Just as they said it now. He couldn't go back on his promise to her any more than he could hold her in his arms against her wishes. His thoughts turned to Hans, struggling to accept what Fate had thrown at him and his realization that, had the accident never happened, his life would be very different. The knowledge Ethan had been holding down by force bobbed to the surface. *If Zane hadn't died saving Obadiah's life, if he had lived to come home from the war, how very different our lives would be. Without a shred of doubt, Larissa and I wouldn't be married.*

The noise of a rig on the drive jolted him from this unthinkable certainty. Glancing out the door, he saw Doc's buggy navigating the curve. Some of the tightness around his heart eased. Surely, Doc would know what to do.

Spotting him in the doorway, Doc guided Bella over. "I passed Hans and the girls. I told him to go ahead to the office. You look like hell," he added cordially. "Couldn't sleep after the big news, I take it."

"I figured word would be all over town by now about Obadiah," Ethan said sourly.

"You know Fairvale," Doc agreed cheerfully. "Tongues tied in the middle and both ends wagging. But I wasn't talking about Obadiah's return from the dead. How's Larissa? I sure hope she looks better than you do."

"She's not taking it well at all." It was a relief to say the words aloud.

Doc eyed him curiously. "Larissa?" He frowned. "You mean she didn't tell you?"

Since Larissa hadn't spoken more than a dozen words to him all night, the odds were good she hadn't mentioned whatever was causing Doc to cluck like a broody hen with one chick. "Tell me what?" Fear fizzed through him. "Is she sick?"

"No, she's not sick." Doc's sarcasm couldn't hold a candle to Ethan's swift gratitude.

Doc's mind, however, was a train on a single track. "I hope you're not trying to tell me that as soon as you got home from the blacksmith shop yesterday, you barreled in and started rattling on to her about Obadiah?"

Ethan's tired brain was having a difficult time keeping up with this conversation. *How could Doc know I did just that?* "Well, yes, but—"

Doc's glare would have scorched the hide off a moose. "Ethan, you're one of the smartest men I know, but sometimes you sure can act like a lunkhead."

He wasn't in the mood for Doc's evaluation of his personal characteristics. "What are you getting at?" He didn't care how much his annoyance showed.

"I don't normally go around telling this to folks. I mostly leave it to them. But in this case, I guess I better clue you in, if you'll keep your mouth shut long enough to listen. She's going to have a baby."

Ethan looked as blank as if Doc just announced Larissa was going to hold her breath until she turned blue. It took a second try before he produced something besides a croak. "Doc, she didn't—I didn't—"

"I'll lay bets a couple of months back, somebody did," Doc said dryly.

"Is everything—is she all right?"

"Shining like a new penny when she left my office yesterday. I can only guess the state she's in, now, thanks to your blabbering. You'd better clue me in on what happened."

With Doc's news and his own heartbeat thumping like a drum, Ethan was in too much of a fog to take offense at the tone or words. He outlined, as rationally as he could, how it had been between them last night.

Scowling, Doc listened silently until Ethan ran down. His lips pursed as thoroughly as if he'd just swallowed an extra-large dose of castor oil. "I'll give you credit. Only a few hours after she left my office, happy as a meadowlark, you managed to stir up one fine mess."

"You don't have to tell me. My list is probably a lot longer than yours when it comes to reasons for kicking myself. What have I done to her?"

Doc snorted. "And you a farmer! Well, according to my handy-dandy medical book—"

"Doc!" Ethan was too worried to be amused by this backhanded attempt at humor. "With all this pulling at her, will she come to harm?"

"She shouldn't. Unless you intend to make a career of upsetting her."

"I don't. I'm just a farmer from here on out."

"Then I hope to God you're smarter about animal doings than you are about married folks' ways. If looking at the pictures in my doctoring book will help, I'll be happy to explain them to you."

Ethan turned approximately as red as his flannel shirt, and Doc finally took pity on him, but not much. "Sure as green apples make bellyaches, you can't undo what's done. But in the future, try not to make as big a mess of things as you have this time." His brows drew together. "You may be a lunkhead, but you're not a damned fool."

This time Ethan managed a rueful smile at Doc's medical assessment. "You're probably giving me too much credit."... *nor all your wit shall cancel half a line...*The brief lightness faded. "I have to go to her."

"Go, then. Quit wasting my time."

Already half turned away, Ethan hesitated. "Will you wait? Just to make certain she's all right?"

"I have sick folks to tend. I can't sit here twiddling my thumbs while you operate to remove your big foot from your mouth." Doc's contrariness level was almost back to normal, but as he shook out the reins, his scowl softened. "You're one rare-lucky man. There's some would give their eyeteeth for what you have. Don't you lose sight of that." He flipped the reins and was down the drive before Ethan could reply.

Not even waiting until the buggy disappeared around the curve, Ethan sprinted toward Mill Creek, certain he would find her at the Sitting Seat. On the way, his thoughts outpaced his hurrying feet. Believing in each other's words and actions, no matter what, formed one of the cornerstones of their marriage. Was she relying on that, trusting him to keep his distance even if he didn't understand why? What would she do when she saw him and knew that, in spite of his promise, he had come to her, anyway?

He shook the thought away. Knowing the truth now, he would wait for her to come back to him. But while he waited, he wanted to be damned sure she knew she could take the time she needed, without any more of his fancy ultimatums. He just hoped he would get the chance to try not to make as big a mess of things as he'd managed to so far.

He passed the springhouse and neared the peach orchard, its bare branches etched against the sky, but holding springtime protectively within. Abruptly, his feet stilled and his heart started racing. She wasn't at the Sitting Seat. She was walking slowly toward him along the edge of the autumn-bare orchard.

Watching the rough ground at her feet, she was still half a dozen rods off when she raised her head. She froze. She looked weary, which didn't surprise him. She had been crying, which dismayed him. But her face no longer held last night's blank-of-all-emotion expression, which sent relief shooting through him in all directions.

Go to her.

I promised I wouldn't bother her.

Go to her.

I promised she would have her time, and what makes you so sure she's coming to me?

The question jabbed into him like a wooden splinter stabbing into his thumb. He closed his eyes as a brief, wordless plea rammed through his mind. He opened them, and she was coming toward him. The gladness lighting her reached across the grass-wet space between them.

You promised when she was ready to talk, you'd talk.

Exhilaration so sharp it was physically painful shot through him. Taking the last steps between them at the same time she did, he drew her to his heart. Her arms clasped around his neck, and she raised her face to his. There are many ways to talk, and some of them say more than a thousand words ever could. He bent his mouth down to hers.

As their lips met and clung, he felt the pulse in her wrists beat wildly against his neck. Time had no meaning as his arms and his body remembered the feel of her against his heart and his mouth remembered the warm sweet taste of her lips.

She shivered, startling him back to the peach orchard and the wet grass at their feet. "Lizzie, are you all right?"

"I was cold, but not anymore."

"We're not taking any chances." At his rock-hard finality, she eyed him questioningly, but he was already leading her toward the springhouse. He stopped at the bench where they'd sat after Mac's departure for school, when she was so certain she'd offended him. Settling onto the sun-warmed seat, he tucked her close to his side, and she leaned her head on his shoulder. Neither one spoke as they simply absorbed the contentment of being together again.

Finally, she stirred. "About last night. I'd better explain. I'm not sure how long my brave will hold out if I don't tell you now."

He stared without seeing at a beetle crawling along the pebbly path. "Doc came by earlier," he confessed, "and described, in painstaking detail, my lamentable lack of sound judgment. In a nutshell, I talk too much, don't listen enough, and don't shut up when I should. So if you want to talk, I promise to listen. If not, that's all right, too."

She hesitated, as if uncertain how to begin. "I was so happy when you came home last night. Then you told me about Obadiah." She stumbled over the name. "I thought I'd put it behind me. But when you said he'd come back, pain poured into me, like a bucket of icy water, and kept pouring, until it seemed I would burst. I was afraid I'd start screaming and not stop, if I said or did anything, or allowed myself to feel any emotion at all. Even for you." He could barely hear her.

"Especially for you, Ethan. When you hold me, it makes everything bearable. I knew how strong and supportive and caring you would be, just as you've always been." He touched her hair, a feather-light gesture, but, as he'd promised, said nothing, simply waited for her to continue.

"I told you how, all my life, someone's been here to prop me up when I needed propping. My parents, Zane, you, rather like shoring up a sagging clothes line," she said morosely. "But this time, the answer had to come from within me, not through anyone else. Everything began and ended with Obadiah. If I was ever to be free of him, I had to fight him by myself. So I shut you out, when you'd done nothing to deserve it."

His breath slid out in a sigh of relief he couldn't disguise as she continued. "I've resisted so long and hard against anything to do with Obadiah. You said he's sorry, but all the apologies in the world won't bring Zane back, or erase how and why he died so far from home. He went away, and I never saw him again. He died, and I wasn't with him." Her voice broke, but the flow of words, having breeched the wall holding them, spilled out.

"Knowledge that Obadiah was there, and I wasn't, it tore at me. *I should have been the one to be with Zane when he was dying.* Obadiah has something that should have been mine but never will be. And it hurt so much."

Tears streamed down her cheeks. He pressed his face to her hair, his own eyes wet. He'd assumed he possessed some understanding of her anguish at Zane's death. *How pitifully little I comprehended.* Through those last minutes with Nettie, he'd knelt beside her, spoken to her, and held her hand. She died in his arms. *And I hadn't endured two cruel years of separation from her when it happened.*

Larissa swiped at her wet cheeks. "I resented Obadiah so much. But as long as he wasn't around to remind me, I was all right. When you said he'd come back, all the pain of Zane's death came back, too. I had the strangest feeling of being married to you, but still married to Zane and grieving for him as if it had just happened."

Looking down at her hands clasped tightly in her lap, she didn't see the effect of this revelation on Ethan. To keep from blurting out the protest flooding his throat, he bit down on his tongue so hard that he tasted blood.

"The strength of that grief frightened me." Her hands gripped together even more tightly. "That's why I went to be alone. I knew if I didn't work it out then, it would destroy us. I thought about a lot of different things last night. With all the bits and pieces floating around, one fact stood out very clearly. You said you weren't telling me what to do, but you were asking, for us. Even then, I fought to keep you at a distance so that I could find my own solution. But when we were in bed, I—I just couldn't keep on with it. I couldn't destroy the 'us' we have."

At this confession, he slumped as if one of the boulders down by Mill Creek had just rolled off his shoulders.

"After you said I would have my time, and you left, I realized I couldn't shut you out of my heart, to keep you from interfering in 'my' decision, because you're already there, and nothing will ever change that."

With perfect clarity, memory replayed for him the anger in his voice last night as he thrust those final wrathful words at her. All that time, she had been fighting an inward battle, the pain of which he couldn't begin to grasp. He could only hold her close against his heart, now, as she continued.

"I started thinking how I carried Zane in my heart every minute of every day he was gone. I know I was in his heart the same way. I don't think it. I *know* it. If he was in my heart, and I was in his all those days we were separated, then, for a certainty, I *was* with him when he died." Her chin lifted with sure, deep confidence. "Obadiah was with him, physically. But through the love Zane and I shared, I was with him, too. Do you see? I can be all right with Obadiah's being there instead of me. I don't have to resent him anymore."

A lump the size of two double-yoke goose eggs blocked his throat, so his words came muffled. "I ... do see, Lizzie. I'm glad it was ... that way for you ... and for Zane. For a fact, he wouldn't want you to grieve about something you had no control over."

"I can accept that, now. I feel like I can take the pain I've been getting from Obadiah and let it go. I battled myself and won. I'll never have to be afraid of me again." The words sighed out as she nestled her face against his neck. "I'm so glad you understand why I have to see Obadiah."

He couldn't prevent the head-to-foot jolt that twisted through him. He sat her back and put his hand under her chin, tipping her face up to look directly at her. The stony grief was gone. Her eyes were serene. "You're not doing it because you think you have to?"

270

She shook her head slowly. "I'm doing it because my heart wants to."

"Do you want me to go with you," he asked carefully, "or is this another of those 'must do it yourself' times?"

Her mouth curved upward. "I would very much like you to go with me. I know now, no matter what, you are with me, a part of me, letting me make my own decisions, but cheering me on. With the messes I get into, there go your future years of peace and quiet."

"It's still a two-way deal," he said firmly. "If you can put up with me, we should plan to make this a very long-term arrangement."

"How long?" she asked innocently. "Until we're old and gray, rocking on our front porch, watching our grandchildren rocking on their front porch while they watch *their* grandchildren?"

His eyebrows scrunched in a frown of concentration as he calculated the time-span. He finally nodded. "That should do for starters." He drew her head back to his shoulder. "Assuredly, we have a good jump on the 'children' department. I suspect they'll be supplying us with the aforementioned grandchildren before we can turn around twice. It'll be a real shame if we're out of practice and can't remember how to tend a young one." He shook his head mournfully at this disgrace, then brightened. "I wouldn't mind remedying the situation. And I don't know of a better time to start remedying than right now."

She became very still in his arms, before she looked up at him searchingly. "When you and Doc chatted about your various shortcomings this morning, did he mention the news I wanted to tell you last night?"

The wonder in his eyes and the tenderness in his smile answered her. Disappointment flicked across her features. "This isn't the way I wanted to tell you about the baby."

"It's all right, love. It's more than all right. Doc didn't want to tell me. I guess he figured it was the only way to get through to me how—and why—it was with you." He gave her a crooked smile. "He really sheared my wool right down to the skin. I don't think he's going to forgive me any time soon, either. But it will still be sooner than I'll forgive myself. If I hadn't been, in his words, such a lunkhead last night, we could have had the happiness you anticipated. I guess we'll just have to make up for lost time, now."

Her disappointment vanished and her eyes recaptured the glow that had been there when he arrived home all those hours ago. "We really will have to put off our future years of peace and quiet for a while. Do you mind?"

His lingering kiss gave its own answer. "We'll just have to be given more years than we're already scheduled for, to make up for it. And that suits me just fine."

He glanced up as a cloud covered the sun, darkening the world around them. "Looks like we're in for a cracking-good storm. We'd better get to the house before it breaks." He pulled her to her feet and circled his arms around her. "Are you truly all right with everything now, Lizzie?"

Her eyes shadowed to a deeper blue. "You were so angry. I have to live with knowing I hurt you so much, that I put my pain above yours."

He stared past her, shaping his new knowledge into words. "You had to work it out, and you did. I've been thinking about that poem you read from the newspaper. *The moving finger, having writ, moves on...* It's what we have to do. Move on. At least it's over and done now, and won't suddenly spring up to haunt us in the future."

"Are you sure, Ethan? Are you very sure?"

He touched a wisp of hair at her temple. "I'm very sure."

For all her new-gained serenity, her eyes remained shadowed. "Everything is so right and good. If only...."

His heart gave a hard bump. "'If only' what?"

"If only I could —" A nearby grumble of thunder reminded them of the fast-approaching storm. "Ethan, I didn't realize it, but suddenly, standing out here, I'm cold."

Her abrupt switch in topics and the first drops of rain splatting on them distracted him. In his haste to get them out of the wet, he didn't realize she hadn't finished voicing her thought. Once in the kitchen, he stoked the fire in the range and in the heater stove he'd just reinstalled for the winter. When both fires were sending out tongues of heat, he brushed ash dust from his hands. "Does that help?"

"Some. But I was so much warmer when you were holding me."

Doc's unflattering diagnosis of his intelligence notwithstanding, he didn't need her to say it twice. He pulled her to his heart. "Better?"

Her head bobbed against his chest. "Yes. But still not all the way to my toes." Slipping her arms around his neck, she pulled his head down and kissed him with a thoroughness that spoke volumes. When she finally released him, such ardor and bemusement filled his expression, she tightened her arms around his neck to pull him close again. "I think I'm getting a little warmer, now."

"Jumping jackrabbits, woman!" he managed to murmur before her lips again closed over his. When she moved back a bit, he brushed his fingers lightly against her cheek. "You do have some fine ideas on toe warming," he managed raggedly.

"I have some others, if you're interested."

"Oh, I'm interested, Lizzie. I surely am." He swung her up into his arms. She buried her face against his neck to stifle a joyous laugh as he carried her to the bedroom door that, this time, stood wide open.

CHAPTER THIRTY-ONE

Her encounter with Obadiah Beldane took place the following afternoon. Shawn arranged the meeting at the parsonage, in his study. After all that had happened, Ethan's mood was much less forgiving than Larissa's.

Her new-found assurance carried her all the way to the parsonage's front door. Then she gripped Ethan's hand more tightly. Feeling her hesitation, he turned her to face him. "You're certain you want to do this? It's not too late to leave."

Her clasp on his hand tightened. "I'd like to run like a mouse trying to avoid becoming the main course at a cat's dinner party, but I need to do this."

"I love you." He gave her fingers a final encouraging squeeze, and rapped the brass knocker.

Martha opened the door. With none of her usual merriment, she welcomed them and showed them to the study. Before she retreated, she pressed Larissa's wrist, a movement so subtle it went unnoticed by Ethan or Shawn, who, his hand out in greeting, approached them with a warm smile. Immeasurably comforted by her friend's touch, Larissa's chin lifted as Martha discreetly slipped away.

Shawn shook with Ethan and clasped Larissa's hand firmly between both of his. He gestured them into the study. "Why don't you sit on the sofa? Since Obadiah is here, we may as well start."

Keeping her hand on Ethan's arm and her attention strictly on Shawn, Larissa entered the room. Throughout the process of removing her dark blue cape and settling onto the sofa beside Ethan, she avoided looking at the man who rose clumsily at her entrance. No longer able to postpone the moment, she turned from thanking Shawn. For a heart-stopping instant, she was seated beside Zane that April morning more than seven years ago when Obadiah Beldane had burst into church, shouting that Fort Sumter had been fired on and the War begun.

Seeing him for the first time since that day, shock zigzagged through her. She'd been picturing him as the muscular blacksmith she'd known before he and Zane left for war. She recalled his way of forever rattling on about something to anyone who was listening, and quite a few who weren't. His once-black hair was white, although she'd always assumed he was about Zane's age. He'd shriveled so, he appeared to weigh no more than Larissa. His coal-black eyes, once glinting with humor and mischief, were dull, as if he'd forgotten how to enjoy life.

Their eyes met. What he saw in hers, she could not know. After her first stunned realization, she simply felt relief because the moment of meeting him, that she had so dreaded, had passed.

Limping heavily, he crossed to her and put out his hand. That he might seek to touch her, even in greeting, had not occurred to her. Ethan stiffened. He shifted protestingly, and she knew he had not anticipated this gesture, either. As her fingers pressed his arm, he sat back, but the glitter in his eyes shot an unconcealed warning to Obadiah.

Slowly, she put out her hand. "Mr. Beldane."

He stared at her blankly, as if disbelieving her reaction. He grasped her fingers as awkwardly and carefully as if she might break at his touch. "Miz ... Michaels." His eyes slid to Ethan's face at thus naming her as his wife. However, he gave no sign of noticing Ethan's clamped jaw as he swiftly returned his attention to her.

Shawn stepped forward. Larissa had forgotten his presence, and so, apparently, had Obadiah, who released her hand and shuffled back to his seat. Instead of taking his own chair, Shawn rested his hands behind him on top of the desk and, without haste, leaned back. He glanced at Obadiah, sitting rigidly, clutching his ancient hat in shaky hands. Larissa's wide skirts covered the short space on the sofa between Ethan and her, concealing their tightly linked fingers.

"Thank you for coming. It can't be easy for any of you." Thus Shawn quietly included Ethan's presence and emotions. "Perhaps everyone will be more comfortable if we get right to the matter at hand. Larissa, you need to be aware that Obadiah and I have talked, but this meeting is between the two of you. I'll leave it to each of you to express your feelings. Would you prefer that Obadiah go first?"

With a swift mental prayer that her voice would emerge with composure, she said quietly, "Yes. Thank you."

When Shawn gestured, Obadiah's panicked expression suggested he'd rather face a herd of stampeding buffalo than the pain in the wide, violet-blue eyes of the woman waiting for him to speak. Leaning forward, still gripping his battered hat, he said nervously, "Thank you for seein' me, ma'am. I know you've had other reports, but it was Zane and me there, no one else to know how it really was." His Adam's apple bobbed with his audible swallow. "I reckon Zane wrote you about the stage station. When a stage or freight wagon come in, we took up positions around the building in case of Indians attackin' during the unloadin'. That last—that mornin', Zane got a letter from you."

Larissa couldn't prevent the small sound that escaped her throat. Until this moment, she hadn't known whether Zane received her last letter.

"With the noon stage comin' in, we took our positions same as always. I was coverin' the east side of the station and Zane the north. When those red devils blasted down on us from the east, I took a arrow in my leg. Zane helped me get back 'round the north corner. Things eased up on our side, but all hell busted loose on the west side. Zane started that way and wasn't but a couple of steps from bein' clean around the side of the building. That's when three bucks slid around the corner in front of me. I yelled for Zane and he turned back. I got one of the ornery skunks. With our rifles bein' single-shot, 'stead of those fancy new repeatin' guns, I had to reload. Zane got one that was aimin' his arrow square down my nose. Before I could finish reloadin', the third one zeroed in on Zane. I swung the butt of my rifle at him, but my damned leg held me back."

Voice now shaking, thrust back into the black unreality of that springtime day, he stared unseeing past Larissa. "The dirty devil let his arrow off a split second before I bashed his head with my rifle. Not more'n a split second," he repeated, unaware how the self-reproach and remorse in his voice conveyed to his listeners the enormity of his burden of guilt. "If I hadn't yelled for Zane to come back—if I'd moved faster— leg or no leg—"

Larissa was not aware of the tears pouring down her cheeks or of Ethan's bone-crushing grip on her hand. Nothing in the world existed except Obadiah's misery-filled voice and the words, like drops of blood, spilling from his mouth.

"I crawled to him and called his name. He took a couple more breaths an' that was all." Obadiah's hands clenched his battered hat in a death grip. "I tried. God, how I tried. But I wasn't fast enough. Two years of fightin' and each watchin' the other's back, all the rough spots we come out of without a scratch, and then *I failed him.*" His voice crumbled. "I ain't askin' you to forgive me. I know no one could do that." He raised his head and his torment swelled the anguish in Larissa's heart. "That's not why I'm here. I come to apologize, and I come because I figured you have a right to know, that God-awful as it all was, he died peaceful."

She stared at him as if, accepting everything else he'd related, this pathetic attempt to comfort her now smeared doubt over all the words that had gone before.

Seeing her disbelief, he squared his shoulders. "I swear before God, he wasn't at all like the men I seen that died screamin' in pain."

A thousand times, Larissa's imagination had walked the path of Zane's last moments, a path forever stretching just out of sight ahead of her, with no signposts to point out what lay at the end of that road. Always in her mind was the fear that Zane's death had come precisely as Obadiah's last words so crudely and vividly portrayed.

Obadiah, in his need to unburden himself, was oblivious to Larissa's violent inward struggle. "When I called out to him, he didn't say nothin', but it's God's own truth, there was nothin' to show he was hurtin'."

With sudden, blinding comprehension, Larissa lurched to her feet and fled the room before the others could react. Across the hallway, a door stood ajar. She heard Ethan shout her name, but without pausing, veered into the haven of Martha's sewing room. Jamming the back of her hand to her mouth in a futile attempt to stifle the formless sounds escaping from deep within her, she bent forward. Strong arms circled her from behind and Ethan's voice fell urgently against her ear. "Larissa!"

She whirled in his arms and buried her face against the soft wool of his black suit coat. She tried to speak but couldn't get any words past the spasms jolting her. He held her tightly, swaying her body with his, under his breath cursing bitterly that it had come to this. Finally, her struggle for breath eased enough for him to understand her broken phrases.

"I've been so afraid for him that he died in agony. That's what I wanted to tell you yesterday out by the orchard. 'If only I could know he didn't suffer horribly at the end.'" She raised her head. Yesterday's shadow that, in spite of her new, hard-won serenity, had lingered, the shadow that had lived in her eyes since the day she learned of Zane's death, was gone. "I don't have to be afraid for him anymore. Knowing his last breaths were sheltered by peace, not pain, at last I can let him go in that same peace."

CHAPTER THIRTY-TWO

On a softly warm morning the following May, Larissa trudged to the springhouse to fetch the eggs and butter to make a pound cake for the night's dessert. Within days of having the baby, she found, to her chagrin, she tired more easily at this stage than she remembered with Mac and Rose. She certainly didn't recall feeling this awkward back then when she attempted to do the routine household chores. *Not that I'm allowed to do much these days.*

If Rose, Charity, or Hans was nearby when she reached for the broom to sweep the porch or stooped to replenish the fire in the kitchen stove, they leaped to help or simply elbowed her out of the way. *Ethan is even worse.* Solemnly agreeing that keeping active was good for both her and the baby, he would then tramp to the smokehouse, the icehouse or down cellar to retrieve whatever item she needed.

She pressed her hands to her aching back and darted a glance around to make certain Ethan hadn't seen the gesture. He'd probably carry her back to the house, instead of letting her walk. *Or waddle.* No one said so, but she had the distinct feeling that, from the rear, she strongly resembled a tipsy mother goose leading her goslings to Mill Pond. Reaching the springhouse, she eased onto the wooden bench to rest for a moment before retrieving the eggs and butter.

In spite of her exasperation over being treated as if she were as weak and fragile as a newborn kitten, she truly appreciated the help Rose and Charity, and Hans, too, had given her these past weeks. Enthralled by the news of the baby, the girls had immediately begun making all sorts of plans to care for it. When Ethan inquired innocently whether those plans included two o'clock in the morning diaper changes, their initial enthusiasm dwindled into caution about making such a dire guarantee. But they promised "to do everything else that needs to be done," in blissful ignorance of all the work it took to keep a baby sweet-smelling and happy.

The past year had wrought changes in both Rose and Charity. Rose had turned fifteen this last Christmas and had, for a certainty now, inherited Larissa's short stature. Her violet-blue eyes, her blond hair now taking on a soft chestnut shade, sometimes caught Larissa by surprise at glimpsing this young version of herself. Rose had matured rapidly these last months. *Just how much has her hearing loss contributed to this process?* Not for the first time, Larissa wondered. After her initial bitter rebellion, Rose had accepted the unchangeable, and her tranquil disposition reasserted itself. Sometimes, however, particularly after being in a large group of happily chatting-away people, she became more quiet than usual. Larissa had seen her slip away, sketchpad under her arm, headed for the orchard or Mill Pond on sunny days, the barn loft on cold or rainy days. After a time, she returned to the house with a new drawing and renewed serenity.

Charity, who would be sixteen in a couple of weeks, had grown slender and had added several inches to her height, so that she was now taller than Larissa. Her hair had darkened to a rich honey-gold, and she and Rose invested a large portion of their free time discussing various styles for her to wear it "pinned up" when the great day arrived.

Uneasiness scraped at Larissa's heart. Subtle at first, but more apparent as the months passed, she and Ethan had sensed a growing restlessness in Charity. They were reasonably certain it didn't have anything to do with the baby's imminent arrival, and so had been diligently attributing it to a natural uncertainty of her rapid approach into full womanhood. Despite this agile mental contriving, they were fully aware they wouldn't be able to avoid the truth for much longer.

Mac had hovered in the background of her thoughts all during this unproductive fretting. Finally, she allowed him to come forward. A rush of pride filled her. Completing his third year of medical school, he was, according to the abbreviated reports Doc Rawley relayed from Dr. Terrill at the University, "making a tolerably good accounting of himself." For Doc, hiding his gratification beneath matter-of-factness, this restrained assessment was the highest of praise.

Mac, himself, had retained his dedication toward his goal. His letters were usually brief, but filled with enthusiastic reports of his medical studies. He and Jeff Kinsley had remained friends. He had admitted to Larissa that the genial competition to see which of them would earn a higher grade "keeps both of us on our toes."

After Mac had introduced them to Amity Terrill in Philadelphia, occasional comments concerning her had popped up in his correspondence. "Once a month, Dr. and Mrs. Terrill invite a group of students to a formal supper at their home. Last week, it was Jeff's and my turn, along with four other fellows. I sat next to Miss Terrill at supper and she casually mentioned *Great Expectations*. I must admit I was glad Ethan is so partial to Charles Dickens. All those books he read aloud while we were growing up allowed me to carry my part without falling flat on my face!"

Over time, "Miss Terrill" appeared with increasing frequency. "Last Sunday afternoon, three other students and I attended a Bach musicale with Miss Amity, her parents and sister." Lately, she merited mention in nearly every letter. "The University held its annual Spring Ball two weeks ago. My dancing is definitely improving with practice. I didn't step on Amity's toes once!" *If Charity still secretly harbors those long-ago feelings that caused such a commotion after Mac left for Philadelphia, it's no wonder she's acting perturbed.* Larissa winced at this unguarded admission that edged far too close to the explanation for Charity's unsettled behavior.

Now's just not a good time to deal with it. We'll face it after the baby comes. This promise was directed to the patron saint of parents dealing with the difficulties of on-the-verge-of-adulthood children. It was tinged with embarrassment for evading the issue. It was also deeply sincere.

Mac's last letter certainly hadn't cured the problem. She'd read it so often, the words were stored in her heart. Nevertheless, once again, she pulled them out to pore over.

"So many new medical techniques came out of the War, from both the North and the South, the school is hard put to fit everything into the standard three-year curriculum. Rumors, of course, are always floating around among the fellows, and one of the latest is that, before long, four years will be required for a medical degree. Perhaps it was with this in mind that Dr. Terrill urged me to take additional classes this spring. According to him, my professors felt 'it would be extremely beneficial to my future medical career.' How's that for high-sounding words? Theirs, not mine, I promise you, Ma."

At this point in the letter, Ethan had interjected with amusement, "I remember Doc informing Mac that his hat better still fit when he gets home or Doc'll personally perform the necessary surgery. Sounds like he's living up to Doc's orders and not getting a swelled head about all this."

Larissa's fingers had clutched the paper more tightly.

"Doc Rawley's last letter casually mentioned that he'd written about me to Dr. Terrill, who just happens to be the head of the University's Board of Directors, as well as the head of the school. Doc didn't give me a clue what it was about, and I was more than a little nervous. You know he never minces words, and these men have the power to end my studies here as easily as snapping a red pencil in two.

"Sure enough, this morning the Board called me into their meeting. They said they wanted me to see Doc's letter, and were solemn as judges pronouncing sentence when Dr. Terrill handed it to me.

"As I feared, Doc bluntly assured them it would be to *their* benefit to keep me on here as long as they had anything new to fill my head with. That *I* might even be able to teach *them* a thing or two if they weren't too puffed up with their own importance to listen.

"Eight pairs of eyes stared at me grimly as I read. Six of the powers possess bushy beards similar to Doc's. I couldn't make out the set of their mouths, which was probably just as well, considering the two that I could see. Courtesy and responsibility are heavily stressed here, since these traits will influence all our future medical actions. Clearly, these distinguished men believed I had used their long-standing friendship with Doc to bully them into extending my coursework to include this advanced instruction, whether they deemed me qualified or not. Such insolence was more than enough reason for them to cut me from the program, and my heart sank into my socks.

"As it turned out, far from taking offense, Doc's pompous bluntness really tickled them. I was so amazed to hear these ultra-dignified men actually chuckling, that I missed part of the explanation. It seems the most sour-faced doctor in the group instructed Doc Rawley all those years ago. When he finally quit wheezing enough to inhale some air, he informed me that Doc had been 'one to speak his mind' even then.

"After they quit poking one another in the ribs, one remembered to mention they want me to continue at the University for another year, to take part in the advanced studies program they will be offering next term. You wouldn't have convinced me by their earlier just-smelled-a-dead-fish expressions that they found Doc's highhandedness amusing, but I was too relieved at being asked to stay on to really care about their weird sense of humor.

"Ma, I know you've been expecting me to come home this summer, but I can't pass up the opportunity to continue learning from some of the finest doctors and surgeons in the country. I know you'll understand."

Larissa had laughed shakily. "Confident, isn't he?"

"I think he knows his mother very well," Ethan had said quietly.

She'd blinked, sniffled, and continued reading. "I must close for now and get back to studying. I don't dare let Doc down, after reading his opinion!"

Now, sitting in the May sunshine, Larissa tucked the words of Mac's letter back into her heart, along with her regret over his not returning for many more months, and her overwhelming joy and pride at his accomplishments.

Rose had accepted the news with disappointment that he wasn't coming home right away, but also with good grace for the larger picture of his continued opportunity to study.

Charity must certainly be aware that Mac's lengthened stay in Philadelphia will prolong his contact with Amity Terrill and strengthen any emotions budding there.

No! Not now. With an impatient shake of her chin, Larissa determinedly pinned her thoughts on Mac's reaction to news of the baby. He would welcome a new sibling, his letter had assured them. His only stipulation was that it must be a boy, because he'd been two against one in the brother-sister relationship for long enough. "Now it's time to even the score, several scores, as a matter of fact." He had then proceeded to give Larissa a lengthy paragraph of advice for taking care of herself during the coming months.

Larissa's mouth had resembled the lip on a milk pitcher. "What does he think I did before he was born? Dance on the roof? Seems to me *he* got here safely enough."

Ethan had known better than to laugh. Instead, he asked mildly, "Is he correct in his medical recommendations?"

Larissa rolled her eyes. "Yes. As correct as if he's given such advice a hundred times."

"Maybe he has, by now."

"Maybe he has. But I think I liked it better when he was seven years old, mending broken bird wings and patching up the barn cats after they had a difference of opinion. It was much less complicated, then, telling him what to do, rather than the other way around."

"Would you really trade his 'now' for his 'then'?"

Larissa had wrinkled her nose at him. "You and Mac! Just what I need, two men who always come up with a good answer, whether I like it or not. And Hans, too, standing shoulder to shoulder with you. Heaven help us if little Sweetpea is a boy. We women won't stand a chance, then."

"Lizzie?" Ethan's voice, as he hurried toward her from the smokehouse, shattered her musing and brought her sharply back to the present. "I was on my way to the tool shed for a hammer and saw you. Are you all right?"

"I'm fine. Just enjoying the sunshine."

"If you don't mind some company, I'll join you for a minute." He dropped down beside her on the bench and stretched out his long legs.

In the months following Obadiah Beldane's revelations, they had spoken only briefly of that encounter. For Larissa, in spite of the peace she had gained, the events preceding it were still painful to dwell on. Ethan had pointed out that they needed to move on. They had done so, and the last thing she wanted was to needlessly stir up those memories for him.

For herself, she remembered Ethan's telling her once how he always had to debate the two sides of an issue before one of him won or lost. That desolate night last October, her soul and her deepest emotions had fought each other fiercely. The meeting with Obadiah had taken every ounce of courage she possessed as she sat listening to Zane die.

Strangely enough, however, she didn't feel that either side of her had "lost" in these encounters. She had gained in understanding and love, the two attributes so tightly stitched together that she couldn't tell where one ended and the other began. With this new awareness, for the first time since Zane's death, the essence that was herself was whole.

Ethan stirred and stretched. "Guess I'd better be getting back to work. That loose board in the smokehouse won't mend itself." He helped her to her feet and slipped his arms around her waist. He could still reach, but barely.

"I have a feeling somebody forgot to explain to little Sweetpea how babies are supposed to go up and down, not front to back," she said ruefully.

The corners of his mouth curved up. "Hopefully, this doesn't mean we have another 'independent spirit' on our hands. We've finally got Charity to the point where mature behavior wins out over stubbornness, most of the time, anyway. Are we prepared to go through it again for another sixteen years?"

"I guess we should look on the bright side. We've had lots of practice handling independent spirit situations."

"That we have." He bent his mouth to hers for a long moment. Raising his head, he whistled sharply. "Lord a' mercy, Wife! If we keep this up, we might just end up with a half-dozen 'independent spirits' to test our parenting expertise."

She raised her eyebrows. "Does that thought worry you?"

"Not a bit," he said unconvincingly. "Not one bit."

CHAPTER THIRTY-THREE

The next afternoon, Larissa stood at the worktable, as close as she could get, anyway, kneading bread dough. Ethan poked his head around the back door. "I'm on my way to pick up the girls. Shall I get anything for you while I'm in town?"

Her hands continued to work the floury mass. "Will you ask Doc to stop by about suppertime?"

It took him a moment for the significance of her request to sink in. She abandoned the dough as he crossed to her and turned her to face him. "Lizzie?" She nodded and he cupped his palm to her cheek. "Are you all right?"

Her lips curved in a soft smile. "I'm very much all right. You can tell Doc the pains started about an hour ago."

He pressed her floury hand to his lips. "I'll tell him." He bent his mouth to hers for a brief, tender moment. "Be back quick as I can. I love you." He was outside and down the steps before she reached the door he'd forgotten to close.

He'd hitched up Andromeda and Pegasus before coming to the house. It's probably just as well, she decided, watching him urge them to greater speed around the curve of the drive.

Moving slowly, she finished shaping the bread dough in the pans for their final raising, cleaned the kitchen, and set out the baby articles Doc would need. Ethan had not yet returned. She slid the loaves into the oven and, to keep her attention off the increasingly nagging pains, assembled the items for a chocolate layer cake. Fortunately, before she actually began mixing the ingredients, she heard the buckboard rattle up the drive and Ethan's boots pound across the porch.

He burst into the kitchen. At sight of her, relief thrust aside his poorly disguised worry. Behind him, she caught a fleeting glimpse of Rose and Charity crowded in the doorway. Ignoring them, reaching her in four strides, he slipped his arms around her. "Doc and Hans are right behind me. Martha's on her way, too."

Grateful as she was for his presence and this information, she didn't answer as another pain gripped her and she bowed her face into his shirtfront. He held her, cupping her head against him until it passed. "I think I'd better lie down."

After this plainly understated remark, events became a little hazy for her and time jumped in uneven spurts. Doc bending over her, all his grumpiness and bluster magically faded into the gentle sureness of his voice and hands. Martha standing at the other side of the bed, holding

Larissa's hand in the warm comfort of her own, and smiling in compassionate understanding and support....

Ethan, unceremoniously demoted to the kitchen when Doc and Martha arrived, felt a stab of panic as he shut the bedroom door behind him.

"Pa?"

At Charity's pinched voice, he looked up to find two sets of wide, startled blue eyes staring at him. "It'll be all right, girls." He spoke with as much assurance as he could, considering that his stomach felt as if every moth in the vicinity was flapping around in there.

In spite of his confident tone, the stunned-deer expression continued to look out at him from both faces. They were farm children. From a young age, they knew the reality of life, and death, too, among the animals under their care. *Clearly, however, they had not related the birthing process of foals and lambs to Larissa's present pain. Was there, behind the shadowed questioning, a foreknowledge of a time to come for them?* He held out his arms, and they scooted into his hug.

He released them and realized Shawn was sitting at the table, with Hans on his far side. Doc had, early on, made it unarguably plain that Hans would not assist him in this particular medical matter. Who was more relieved, Larissa or Hans, would have required a coin-toss decision. None of them, Doc included, ever mentioned the subject again.

Shawn grasped Ethan's hand. "We figured you could use a spot of company along about now."

Ethan returned the grip and managed a weak smile. "I'll take all the spots you can spare."

The five waited in silence until it dawned on Ethan that he should get out to the barn. It never seemed so far away before. He stood, reluctantly, and Hans leaped up, signing that he would do the chores.

With a swift memory of that night last October, and his brushing Hans' proud assistance aside when he had done the barn work by himself, Ethan conveyed his relief at the offer. Hans beamed and raced out the door.

Rose and Charity, in total and unaccustomed silence, had rescued the well-done bread from the oven, mixed the chocolate cake batter, and were putting supper together when Hans returned with the evening milk. At his wordless inquiry, Ethan shook his head and, this time, made certain to express his thanks for Hans' contribution.

Charity and Rose were setting the steaming platters and bowls on the table when Larissa's stifled cry of distress made all of them jump. Ethan leaped to his feet, but before he could go to her, Shawn gripped his arm. "No, Ethan."

"But—"

"Whatever's happening, you have to leave it to Doc. It won't help anything if he has to trip over your big feet. Remember, Doc's the best there is. Trust him." Shawn's brown eyes were full of sympathy, but his grasp on Ethan's arm was unyielding. Ethan stared at him as if he'd come from the other side of the moon, and dropped back into his chair. Shawn's shoulders slumped in relief. He let go of Ethan's arm, and sank onto his own chair.

Ethan didn't take his eyes from the bedroom door. *Nothing this side of hell or the other side, either, will keep me from holding her.* His thoughts from so many months ago slammed through his mind. He heard Shawn murmur soothingly to the girls in response to their fright over Larissa's broken cry. He couldn't bring himself to turn away from the door to offer any words of encouragement to them, even if he'd had any.

From beyond the closed panel, the silence continued.

***

Larissa, her task accomplished, laughed breathlessly up at a beaming Martha. As she did so, her heart waited for the baby's first explosive squall. It didn't come. Fear stabbed her with brutal intensity, and she tried to stretch up to see Doc who, his back to her, was perched at the foot of the bed. Martha's firm hands, pressing against her shoulders, wouldn't let her raise up. "Doc!" The single word was a wail from the depths of her soul. She clutched Martha's hand so tightly she was in danger of breaking the bones.

All Larissa could see of Doc was the wrinkled white shirt covering his shoulders. She watched, terrified, as those shoulders lowered, then raised, then lowered and raised again. All the agony of the moments following Rose's birth, when her baby hadn't made a sound, hit her with bruising force. *Not again. Please not again!*

As Doc straightened, he turned a little so that Larissa glimpsed the fierce concentration stamped on his face. He murmured something that, to her anguished hearing, was, "Come on, little one. Breathe."

A gurgle, a gasp, and the baby's squeal filled Larissa's ears and filled the room. Doc's single-minded focus became overwhelming relief, and he looked around at Larissa with an ear-to-ear grin. "Took a bit to get the engine started, but it's going full-throttle now."

Martha squeezed Larissa's hand joyfully and picked up a soft blanket from the articles so carefully arranged for the baby's arrival. She hugged the small bundle to her heart, then laid the now-howling infant into Larissa's reaching-up arms.

Gazing down into the red, scrunched-up, furious little face, Larissa knew the features to be as beautiful as Mac's and Rose's had been.

Utterly absorbed, she scarcely paid any attention to Doc's activities until he eventually materialized beside the bed, drying his hands. "I'm getting too old to be having my suspenders snapped like this," he growled. "I hope this is the last time you intend to put me through it." The baby had now quieted to hiccupping whimpers. With a large finger, he gently stroked the back of the tiny hand that had escaped the confines of the blanket and was fluttering aimlessly.

"Thank you, Doc. Again." Larissa's voice caught on the last word.

He said gruffly, "It had to work. Just like when I pushed my breath into Rose after she was born. Guess it was so off-putting, she and this little one both started using their lungs out of self-defense." He cleared his throat. "Don't you think it's about time to tell that husband of yours to quit chewing his nails and get in here?"

Martha opened the door, told Ethan he could come in, and hastily dodged as he barreled past her to Larissa's side.

"Lizzie, are you all right?" He took her hand and pressed it to his cheek.

"I am, now. Don't you want to say hello to your—" She stopped and her eyes grew wide as she realized she hadn't even asked whether the baby was a boy or a girl.

Doc snorted. "I was beginning to think you'd never get around to inquiring whether 'Mary' or 'Thane' would be more suitable." Martha, and Shawn who had entered as far as the doorway, stifled their laughter at the new parents' baffled expressions. Doc studied the baby solemnly. "It's a good thing I've had more practice than this young lady has at being cantankerous. She—"

Whatever else he said was lost to Larissa and Ethan as they gazed with awe at their daughter. Handing the baby to Ethan, she saw Charity and Rose hesitating in the doorway. She held out her arms and they tiptoed to the bed. Behind them, Hans had been hanging back uncertainly. Now, he followed, stopping a little distance away to peer around the girls.

Doc put a hand on his shoulder. "I'll admit I had a few nervous moments, but everything worked out fine," he said in a low voice. "We'll talk it over later. Right now, why don't you say hello to the newest member of the family?"

Hans scuffed his feet, but Doc propelled him forward. He studied the baby now snuggled in Rose's lap, and broke into a big grin. "Mary is a beautiful name. But she certainly didn't sound very merry a while ago," he signed.

For the space of two or three heartbeats, everyone froze, before Larissa ducked her head, Ethan grinned, and Rose and Charity stared at him as if he'd just announced he was going to dye his hair green. Seeing their reactions, he drew back self-consciously, then joined in their burst of laughter.

The baby, now transferred to Charity's arms, blinked sleepily, oblivious to the amusement swirling around her. She had no awareness, either, that she had just received the name that, her baptismal certificate notwithstanding, would follow her all the days of her life.

CHAPTER THIRTY-FOUR

In the months before Merry's birth, Larissa's and Ethan's mood swings naturally but unpredictably varied between high and low. Aware of this lopsided emotional stability, they had agreed to wait until after the baby came to tackle the dilemma of Charity's feelings for Mac. Merry put in her appearance as scheduled, but a telegram from Mac, arriving before they could talk to Charity, annihilated their good intentions.

The girls, laughing and chatting to Larissa, were perched on the bed, Charity holding Merry, when Ethan extended the yellow envelope to Larissa. She didn't say anything, but dread loomed large in her eyes. Loved ones died in telegrams. Rose and Charity became very still and regarded him unblinkingly. "It's all right, Lizzie. It's not bad news."

Reassured, curiosity swiftly replaced her alarm as she took the envelope. The girls ceased to be still as the statues in Fairvale's cemetery and became their usual inquisitive selves as Charity urged her to "Open it, Ma. Quick."

Ethan raised his eyebrows at this mangling of the English language, but she merely flashed him a guilty grin and focused her attention on Larissa's hands unfolding the paper. Larissa stared at the words, then broke into a smile. "It's from Mac."

Charity swiftly translated, and both girls leaned forward in anticipation. "He says, "'Happy Birth Day to my newest little sister. Love, Mac.'" Rose's face lit with pleasure. Charity looked as if death had, after all, come in the telegram. She ducked her head and became very busy arranging Merry's flannel blanket. Larissa's eyes met Ethan's. To Charity, clearly, it *was* a death announcement—the death of her long cherished, stubbornly held hope that some heaven-sent day Mac would return her love.

Rose's chirping exclamations about the message covered Charity's sudden silence. For the space of several heartbeats, she sat unmoving, eyes fastened on the paper in Larissa's hands, before she stirred and handed Merry to Rose. Finding the three of them watching her questioningly, she squared her chin. "I have to go out back." With a dignity Larissa and Ethan had never seen, she slipped off the bed and walked to the kitchen. They heard the back door close and the sound of swift footsteps across the porch.

Larissa raised up, but Ethan stopped her. "She has to do this one by herself." She sank back, unaware of the harsh inner knowledge with which he spoke the words.

***

On a perfect morning in late May, with caring for the baby a joyful addition to her daily household routine, Larissa found it impossible to stay confined to the kitchen. Bundling Merry snugly against any chance chilly breeze, she paused on the porch. She wished she could go to the Sitting Seat by Mill Creek, but the too-vivid picture of her trying to scramble to the top of the rock, all the while clutching Merry, convinced her to settle for the springhouse bench instead.

Ethan found her, head resting against the wall, eyes shut and her face tipped to the early-summer sunshine. Her body gently swayed the baby nestled against her shoulder. To keep from startling her, he backed off a few steps. "Lizzie?"

Giving her a moment to get her bearings, he sketched a bow. "May I join you two beautiful women?" He bent over the baby, who stirred and stretched, but did not wake. "She's sleeping peacefully enough, now," he observed glumly.

"Of course she is. It's not two o'clock in the morning." Inching over, she made room for him on the bench. Brushing a kiss against her mouth, he dropped down beside her. "Rose and Charity want to do everything else for her," she reminded him. "Think we can get them to teach her how to tell time?"

He carefully nudged his thumb under Merry's tiny hand, and her fingers curled around it. His head was bent so that his face was partially hidden, and he didn't answer this sprightly remark. "Ethan?"

He shifted his feet. "Speaking of time, we promised that once the baby came, we'd face Charity's feelings for Mac."

In spite of the sun-warmed breeze touching Larissa's face, she felt a chill, and her arms tightened around Merry. "I've thought and thought, but I honestly don't know what to do. Maybe we should start by following Doc's advice when she had that temper tantrum after Mac left. Acknowledge flat out she loves him and has for a very long time."

Instinctive protest leaped into his eyes, then faded. "'Ignore it and it'll go away' certainly hasn't worked," he muttered. "She's one willful young lady. She can't get it from me. I still have all *my* orneriness." He intended it as a teasing observation, but vivid remembrance flashed through him. He'd loved, and continued to love Larissa, even when honesty, that meddlesome keeper of his conscience, had insisted it was impossible that she would ever return that love.

"Have we ever really looked at it from her viewpoint?"

Larissa's question was so close to his own thoughts that he gave a start. "I'm beginning to, I think." *I just pray to God she doesn't ache the way I did.* He snapped off the thought that hit too painfully close to home in his recognition of his daughter's feelings.

Merry squirmed and Larissa shifted her. "I can't be certain, of course, but I think Charity's planning to leave home before Mac comes back."

"What?" All the air shot out of him with that lone word.

"She hasn't said anything," she assured him quickly. "She's definitely not the chatterbox she used to be. Remember how we talked at supper about several of the things Anne Clayton casually mentioned in her last letter? That they now live in 'Wyoming Territory' instead of 'Nebraska Territory' and how all anyone can talk about is that women there might soon be able to vote. She just as casually mentioned they're wondering where they can hire a teacher for their new school. Since then, Charity's been even more reserved, but not in a forlorn way."

She glanced at him and pushed the words out. "It's more like she's waiting for something. I think she's getting it set in her mind to go out to Wyoming Territory and teach in that new school."

One swift look at her assured him she wasn't joking. He opened his mouth, but no words emerged. They were too busy slamming off the walls of his mind to have time for utterance. His voice, when it came, sounded as gritty as if he'd just swallowed a mouthful of fresh-ground cornmeal. "She wouldn't do something like that! Would she?"

"We know how she's always wanted to teach, but now she's more determined than ever. Have you noticed that lately she hasn't talked about Mac? She changes the subject if anyone else mentions him. You saw her when the telegram came about his 'newest sister.' She left the room as soon as she politely could. I don't know for certain going away is what she has in mind. But it is what I'm sensing from her."

"Not without our permission," he said flatly.

"She's sixteen. Old enough to marry next year, whether we're ready for it or not. Ten years ago, you could dictate to her. At this point, can we really hold her back from choosing to live her life according to her own plans?"

He didn't answer immediately, because his thoughts had snagged on the words "old enough to marry next year." She'd been such a little thing when they came to Ohio to escape his inescapable torment after Nettie died. *How has she suddenly become old enough to marry? Old enough to make her own life choices?*

He set his jaw, determined not to finish such a line of reasoning. He looked at Larissa and the line of reasoning chugged on, regardless. *If you hadn't followed your heart's instinct to come to Ohio, you wouldn't be sitting here right now beside Larissa. But when I made that decision, I was older than Charity is now.*

The voice of argument didn't even clear its throat at the feeble plus point. *Doc asked you once how old you were when you first knew you loved Nettie. You didn't admit you were younger than Charity is now.*

He gritted his teeth. "How can we grant our blessing if she plans to go so far away? It was hard enough to let Mac, a young man, leave. For a young woman, it's literally an entirely different set of circumstances, even knowing she'd be with good people." The assertion stuck in his throat, preventing his putting words to their greatest apprehension of all. *People aren't always good.*

Neither one spoke for a long while. They could not, with certainty, provide an answer to that always-present knowledge of good and evil, whether Charity stayed in Fairvale, or went to far-off Wyoming Territory.

Finally, Larissa stirred. "We need to remember she hasn't actually told us she's going to do this. Maybe we're putting the cart before the horse."

He shook his head. "We're used to facing facts. I suspect now isn't the time to break that habit." He paused. "Think how easy it would be if we could only map out our children's lives, just as we see fit."

"But we can't," she said softly, "any more than we can set out our own futures."

Carefully, so as not to disturb Merry, he drew Larissa's head onto his shoulder. "At least we're aware of the possibility, instead of being caught flat-footed. If she decides to go through with it, all we can do is face it day by day, and pray to God that the words we speak to guide her are the right ones."

EPILOGUE

That night, as so many times since she and Zane came to this place twenty-two years and a million memories ago, Larissa stood at the window, looking out on the moon-and-starlight speckled farm world. How deeply Zane had loved this place. It had been so much a part of him, and he of it. Sometimes, as she walked through the springtime-blossoming apple orchard or passed by the heavy-laden stalks in the rustling cornfield, she had a sense he would step out and meet her at the end of the next row, just as he had in life.

She touched her fingers to the glass, against the faint reflection that was herself. She had not been much older than Charity was now when she first came here. Those young days of breathtaking happiness with Zane had come only after her parents had reluctantly—she well knew now—given their consent for her to marry him.

You know well enough that Charity's not getting married. But was this quest to leave behind the bindings of an unreturned love, to free herself to grow in another direction, any different, really, from what Larissa had done? She had left behind the bindings of childhood and freed herself to grow in the direction she had chosen, a deeply rich and fulfilling marriage.

Charity's struggle brought to mind Mac, rescuing broken-winged birds when he was so small they were large in his hands. He had placed them in sturdy cages to protect them from harm while they recovered. In the process, invariably, the day came that the break was healed and the patient ready to try his mended wing in the outside world. And always on that day came Mac's momentary hesitation. Keep them safe in the cage or set them off into the unknown to soar free?

If Charity soared free, what about Rose? Day by day, the door through which Charity must pass to reach her teaching goal inched open a little wider. For Rose, however, it was a door through which she could neither walk beside nor follow Charity, because her own teaching dreams would not, now or ever, be fulfilled.

And Mac's future? How much had the decisions she and Zane, and she and Ethan made affected him? Doc once said that Mac had had the finest of examples to follow in seeking his life's choices. If so, why were her mother-instincts so concerned about him now?

She remembered Ethan's words outside the springhouse about taking things day by day, and doing the best they could. Now she knew why it sounded so familiar. Ethan, and David in his Psalm of Thanksgiving, had come to the same conclusion.

Day unto day uttereth speech ... Let the words of my mouth, and the meditation of my heart, be acceptable in thy sight, O Lord.

"Lizzie?"

Comfort, warm and sweet as the sound of her children's laughter echoing down the years, welled within her as she turned and walked to Ethan's waiting arms.

About the Author

How does one piece together the life events that make up a biography? How to choose this event or that one when one incident flows into another so subtly that, suddenly, decades have been spanned and the adult we are looks back at the child we were. And we shake our heads in wonder at the swiftness of the journey.

I was born in the Sacramento Valley in the midst of peach picking time and now live in Washington state, where I can see Canada from my back door. I began writing my first novel in my spare time when my children were small. Mixed in with the joy of writing, I worked nights in a nursing home to be with my daughters during the day. In the intervening years, I worked on three more novels, found employment in a law firm, received my B.A., took sign language classes, and learned to square dance. I was also the public relations representative for our county unit of the American Cancer Society's Relay for Life for many years. My daughters grew up, and my older daughter chose to go to college in Missouri. Her first phone call home after she had been there three days: "Hi, Mom, guess what? We just had a tornado!"

The novel that I began writing when my younger daughter was three months old was published just a month before her twenty-fifth birthday. My "spare time" had ended up being a lot sparer than I had imagined!

PUBLISHING CREDITS/AWARDS

1985: *Eight Letters* published in *Tidepools*, my college literary magazine. This non-fiction article received a "Communications Day" award in the college-sponsored competition.

1988: Received a Third Place award in *Literary Lights* contest for my adult essay *Wherever I Am.*

1989: Received a Finalist award for my adult essay *Chris's Legacy of Laughter* in the Pacific Northwest Writers competition.

1989—2002: Publicity Representative for our county unit of the American Cancer Society, writing radio and newspaper articles detailing cancer-related activities. Our Unit won several "Excellence in Communications" awards during this time.

1990—1992: Received my B.A. in Human Services from Western Washington University. Emphasis on writing papers (26 the first year). Administrator/President of Human Services Program authorized my reading of *The Windows of His Heart—Chief Joseph of the Nez Perce*, my critique of leadership qualities, to the Human Services students at another college; he also urged me to expand the paper for my thesis.

July 1991: Received a Finalist award for my adult essay *Wherever I Am* in the Pacific Northwest Writers competition.

July 1994: Received a Fourth Place award for my novel *The Longing of the Day* in the Pacific Northwest Writers competition.

1996—2001: Recording/corresponding secretary for my local square dance group and club editor for *Footnotes*, our state council's square dance magazine.

July 1996: My nonfiction article, *Eight Letters*, was published in *Grit* Magazine.

July 1997: Received a Finalist award for my adult essay *For Terri ... For Helen ... For Sally ...* in the Pacific Northwest Writers competition.

September 1999: *Chicken Soup for the Single's Soul* included my story, *A Faded Card*.

December 1999: *Grit* Magazine printed my story *A Ten-Cent Christmas*.

August 2000: Ogden Publications, in conjunction with *Grit*'s Fireside Library, published my novel, *The Longing of the Day*. *Longing* is "a tale of bittersweet love and savage challenges in Wyoming Territory" according to the book cover. The first print run sold out in just six weeks. The second print run continues to sell.

September 2001: Ogden published *Day Star Rising*, the sequel to *The Longing of the Day*. *Day Star Rising*, billed as "a tale of healing love against slander and suspicion in Wyoming Territory" also sold extremely well and is still selling.

November 2007: Treble Heart Publications published my third novel, *Days of Eternity*, a sequel to *Longing* and *Day Star*.

June 2010: Received a Second Place award from Wyoming Writers competition for *The Windows of His Heart—Chief Joseph of the Nez Perce*.

November, 2010: Short fiction work *Night Shadows* selected for inclusion in *Aesthetica* Creative Works 2011 Commendations List.

ALL THINGS THAT MATTER PRESS ™

FOR MORE INFORMATION ON TITLES AVAILABLE FROM
ALL THINGS THAT MATTER PRESS, GO TO
http://allthingsthatmatterpress.com
or contact us at
allthingsthatmatterpress@gmail.com

6737781R0

Made in the USA
Charleston, SC
02 December 2010